To S

I

for

Death

Now you've got the time,
I'M sure you could
write one ....!

DIARMID MACARTHUR

VERY BEST WISHES

Diarm

Contents

I

The lady in red...is dancing with me..."

God, why is that in my head, I've never liked that song; in fact, I've never bloody liked red...

She likes red though, it's her favourite colour, apparently, although I sometimes wonder if she just says that to annoy me...

She says that red is the colour of love, the colour of sex...red light spells danger (another song I don't like, by the way)

But, to me, red is the colour of fire, the colour of blood, the colour of death...

"Still...I feel the red in my mind, though the drums are out..."

II

"When the suspicious head of theft is stopped…"
William Shakespeare, Love's Labour Lost.

It wasn't her fault—it was *never* her fault!

Amanda Duff held the slinky, black jump-suit in her hands and swore; life was always so fucking unfair; but it wasn't *her* fault…

As always, the bitter, painful memories flooded into her mind, a subconscious mechanism that allowed her to justify her actions. It hadn't been her fault that she had had to move primary school at the start of Primary 7. That little bitch, Thea Crowner, had deserved exactly what she got; after all, you can't go lording it over others just because your parents had a minor lottery win. It hadn't been her fault that she got in with the wrong crowd at high school; if she hadn't been moved, she would still have had, her friends from primary school, right? And, when her "new" crowd did drugs up the back path, it wasn't *her* fault that she had developed a liking for the illicit substances on offer. It had been tactfully suggested by the School Head that she leave school early and look for a suitable college course, but that wasn't easy, as she had very few qualifications. Of course, that hadn't been *her* fault; if she'd been allowed to stay on, she was quite sure she'd have done a lot better. The college course hadn't worked out and she had ended up bumming about for a year or two, picking up casual work in a variety of retail outlets. These jobs usually lasted for only a few months, until something (although nothing that was ever *her* fault) went wrong.

She screwed up her eyes as if trying to block it all out, but to no avail; here she was, nearly twenty-three, with no job, no money, no boyfriend, and still living with her long-suffering, respectable parents in a nice, respectable house in Elderslie.

It was hell.

Her parents didn't understand her. Colin, her father barely looked at her these days; mind you, he barely looked at her mother, Christine, either! He only had time for her eighteen-year-old brother, Bruce, who seemed to be excelling at every fucking thing; school subjects, the guitar, rugby—the smarmy little shit even had a pretty, snobby little "private-school" tart in tow these days. Amanda could feel the familiar anger and resentment start to rise and she stood up, still clutching the coveted jump-suit.

But it really *wasn't* her fault, she knew that. On the various (and numerous) occasions that she had been in trouble, she had often overheard her father say to her mother that it was "in her genes", although she wasn't entirely sure what he meant. Colin's own father was still alive, a retired physiotherapist and a pillar of his church. Her mother had been orphaned at an early age and had no living relatives that Amanda knew of. But, apparently, there was "something in her genes" which meant...it wasn't *her* fault!

Amanda had been invited to a twenty-first birthday party that night and she hadn't anything decent to wear. The jump-suit was thirty-four pounds and she knew only too well that her purse contained one solitary twenty-pound note. It had contained more until that little shit, Deek Barrowman, had offered her an unmissable deal on a little bag of Charlie (in return for a quick hand-job) that had used up most of her reserve. She considered her options; unfortunately, they were limited.

She could wear something from the meagre contents of her wardrobe but she immediately ruled this out; there was a particularly hot boy going to the party that she wanted to impress and the jump-suit would do just that. Her wardrobe consisted mostly of jeans, t-shirts and a few ridiculous items of clothing that her mother had bought for her—as if she'd wear any of *those* to a twenty-first!

She could look for something within her budget, but there wasn't much and, anyway, the jump-suit looked fantastic on her, emphasising her lithe body and highlighting her thick, dark hair; two of the more welcome assets that she had inherited from Christine.

She could try and "do a runner." She was reasonably fast on her feet but the problem was the security tag; there was no way that she could get it off in the shop and she had the suspicion that it was of the type filled with dye that would ruin the garment as soon as she tried to prise it apart.

She sighed; it was hopeless, as always. Angrily, she pulled the changing room curtain aside but, as she stepped out, a slightly dishevelled woman, wearing an ill-fitting crimson dress, rushed past and smiled at her, causing Amanda to take a step back.

'Oh, sorry, love, just looking for this in a fourteen. Don't you just love it when you've dropped a size without realising?

The woman disappeared round the corner, leaving Amanda standing shaking her head, a cynical sneer on her lips. She had been a size ten for her entire, if short, adult life and didn't intend on getting any bigger. No, her problem was affording the fucking stuff in the first place! Shoulders slumped, she turned to follow the woman out of the changing area then, on an impulse, she turned and looked back along to the recently-vacated cubicle; although the curtain was only half-open, Amanda could see that there was a handbag, slightly agape, sitting on the bench. She allowed herself a sly smile and looked about; the two adjacent cubicles had their curtains tight shut but there was no apparent movement inside them. The woman would be a minute or so—it would take Amanda about ten seconds, then her problem would be solved!

With great stealth, she moved along the short corridor, into the cubicle and, reaching into the half-open handbag, briefly rummaged about then deftly lifted out the purse that was buried amongst the other contents of the bag, gratified to feel that it was comfortably heavy. She experienced only the briefest pang of guilt but she shook it off easily; after all, it wasn't *her* fault, it was the woman's own stupid fucking fault for leaving her bag lying unattended.

She grinned wickedly as she pocketed the purse. She'd come back for the jump-suit later and, hopefully, have a wad of cash left over to ensure that she *really* enjoyed the party; before she could turn, however, she was aware of a movement behind her.

Oh shit...

Excuses flashed rapidly through her mind. She had found the purse and was putting it back; she was checking store security; the ability both to lie and to think up instant explanations were two of Amanda's life skills. However, before she had a chance to use either one, suddenly and inexplicably she found herself unable to breathe. In desperation she grasped at the ligature that had appeared around her neck but her struggles quickly became less frenzied as a wave of darkness engulfed her; Amanda Watt's last conscious thought was that, for perhaps the first time in her life, it really *wasn't* her fault...

CHAPTER 1

Somewhere, a phone was ringing, irritatingly, incessantly. He ignored it—after all, it was Sunday morning—– until, finally, it stopped; then it started again. He dragged himself from the deep morass of sleep and into the light of the morning; the ringing stopped again, then started for the third time. He reached out to the bedside cabinet; his mobile wasn't there.

Shit...!

He pulled down the duvet and made to sit up but, to his utter astonishment, he found the movement impeded by a graceful, naked arm that lay across his chest, the slim fingers entwined in his prolific chest hair. He followed the arm upwards and found himself staring at the woman lying beside him; as he gaped, she opened one eye and smiled.

'Good morning, Mr McV. Aren't you going to answer your phone?'

Just under half an hour later, DCI Grant McVicar stepped out of Bluebell Cottage and into his well-used and mud-splattered Toyota pick-up. He pulled out of the drive, heading through the hamlet of Newton of Belltrees and down the narrow country road that would take him on to the considerably busier A737.

He was in a state of shock.

He rubbed his dark, neatly-trimmed beard as he tried to re-construct the previous evening's events, then winced as the excruciatingly painful memories returned. Deciding that it would be best to concentrate on today's considerably more pressing situation, he put his phone on speaker and dialled DS Briony Quinn's number; she answered almost immediately.

'Boss. You okay?'

'Aye, not bad, Bri...listen, I was half-asleep, don't know if I picked you up right; run this past me again...'

There was a long pause, as if Briony was collating her own thoughts.

'Well, as I said, we've got a body—a probable murder—in Asda's Linwood branch...'

'Right, I got that part, it's the next part that I can't quite get my head round.'

Another pause.

'So, it seems this woman went into the changin' room and found said body; problem is, she then had a complete melt-down—ran back out an' started screamin' blue murder. Next thing, the whole shop thinks it's a terrorist attack, they all went into a blind panic and charged out as quickly as they could. There were a few minor casualties with folk bein' knocked over but nothin' serious, fortunately.'

Grant shook his head in astonishment; it was certainly proving to be a morning of bizarre events!

'God, that's all we need. But the bottom line is there's a body in a changing room, probably a murder.'

'Aye, Boss; I've just arrived an' it's bloody chaos but, fortunately, we've still got the woman who discovered it; she collapsed in shock, apparently, got a bit o' a knock on the head. The store manager's kept the place closed up and secured the locus as best she could. I spoke to her on the phone, she seems pretty capable and knows the score. But it's bedlam; because one of the staff phoned it in as a possible terrorist attack, the armed response unit are there, the place is in lock-down, helicopter, the whole she-bang.'

He let out a long sigh; bizarre events indeed...

'Any other witnesses?'

Another pause.

'Other than a few staff members, no. Seems everyone ran out when the screamin' started. I suppose you can't blame them, eh.'

Fuck...!

'Christ, it's going to be a bloody long day, by the sounds of it. Right, Bri, you know what to do; I'm on the 737 but I doubt I'll get near the place at the moment. I'll be there as soon as I can.'

'Okay, Boss. I've phoned the troops, they're all on their way; Sam's in Dundee but she's comin' back over.'

This, at least, was welcome news; his team were often otherwise engaged at weekends and it would be good to have the full crew involved. He spared a brief thought for the new recruit to the team; it would be her first murder enquiry and he hoped that she was up to it.

'Good stuff, Bri. Right, I'll see you as soon as. Cheers.'

He ended the call and stared unseeingly at the road ahead—— murder always brought back bad memories...

Sandie Pollock carefully pressed the final crease into the sleeve of the pristine white Oxford shirt and placed the iron back on the ironing table, the sigh of steam coinciding with her own sigh of... sadness? Despair? She shook her head—she really didn't know anymore. She lifted the warm shirt off the ironing board, placing it carefully on a hanger before hanging it on the adjacent electric clothes airer, where the garments would remain until they were fully dried out. Sandie took great pride in her ironing; she had always liked to see her husband, Neil, head off to work in crisp, white shirt and well-pressed trousers. Neil liked it too, and not just the end result! Even after nearly thirty years of marriage he still told her that she often looked her sexiest when busy at the ironing board. She could never quite understand it herself but, if it pleased Neil, it pleased her—she gave a sad smile.

Until recently...

She switched the iron off at the wall, unplugged it then sat down on her comfortable, if slightly worn, tweed armchair and stared out of the tall bay-window at the grey sky outside. She loved this bright, spacious room, with its high, heavily-corniced and original ceiling; in fact, she loved every part of their house. Just before they had viewed it, she had discovered that the original owners had shared the surname of Pollock. She felt it had been an omen, compounded by the urban tale that the ash and lime trees in the back garden had been at the entrance to the original farm where the lady of the house had lived prior to her marriage. It was a romantic tale and Sandie loved romantic tales...

~~~~

They had met when they were both pupils at the once prestigious Greenock Academy, in the days when the boys had all been addressed by their surnames and woe betide any girl arriving at school in a pleated skirt any more than an inch or so above the knee. How times had changed.

She had known who Neil Pollock was, of course; he lived just round the corner from her in nearby Brisbane Street and he happened to be one of the school heart-throbs. Two years older than Sandie, during her first three years at high school the age difference had seemed vast. However, once she found herself in fourth year, the gap in years didn't seem quite such an issue and it was at a senior dance that she and Neil finally became an item. The dance, in the Academy's assembly hall, had featured the acclaimed local rock band, the unlikely (and somewhat pretentiously) named 73-96, apparently the house numbers of the two founding members. Apart from being highly accomplished musicians, the band also possessed a prized (and mightily expensive) Hammond organ, allowing them to give a near-perfect performance of the classic Yes track, "Yours is no disgrace". An ardent fan, Neil had stood spellbound and Sandie had sidled up to him, equally captivated by the performance. Somehow, and without a word being spoken, he had taken her hand, then, as the band reached the climax of the lengthy song, he had turned and snogged her; the rest, as they say, was history...

They had married not long after University. Sandie had studied as a pharmacist and, despite an offer of a place at Glasgow's prestigious School of Art, Neil had opted to study the then near-mystical science of computing, from where he had entered the giant international firm, IBM, whose massive plant in Greenock's Spango Valley employed about ten per cent of the local population. Neil rose up the ladder quickly while Sandie progressed at a more sedate pace with Boots the Chemist; then came the children...

She sighed, stood up and went through to the kitchen. Time for coffee.

Or maybe...no, Sandie, not yet...

Mug in hand, she returned to her favourite chair and let her mind wander through the years. The eventual move up-river to their beautiful detached villa in Craw Road, one of Paisley's most exclusive streets. Three wonderful children, now all successfully making their own way in the world. The effective closure of the mighty IBM plant, the worry as Neil was made redundant, her return to work three days a week for a local pharmacy. Then, a few years ago, Neil's new position as an IT specialist for the NHS. The only drawback was the travelling; although primarily based at Meridian House in Glasgow, he was required to go wherever there was an IT problem. Still, he appeared to love the job and it seemed that their financial worries were over. The mortgage was paid off, the kids were happily self-sufficient, early retirement should have been beckoning, until a few months ago...

She placed the coffee mug on the mantelpiece and tried in vain to stop her train of thought. She had gone over it so many times that it seemed like one of her old vinyl long-players with a scratch—it just kept repeating, repeating...

She shook her head and stood up. Time to put away the ironing...

'MORON!'

Grant held his hand on the Toyota horn for about ten seconds, furious at the impatient driver who had cut in on him, causing him to brake violently; as expected, the incident at Linwood Retail park was causing serious delays on the adjacent A737. Finally, he relented, switching on the concealed blue lights and the siren; technically, this wasn't an emergency but he'd had enough! The traffic parted and ten minutes later, he pulled up on the side of the dual carriageway, just before the access roundabout for the retail park, reckoning that this was probably as close as he would get. Leaving his hazards on and the blue lights flashing, he exited the car, locked it and trotted along the road.

By the time he reached the large Superstore (having had to show his warrant card three times) the operation was beginning to stand down. The armed response unit were already leaving, having satisfied themselves that the incident had been a false alarm. Chief Superintendent Cuthbertson, whom Grant assumed to be the officer in charge, was standing at the deserted doorway, an imposing and solid presence in his Kevlar vest. Grant approached him.

'Morning Sir.'

'Oh, mornin' Grant. Right bloody carry on this– I take it you heard what happened?'

'Aye, my DS told me. False alarm right enough then?'

'Yes, thank Christ. Big time, though—mind you, I can see why it happened; by all accounts the woman who found the body was pretty vocal and everyone just panicked; shows you just how easily these things can escalate. The only positive outcome is that it gave the team a pretty good exercise, in case the real thing ever does occur. God forbid...'

The two officers remained silent for a few moments; each knew that the possibility of a genuine terror incident was always present and each dreaded it. Finally, Cuthbertson continued.

'Anyway, looks like it's over to you now, Grant. There's a body in the changing rooms—I had a quick look in, just to check, looks like the poor woman's been garrotted! Listen, I'd best get away and get on with the bloody report, it'll take ages. Good luck with the case.'

'Aye, thanks Sir. Cheers.'

Grant turned and entered the eerily quiet store, ducking under the various lengths of blue and white police tape and showing his identity card one last time; finally, he stood, hands on hips, surveying the scene. The store looked as if a bull had run amok; goods were strewn everywhere, there were overturned trolleys, smashed bottles and containers, racks of clothes were knocked over. DS Quinn was standing beside a tall, business-like woman with short, greying blonde hair who, in turn, was issuing instructions to a group of staff in a no-nonsense Northern English accent. As Grant walked towards them, the woman turned and, seeming to recognise his authority, extended her hand.

'Good mornin'. I'm Norma Hanton, store manager.'

'DCI Grant McVicar. I take it you've met my sergeant?'

Norma Hanton smiled.

'Yes, indeed, Briony and I are already acquainted.'

Grant smiled back; his impression was of a warm, capable and friendly woman, quite obviously good in a crisis. He took the proffered hand and returned the firm grip.

'Grant, please; bit of a mess in here, Norma.'

'Aye, it is that, Grant, but we'll get it sorted. Fortunately, no-one's been badly hurt, that's the main thing. Well, apart from... which is why you're here, of course.'

'Yes, I'm afraid so.'

'Right, follow me. I've got one of me lads outside the changing rooms, keepin' the place secure as I knew you wouldn't want folk tramplin' all over your crime scene.'

As they made their way through the deserted, chaotic aisles he reflected briefly that Norma Hanton might have made a good cop!

They arrived at the rear corner of the store; a young, dark-haired employee was standing beside a chair, in which a slightly older woman, with mousy-brown hair and wearing a rather slinky scarlet dress, was sitting with a steaming mug in her hand. Her face was white as a sheet and Grant immediately recognised the symptoms of shock. A uniformed security guard was standing at the entrance to the changing area, strips of blue and white police tape deterring any unauthorised entry; he kept glancing nervously behind him as if the body was going to suddenly appear in the doorway. Norma Hanton pointed to each employee in turn.

'This is Kim Chang—she was on duty when the lady came runnin' out—but she's a good lass, Grant, she kept her cool and stayed put—'

Grant could see the young woman smile as her Boss's warm praise hit its mark.

'...and Tom McFall has been keepin' a watchful eye on the place, just in case.'

Briony immediately headed towards the figure in the chair; with a background in victim support, Grant knew that the shocked-looking woman would be in capable hands. He turned towards McFall.

'I take it nothing's been touched?'

'No, Sir. Just stood here like Miss H said, makin' sure that naeb'dy went in after the boys in uniform went away.'

Grant frowned—personally he'd have left an officer guarding the doorway, although he realised that these were rather exceptional circumstances and resources would have been required elsewhere; anyway, McFall appeared reliable enough.

'Good. So, apart from this woman...' he indicated the lady in the chair. No-one has seen or touched the body?'

McFall shook his head.

'Well, just one o' the uniformed boys—think he wis an inspector or somethin'— he went in an' checked, just to make sure the lassie wis...well, you know...but naebody else has tried tae get in since Ah've been standin' here.'

The guard looked nervously over his shoulder again.

'That's fine, Mr McFall, I've already spoken to the officer, I just needed to check...'

He turned as he heard someone approaching and saw two paramedics striding purposefully towards him. He recognised one of them as Karen Walker, a woman not to be trifled with...

'Mornin' Grant! Been diggin' up more bodies for us then?'

'Seems so Karen, although I've not actually seen the victim yet.'

'Aye, well, on you go. We'll take care o' this poor woman first, looks like she's in shock—at least we can do somethin' for her.'

'Okay, Karen. I'll let you know when we're done, although I daresay the pathologist will be along soon to confirm things. Don't think There's any doubt that she's dead, though.'

He looked questioningly across at Briony, who had stood up as Karen Walker had arrived. She nodded.

'Aye, it's Dr Napier that's on duty today an' she's on her way. Be nice to catch up...'

The sarcasm wasn't lost on Grant. Dr Margo Napier frequently lived up to her nickname "Nippy", and he gave a half-hearted smile.

'Och, she's all right underneath the prickly exterior! Right, Bri, let's go...' he looked across the store Oh, good stuff, here's the SOCOs...and Cliff and Grace bringing up the rear.'

He breathed a sigh of slight relief; things were starting to move and, as always, there was the slight frisson of excitement. After all, this was what they were trained for. He stepped over the Police tape, closely followed by his sergeant. It was time...

∿∿∿

If he could, Grant always liked to take a few moments to get what he thought of as the "feel" of the crime scene; to take in the details before anyone else arrived, to look for something out of place. The immediate area, the position of the body, the smell, the sight...death was never pretty but murder was always worse and, as he surveyed the sad little scenario, he asked himself the question that was seldom answered satisfactorily.

Why...?

The victim was young, Grant reckoned, probably in her twenties. Her long dark hair lay across her face but, underneath, he could see that her eyes were wide and staring, a look of surprise...fear., panic set on her reasonably attractive features. There was a livid red mark around her neck and, where the skin had been broken, a few rivulets of blood had run down and on to her white t-shirt, where they had formed small stains, almost like a pattern around the neck-line. He shuddered—what had she done to deserve this? Was she just in the wrong place at the wrong time? He took in the other details; there was a handbag lying on the floor, some of its contents spilled out. Lying beside the dead girl's feet were a purse and an item of clothing, something black and silky-looking. Briony came in to the cramped space and stood beside him; he turned and looked at her—her expression was grim. He spoke quietly, respectfully, as if afraid he might disturb the corpse.

'Thoughts, Bri?'

She had a pained expression on her face as she replied.

'Don't know, but there's that, for a start.'

She pointed; the victim's jeans had been pulled almost to her knees and her brief, cream-coloured panties were around her thighs, as if someone had tried unsuccessfully to remove them.

She shook her head, biting her bottom lip, but said no more; he could understand why.

'So, what's the story with the woman who found her?'

Briony looked up at him.

'What? Oh, em...Susan Fielding, forty-three years old. She'd tried on a dress and had gone back for a smaller size, saw the victim come out of a cubicle as she rushed past. When she came back with the other size she went into her cubicle and found the body. She can't remember much after that. I think she went into a blind panic and started screamin'. That's about it. I'll have another chat in a wee while, once she's calmed down a bit more.'

She paused and looked at the floor.

'Oh, and she said that she'd left her bag behind...'

Their eyes turned to the purse that was lying on the ground beside the victim. Grant looked back at Briony and raised his eyebrows. She nodded.

'Looks like the victim was stealin' Susan Fielding's purse...'

'Excuse me, but if you two have quite finished contaminatin' my crime scene...'

Grant and Briony turned to find SOCO Gordon Harris grinning amiably at them. An experienced and highly competent forensic scientist, he and Grant knew each other of old and held each other in high regard.

'Yer arse! Just having a wee nosey, Gordon. You know how I like to get a sniff of things before you start shifting them about.'

Gordon Harris grunted something unintelligible then turned his gaze to the victim.

'Hmm. Mind you, I know what you mean, Grant, the smell of death...poor lassie, looks like she's been garrotted!'

Grant nodded; it was the second time the phrase had been used.

'Right, Gordon, I'll leave you to it. We'll go and get some statements taken...'

'There's no-one left, Grant, in case you hadn't noticed!'

Grant glowered back at Gordon, who merely grinned back.

'Huh, tell me about it; I take it you know what happened?'

'Aye, they heard you were coming and buggered off sharpish...'

Finally, Grant smiled; he couldn't help himself.

'Och, away and get on with your bloody dusting, Gordon.'

As they left the white-suited SOCOs to get on with their job, Briony had the impression that there was something different about her boss; she couldn't quite put her finger on it but her feminine intuition told her that, somewhere, a woman might just be involved...

They returned to the area outside the changing room, where Susan Fielding looked as if she was beginning to recover. DC Cliff Ford nodded across and gave them a smile; he was looking around the vicinity, checking for anything that might be relevant. The DC's enthusiasm seemed boundless and, despite the occasional slip-up, Grant reckoned he would soon be on track for a well-earned promotion.

DC Grace Lappin, the newest member of their team, was chatting to Briony; the attractive young officer, recently transferred from uniform, was still finding her feet but she had the makings of a decent detective constable. She nodded at Grant; he realised that she was probably nervous and he briefly wondered if she had ever actually seen a murder victim. He walked across.

'Morning, Grace. You okay?'

She attempted a half-hearted smile.

'Em, yup, Boss, I think so.'

'You'll be fine. Listen, just stay out here until...'

She shook her head.

'No, I need to do this—after all, if I'm going to be a decent detective, I can't afford to be squeamish, can I?'

He was impressed by her attitude and gave her a friendly grin, ignoring Briony's surprised glance. He wasn't always known for his empathy.

'That's the attitude, Grace. First is worst. We'll wait for the SOCOs to finish then we'll have a look again, see if we can pick anything up. Right, we'll need another word with—' He glanced at Briony and raised an eyebrow.

'Susan? D'you want me to speak to her again, Boss?'

'Aye, okay, Bri, but I'll listen in. Grace, why don't you go and have a chat with the girl who helped her, Kim Chang, I think the manager said. See if she can tell you who went in and out. The time frame for the murder must be really short if it happened between Susan going out to get the dress then coming back and finding the body. I suspect our killer must have been in one of the other cubicles.'

'Okay, Boss' Grace replied; she paused then looked up at him. He frowned.

'What, Grace?'

'I was just thinking, Boss. If someone *was* already waiting in the changing rooms, who were they waiting for? I mean, was *Susan* maybe the intended victim? Just a thought...'

He considered this for a moment.

'Aye, fair point, Grace, I'll bear it in mind. Right, you go and talk to Kim, see what she has to say.'

As Grace turned away, they walked across to where Susan Fielding was still sitting, looking somewhat ridiculous in the slightly-oversized red dress. Karen Walker glared at their approach—as usual, she was on the defensive, the well-being of her charge was her first concern and she knew that Grant would want to question the woman. He smiled at her but it had no effect.

'Can it no' wait, Grant?

He shook his head.

'It's a murder, Karen, you know it can't, I'm sorry.'

The paramedic grunted something that sounded like "unsympathetic bugger", but Grant ignored it. Although he and Karen didn't always see eye-to-eye, he had great respect for her and her ability to do the job. He looked around for a chair but couldn't see one and, as Briony had already crouched down beside the woman, he did the same, feeling a slight twinge of pain in his right knee as he did so. He ignored it.

Briony laid her hand gently on Susan's arm as she spoke, softly and sympathetically, to the still-shocked woman.

'Right, Susan, this is my boss, DCI McVicar. I've told him what you told me already but I need you to think very carefully about anythin' else you may have seen. Did anyone go in or out of the changin' area while you were there, eh? Did you see or hear anythin' unusual? Did you notice anyone hangin' about?'

The woman looked at Briony with the expression of a rabbit caught in headlights and Grant could see tears welling up in her eyes. He felt a rush of sympathy for her as she shook her head rather violently, causing her lank brown hair to flop across her face.

'No, no, I don't think so. I mean, I'd tried on this lovely dress... we're going to a party next Saturday and I didn't have...it was so nice, you see and I'd tried my usual size but it was too big and I was really chuffed, you see, because I've been trying so hard...'

Briony smiled at her as the words tumbled out.

'It's okay, just take your time, that's it, take a deep breath...and out...and another. There you go. Now, let's go through it all again, eh. Nice and slowly, That's it...'

Grant envied his sergeant's ability to calm down a near-hysterical witness as Susan managed to compose herself slightly. Her background in victim support had frequently proved its worth.

'Well, okay, so I saw the dress and I decided to try it on. I took a sixteen—that's what I usually am, you see—but it was too big! Well, you know how good that feels...'

Despite her state of shock, she regarded Briony's lithe form with a woman's critical eye and gave the DS a slightly rueful, watery smile.

'No, you probably don't, do you? Anyway, I was in a bit of a rush as I hadn't actually done any of the normal shopping. I dashed out to get the fourteen and this girl...'

Grant saw her face start to crumble; he had already realised that, apart from the murderer, Susan would probably have been the last person to see the victim alive. Briony gave the woman's hand a squeeze.

'It's all right, love, take your time.'

Susan sniffed back the tears and continued.

'Well, she came out of the cubicle next to mine, she was quite pretty, nice figure...anyway, I noticed that she was holding something— I think it was black—and she looked...well, sad, I suppose, really. But I was in a rush, I said something to her about the size and dashed out to find the fourteen. It was only when I was coming back that I realised I'd left my bag sitting but I was sure it'd be okay.'

For the first time she looked at Grant, her eyes widening in a silent question. He nodded his head.

'Susan, we think that the victim may have been in the act of stealing your purse; it was on the floor beside her body.'

Susan Fielding winced at the use of the word and Briony gave him a sideways glance. He decided to let her continue.

'So, what then, Susan? What else do you remember? Did you see anyone else goin' in, eh?'

She shook her head again.

'No, I don't think so. The young assistant was outside and she smiled at me as I went back in. To be honest, I was in a bit of a panic when I realised I'd left my purse behind.'

'Okay, that's good. Now, can you think back to when you went in the first time? Did you see anyone else go in or out then?'

Susan considered the question for a moment.

'Em, well, there was the young girl at the door, as I said. Oh, and there was a blonde woman who came in just behind me...'

She furrowed her brows slightly.

'Actually, now I come to think of it...'

'What, Susan, what is it?' asked Briony.

'Well, I think she might have been looking at the same dress as I was; when I took it in, I had the feeling I'd just seen her, if you know what I mean. Oh—'

Susan's eyes widened and her bottom lip started to tremble.

'What, Susan?'

'I saw her again just as I came back to the changing room. She was walking away and seemed to be in a bit of a hurry—well, I suppose I was too, but—oh, my God! Was she the...did she...?'

She started to sob again and Briony squeezed her hand.

'That's all right, Susan, you go ahead and have a wee cry, it's fine, you've been a big help.'

She looked at Grant and held up her free hand, gesturing for him to back off. He stood up, his knees giving another loud crack as he did so. He looked over at Grace, who appeared to have finished taking the statement from Kim Chang. She walked back across and he raised a questioning eyebrow.

'Well, Boss, Kim seems to be a pretty credible witness. They weren't too busy. She remembers the lady there...' She indicated Susan...going in with the red dress then, just after her, she remembers a tall, blonde lady going in with a pair of trousers. An older woman took in a skirt but came back out fairly quickly and left it on the rack. Then she remembers the victim taking in a black jump-suit. She's given me pretty good descriptions.'

'Good; let's hear more about this blonde.'

Grace paused.

'You think it's her, Boss?'

'Too early to say, Grace. What did Kim say?'

Grace consulted her notes, written long-hand in a small, neat script.

'Well, Kim reckons she was tall—maybe about five-ten—and seemed...'

She consulted her notes with a slight frown.

...well-built and strong-looking," was her impression. She had long, straight blonde hair, very shiny and nicely styled. Apparently, she didn't say much, just went in with a pair of black trousers. She was wearing white jeans— Kim said they looked a wee bit tight on her—and a green, silky long-sleeved top. Actually, the way she put it was that the woman looked a bit "tarty", if you know what I mean?'

Grant nodded; he knew.

'So, Kim didn't take much notice but she reckons that the blonde was in for a good wee while. Susan came back out, saying that she was going to change the dress for a fourteen. Apparently, she seemed really happy as she'd said she needed a smaller size than usual. Then, quite soon after that, the blonde woman went back out, handed Kim the trousers and left.'

'Did she say anything?'

'Just mumbled "thanks" then walked off, Boss.'

'Did Kim say if she was in a rush?'

'Em, I didn't ask. Listen, I'll go and have another wee chat.'

'You do that, Grace. See if she can remember anything else about this blonde—at the moment, she could be our prime suspect. Get a more detailed description if you can...'

Suddenly Grace's expression changed very slightly, her lips twitching upwards in a smile. He turned; another of his team was approaching, his young tech-guru, be-turbanned DC Fasil Bajwa. He smiled over at them, his white teeth gleaming through his dark beard.

'Morning, Boss. Hi Grace.'

Aye aye...!

There had been a time when a relationship between fellow officers would have been strongly discouraged, but nowadays? Well, things had certainly changed since Grant's early days in Paisley's "K" Division, although his own relationship at the time would still be strongly and actively discouraged...he suppressed the painful thought.

It had been Grace Lappin, then stationed in Partick, who had provided the initial information on the Domestic Services Agency, three of whose young men had been brutally murdered; and it had been Faz Bajwa who had suggested that Grant recruit her as a detective constable. Grant was well aware of the growing chemistry between the two young officers before he had offered her a transfer and he had felt it necessary to discuss the situation with DC Bajwa...

~~~

'Right, Faz. I'm taking Grace on as part of the team, very slightly against my better judgement, I have to say.'

Faz had looked at his boss uneasily as he continued.

'Listen, we all know the stresses and strains that come with this job, none better than me. And, yes, there's an argument that a relationship with a fellow officer can lead to a better element of understanding, a more sympathetic partner...but my worry is this; if things *do* go wrong with your relationship, I can't afford to have personal issues affecting your ability to function as a detective...'

And, even as he had spoken the words, he had realised the irony of them; after all, it hadn't been that long since his own personal issues had nearly led to his suspension from a murder enquiry...

~~~

Grant stood thoughtfully rubbing his beard as he surveyed the scene. He was aware of considerable activity in the store as the staff worked hard to restore order from the earlier chaos. He could hear Norma Hanton issuing orders in her rich, warm Lancashire accent and he could sense the loyalty to her amongst the staff, the desire to help—not unlike his own little team, he realised with a surge of emotion; they were a bloody good bunch...

He had sent Faz and Grace to the security office to check the CCTV recordings; at present, everything seemed to be indicating that the anonymous blonde woman was their main suspect and he wanted to see if there were any usable images of her. Susan Fielding was changing back into her own clothes, about to be taken to Paisley's Royal Alexandra Hospital, more due to her collapse and the possibility that she had concussion rather than her state of shock. Briony was still chatting to Kim Chang while Cliff and DC Kiera Fox were looking about for anything that may be relevant. They had already retrieved the trousers that the suspect had taken into the changing cubicle and, along with the hanger, they had been carefully bagged to check for any fingerprints or DNA, although Grant thought that the latter was highly unlikely. If the woman had been planning a murder, he doubted that she'd have bothered to try on the trousers in the first place. He was waiting for the SOCOs to finish, then he and his own team would get a better look at the victim and the immediate area. He was about to turn away when he noticed a slight, wiry female striding towards him. Smartly-dressed, tightly-permed dyed-blonde hair, pursed smoker's lips, the characteristic frown...

Dr Margo "Nippy" Napier.

He smiled, with little hope of receiving a response then, just as she approached, his mobile rang. He ignored it—Dr Napier detested mobile phones and became decidedly "nippier" when they interrupted her.

'Good morning, Doctor.'

'Grant. You're well?'

'Yes, thanks. I'm good. And you?'

'Well, I could do without this, of course. Fortunately, I'd just left church but the minister had invited me to lunch. To be honest, I don't know why I don't retire.'

Grant did; death was the woman's life. Despite her protests, she lived for the job and she was a highly qualified and respected pathologist who was a formidable presence in court, a match for even the best defence counsel.

'Anyway, what do we have?'

'Well, the SOCOs are still in, so I've only had a brief look. A young girl, twenties, I'd say, looks like she's been strangled. The odd thing is that her jeans and underwear have been pulled down...'

Dr Napier frowned.

'Hmm...doesn't sound too pleasant. Sexual motive, do you think?'

'I couldn't say, Doctor. At the moment, it appears that the victim was in the act of stealing a purse. The cubicle had just been vacated by a lady who was fetching a smaller size of dress and we don't actually know which woman was the intended victim, or if it was just a random act.'

'Oh well, I suppose that's your job...is there anywhere I can get a cup of tea, do you imagine?'

Grant smiled inwardly; this was often Nippy's first priority and he could certainly do with one himself.

'I'll have a word with the store manager, she's a good sort.'

His phone rang again and Margo Napier glared up at him.

'Aren't you going to answer that?'

'Oh, em, yes...sorry...'

He pulled the phone from his pocket and saw that the call was from Osprey House, home to the Major Investigation Teams; technically, his "head office". As he swiped to answer it, he turned and saw that Briony was also on a call—she looked across at him, her eyes widening in surprise as he answered his own phone.

'McVicar.'

ᒧᑌᑌᒧ

"All in red, she's all in red, she's all...all in red..."

Oh God, another bloody "red" song. Why do they come into my head like that?

Who was it again? Oh, yes, "It Bites." —I quite liked them, especially "Calling all the Heroes..."

Anyway, let's think. Red... Red or dead...

That's more like it...

"...the red in my mind..."

CHAPTER 2

It really was a lovely dress.

And, of course, like so many lovely things, it was quite unnecessary; in fact, it was debatable if there was actually space in her wardrobe. But it *was* only nineteen pounds...

Natalie Wheeler sighed and did a quick mental calculation; she had only been about half-way through the weekly shop in Tesco's Linwood branch but her trolley was already well-laden; still, the budget might just stretch to it. She had recently started using the "scan as you shop" system and the running total was standing at £67.59, with a good number of items on her list still to be purchased; she had long since learned just how expensive the upkeep of two teenage boys could be. She held the dress up against herself; it looked a nice length (she had shapely calves and slim ankles) and a nice cut (she always felt she could do with some emphasis on her slightly narrow hips). And she *did* love red...

She put it back on the rack and moved away; she could always look again next week.

But what if the size twelve has gone...oh bugger it...

She turned back, took the dress back off the rack and walked purposefully towards the changing area. Lifting her handbag from the trolley she stepped into one of the small cubicles which, today, appeared to be lying unlocked; although it was only just before lunchtime, the space was already untidy, with a few labels and broken hangers strewn on the floor. She unfastened her belt, sat down on the little seat, removed her trainers then stood up again and stepped out of her jeans. She pulled her t-shirt over her head, catching a glimpse of herself in the mirror. Her boobs were full and round (helped somewhat by the black push-up bra), she had good legs and, although she was a bit skinny round the hips, her bum was reasonably shapely (the slinky black thong helped, of course!)

Not bad, Natalie, not bad, you've still got it, girl. If only bloody Tommy would notice a bit more often...still, maybe the dress...

She grinned; red also happened to be Tommy's favourite colour. Red for danger...red for sex...surely nineteen pounds was a small price to pay?

She lifted the slinky little number—it was made of a silky, viscose material that she knew her husband liked—and slipped it over her head. Perfect! Well, almost.

It really was a lovely dress...and the twelve was just a wee bit too big!

Happy days...!

She decided to try a size 10 instead, knowing her figure would allow her to get away with it being slightly tight; anyway, she now had it in her mind that she was purchasing it more for what she termed "recreational purposes" than to wear out. She smiled and gave a little anticipatory shiver at the thought of Tommy's strong hands caressing her...

Oooh, you naughty girl...

She slipped on her worn, grubby trainers (which did nothing to enhance the outfit), grabbed her handbag again and trotted back out to the clothes racks, where another two women were now looking at *her* dress. One, a tall, blonde and somewhat more generously-sized female, lifted up a size 14; Natalie smiled inwardly.

In your dreams, sweetheart, in your dreams! No way you're a fourteen...

She said nothing but, as if reading her mind, the woman put the dress back on the rack and walked away without a backward glance. The second, a slightly older woman, was holding a size 10 and, as Natalie's gaze searched the rack, she realised that it was the only one left.

Oh no!

The woman smiled at Natalie and shook her head.

'Hmm, I'm no' really that sure about it. Looks nice on you, though, pet.'

'Oh, thanks—'it's just a bit big though. I was going to try a ten, but I think that's the last one.'

Natalie pointed to the dress and the woman handed it to her, a wistful look on her face.

'Here, hen. It's no' really ma colour, to be honest. Go on, knock him deid!'

The older woman winked and Natalie smiled back at her, grabbing the dress with unbecoming haste.

'Thanks, I will.'

She dashed back to the cubicle, clutching her prize but, as she closed the door behind her, she was suddenly aware of a movement and, to her horror, she realised that someone had been standing behind it. She opened her mouth to scream but, before she could, she felt something thin and cold being placed round her neck, pulling tightly and painfully against her skin. She tried to pull it off but, already it was biting into her flesh—she could feel the dampness of her blood, warm and sticky. In desperation she kicked at her assailant's legs as she tried to break free but their hold on her was too strong. As the panic rose inside her, the unidentified object started to tighten even further and the image in the mirror of the attractive girl in the lovely red dress started to swim. As her life slipped away, she was overwhelmed with a feeling of great sadness that Tommy would never get to see her in it.

For FUCK *sake...*

Grant ended the call and looked across at Briony who, like him, was standing with her mouth agape. He slid the phone into his pocket and, ignoring the glare from Margo Napier, took the few steps across to his sergeant.

'You got the call too, Bri?'

'Aye, they tried you first, then me.'

'Didn't answer...was talking to the doctor...Christ, this is all we bloody need.'

He thought for a moment, his dark brows furrowed. He reached a decision.

'Right, you and Kiera stay here, Bri, you take charge. I'll leave Faz to look at the CCTV and take Grace and Cliff with me; they've had a good look round here, they might notice if there's any visible similarities. Listen, can you get some more uniforms to secure the locus at Tesco while I'm on my way over; the pickup's bloody miles away so it may take a wee while to get there. We need to hold on to as many shoppers as we can, there might be a better chance of finding a witness given that there's not been a mass evacuation of the premises this time. Oh, and we'll need to try and get more officers to help take statements too. Can you phone The Mint and see what she can rustle up?'

Superintendent Patricia Minto was their superior officer and, despite their occasional differences, Grant knew that he could rely on her to do what she could to ensure that they had sufficient uniformed cover for the investigation.

'Will do, Boss. Em, I think the doctor's wantin' to speak to you, eh—...'

Grant turned round. Dr Napier was wearing a thunderous expression as she spoke.

'I haven't got all bloody day, Grant. The SOCO's look like they're nearly finished and they're waiting to talk to you; could we get a move on, if it's not too much trouble?'

He suppressed an angry response to her sarcastic comment.

'Aye, sorry Doctor. Bad news, I'm afraid.'

'Oh? What?'

'There's been another body found, in Tesco, just along the road.'

He saw the doctor's eyes widen slightly in surprise.

'God Almighty, what's the world coming to? This was what happened last time, if I recall.'

Her voice tailed off as the troubling memories played out in her mind...just as they did in Grant's. She gave a heavy sigh and continued.

'Oh well, I'd best get started here, I take it you're heading over there now?'

'Yes, I'm leaving Briony in charge here. You know where it is, just the other side of the A737?'

'Yes, I *am* familiar with it, Grant. Right, off you go, I'll be along as soon as I'm done here. Let's hope this is the last—'

Aye, let's hope...

∿∿∿

As Grant had suspected, the short journey from where he had left his Toyota pick-up to the nearby Tesco took about twenty minutes. Finally, he took a right turn off the main road and nosed the bulky pick-up into the supermarket car park, which was being guarded by a young female uniformed cop. He showed his ID, which she checked carefully.

'Okay Sir, that's fine. Just mind how you go, though. Despite our best efforts, it seems everyone's trying to do a runner—'

They turned and looked towards the exit, where another, rather jaded looking policeman was being harassed by the female driver, fag in mouth, of an ageing four by four that had clearly seen better days.

'Listen, Ah'm in a hurry, pal. Ah've got a load o' frozen stuff an' three weans.'

'I'm sorry Ma'am, but we just need a few details and a statement.'

'Ah don't give a flyin' fuck, if you'll pardon the French. Ah huvn'ae done nuthin.'

The weary, middle-aged cop changed his tone.

'I'll have to ask you to tone it down a bit, Madam. Pull your vehicle over there and my colleague will take a few details. If not...well, we have your registration and we'll...'

Grant looked back at the young constable and winked.

'Aye, best of luck. Cheers.'

He drove on, parking as close as he could to the store entrance, already cordoned off with blue and white Police tape. As they approached the entrance, they could see a group of mutinous-looking shoppers giving the two uniformed cops at the door considerable verbal grief and Grant strode quickly across, his tall, well-built physique and his authoritative demeanour immediately causing the rowdy ensemble to quieten down. He folded his arms and glowered at them for a few seconds.

'Right, if I can have your attention please, ladies and gentlemen.'

They fell silent.

'As you probably know, an incident has taken place in the store. We need to take a statement from each of you.'

There was a collective groan.

'...quiet, please. Now, this will be brief, mostly your personal details and any additional information that you can give us that may be of use. I'll get as many officers as I can on to this to avoid you being delayed any further. Now, if you could just wait here please, I'll speak to the manager and see if we can arrange somewhere more convenient. Thank you all for your patience, you should be on your way shortly.'

As he spoke, he looked across at the cafeteria that occupied the right-hand side of the store—that would do nicely! He turned to Cliff.

'Cliff, can you organise taking the statements over there in the cafeteria. Oh, and if there was, by any chance, a coffee.'

Cliff managed a grin; he knew his boss's needs and requirements only too well.

'Aye, on it, Boss.'

Grant then turned to the nearest uniformed officer, who was looking at him with an almost reverential expression.

'Any idea who or where the manager is?'

'Yes, Sir, he's at the clothing department, where the body was found. I can take you over.'

'Just hang on.' He looked at the assembly once more.

'Right folks, just give me a minute and we'll get all this sorted out.'

He turned to his constable.

'Okay Grace, let's go and see what we've got.'

The two detectives followed the uniformed officer across to the clothing area that sat adjacent to the checkouts; a tall, bearded man with receding grey hair, was standing with a decidedly troubled look on his sharp features. The constable turned to Grant.,

'This is Mr Patrick Queenan, the store manager, Sir. Mr Queenan, this is...em—'

Grant extended his hand.

'Detective Chief Inspector Grant McVicar. How do you do, Sir.'

The man stepped forward and took Grant's hand, speaking in a polite, northern-Scottish accent.

'How do you do, Chief Inspector. Nice to meet you, thank you very much for coming.'

Grant was used to people in such situations saying slightly inappropriate things; on this particular occasion the store manager made him feel as if he was arriving to opening a fête!

'And this is my colleague, DC Grace Lappin.'

Patrick Queenan duly shook Grace's hand, giving her a nervous smile. Grant spoke again.

'I'm sorry to have to meet you in such circumstances, Mr Queenan, but if you could tell me what's happened so far.'

Patrick Queenan adopted an even more sombre expression; unlike Norma, his Asda counterpart, Grant thought the man would have been better employed as a funeral director.

'Well, normally the changing room doors are locked and a member of staff has to open them if anyone wants to try something on. You see, it's just to prevent people from putting garments on under their own clothes then walking out of the store—'

Grant nodded, remembering his years as a beat constable in Paisley. There was little that surprised him.

'...but we had a couple of staff phone in sick today so we had to re-deploy the others and it left us a bit short in the clothing department. I said just to leave the cubicles open until we managed to get a few more bodies... Oh, sorry, that's a bit inappropriate, I suppose—'

'It's fine, Mr Queenan, don't worry.'

'Well, em...anyway, Kimberley, the department manager, was checking to make sure everything was okay—you'd be surprised how quickly the place gets untidy—she walked into the cubicle and there she was...'

The man was now visibly upset and Grant felt decidedly sorry for him; he didn't seem to be coping nearly as well as Norma Hanton. He wondered if Mr Queenan had heard of the earlier incident but decided not to mention it for the moment.

'Okay, well, we'll need to have a word with Kimberley, of course. How's she bearing up?

'Em, reasonably well actually, all things considered. You see, she was in the fire service for about twelve years, so she's made of stern stuff, our Kimberley; probably not her first body...a nice girl too; she's in the staffroom. Do you want a word now?'

'No, not just yet, Mr Queenan, Listen, if it's okay, why don't you go and tell Kimberly that we'll be along in a bit, I'll just have a look about here and get a feel for things, if you don't mind.'

A look of relief spread across Patrick Queenan's gloomy features; the man was obviously glad to get away from the scene.

'Oh, no, no, of course not. Em, what about the customers though? Your officers have stopped them from leaving and things seemed to be getting a bit fraught. People don't like being caught up in events like this, you know...'

'No, I fully appreciate that, Mr Queenan, but I have the situation under control now. I've asked another of my officers to organise the taking of statements in the cafeteria, if that's okay; the uniformed officers will have started taking them as we speak, then once they've got all the relevant details, your customers will be allowed to leave. Listen, I fully sympathise, Mr Queenan; I know this is the last thing you want on a Sunday morning and, believe me, murder is the last thing we want too. We'll get it all over with as soon as we can and let you get back to normal.'

Grant knew that it would some considerable time before "normal" returned to the store, as people were always understandably reluctant to return to the scene of such macabre events; well, apart from the thrill-seekers! The manager gave him a fleeting smile then turned and walked away. Grant looked at

Grace, she seemed to be bearing up reasonably well, he thought, but the next few minutes would be the *real* test...

This time, a uniformed constable was standing outside the door to the changing room and he nodded as Grant and Grace approached. They stopped in front of him.

'In here?'

'Aye Sir,' said the cop. No' a pretty sight, I'm afraid—'

Although the officer looked at Grant as he made this statement, he rolled his eyes very slightly in Grace's direction. Grant glanced at his DC, who had turned white.

'You're sure you're okay, Grace?'

She swallowed hard and looked up at him.

'No, Boss, I'm not okay, not really. But if I can't face the sight of a murdered body, what use am I going to be to you?'

He gave her a rare, kindly smile.

'Fair point. Right then, let's get it over with. Gloves on, don't touch anything unless you have to. Tread very carefully, watch you don't disturb the crime scene or the SOCO's will be down on you like the proverbial ton of bricks. Oh, and one more thing—'

She had turned even whiter as she pulled on the thin latex gloves. As she replied, he could hear her voice quaver and his heart went out to the nervous young woman; he could still remember, all too clearly, his own first murder investigation—hence the warning!

'What, Boss?'

He winked at her.

'If you plan on throwing up, can you do it outside the room, please?'

Grant surveyed the sad sight that greeted them; he could hear Grace breathing deeply beside him but she seemed to be holding up. The victim had been an attractive woman in life, she was attractive still, apart from the bulging eyes, the pallor of death and the angry red mark around her neck; again, there was that slightly surprised, or shocked, look on her face. She lay where she had fallen, undignified and pathetic, on the floor of the changing room, the red dress hoisted above her waist, her naked buttocks facing towards the door and a pair of grubby trainers on her feet. Her handbag, apparently unopened, lay beside her where it had fallen and a second, identical dress, still on its hanger, lay beside it. He exhaled slowly, feeling a wave of pity and sympathy for this seemingly innocent woman whose life had been so violently cut short. Was she married? Did she have kids? Once again, the massive boulder that was murder had been cast into the small, tranquil pool... he sighed wearily and asked himself the question once again.

Why...?

He lowered his voice and spoke to Grace. He knew it was important to keep her focussed, to prevent her from dwelling too long on the brutality and tragedy of the situation.

'Right. Tell me, Grace, what do you see? What's important here, what wee details might give us a clue. Anything. Look around, look for something—well, other than the body, of course, but something that's odd, something that doesn't fit.'

Grace Lappin squared her shoulders and did as Grant asked. She was fighting it, she could feel the bile rising in her throat, but she was determined not to let herself, or her boss, down. She replied, hesitantly at first but with a growing confidence.

'Em, well, it looks as if she's been strangled, of course...and she looks surprised. Oh, but maybe—'

Grant interrupted.

'No, it's not always the case. She *does* look as if she'd been surprised. Go on.'

'Oh, okay; well, of course, there's the fact that she's not wearing pants. That's kinda odd.'

'Is it?'

'Oh yes, I'd say so, Boss, especially if you're just out doing the weekly shopping; and if you suddenly decide to try on a dress.'

'But how do you know she *was* just out shopping, Grace?

She looked up at him, narrowing her eyes.

'Well, there was a half-full trolley just outside, with a list sitting on top. I'm assuming it's hers—'

Grant hadn't actually noticed this.

'Well spotted—I'd missed that! We'll check, of course, but you're probably right. So, if she *was* just out doing the weekly shop, she'd be unlikely to be, em—'

'Native?' Grace managed a small smile, she was beginning to relax slightly and, to her great relief, the feeling of nausea was starting to pass. Yes, I'd think it would be very unlikely. She was wearing jeans and a t-shirt, by the looks of it; she wasn't dressed to impress, she was dressed for comfort and I'd be almost certain that she'd have been wearing some kind of underwear. She'd have been quite uncomfortable otherwise.'

'So, the murderer may have removed them. That's interesting.'

Grace gave him a questioning look. He realised that she hadn't been into the Asda changing room.

'You didn't see the body in Asda, did you?'

She shook her head.

'Well, the victim there was wearing jeans but they'd been pulled down to her knees and her pants were half-way down her thighs, as if the murderer had tried to rip them off.'

'Right...' Grace replied....so, trophies, maybe?'

'Hmm, maybe. Strange, though. You see, we're not sure if the murdered girl in Asda was actually the intended victim, seems she only nipped into the cubicle to steal Susan Fielding's purse.'

'Really? Wait—the dress that Susan Fielding had tried on— wasn't it red too, although a darker shade than this one?'

Grant thought for a moment.

'Aye, it was, you're right enough. So, we've got two female victims, both trying on red dresses, with apparent intent by the murderer to remove their underwear after they were killed.'

Grace Lappin remained silent for a moment.

'There's something else, Boss, something that seems a wee bit odd. Maybe just a co-incidence, but—'

'What's that?'

'Well, in both cases, it seems that the dresses were too big and both victims—well, if Susan *was* the intended victim, I suppose—had gone to get a smaller size.'

'What makes you say that, Grace? How do you know this victim had gone for a smaller size?'

She considered the question for a moment—what *had* made her say it? It was just a feeling she had, an instinct...

'Well, my first thought was that the dress she's wearing looked to be on the big side and she'd gone to get another one, presumably in a smaller size– she'd put her trainers back on, you see. She must have taken them off when she took off her jeans.'

'Right...so what's the significance there?'

Grace looked up at her boss.

'In my experience, the sizes stated usually tend to be on the small side. So, I'm usually a size ten but sometimes I need a size twelve, depending on the fit, the brand, the shop it's in, do you see what I mean?'

He had a vague idea; he nodded and let her continue.

'So, presumably, both women would have selected what they thought was their correct size first, with a slight expectation that they might be a wee bit tight. Then, once they try the dresses on, they find that their normal size is actually a bit big, so they both had to go and fetch a smaller size. That *is* unusual, especially in different shops; oh, and, of course, with similarly-coloured dresses. Listen, Boss, is it all right if I have a wee look?'

'Aye, but remember what I said, Grace.'

She stepped carefully towards the body then stopped. Could she actually touch this poor girl? She gritted her teeth; she was buggered if she was going to let her nerves get the better of her. She knelt down, reached forward and very carefully turned over the neck of the dress, reading the size label.

'Okay, it's a size fourteen. Hmm...looking at her build, I'd have put her about a twelve, maybe slightly less—'

She turned over the collar of the dress that the victim had been clutching.

'So, this one *is* a twelve. Why would she have tried on the bigger size first, I wonder?

She stood back up and shook her head.

'Seems odd, Boss. Most girls know their size pretty accurately... hang on...'

She knelt back down and looked at the hanger that was tangled up in the second dress. She turned and smiled up at him.

'And here's the reason. The second dress is a twelve but the hanger says it's a ten. Now wait...'

She stood up and crossed to the peg on the wall.'

'So, if this is the hanger for the dress she's wearing—'

She looked at it.

'That's it.'

'That's what?' asked Grant, somewhat mystified; the sizing of women's clothing was unfamiliar territory.

'She tried on what she though was the correct size, a twelve. But, although the hanger says size twelve, the dress is actually a fourteen, a size up. The second dress *is* the correct size, but the hanger says it's a ten, which should normally be a size too small.'

'Right...but what's the significance of that?'

She smiled, the nerves and the nausea now completely forgotten.

'Well, Boss, most women wish they were a size smaller, guys probably do too, I suppose. So, you go to try on a dress—well, a pair of trousers, in your case— and you take what you think is the correct size. You expect them to fit or, at worst, to be a bit tight, but the last thing you want is to have to go up a size, it's kind of an admission of defeat, yeah?'

He nodded; he knew the feeling.

'Okay, so, if it's too tight, you feel pretty fed up and you probably just put it back. But when you try on your normal size and it's too big? Well, that's always good news and the first thing you want to do is rush out and find the smaller size, to prove to yourself that you're heading in the right direction.'

'So, are you suggesting that the dresses were deliberately placed on the wrong hangers? But surely, they would all have to be the same? Anyway, what if it's just a mistake that the store made?'

'Yes, of course, Boss, you're right, even just a customer putting them back the wrong way round. But it's a bit of a co-incidence that the two sizes are mixed up then, when she gets back, someone strangles her...'

She stopped mid-sentence, a doubtful look on her face.

'Sorry, am I getting ahead of myself here, Boss?'

He shook his head; he was much impressed by his new DC's intuition and her train of thought.

'No, Grace, you're doing great; and there's one way to find out. Come on...'

A quick examination of the rack containing the red dresses had shown that they were, indeed, all wrongly sized; they ranged from a size twelve to a size eighteen and the garment on each hanger was one size up from the size stated. Grace was now searching for the three size twelve dresses that, presumably, had been placed on the spare size eighteen hangers elsewhere in the department.

Grant had questioned Kimberley Smart, the department manager, a tall, short-haired woman that he placed in her late forties. She had assured him that they had been correct when put out on display—despite a rather masculine demeanour she gave the impression that she took considerable pride in her job—but, other than the discovery of the body, the woman had little to add. Although she seemed to be coping well enough, there was a vague, distant look in her eyes that Grant recognised; he remembered Patrick Queenan saying that she had been in Fire and Rescue and he wondered if she had possibly had a breakdown of some sort, or was even suffering from post-traumatic stress disorder.

However, although her statement was both coherent and concise, it added little of relevance; she hadn't seen the mysterious blonde woman and, due to the staffing problems, she had spent most of the morning working in the stockroom. Gordon Harris had arrived with another SOCO, having left two of his colleagues finishing off at the Asda crime scene, and had started his meticulous examination of the body and the surrounding area. He had brought Grant up to date with his findings, including the identity and address of the first victim. It was time to catch up with his sergeant; he took out his mobile.

'Hi Boss, how's it goin' at Tesco?'

'Aye, very interesting, Bri, very—'

'And how's Grace holdin' up?'

'Grace...?'

He paused briefly.

'...well, to be perfectly honest, she's been great so far!'

'Really? An' she was fine with the body an' everythin'?'

'Yup. Turned a wee bit white at first but got over it very quickly. Listen, Bri, I need you to check something for me.'

'Okay Boss, fire away.'

'I need you to check the size of the red dress, the one that Susan Fielding was trying on, against the size on the hanger. Check the stock on display too, I think that young Grace might just be on to something. By the way, Gordon tells me he's identified the first victim.'

'Aye, her name was Amanda Duff, home address in Elderslie. I've checked, she's got no form but there was only a twenty-pound note in her purse, no credit or debit cards and the play-suit thingy she was holdin' was thirty-four quid. Bit o' a shortfall, eh?'

'Hmm. As good a reason as any to steal Susan Fielding's purse, I suppose. Looks like an opportunist theft, then. So where does that leave us with Susan? Was she the intended victim, do you think?'

'Hard to know, Boss. I put it to her as gently as I could before the ambulance took her away, but she just fell apart again, says she has no idea why anyone would want to harm her, she was in an awful state. So, what's this story with the dress sizes, then?'

'Well, turns out the victim in Tesco was also trying on a red dress, which is a co-incidence in itself. The modus looks the same, although I'm sure Nippy will keep us right...anyway, all the red dresses here are sized wrongly, the actual dress is one size up from what it was on the hanger, if you see what I mean...'

'Aye—listen, hang on a moment...'

He heard Briony speaking and waited a few seconds. She spoke again.

'Well, that *is* interestin', Boss. Remember Susan ran out to get a smaller size? Well, she said in her statement that she's normally a sixteen but the one she tried was too big. The hanger on the second one says that it's a fourteen, but the dress is actually a sixteen, her correct size. The one she was still wearin' is an eighteen; Gordon's bagged up and taken the hanger but she said it was definitely a sixteen she lifted. I'll get Kiera to go and check the stock on display and see if they're all the same. I suppose we should take the second dress and hanger that Susan has, just in case.'

'Aye, do that, Bri; God, I'm learning fast about women's clothes sizes!'

He paused, then spoke more softly.

'Oh, and it looks like you and I are going to have a rough afternoon, you know...'

Briony Quinn sighed, knowing only too well what he meant; her sympathetic nature meant she was usually the one left to break the tragic news.

CHAPTER 3

Osprey House was one of several generic, brick-built buildings sitting just off Paisley's Inchinnan Road. Most people driving past would just presume it to be part of a small industrial development, one of many dotted about the area in an attempt to replace the long-gone heavy industries. The only give-away was the high security fence and the barrier controlling the entrance, under which Grant's Toyota pick-up was now passing. Being a Sunday, the car park was fairly empty and he pulled in to a space near the main entrance. As he climbed the steps, his phone rang; he pulled it out of his pocket, staring at the screen with a mixture of surprise and shock; he had completely forgotten that, when he had left Bluebell Cottage that morning, he had also left a woman in his bed. He let it ring until, finally, it fell silent; then, as he stood outside the entrance, he closed his eyes, trying in vain to block out the memories of the previous evening...

It had started the previous year; following the case that had come to be known as "the bodies in the loch", he had subconsciously avoided Castle Semple Loch. However, in late October, wakening to a bright and crisp autumn morning, he had decided that it was time to dust off his trusty mountain-bike and try to lay another ghost to rest.

It took him the best part of an hour to get the machine roadworthy but, eventually, he was cycling on the once-familiar circuit that took him down through the village of Howwood, then onto the cycle track that skirted the western edge of the loch. As he cycled past the rowing club, he stopped for a breather but, as he took a long drink from his water bottle, a figure came up behind him.

'Well, well, look who it is.'

He turned; the voice was vaguely familiar but he couldn't place the attractive, athletic-looking woman who was smiling at him; sensing his slight embarrassment, she extended her hand.

'Tina Sturrock. Captain of the rowing club...?'

'Oh, of course, sorry, Tina—it's been a while.'

They shook hands.

'It has, and you can't be expected to remember every witness, I suppose. Anyway, how are you, Grant...?'

Forty-five minutes later, and very much to his astonishment, he had found himself cast adrift on the loch, in a long, narrow rowing boat (a training single, Tina had informed him) with two floats attached (apparently to stop him from capsizing, although he was very much doubting it) and a pair of oars (or blades, as Tina had called them) that appeared to be too long and had to cross over each other as he attempted to row.

It had been one of the most difficult things he had ever attempted!

∿∿∿

The door to Osprey House opened and two detective constables exited, holding it open for him.

'Afternoon Sir.'

'Oh, afternoon...Cheers...'

He entered the building, pushing the thoughts out of his mind and trying to focus on the case in hand. He had just reached his office when his phone pinged with a text message. He looked at the screen.

"Hi babe. Just wondered when u'll b home so I can have something HOT waiting for u! xxxx"

Fuck...!

∿∿∿

Grant had found that he really enjoyed the challenge of rowing (or sculling, as it was known) but after a few months, he had realised that he was more looking forward to spending time in the company of Tina Sturrock. As he had walked along the car park with her, following the previous day's training session, they had chatted with a comfortable familiarity. Finally, as they had headed towards their respective vehicles, on an impulse he had turned back towards her.

'Em, Tina...'

She spun back to face him.

'Yes, Grant?'

'By any chance are you free toni—'

'Yes, I am, as it happens.'

'Oh great, em, right...listen, I wondered if you fancied dinner...'

She grinned wickedly.

'Grant McVicar, are you asking me on a date?'

He could feel himself start to blush.

'Em, yes, I suppose I am, Tina. So...'

'I'd love to, Grant. What time?'

'Well, let's say I pick you up at seven?'

'Why don't we just say we'll get a taxi and have a bottle of wine...or two?'

He smiled back at her.

'Yeah, that sounds like a plan, Tina. Okay, seven at yours. Em, where is "yours" by the way?'

Once she had given him her address, he had set off towards his pick-up, his head held high, his back straight and a spring in his step. He was trying desperately not to grin like the proverbial Cheshire Cat!

~~~

He was sitting at his desk, trying once again to keep his mind focussed on the investigation, but the message he had just received kept insinuating itself into his thought process; what, exactly, did she mean by "something HOT"? His mental turmoil was interrupted by a knock on his door, followed by Briony's head appearing round it.

'Hi, Boss.'

She gave him a scrutinising look.

'Everything okay, eh?'

'What...oh, aye, just thinking about what we've got so far, Bri. Anything fresh turned up?'

Grant had left the Tesco store first, arranging to meet Briony back at their headquarters. The rest of the team had remained at the two crime scenes but he and his sergeant still had to perform the difficult task of informing the families of the victims. It was something that he always dreaded.

'Well, I spoke to Nippy, she says she'll carry out the post mortems first thing tomorrow and let you know. Faz says there's a good bit of CCTV footage of this unidentified blonde woman; oh, and we checked the red dresses on display in Asda. It's just like you said, they were all sized wrongly. The CCTV shows our suspect hangin' about the clothin' department for about half an hour before the body was found, presumably swappin' the sizes.'

Grant sat in silence, considering this new piece of information. It was extremely perplexing; there was obviously a considerable amount of pre-meditation involved if the suspect had gone to the trouble of changing all the dresses on their hangers in both stores. But she would have no way of knowing the identity of who would be trying these on, which suggested that the victims were chosen entirely at random. Finally, he replied.

'I just don't get it, Bri. Why would this blonde female go to all that trouble to murder two presumably unknown and innocent women? I mean, she must have calculated that, sooner or later, someone would go out for a smaller size but, let's face it, it was a bit of a long shot, wasn't it? And what, in God's name, was her motive? Strangling two random female victims? Doesn't really make any sense, does it?'

'No, it doesn't, Boss. Maybe she just had something against the colour red, eh?'

'Aye, maybe, given that the dresses in both locations *were* red. I take it Faz is heading to Tesco next to check the CCTV there?'

'Aye, he was just leavin' after me. He'll be on it by now, I'd think.'

'Good. Be interesting to see if it's the same story. Right, Bri, we've got a job to do. Best get it over with, then we can get on with the investigation.'

Before they had left to perform their painful duties, Grant had been vaguely aware of his stomach grumbling; now, their grim task completed, his appetite had deserted him completely. As he and Briony drove back to Osprey House in a despondent silence, once again he was extremely thankful for the skills—not to mention the company—of his detective sergeant...his friend.

They had visited the families in the order that the victims had been found. Colin and Christine Duff lived in a smart, semi-detached red sandstone villa in the nearby town of Elderslie, a sparkling black BMW saloon and a white Ford Fiesta in the drive, its garden neat and well-tended. The epitome of successful suburban life...

They had been shown in to a comfortable and well-appointed living room; somewhere in the background, an acoustic guitar was being played, rather proficiently, Grant thought. The Duffs had sat together on the couch, albeit at separate ends, their expressions alarmed but, somehow, not completely surprised and Grant wondered if there had previously been trouble of some sort in their lives. After a few banal formalities, Colin Duff spoke, his manner rather offhand.

'I'm assuming this is about Amanda? What's the girl done now?'

Christine Duff gave him an angry sideways glance and shook her head.

'Mr Duff, Mrs Duff, I'm afraid I have bad news...'

∿∿∿

Christine Duff had simply started to cry, softly and silently; no hysterics, no fuss, just a steady stream of tears running down her careworn cheeks. Colin Duff had stood up and walked to the window, staring out at the tidy garden, then, without a word, he strode across the room and left. A few seconds later, the gentle guitar soundtrack had stopped; there was a raised voice, footsteps in the hall, then the sound of the front door slamming shut. Colin Duff came back in to the room, his expression hard to read.

'I told Bruce—he's gone out to see Hannah.'

Briony looked up at him, then across at his wife, who was still weeping, although her husband appeared oblivious, showing no intention of comforting her. Finally, Briony stood up, crossed over and sat beside the grief-stricken woman, pulling her head gently on to her shoulder.

'There now, my dear, there now...'

Grant had stared at the floor, unable to contribute in any meaningful way.

The second visit had, if anything, been worse. Natalie Wheeler had lived in a smart modern house in the little Renfrewshire village of Crosslee, with her husband Tommy and their two teenage boys, Paul and Andy. As soon as they entered, they could see the feminine influence at work in the home and they knew the devastation that their news would wreak; alas, they underestimated it considerably.

Tommy Wheeler had broken down completely. Andy, the eldest boy, had tried to comfort his father but he seemed completely powerless; Tommy Wheeler was hysterical and completely inconsolable. Finally, Briony took the lad aside.

'Andy, is there someone I can call, a family member, anyone, eh?'

The boy, although obviously devastated, seemed to be coping considerably better than his father.

'Em, aye, there's my Auntie Ann, my old ma...sorry, my dad's sister, she lives in Houston. D'you think I should call her?'

'Yes, but let me speak to her please, Andy, I'm more used to this kind of thing.'

Auntie Ann had arrived fifteen minutes later, her husband Harry with her. They seemed solid, dependable people and Ann had immediately taken control of the situation, sending Harry out with Andy to find his younger brother. Finally, Grant and Briony had taken their leave, their job done, the havoc wrought, the door closing with a thump of finality behind them.

They arrived back at Osprey House, having spoken not a word on the journey. Grant pulled into a space and turned off the engine. Staring straight ahead, he spoke, softly and with considerable emotion in his voice.

'Bri, I don't know how I would have got through that without you. Honestly, you—'

She didn't reply; he knew she was crying. He realised that he, too was close to tears but he managed to hold them back. His emotion surprised him; way back, when he had been told about the death of his friend, DS Brian Thackray, he had felt completely numb, unable to shed a single tear. But now...? He shook his head sadly.

Sometimes this job is just total shit...

Having regained their composure, Grant and Briony entered the slightly cramped room that the team used as their meeting room. Fortunately, the Police Scotland budget had managed to set aside funds to have the air-conditioning system repaired and the room now remained at a comfortable working temperature. They were all seated, discussing the case. Cliff Ford, in anticipation of his boss's needs, was clutching a marker pen and had two white boards ready to write down the salient points; Grant still liked to see things set down clearly before him. Faz was sitting at a computer, uploading details on to HOLMES, the national Police computer network. DC Kiera Fox was running her fingers savagely through her mop of unruly red hair, pondering over some notes she had taken and chatting to Grace Lappin, the new recruit. Grant had noticed that Grace had won the confidence and the friendship of her colleagues quickly and easily, a trait that he hoped would prove to be an asset. His train of thought was disturbed when the door banged open and Sam Tannahill, the final member of the team, entered, clutching her handbag and a Costa coffee cup. She was slightly harassed-looking as she gave Grant a nervous smile.

'Sorry Boss, I was over in Dundee.'

It hadn't been that long since his behaviour towards the attractive young DC had nearly caused her to return to uniform.

'No problem, Sam. Are you up to speed?'

She nodded.

'Cliff gave me a call on the way, Boss, so I've got the general picture.'

'Good stuff. Listen, I appreciate you coming back over at such short notice.'

As Sam pulled over a chair, Briony gave him a brief nod. She remembered the incident too...

With the arrival of their superior officers, the team had looked up from their respective activities in anticipation. Grant and Briony sat down and the room fell silent; he took a deep breath.

'Right, Cliff, you ready?'

'Aye, Boss.'

He removed the lid from his marker pen.

'Okay. Two victims—put one on each board, Cliff. Amanda Duff, aged twenty-three, unemployed, unmarried and living at home with parents Colin and Christine. Young brother, Bruce, aged seventeen. Still at school.'

He paused, the only noise the sound of the marker scraping on the board.

'I have the feeling that there's been trouble there in the past; can you check for any previous form—Sam?'

She nodded her blonde-curled head; she was still keen to make an impression on her somewhat fearsome superior officer.

'Yup, will do, Boss'

'Good. Next, Natalie Wheeler, aged forty-two, married to Thomas, or Tommy, living in Crosslee. Two sons, Andy and Paul, aged sixteen and thirteen respectively. Works...sorry, worked...as a dental receptionist.'

Another pause.

'Neither victim has any previous record, although, as I mentioned, I suspect that Amanda may have had a few scrapes and the evidence suggests that she was in the process of stealing

Susan Fielding's purse—you may as well put Susan down too, Cliff, she may actually have been the intended victim...'

∿∿∿

The boards were filled with the information that they had gleaned to date and, as Grant surveyed it, he realised that it didn't amount to very much. Two victims, found in separate store changing rooms, both strangled. The strong, but unproven, suggestion that Susan Fielding may actually have been the intended first victim and that Amanda Duff just happened to be in the wrong place at the wrong time; the significance of the red dresses and the changing of their hangers. Most of all, the unknown blonde woman who had been seen at the time of the Asda murder and whose image Faz had also located on the Tesco CCTV system. Grant leaned back, putting his hands behind his shaved head.

'Right. We need to find out who the hell this blonde woman is and that's not going to be easy; however, at the moment, she's our prime suspect. We need to establish if there's any connection between Susan Fielding and Natalie Wheeler, although I seriously doubt it. Oh, and probably Amanda Duff too, just in case. If these are just random killings, purely for the sake of it, then it'll be bloody difficult to get a result.'

He looked at his watch; it was nearly six-thirty.

'Right, at some point we'll need to have another word with the victims' families...'

He caught Briony giving him a look.

'...but probably not today. Faz, can you check HOLMES to see if there's anything relating to any of the three women involved, anything that might form a link?'

'Sure thing, Boss.'

'And can you check the external CCTV for both stores? This blonde must have had a vehicle and if we can track her outside, we might be able to get a registration.'

'No problem, Boss.'

'Good lad. Now, we'll need to check all the prints; the hangers that the dresses were on, the cubicle that the blonde woman was in...at the moment, that might be the only way we can track her down. Faz, were there any usable facial shots from the CCTV?'

DC Fazil Bajwa shook his head.

'Not really, Boss. We can make out what she was wearing and get a good idea of height, build, etcetera. But her facial features aren't particularly well defined; it's just a standard security system, pretty low resolution and she seems to walk with her head down, as if she knows she's being caught on camera.'

Faz turned and looked at his laptop.

'As I said earlier, I reckon she's about five-ten, pretty well-built, shoulder-length blonde hair...'

Grace had crossed over and was standing behind him, her hand placed affectionately on his shoulder, Grant noticed. She peered at the image.

'Hmm...if you were to ask me, I'd say it's definitely dyed.'

Faz turned to her.

'You think?'

'Yes, it's just too perfect. Looks as if it's just been done, too, it's... well, I'm not sure exactly...but it just doesn't look natural, I'd say.'

Grant was intrigued, both at Grace's thought process and at the interaction between the two officers. He cleared his throat and they turned towards him, a look of slight embarrassment on their faces. Briony's lips twitched as she suppressed a grin.

'Okay, that's a good point, would it be worth checking with hairdressers in the area, see if anyone's been in, say—'

He looked at Grace and raised an eyebrow.

'Em, maybe Saturday, but probably no earlier than Friday, Boss. As I said, it looks like it's just been done, whatever "done" means, I suppose—'

'Okay, let's work on that basis. Grace, you can get on to that tomorrow.'

'Might be a problem, Boss,' said Kiera.

'Oh? Why?'

'Most hairdressers round here shut on a Monday.'

Fuck...!

Seven-thirty; they had collated all the evidence that they had to date, Faz had run a check on HOLMES, the police computer and database to see if the description that they had of the mysterious blonde woman appeared elsewhere; it didn't. Grant rubbed his face.

'Right, guys, let's wrap it up for now. We're not going to get anything else until tomorrow—well, if we're looking at hairdressers, Tuesday—so let's call it a night and we'll tackle it afresh in the morning.'

It was eight-thirty by the time Grant arrived back at Bluebell Cottage, tucked up a narrow road in the little Renfrewshire hamlet of Newton of Belltrees. As he approached his house, his first thought was that he had forgotten to turn off the lights. Then, as turned his pick-up into the gravelled drive and saw the unfamiliar car parked there, he remembered...

He locked his vehicle, walked wearily towards his front door and entered the warmth of his home; his heart was pounding.

'Hi sweetheart! In the kitchen!'

Sweetheart!

He closed and locked the door, hung his jacket in the hall cupboard then followed the delicious aroma of cooking that was emanating from his bright, modern kitchen. He pushed the door open and there she was...as she put her arms round his neck and kissed him, he noticed that she smelled of both perfume and garlic; oddly, it was rather appealing...

Mother's ruin...

The words of Sandie Pollock's own mother sprang into her head as she poured her second measure of Tanqueray Ten gin over the ice cubes, causing them to crackle enticingly. She topped the glass up with premium tonic, popped in a slice of red grapefruit and took a large mouthful, hoping it would make her feel better.

It didn't.

She took her drink back through to the lounge, now bathed in the soft light of four tasteful side-lamps. She dropped back down in her comfortable chair, took another slug of "ruin" and laid her head back, desperately trying to block out the last few day's events...

Neil had left on Friday afternoon for a weekend conference in Edinburgh; since he had started working for the NHS, there had been a few of these so-called "team building" events. Although he considered them to be a bit of a waste of time, he was obliged to attend and nearly always stayed over, as there was usually a shindig of sorts on the Saturday night, fully funded by the NHS, of course—so much for the tight budget! However, as Sandie didn't work on a Friday, they had spent an extremely pleasant morning together; the night before, she had prepared a flask of coffee and a couple of croissants, taking them up to the bedroom so that they could have a leisurely coffee in bed. They had read for a short while then made love, gently, sweetly and with the comfortable familiarity of many years of intimacy. They had showered, had a light lunch then he had left mid-afternoon, following the usual ritual...

'Right, have you got everything, Neil?'

He would grin.

'Think so, Sweet Pea'

That had always been her nickname, even before they were married; her maiden name had been Phillips, her initials S-P.

He would then place his hand on his forehead, down to his crotch and then across his chest, as if in genuflection.

'Spectacles, testicles, wallet and watch...'

They would both laugh, "Nuns on the Run" having been one of their favourite films...in the early years...

'Aye, wallet, phone, toothbrush, spare socks—'

'Only because I packed them, though.'

He would grab her in a bear hug and kiss her passionately.

'I know, Sweet Pea. What would I do without you?'

'Forget things, maybe, love?'

He would walk out the door then, half-way down the steps, he would turn and grin again. Even after all these years, even with the thinning hair and the expanding waistline, that smile would give her butterflies in her stomach.

'Love ya, Sandie P. See you Sunday night.'

Then, as his Racing Yellow Porsche crunched down the short gravel drive, he would peep the horn twice (often to the annoyance of their elderly next-door-neighbour) and he would be gone.

~~~

She sighed, realising that her second gin and tonic was nearly finished. Should she have another? She sat forward and, as she did so, the tears started to run down her cheeks. Tears of humiliation, tears of heartbreak, tears of anger...

The bombshell had struck several months previously; out of the blue, unexpectedly...

She had been at home and Neil had been at work; just an ordinary weekday afternoon.

'Hello.'

'Hello Sandie? It's Carole here. How are you?'

Carole McKillop was a local GP, a woman with whom Sandie was reasonably friendly; they had met at a few training courses, she had occasional dealings with her in the pharmacy where she worked and, for a short while, Carole had joined Stage-Right, Sandie's beloved amateur dramatics company. However, even now, Sandie still wasn't entirely sure whether the phone call had been malicious or altruistic.

'Oh, hi Carole, I'm good, thanks. How's things? Haven't spoken to you for absolutely ages!'

'I know, I know, but you know what it's like; plus, I hurt my back a few months ago and I've not been able to make rehearsals... listen, Sandie, I hope you don't mind me calling... em...well, it's a bit awkward...'

Sandie was slightly puzzled; Carole was normally pretty forthright but, on this occasion, she seemed uncharacteristically hesitant.

'Gosh, what's the matter, Carole? Is everything all right?'

'Oh, God, I don't really know how—'

She paused and Sandie remained silent.

'Okay, so, the thing is, I was through in Edinburgh at a training course at the weekend and I'd stayed over on the Saturday night. We were staying down at Leith, There's a Premier Inn there, it's nice and quiet—...'

Sandie wondered where this was leading, her stomach was starting to churn.

'So, I'd just arrived and checked in. My window overlooked the car park and I happened to look out and I saw what I thought was Neil's Porsche. It's bright yellow, isn't it?'

'Em, yes, it is, but they're not *that* uncommon, especially through there—'

'No, but I'm sure it was his number, ends in 753. That's his, isn't it?'

Sandie could feel both her pulse-rate and her hackles rising. She had the vague feeling that Carole McKillop was enjoying this ever so slightly, whatever "this" was.

'Yes, that's Neil. But he was through at a conference too, there's nothing unusual—'

'Well, that's the thing, Sandie. As I was watching, someone went out to the car, opened it and took a bag out before heading back into the hotel. But it wasn't Neil.'

Sandie didn't respond. She knew Carole was going to tell her anyway.

'Em...so...it was a woman. Tall, long blonde hair, well-made, if you know what I mean. Dressed to the nines...well, to be honest, she actually looked pretty "tarty!" A flouncy white blouse, high heels, a short skirt with black stockings—'

'How do you know they were stockings, Carole?'

'Oh...em...well, of course I don't but...'

'So, you're just jumping to conclusions; as you are with the rest of it. It was probably just a work colleague, maybe he gave them a lift, I don't know. What I do know is that I trust Neil implicitly and I know he's not playing around, if that's what you're getting at; which it is, by the sound of it.'

Sandie's voice had a harsh edge to it; there was another pause then, when Carole McKillop responded, her voice was similarly frosty.

'Listen, I'm just telling you, Sandie, don't shoot the messenger. It might be nothing, for all I know...or care.'

Ouch...

'Okay, well, thanks anyway, Carole, I appreciate you letting me know, but as far as Neil is concerned, I don't have any doubts. Bye.'

$\sim\!\sim\!\sim$

But the damage had been done. Sandie couldn't help but have doubts and she had started to look for the signs, but there were none, Neil was the same, kind, loving husband he had always been. After a few weeks, she had started to forget about the phone call; after all, she knew that Carole McKillop had just been ditched by her second husband. Maybe she had an axe to grind, maybe she was envious of Sandra and Neil's marriage...but there had still been that tiny, niggling doubt.

Oh, you bitch, Carole McKillop. You fucking bitch...

She swallowed the last mouthful of gin, mostly now just melted ice. Maybe just one more...

$\sim\!\sim\!\sim$

She had watched Neil leave that Friday, promising herself that she would trust him. A vague memory stirred from her early amateur dramatic days, a song from "The Pyjama Game", something silly about a man learning to trust his woman— 'I'll never be jealous again." Up until now, she never had been...

He had phoned on the Friday night, before he went out for dinner with a few business associates. He had promised to phone on the Saturday night, with the final proviso

'And don't you go hitting the gin, Sweet Pea, I know what you're like when I'm not there...'

He had laughed light-heartedly, but how *did* he know...still, it had all been so normal, so routine. If only she hadn't opened Pandora's box. If only she hadn't phoned yesterday...

She swallowed a large mouthful of the fresh glass of G&T—she had made it a double...

Why did I? Why, you stupid cow?

'Hello, Midlothian Hotel Edinburgh, how may I help you?'

'Em, hello, I wonder if you can. My husband is through at a conference today and the silly idiot's forgotten his phone. Could you possibly put me through to his room?'

'Certainly, Madam. What are they like? We're always running about after them...now, what's your husband's name?'

'Oh, em...it's Neil Pollock.'

'One moment, please.'

A pause.

'I'm sorry, but we don't seem to have anyone of that name staying at the hotel.'

'Oh, em, well, he's attending an NHS conference there, some IT thing, apparently.'

'Oh, right. When is that, Mrs Pollock?'

'Today, I think.'

'Em, no, I'm afraid the hotel is fully booked for a wedding today, I'm sorry.'

'Oh, maybe it's tomorrow, then.'

Another pause.

'...no, I'm sorry, we do have a training day booked tomorrow but it's for opticians. Nothing else on, I'm afraid.'

'Oh, um...well, maybe I have the wrong hotel. Is there another Midlothian Hotel in Edinburgh?'

'No, I'm sorry, this is the only one. Are you quite sure it was the Midlothian Hotel, Madam?'

She was—well, Neil had told her that was where he was staying...

Finally, she had hung up, her cheeks burning with hurt and embarrassment. She was only too well aware that the friendly receptionist had realised that she was "checking up" on her husband—and had found that he was lying!

Neil had phoned her, just before six, just as he had promised; he was his normal cheerful, funny self.

'Hey, Sweet Pea. How was your day?'

Somehow, she managed to retain her composure.

'Och fine, the usual, I did a bit of ironing, pottered about in the garden. Well, until the rain came on, I phoned Dawn.'

They had made small-talk for a few minutes, Sandie chatting about the grandchildren, Neil making his usual complaints about his work colleagues and about how boring the course was. Then he paused, as if hesitating slightly.

'Listen, Sandie...em, they're wanting me to go over to head office at The Gyle on Monday to help with some upgrading installations.'

'Oh...'

'So, I thought it was a bit daft coming all the way back over to Paisley on Sunday then all the way back through again on Monday morning, so I booked an extra night. Is that okay?'

Sandie bit her lip.

'Of course, love, you're right, it'd be daft. It's fine, really.'

It was very far from fine; Sandie heard her husband, Neil, breathed an audible sigh of...relief?'

'Great, Sweet Pea, I knew you'd understand...'

She understood all too well.

'...listen, I should be home late afternoon on Monday. I'll make it up to you, promise.'

'Pinkie promise?' she heard herself say, in a light tone.

'Pinky promise. Listen, I'll call when I'm nearly home and you can get...ready!'

The last word was emphasised; she knew exactly what he meant and, somehow, it made her shudder.

The call had finished, as always, with an assurance that he loved her. In disgust, she threw her mobile on to the couch and, as she did so, she briefly reflected how useful her amateur dramatics had proven to be—it had been a superb act!

~~~~

The gin was finished once more and, with a heavy heart, she decided that it was time to head upstairs to bed, although she knew that, despite the alcohol, sleep would be a long way off. She had tried desperately not to wonder where he was, who he was with, what he was doing...

She turned off the lights then, after checking that the front door was locked, she plodded wearily up the stairs to the spacious top landing. The house had four generous, high-ceilinged bedrooms; theirs, the largest, was at the front, the other three having been occupied by their children. Now that the kids had flown the coop, they retained two spare rooms (for their return, along with the adored grandchildren) and one, a south-facing rear bedroom, had been adapted for Neil to use as his art studio. He still painted; in fact, he was rather accomplished and he often expressed regret that he had decided against Art School in favour of computing. Hanging on the wall in their bedroom were four wonderful charcoal sketches that Neil had done whilst Sandie was pregnant with Dawn, their first child. She could still remember posing for them, naked, glowing and lying on the couch in their lounge. They were flowing, sensual drawings, highlighting her soft curves, her round belly and her firm, swollen breasts. She had always said that, in the event of a fire, these would be the first thing that she would grab (well, after Neil and the kids, of course!)

She stood for a moment, lost in her thoughts. Neil had always liked, and benignly encouraged, the privacy of his studio, his own "space", as he called it, and she had respected that. It had only been after the phone call from the "bitch" that Sandie had been tempted to have a look but she had refrained; after all, she trusted Neil, didn't she? But now? Once more she was inexorably drawn towards the room, wondering, dreading what she might find...

She turned towards the bedroom door, hesitated, then turned the handle, pushed it open and switched on the light. The room had a comforting smell, a nice smell, of pencils, paint, thinners; a slightly heady aroma, the smell of creativity. It all looked so neat and tidy; there was a half-finished, and quite superb, sketch of Dylan, their eldest grandchild, propped on an easel. She looked about, her gaze resting on the large cupboard that was secured with a hasp and a small combination padlock. Ostensibly this was to prevent the children—and now the grandchildren— from tampering with any of the paints or chemicals which, in the wrong hands, could prove to be disastrous. She took a few hesitant steps towards it...

It was almost half an hour later; she had tried all the birthdays, their anniversary, none of them had been correct. She had racked her brains, assuming it must be some random number known only to Neil. Then, with an almost subliminal flash of inspiration (and in near-desperation) she tried the pretentious and rather peculiar title of the band that had played, all these years ago, the soundtrack to their first kiss...

7396

And Pandora's box had opened...

CHAPTER 4

Detective Sergeant Briony Quinn knew her boss well enough by now to realise that something was...well, different! It was just over a year since she had transferred to Paisley's "K" division to work with DCI McVicar, a position that she had specifically requested and that had been partially facilitated by her mother's partner, retired divisional commander Alastair Young. She was now aware of the reason for Grant's lapses into self-doubt and self-pity but, recently, he seemed well along the road to recovery from the tragic accident that had claimed the life of his best friend, DS Brian Thackray. Today, however, she couldn't quite read his mood as he entered the office, where the team was already assembled.

'Mornin' Boss, everythin' okay, eh?'

He looked at her, rather distractedly, she thought.

'What...oh, em, aye, Bri, just didn't sleep well.'

She raised a questioning eyebrow and he shook his head.

'Long story...' He clapped his hands together and Briony knew that he would say no more—until he was ready.

'Right, morning troops, let's see where we are. Doctor Napier should be carrying out the post mortems later today, although I think it's pretty clear how both women died. What we need to do is to try and establish some connection between the two deaths and to try and find a motive.'

Kiera looked up from her mobile phone.

'Boss, what if there *is* no motive? I mean, is there a possibility that these are just random killings, you know, by some, em, psychopath?'

Grant sighed. She could easily have added "like last time" although that wasn't strictly the case; in the end, Francesca Hope had been deemed mentally ill and unfit to stand trial.

'Unfortunately, that's a possibility we have to consider, Kiera, which could make the case pretty tough to crack.'

'What about this Susan Fielding woman?' asked Sam. Do you still think she might have been the intended victim? After all, she and the Tesco victim were both wearing red dresses, weren't they?

'Yes, they were.'

He paused, almost reluctant to consider this possibility. When he spoke, he mumbled, as if talking to himself.

'So, do we have a psychopathic killer with an aversion to the colour red?'

He shook his head; he had a feeling that this wasn't going to be a straightforward case. He looked back up and spoke, more clearly this time.

'Sam, could you and Kiera go and have another chat with Susan Fielding, she should have recovered sufficiently by now and I'd imagine they won't have kept her in hospital for any longer than necessary. See if she can give us any more information; you need to ask tactfully if there's any reason why someone might want to kill her. Check the backgrounds of the two women; did they ever work together, did they socialise, anything that might connect them.'

'Could be something like a gym membership, maybe they didn'ae even know each other but the murderer knew them both from a common location?' suggested Cliff.

'Good point, Cliff. We'll need to try and talk to Tommy Wheeler again too, although the chances are the poor bugger's still in no fit state to give us a coherent statement. But we need to try and establish a connection, if there is one. Bri, maybe you and Grace...?'

Briony Quinn sighed.

Aye, the price of having been in victim support...

'Okay Boss, but I'll phone and see if he's up to being interviewed first.'

'Fair enough. Right, Faz, can you go back and check the CCTV in both stores, see if there's any images of this mystery blonde leaving the store and getting into a vehicle. That would be a major step forward. Cliff, you go along as well, two sets of eyes...'

'Sure, Boss.'

As the team left to carry out their assigned tasks, Grant went through to the small room that served as a kitchen and made himself a coffee before returning to his office. There had been times in the past when his team had seemed to be overstretched; now, with Grace Lappin having joined their ranks, there were occasions where he almost felt redundant. He sat down, took a sip of the liquid and stared out of the window; he was soon deep in thought, although not necessarily about the case.

Sandie Pollock was sipping her second coffee of the day. She, too, was staring out of her window at the same leaden-grey Paisley sky and a deserted Craw Road; the rain wasn't far away and it matched her mood perfectly. She hadn't slept well and she had a hangover but, fortunately, she had arranged to have the day off as she had planned to spend it with Neil.

Therein lay the problem; her beloved Neil, her husband, best friend and one-time soul-mate. Now? Well, she really didn't know; in fact, she wondered if she really knew him at all.

It wasn't the extra day away that bothered her; after all, this wasn't the first time that he had decided to extend a weekend conference to save travelling back to Edinburgh and it made sense. It wasn't the contents of the cupboard either; she could live with that, although she had shut the matter away in a corner of her mind labelled "to be addressed..." No, this time, she had caught him out in his lie and she couldn't help wondering if the other times had been lies as well. To make matters worse, in a few hours he would be home, expecting her to...

She shook her head; she didn't know if she could any more. She stood up and headed back towards the kitchen; she would have another coffee, maybe with a wee shot of vodka, just for a bit of Dutch courage, of course. Just to help her through the day...

Helena Pettigrew placed her mobile phone back in her handbag and leaned back in the comfortable wicker couch. She stared out of the conservatory window, impervious to the incessant drumming of the rain on the roof. Her eyes ached; she had shed a lot of tears over the past few days and it seemed there were none left to assuage the pain. The large, secluded garden looked drab and dreary; although she liked to potter about in it when the weather was nice, today nothing could have been further from her mind. She chewed at the skin on the side of her thumb; suddenly, there was a small stab of pain.

Fuck...

She looked down at the blood that was dripping on to her hand, then she pulled a tissue from the sleeve of her black cardigan and wrapped it round in a makeshift bandage.

Coming on top of her own tragedy, the phone call had both shocked and disturbed her; firstly, the identity of the caller, someone she hadn't spoken to in years and, in all honesty, had doubted if she would ever have spoken to again. Secondly, the news that the caller had imparted had, for some strange reason, really upset her. She would normally have gone immediately to speak to Michael but not now, not any more...she shook her head in despair. For almost the first time in her life, she didn't know what to do. She reached into her bag and rummaged about, bringing out a crumpled packet of cigarettes and a cheap plastic lighter.

One won't do any harm...

She had just lit the cigarette when she heard the conservatory door open behind her; she looked around in desperation for somewhere to hide the offending white cylinder as she vainly tried to waft away the smoke.

'Mum!'

'Whit? Och, it's just the one, Ronnie, for God's sake...

'I thought we agreed, you bloody promised me, Mum. For God sake, it's bad enough losing Dad...I don't want anything to happen to you too.'

Helena Pettigrew leaned forward and lifted a crystal ashtray from the lower shelf of the wicker table, then violently stubbed the cigarette out. She glared up at her daughter.

'There! Are ye happy now?'

Ronnie Pettigrew shook her head in despair, her long, dark, glossy hair swinging about. She sighed.

'Aye, mum, thanks. But you know fine well you shouldn't—the doctor told you...'

'Aye, Ah know what the doctor told me, Ronnie. But there's bugger all pleasure left in life these days...'

Ronnie sat down beside her mum, gently taking the older woman's hand in hers. She tried not to wrinkle her nose in disgust; she hated the smell of cigarettes.

'I know, Mum, I know, and it's awful what's happened but, for my sake at least, you need to stay healthy.'

Helena nodded and stared back out of the window at the rain. Ronnie turned and looked at her mother.

'Who was that on the phone, Mum?'

'What? Oh, em, just a friend, Ronnie, just seein' how Ah wis doin...'

Ronnie frowned at her mum; she wasn't exactly what could be called a sociable woman.

'A friend, Mum? What friend?'

Helena Pettigrew averted her eyes.

'Och, just someone Ah haven'ae seen fur a while. They'd heard about Michael...'

Ronnie shook her head sadly; she knew her mum was lying.

Grant finished his last chip, wiped his hands on a square of kitchen-roll and took a slug of Irn-Bru.

'Aah, that's good. Right, now that we're all fed and watered, are we any further ahead; Sam?'

Sam Tannahill took a final mouthful of her water.

'Not really, Boss, to be honest. Susan Fielding's back home but she's still in a bit of a state and the suggestion that she might have been the intended victim didn't go down too well. She lives with her partner in a nice wee house down in Erskine, he seems a decent bloke and he's certainly giving her plenty of support, but she isn't a member of any gym, or the like. She goes running about once a week and that's it. Just ordinary, respectable people with no reason to think anyone would want to harm her.'

'Hm. what's her job?'

Kiera answered.

'She's a physiotherapist, works full-time in Ross Hall hospital so, after the daily commute, she hasn't got a lot of free time. Her partner's a plumber and, as Sam says, a decent enough bloke. I really don't think there's any avenue worth pursuing there.'

'Fair enough.' Grant paused for a moment; it wasn't sounding hopeful.

'Bri?'

She sighed wearily.

'Well, there's no doubt that Tommy Wheeler's still in a state of shock; couldn't get much out of him but, fortunately, the relatives are still there takin' care of him, poor bugger. I spoke to his son though, the one that was there yesterday. Says his mum was a member of the sports centre at Linwood, she went a couple of times a week. She worked as a dental receptionist down in Port Glasgow. There doesn't seem to be any connection at all with Susan, Boss and, again, just ordinary people...'

Grant rubbed his hand over his head; the information didn't help...

'Doesn't really get us anywhere, though; but that's assuming that Susan Fielding *was* the intended victim—maybe it was Amanda Duff all along.'

'But what about the dresses, Boss? I mean, surely that indicates some sort of link between Susan and Natalie?' asked Faz.

'Maybe, but it's still a pretty tenuous one. Listen, how did you get on with the CCTV?'

'It's really odd, Boss' Faz replied. 'There's reasonable footage from outside both stores, although with the mass exodus from Asda it was pretty hard to identify individuals. But Cliff and I have trawled for hours and there's no sign of the blonde woman outside at either locus.'

Grant frowned.

'You're sure?'

'Aye, positive, Boss.' replied Cliff. We went through it aboot a dozen times, slowed it down. There's just no-one answerin' the description o' this mystery woman. We checked back a good bit to see if we could see her comin' in to either o' the stores but there was still nothin'.'

Grant considered this.

'Did you check afterwards?'

'Afterwards?' Cliff repeated.

'Aye, afterwards, Cliff. Maybe she didn't leave at all, maybe she hid in a toilet or somewhere, waited till the fuss died down then slipped out; well, at Tesco, anyway, I doubt she'd have got past the armed police at Asda!'

'But surely one of the uniforms would have noticed them, Boss? asked Kiera.

'Not necessarily. Remember, we weren't actually looking for her until we'd viewed the CCTV footage so she would just have been another shopper at that point. Go back and check...say, half an hour after the bodies were discovered, just in case...'

Grant's phone rang; he looked down at the screen then back up to his team.

'Doctor Napier.'

He answered the call.

'Good afternoon Doctor. Is it okay if I put this on speaker?'

'Oh well, if you must...good afternoon, everyone, Dr Napier here. I wasn't expecting to be Public Speaking today...'

Grant smiled as he caught Briony's eye

'...anyway, the post mortems are complete and I thought you'd like to know my findings.'

Yes, Doctor, thanks.'

'Well, as you already know, both women had been strangled; they died of hypoxia, as a result of said strangulation. In both cases a ligature had been placed around the victim's neck and pulled tight, breaking the skin and causing localised bleeding. I would say that the killer is probably left-handed, as the force on the right-hand side appears to have been greater where the ligature has been pulled across the neck. Also, from the skin-patterns, I'd say the ligature was a thin, but strong, pliable and braided wire of some sort. I've been fortunate enough to retrieve a tiny fragment that has broken off and I've sent it to forensics for a more detailed examination.'

Grant raised his dark eyebrows; this was encouraging news.

'Great stuff, Doctor, that could be a big help. Anything else of note?'

'Nothing really. Both healthy enough women, neither appeared to have put up a fight, which would suggest that they were surprised and incapacitated before they could resist.'

There was a pause as Grant waited for the morsel that Nippy invariably kept until the end.

'Oh, and just to mention that the first victim, Amanda Duff had ingested cocaine nasally not long before she was killed. I've sent her bloods for a toxicology report to see if she was a habitual user but I definitely found traces of the powder in her nostrils. I don't know if that's of any significance, but there it is.'

'Right, many thanks Doctor.'

'You're welcome, Grant. I'll let you know as soon as I have the reports. Goodbye.'

Grant pocketed his phone and looked up at his team.

'Well, it's not much...but cocaine? Hmm...Cliff?'

Cliff was already standing at the as yet sparsely-populated white board, marker in hand and poised to write.

'Okay, so our killer is probably left-handed and using wire of some sort to strangle her victims; easy enough to conceal in a pocket or a handbag, I suppose. Amanda Duff had taken cocaine not long before she died. That's about it.'

It wasn't much; Grant rubbed his beard.

'Right, Faz, Cliff, can you head back to the stores and check that later footage, just in case.'

Cliff put down the marker.

'Okay, Boss, we'll let you know.'

He waited until the two DCs had left.

'Right, what now? Suggestions, anyone? Yes, Sam?'

'Well, we're assuming that our killer is a member of the public but what if this blonde is a member of staff?'

'Hm... but she was seen in both places, Sam. That wouldn't work.'

'Oh, em, neither it would, sorry Boss.'

'No, it was a reasonable enough suggestion.'

Briony gave a wry smile; her boss now tended to walk on eggshells where Sam was concerned and it wouldn't do him one bit of harm! Before he could continue, Grant's phone rang again and he frowned as he looked at the screen.

'It's the Mint, wants a word. Wish me luck, folks...'

Superintendent Patricia Minto sat in her chair, shrewdly regarding her DCI. He was a good policeman—he was a good man, for that matter—and she felt sorry for him. He had had his fair share of tragedy in his life and it was only in the last few months that she could see any tangible improvement in his demeanour...and his work, for that matter.

Thank God for Briony Quinn...!

He had briefly outlined the results of their enquiries to date. After mulling them over for a minute or so, she spoke.

'So, where do you think you stand with this investigation? I expect I'll have the Fiscal on the phone any time now looking for an update.'

'Well Ma'am, I've just had the PM results. We know the killer strangled the victims with some sort of wire and that she's probably left-handed...'

'You say "she"? You believe that it was this unknown blonde woman who's responsible?'

'Well, she appears in both stores just prior to the killings. CCTV shows her at the dress-racks, where the sizes were swapped and she was seen coming out of the Asda changing room just before

Amanda Duff's body was discovered. I'd be pretty certain that she's our killer.'

'Hm. But who the hell is she? I don't suppose you've got anything showing her getting into a vehicle?'

'No, Ma'am and that's the strange thing. We have plenty of footage of her inside the stores but none outside; I've sent Cliff and Faz back to check later footage in case she stayed inside the store until the fuss died down.'

'Good. We need a quick result here, Grant. Murder never makes good press for us but these are particularly nasty and we've already had the head offices of both Tesco and Asda on to the Divisional Commander. They're saying that this will affect their trade, that women will be frightened to go shopping while the killer's still on the loose. It's a bit of an over-reaction but I can see their point, I suppose. Needless to say, I've had the Commander breathing down my neck so, unfortunately, I'm breathing down yours...'

She gave him a thin-lipped smile.

'By the way, are you still planning on attending the funeral?'

He paused before replying.

'I don't know, Ma'am. Might be worth going along, just to see who shows up.'

'Yes, I take your point but, if you do go, be careful. You'll have a lot of enemies there and precious few friends...if any.'

She stood up, indicating that the interview was over.

Right, Grant, keep me informed.'

'I will, Ma'am.'

As he turned to leave, she started to cough. Patricia Minto had always been thin but today she looked almost skeletal, her grey trouser-suit hanging unflatteringly on her gaunt, bony frame. He briefly wondered if the woman was ill.

Christ, that's all we need...

✿✿✿

Sandie Pollock pushed her half-eaten cheese toastie around her plate. Normally she was a good eater but, today, her appetite had deserted her—and not just that for food! Neil had called to say he should be home sometime after two and it was already nearly one. She could feel the tears welling up in her eyes; how could she, after...

Christ, pull yourself together, girl...

She stood up, cleared away her lunch dishes and swallowed the last mouthful of vodka and coke; if ever Dutch courage was needed, it was today. In an attempt to distract herself, she switched on the one o' clock news.

"...still investigating the murder of two women in Linwood, near Paisley. Police have named the victims as Amanda Duff and Natalie Wheeler, both women having been found strangled in the changing rooms of the town's Asda and Tesco stores respectively, at lunchtime on Sunday..."

Sandie gave a shiver; she didn't normally purchase clothes from either of these shops but it could just have easily have been Marks and Spencer's or Next...she switched the radio off. News of a double murder certainly wasn't going to help her demeanour.

Resignedly, she climbed the stairs and entered the bedroom, where she undressed then slid open the wardrobe door; Neil was a man of fairly simple tastes. She selected a pale cream blouse, a black pencil skirt and some fairly standard black underwear—a bra, suspender belt, stockings and a string. That would have to do...she considered pouring herself another vodka but, although she wanted to be numb, she didn't want to appear drunk and incapable.

She got dressed and sat on the bed; how the hell had it come to this? How had she managed to lose her beloved Neil? Could she possibly ask him? The tears welled up again.

*Fuck it...I **am** having another drink...*

She went back down the stairs, carrying her black stiletto heels; the last thing she needed was a fall or a broken ankle. Once in the kitchen, she poured a hefty measure of vodka into her glass then topped it up with coke; still carrying her shoes, she returned to the comfort of the lounge, sat on the settee and took a long draught of the drink. She placed it on the side table, laid her head back against the cushions and fell fast asleep.

$\sim\sim\sim$

The security camera footage had yielded no further images of the anonymous blonde woman. Grant stared at the two white boards, still discouragingly empty, then looked around at his team.

'Ideas, anyone?'

There was a slightly uncomfortable silence.

Kiera replied.

'We've looked over the witness statements again Boss. No-one else has mentioned her, but I suppose most people wouldn't necessarily be paying attention. Would it be worth talking to them again?'

'Hm, maybe, Kiera. But if she hasn't made much impression, then what else are they going to add?'

'We've checked and double-checked all the footage, Boss' added Faz. 'There's nothing more to add to what we've got and no sign of a blonde getting into a car outside

There was another silence; this time Grace Lappin broke it.

'Em, Boss?'

'Aye, Grace?'

'Just a thought... we're looking for a blonde getting into a car?'

'Yes, we've established that...'

'I know, but I was thinking; remember I said her hair looked almost too perfect, as if she'd just been to the hairdressers?'

Grant frowned.

'So, what's your point, Grace?'

'Well, what if it wasn't actually *her* hair? What if it was a wig? I mean, she could have taken it off on the way out, or in a toilet. Be a good way to disguise yourself, wouldn't it?'

'That's a good point,' said Bri. Faz, were you and Cliff just looking for the blonde hair?'

Faz looked slightly taken aback.

'Em, I suppose, Sarge, but there's loads of footage to go through and I thought that she'd stand out. I didn't think...'

He looked helplessly at Grace, who was smiling at him, then turned back to face Grant.

'Right, we'll go and look again, Boss. Might be difficult to pick her out but, hopefully, the white jeans should help.'

'Unless she changed those too?' suggested Kiera.

Grant considered this.

'I doubt it, it would take too long and she'd want to be well away before the bodies were found, I'd imagine; and it would mean changing at each locus. But a wig would be easy enough to pull off and stuff into a bag. Okay, away and have a look, see if you can trace the clothes rather than the hair. Grace, you go too, keep them right...'

As they left to re-scrutinise the CCTV footage, Briony stood up and walked over.

'Could we maybe put out an appeal for information, Boss? Issue a description on TV, see if anyone saw her getting into a car?'

'Aye, maybe, but let's see what they find first. Anyway, we don't want to show our hand too soon. But I'll speak to the Mint, see what she thinks. Time's rolling on...'

~~~

After grabbing a bite to eat, Grant and Briony had had a discussion about the case; he had seemed preoccupied but, somewhat reluctantly, she had desisted from asking anything further about his private life. Eventually, he had gone to speak to his superior officer, returning fifteen minutes later.

'Okay, she agrees; the Press are looking for a progress statement so that's as good an opportunity as any. But she wants to wait until...oh, hang on, here they come...'

Cliff, Faz and Grace entered the office, their faces clearly showing that they'd had a result. Faz was carrying his laptop.

'Well?' asked Grant.

'We've got her, Boss,' said Faz, his customary grin having returned. 'Here, I'll show you...'

He put the computer down on the nearest desk.

'Right, let me run the first images we got, inside Asda.'

They watched the footage; the tall blonde was looking at the red dresses, her head facing down as if to hide her features.

'Do you think she *is* avoiding the cameras?' asked Sam.

'It looks like it, but maybe she's just concentrating on what she's doing...or what she's about to do.' replied Faz. He pulled up the next piece of video.

'Right, I'm afraid it's not great quality, think There's been a bit of moisture on the external camera, but look...'

They watched as the next set of images played; the clothes were the same, the tight, slightly cropped white jeans, high-heeled shoes and the long-sleeved green blouse. But the long blonde tresses had been replaced by short hair, the colour indeterminate due to the poor resolution.

'Well, well, well...so it *was* a wig!' said Grant, with a smile.

'Strange, though,' muttered Briony. Grant turned and looked at her.

'How strange, Bri?'

'Well, it was pretty chilly on Sunday, wasn't it? You'd think she'd have worn a jacket on a day like that.'

'And it would have lessened her chances of being spotted.' added Grace although maybe she thought a jacket would be in the way when she was...you know?'

Grant continued to stare at the screen.

'Any sign of her getting into a vehicle, Faz?'

'Nope, none, Boss. We've checked and double-checked; she just seems to disappear off camera. No sign of a car anywhere.'

'Have you checked all the footage?'

'No' all of it, Boss,' said Cliff. 'We thought you'd want to see this first. We'll away an' get on with the rest, see if we can get dig up anythin' else.'

'Right, on you go. The Mint's giving a press briefing later so I'll bring her up to date and we'll work out what we want to say. Good job though. You too Grace, that was a smart piece of thinking.'

Much to Grant's disappointment, the remaining footage hadn't yielded any further images of the suspect entering or exiting a vehicle at either store. He had spoken to Superintendent Minto and they had come up with a statement asking the public for any information on the mystery woman. They had decided not to issue a e-fit picture at this stage, relying instead on a detailed description of their suspect. He headed back to the office.

'Right, she'll be on this evening and we'll see if that brings us anything. In the meantime, let's have a round-up of what we've got so far...'

Cliff had updated the white boards with the small amount of additional information that they had gleaned; it still wasn't much. Grant stared at the boards as if willing them to reveal some hidden content; finally, he gave a long, weary sigh. He had been aware of his phone vibrating and, making sure Briony was looking elsewhere, he surreptitiously read the short message.

"Dinner's in the oven. Will you be home soon, love? Xxxx

Shit...

He put the phone back in his pocket, hoping Briony hadn't noticed, then stood up.

'Guys, let's wrap it up for tonight. All of you get off home and have a good think about any other possible avenues we can explore then get a decent night's sleep. Hopefully tomorrow will bring something fresh once the Mint's done her stuff. Good job, all.'

As the team left, Briony came up beside him.

'Boss...Grant, is somethin' botherin' you? You seem, well, a bit distracted, if you know what I mean, eh?'

He studiously avoided her gaze.

'No, just a bit tired, that's all, Bri. I'll be fine...'

As he walked out of the room, he wondered if he should have told her...

It was the scrunch of car tyres on the gravel that had finally caused Sandie to waken; she sat up with a start—how long had she been sleeping? She stood up, very slightly unsteadily, and made her way to the stained-glass front door just as she heard Neil's feet on the step. She opened the door and there he was, same old Neil; or was he...

'Hi Sandie.'

She just stared at him; this was by no means his customary greeting. He would usually grin and say "Hi Sweet Pea, you miss me?" before sweeping her into a passionate embrace. He looked tired, strained...

And no bloody wonder...

He stepped into the hall and placed his suit bag and hold-all on the floor; then, almost as an afterthought, he took her in his arms, placing his head wearily on her shoulder. He spoke softly in her ear.

'Sandie, it's been a pretty rough weekend and the journey back through was hellish, to be honest; listen, sweetheart, I know you've made the effort but I'm exhausted, could we take a rain-check on the sex? I think I'll go and have a bath and change, then see how I feel. I'm really sorry...'

Sandie Pollock didn't know whether to feel relief or worry; this was the first time in years that he had declined the offer of a passionate interlude, something that he had never referred to simply as "sex". She pulled away.

'No, that's fine, Neil, actually I'm feeling a bit off-colour myself. Listen you away up and run the bath, I'll fix us a wee drink...'

He gave her a questioning look.

'A bit early, isn't it?'

She forced a smile; it certainly wasn't too early for her. As he headed towards the stairs, she called after him.

'Any dirty washing, Neil? I can put it on!'

He replied, a trifle hastily, she thought.

'Em, I'll unpack and bring it back down, babe...'

Yes, of course you will...

There had been a lasagne in the freezer and Sandie had heated it up, making a simple side salad to accompany it. Neil had picked at his dinner, eventually managing to eat about half of what she had put out; even his gin and tonic remained unfinished. Part of her wanted to ask what was wrong, just as part of her dreaded knowing.

The meal finished, they had sat together on the comfortable settee, flicking TV channels for an hour or so. Neither of them had much enthusiasm and, finally, Neil yawned and stretched.

'Listen, I'm nearly falling asleep here, love. I'm going upstairs—you coming?'

'Em, no, I had an early night last night and I've had a pretty restful day so I'll stay down and do a wee bit of sewing. On you go, I'll try not to disturb you when I come in.'

He stood up and smiled.

'Okay. You working tomorrow?'

She nodded her assent.

'Right. Goodnight then.'

He bent over and kissed the top of her head. As he went out of the door, he turned back towards her and gave her a weary smile.

'And you *never* disturb me when you waken me up, Sweet Pea, you know that.'

But do I...?

He was gone, leaving behind the ghost of the man she used to know. She turned the volume on the television down, her mind wandering into dark, dangerous corners.

The news came on and she turned it back up slightly; the police were still investigating the murders in the supermarkets and she shuddered, thinking how easily it could have been someone she knew. A gaunt looking policewoman was giving a press interview, asking for information on a person whom they wished to speak to in connection with their enquiries. Sandie thought the woman looked ill.

'...about five feet ten and well-built, with long, straight blonde hair. However, we now know that this was a wig and the woman was later seen to have short, greying-brown hair. She was dressed in a long-sleeved green top and white, cropped jeans and was seen at both locations. Anyone having seen this woman or having any information about—'

Sandie stared at the screen, her mouth open; it was as if something had clicked into place in her brain and she realised that she had stopped breathing. She turned off the set and stood up, listening for any sound from her husband; she opened the door and stood at the bottom of the stairs—she could hear him snoring gently. She tiptoed up the heavily-carpeted steps and stealthily opened the door to his studio; his suit bag had been emptied and was draped over the back of his chair but his holdall was nowhere to be seen. She crossed to the storage cupboard, entered the combination and gently pulled the lock apart to release it.

She opened the door and stared; the contents made her feel physically sick...

∿∿∿

Billy Cook placed his mobile phone back on the bedside cabinet and pulled a face; the caller had been friendly enough but he knew only too well that there had been hidden menace in the man's voice. Still, needs must and, after all, he *did* have a holiday coming up! A chill spread through him.

But just how the fuck does he know that...?

Anyway, as requested, he would be there; after all, it wasn't really a request...He let out a long, slow breath; sometimes he hated this existence, this double life. Maybe it was time for a change; but a change to what?

He picked up his laptop and pressed "play"; as the images on the screen took up where they had left off, Billy Cook did the same...

CHAPTER 5

DS Briony Quinn pulled her Volkswagen into a space outside Osprey House and, after glancing down at the clock on the dashboard, to her slight surprise, she noticed Grant's pick-up parked a few spaces further along. Although he wasn't normally late, he was seldom at the office this early, even during a murder investigation. She wondered at the reason.

A few minutes later, with two steaming mugs in hand, she tapped at the door of his office with her foot.

'Aye?'

'Mornin' Boss, brought you a coffee.'

Without waiting for an invitation, she entered his slightly untidy office, placed the coffees on his desk and sat across from him. He looked troubled, she thought, and tired, certainly; although she knew he didn't always sleep well, he had looked more refreshed over the past few months. But there was something else; she scrutinised him and, suddenly, she realised that he looked slightly smarter than usual. Living by himself, her boss wasn't exactly the most domesticated of creatures, although he was always clean and reasonably well presented; "slightly crumpled" was how she would have described him. Today, however, he was dressed in a crisply-ironed blue checked shirt and neatly pressed navy chinos. She smiled inwardly; again, her instincts told her that, somewhere, a woman was involved and now seemed the ideal opportunity to find out. He lifted his coffee.

'Cheers, Bri.'

He took a sip, grimacing as he burnt his mouth. As he placed the mug down, she spoke, keeping her tone light.

'So, what's the story, Boss? You're hardly ever in at this time, you're the smartest I've seen you in ages; come on, fess up!'

To her surprise, he let out a groan, leaned his elbows on the desk and dropped his shaved head onto his hands. A wave of concern swept over her.

'Grant, what is it?'

'It's a bloody mess, that's what it is, Bri,' he mumbled from between his fingers. As he did so his phone started to ring. Before he could reach it, Briony saw the identity of the caller and looked at him in surprise.

'Delia Donald?'

He rejected the call and turned his phone face down, switching off the ringer as he did so.

'Aye. Delia bloody Donald.'

Her eyes widened in surprise.

'But…'

He shook his head woefully.

'I know, Briony, I know. She just kinda turned up out of the blue on Saturday and…

There was a knock at the door and Faz popped his head round.

'Morning, Boss, Sarge. Ready for…oh, sorry, didn't mean to interrupt…'

'No, you're okay, Faz, Bri and I were just discussing, em…stuff. Right, let's get on.'

As he stood up, Briony gave a sigh. She still didn't know what was bothering her boss other than, somehow, Delia Donald seemed to be involved; she wasn't sure if that was necessarily a good thing…

~~~

Sandie Pollock watched in dismay as Neil's Porsche scrunched down the gravel and roared out into the quiet of Craw Road. He had never been a morning person, but today he had appeared particularly withdrawn and taciturn although, despite her best attempts, she had probably been the same. She returned to the kitchen in a daze; she had to be at work in less than an hour and she would have to get her own act together until she decided what course of action she should take. She looked longingly at the cupboard containing the alcohol but decided against it. The last thing she needed was a drink-driving conviction or, worse, the loss of her job!

As she washed the dishes, she could feel the tears running down her face. Neil, her friend, her lover, her *husband*, for fuck sake! Surely not, surely, he wouldn't? And yet...

An hour later, she was busy dispensing the first prescriptions of the morning. She had managed to pull herself together and put a brave face on, but her stomach was churning. One of the pharmacy assistants asked if she was okay.

'Oh, just a bit tired, that's all, Trish. Neil was away at the weekend and he only came back yesterday...'

The assistant smiled knowingly, the nature of Sandie and Neil's close, loving and often physical relationship being reasonably well-known at her work; Sandie saw Trish's look and turned away, frightened her mask would slip.

$\sim\!\sim\!\sim$

Linda Cameron switched off the television and took a deep draw on her cigarette. She didn't always watch the morning news but the two local murders had both terrified and fascinated her. Today's update, however, had brought the tragic story closer to home; the police were looking for anyone who had seen what appeared to be a suspect and, from the description they had given, she most certainly had.

Not only that, from the picture of the second victim, it seemed likely that she had been one of the last people to see the poor woman alive. She stubbed her cigarette out in the ashtray; although an honest enough person herself, she had an inbuilt mistrust of the Police as there were a few, more distant, members of her family that hovered around the fringes of the criminal fraternity. Finally, she reached a decision, picked up her mobile phone and dialled the number that she had written down; it was time to do the right thing.

$\sim\!\sim\!\sim$

'Right, looks like we've finally got a proper witness, Boss.'

'What? No conspiracy theory, you mean...great stuff, Cliff; what're the details?'

'She's just phoned in; her name's Linda Cameron, she lives in Linwood. She says she's pretty sure she saw our blonde and, apparently, she also spoke to Natalie Wheeler when she was looking for the smaller-sized dress.'

'Brilliant! Right, what have you said to her?'

'Ah said we'd be over right away; here's the address, Napier Street.'

'Okay, you may as well come, Cliff. Briony and Sam are off speaking to the Wheelers again. Where's Faz and Grace?'

'They're double-checkin' the CCTV, in case there's any sightin's of a car that they've missed. Kiera's fieldin' the calls from the cranks; you know, the ones who say they know who did it, it's the woman next door, all that nonsense. There's even been one alien theory that Ah've heard...'

Grant made a face; it never ceased to amaze him how the public responded to such requests.

'Right we'll leave her to it, just in case there are any further bona-fide calls. Come on, let's go and speak to this woman.'

⁓⁓⁓

Twenty minutes later, they were sitting in the small living room of Linda Cameron's flat, which smelled of cigarettes and bacon. The woman was in her late forties, thin and with shoulder-length brown hair tied in a ponytail. She sipped nervously on a mug of tea, the offer of which both Grant and Cliff had declined. Grant had left the questioning to his DC, who had adopted a more formal tone which Grant found mildly amusing.

'Right, Linda, if you can just tell us what you saw.'

She gave him a slightly suspicious look.

'Ah'm no' under caution, or anythin'?'

'Of course not, Linda, you're no'...not under suspicion...'

This wasn't strictly true as, technically, anyone connected with the victim, especially that close to the time of their death, was certainly of interest.

'...we just want any information you can give us on this blonde woman who wis seen at the locus.'

'The whit?'

'Em, the crime scene.'

'Oh, right; well, Ah had this red dress in ma hand, an' this lassie comes up, lookin' for the size ten, but the one Ah had was...'

She looked up at Grant, her eyes watering.

'...that wis her, wisn't it, the lassie whit wis murdered...'

Grant tried to look sympathetic.

'I'm afraid so, Linda. Listen, there was nothing you could have done...'

'Ah know, it's just so sad, though, that Ah wis the last one tae see her, she seemed an awfy nice lassie...'

They sat in silence for a few moments, then Cliff spoke again.

'So, Linda, this other blonde woman—'

Linda Cameron looked up,

'Oh, aye, her. Well, she wis lookin' at the same dress, she was holdin' a fourteen an' I mind thinkin' that there wis no way she'd fit a fourteen—that other poor lassie gave me a smile as if she wis thinkin' the same thing...'

'So, you think she wis...em, was bigger than a size...em, fourteen, Linda?' asked Cliff, rather awkwardly. His knowledge of ladies' clothing sizes appeared to be as limited as Grant's.

Linda Cameron thought about it before replying.

'Aye. Ah'd have said she was aboot an eighteen; a big, well-built wifie, an' a bit tarty, if you know whit Ah mean.'

This seemed to be a recurring theme, Grant realised.

'In what way?' he asked.

'Her clothes were a bit tight, for a start. An' she wis definitely overdressed for goin' shoppin'. Ah mean, tight white troosers, a tight satin blouse, high heels? Who the hell does the weekly shop dressed like that?'

'But did she actually *have* any shoppin'?' asked Cliff, the formality slipping as his questioning continued. A trolley, a bag, anythin' like that? An' did she have a jacket, did you notice?'

Linda frowned as she considered the question and Grant realised that the woman was proving to be a pretty good witness.

'Now you come tae mention it, no, she didn't—all she had was a small handbag. Right enough, that's a bit funny. Mind, it wis cold on Sunday but she'd no jacket on...aye, that *wis* strange...'

'Did you get a look at her face?'

'No' really, she turned away but, from whit Ah could see, she wis kinda heavy-featured, if you know whit Ah mean. Biggish nose, full lips...oh, an' she had a lot o' make-up on, tae; very red lipstick, eye-liner, the works. That wis the other thing that made her look tarty, Ah suppose. An' that hair! Ah'm no' wan bit surprised it turned oot tae be a wig...'

∿∿∿

They had taken their leave and were on their way back to Osprey House.

'Thoughts, Cliff?'

'She seemed pretty reliable, Boss, we've got a much better description o' the blonde woman now.'

'Anything strike you as odd?'

Cliff thought for a moment.

'Aye, now you come to mention it, Boss. If you were settin' out to commit murder, would you no' take a few more precautions to remain anonymous? It's almost as if she wis tryin' to stand out, isn't it? Ah mean, no jacket, bright, distinctive clothin', why did she no' just wear jeans, a t-shirt an' a jacket? It's almost as if she was wantin' to be seen.'

'Aye, that's exactly what I was thinking, Cliff. It *is* almost like she wants us to see her, to notice her—well, her clothes, anyway. Odd, then, that she's gone to considerable lengths to cover her face on the CCTV...'

'And with the make-up, Boss. Linda said it wis pretty caked on. I mean, that's a disguise in itself, isn't it?'

'Aye, it is—so what *is* she hiding? Right, let's get in and see what everyone makes of it.'

No-one else had come forward with any further information on the mystery blonde. The calls had slowed over the morning, the assorted cranks having said their piece, and Grant brought them up to date with the interview.

'Thoughts, then?'

Kiera Fox frowned.

'You know, I wonder if she's actually pretending to be someone else, Boss.'

Grace Lappin agreed.

'I was thinking that too. Her dress, her make-up, it's all pretty blatant; as you said, if you were setting out to commit murder, surely, you'd want to remain as anonymous as possible, but she's gone out of her way to stand out, even down to not wearing a jacket!'

Grant nodded.

'I agree, Thing is, just who the hell *is* she pretending to be?'

He leaned against a desk and folded his arms, a frown on his face.

'I'm not a great fan but I think we need to try and get an e-fit picture, with and without the wig. The first might identify the person that she's impersonating, the second might help track her down. Faz, can you get on to that? You'll have to speak to Linda Cameron again, as well as the sales assistant in Asda. They both got a good look at her.'

'Sure, Boss.'

'And can you get something on HOLMES, a description without the wig, it might just be someone with a record elsewhere; it's a long shot but worth looking...'

His phone rang and Briony noticed the slight look of dismay as he glanced at the screen.

'Em, I'd best take this...'

As he walked towards the door, she heard the tone of his voice change as he mumbled into his phone.

'Hey! How's it going? Everything okay...?'

She rubbed her hand over her short dark hair; something was definitely afoot in the private life of DCI Grant McVicar.

~~~~

Somehow, Sandie Pollock managed to make it through the day; she looked at her watch—it was just after four-thirty, only an hour to go. Her phone pinged with a text message; excusing herself, she entered the cramped staff toilet, closed the door and looked at the screen.

"Hi SP. Sorry, more overtime being demanded, I'm afraid. Another IT crisis, it seems. Don't know when I'll be in, I'll grab a bite here so don't worry about dinner. I'll see you when I see you. Much love, Neil. Xx"

The message seemed stilted; more telling was the fact that he had texted rather than phoning her. Yet again, tears pricked her eyes, but her decision now seemed clearer. She stood up, flushed the toilet and returned to work.

Over the last remaining hour, she feigned a few symptoms until, finally, the manager took her aside.

'Sandie, are you okay? You seem to be getting worse as the day goes on.'

Sandie shook her head sorrowfully.

'To be honest, Mo, I feel dreadful, I'm sure I'm coming down with something.'

Morag Hunter was a sympathetic boss.

'Listen, you get yourself off home. There's only fifteen minutes to go anyway and I suggest you take tomorrow off; see how you feel. I'll get a locum in to cover.'

Sandie looked appreciatively, if slightly guiltily, at Mo.

'Okay, maybe you're right. Hopefully I'll be okay by the weekend.'

'Just let us know, Sandie, I hope you're feeling better soon. A couple of paracetamols and an early night should do the trick!'

Sandie gave a wan smile.

'Good advice, Mo, thanks. I'll see you soon.'

Grant was both frustrated and worried; although he realised that it was still early days, the wheels of the investigation seemed to be grinding very slowly. Since the amalgamation of all Scotland's regional forces to become Scotland's police, as far as he knew there were no unsolved murder cases on their books and he most certainly didn't want to be the one to break that un-blemished record!

Faz, Cliff and Grace had spent the afternoon tracking down the various security cameras around the Linwood area and had started on the painstaking and mind-numbing task of looking for further images of their suspect. HOLMES had yielded no information on the identity of the woman and there had been no fresh evidence from any potential witnesses. It was about four-thirty when his phone rang and, once again, Briony noticed her boss looking at the screen with a pained expression; he looked back up at her.

'It's Louise. I'd better take it.'

It had been just over a year since Grant's former sergeant, and best friend, Brian Thackray, had been killed in a tragic accident and Grant continued to feel that he was, in some way, responsible. Brian had been drinking heavily whilst Grant had been trying to comfort his wife, Louise. Unable to contact either of them, Brian had driven home, blind drunk and imagining that Louise was having an affair; when he saw Grant's car outside his house, he wrongly assumed that the "other man" was his best friend. Just before his car had crashed and he had died in the ensuing fireball, Brian had sent Grant a final text

"You bastard! I thought you were my friend...'

Fifteen minutes later, Grant returned to the main office. Briony immediately recognised the blank expression, the distant look in the big man's eyes...

'Boss?'

'What? Em, listen, I need to go, Bri. Look, I'll be a bit late tomorrow morning. Be in as soon as I can. Stuff to do...'

He walked out of the room without a backward glance. Briony stared after him, shaking her head.

What the hell's wrong now...?

As Grant turned the pick-up off the A737 and onto the narrow Belltrees Road, his head was spinning. As well as investigating the brutal murders of two apparently innocent women, he had now been requested (begged, actually) to attend a meeting with the head teacher of his godson, Finn Thackray, first thing in the morning. Not only that, but he was due to attend the funeral of Glasgow crime patriarch, Michael Pettigrew, the following afternoon; more time away from the case that he could ill-afford...

Finally, as he pulled into his drive, the realisation that he had, somehow, acquired what his mother used to call "a bidey-in" suddenly hit him. He managed a grim smile; at least there was a good chance of a hot meal waiting for him...

Then he remembered; Tuesday night was usually his night for training at the rowing club; he groaned out loud—that was now the last place on earth that he would dare show his face...

Christ, Grant, what a bloody mess...!

Sandie Pollock had little appetite; she was on her second vodka and coke and had forced herself to heat up and eat a pepperoni pizza, which was now giving her indigestion. She swallowed the last of the drink and looked at the brass carriage clock on the mantelpiece; eight fifty-three. She had no idea where Neil was, whom he was with, what he was doing; and, she realised, she no longer cared. No, she had a course of action to follow now and follow it she must, even if it meant...

No, Sandie, you can't think like that...

She went through to the kitchen and poured the last of the vodka into her glass; she slugged it back, without the coke, in the hope that she'd be asleep by the time Neil got home. She'd leave him a note, asking him not to waken her but, as the idea came to her, she realised that it would be the first time in her life that she had done so...and probably the last.

She started to cry.

McTurk's Bar stood on a corner mid-way along London road; a dilapidated, flat-roofed building seemingly cast adrift on a patch of waste ground, the adjacent buildings long since having been demolished in the ongoing regeneration of Glasgow's East End. Somehow McTurk's had survived, one of the few remaining traditional Glasgow working men's pubs in existence, although this was more on account of its ownership rather than its appeal. There were precious few "working men" in this part of Glasgow nowadays.

Billy Cook pulled his car in to the side of the dirty, pot-holed road, carefully avoiding the assorted debris lying in the gutter. He got out and cast a furtive look about; a group of smokers, huddled outside the pub, turned and stared at him as they drew heavily on their cigarettes—no electronic nonsense here! He walked quickly towards the door, the three men reluctantly standing aside as he did so. One of them insolently blew a stream of smoke at him as he passed and he was certain that they had guessed his profession. He cast a final backwards glance at his car before he entered the dingy and sparsely-furnished bar, wondering if it would be intact when he came back out.

If I do come back out, that is...fuck...!

There would have been a time, not too long ago, when the room would have been filled with the blue fug of tobacco smoke; nowadays the air was clear, albeit with a pervasive odour of stale beer and unwashed humanity. Seated at a table was a dark-haired man with a pock-marked face, smartly-dressed in a navy suit and an open-necked white shirt; the man hailed him.

'Billy Boy. How goes it, ma friend?'

Billy Cook looked across; despite the greeting, John Norris was no friend of his. He walked over to the table and sat down across from the man, who was taking a sip of whisky; Cook ignored the second glass which was sitting in front of him.

'Aye, not bad, John. You?'

'Never better, Billy, never better. Business good?'

Cook gave him a sharp look but remained silent.

'Talkin' of which—'

John Norris reached inside his suit and removed a plain white envelope.

'Ma employers are lookin' for a wee bit o' information, Billy. Ah said you were just the man; as and when you can get it, of course.'

He handed Cook the unsealed envelope and the latter opened it, taking out the single sheet of A4 paper. He removed a battered pair of reading glasses from the pocket of his jacket, read the content then looked back over at Norris.

'Shouldn't be too much of a problem, John. Haven't heard anything, mind, but I'll keep my eyes an' ears open.'

'Do that, Billy; ma employers will be very grateful.'

There was a slight, ominous pause.

'How grateful, John?'

Norris gave an oily smile and reached into his pocket for a second time; he withdrew a zipped plastic bag and placed it carefully on the table. Billy Cook leaned over, lifted and unzipped it, then removed the small cardboard folder, marked "Travel Currency." He looked inside then back across at John Norris, who was regarding him carefully.

'Hundred thousand Thai baht, Billy. Another hundred K to follow if an' when you get us somethin'...Ah know how you like your wee jaunts over tae the East and Ah know just how expensive the entertainment can be...'

Billy Cook could feel the colour rise in his cheeks; he wasn't sure if it was anger or embarrassment and he certainly wasn't going to analyse it. He wrapped the letter round the currency wallet and placed both in the envelope, which he tucked safely back in his pocket.

'Aye, well, leave it with me, John. I'll be in touch...'

'Ah hope so, Billy Boy, Ah certainly hope so...listen, are you no' goin' to drink that whisky?'

Cook snorted.

'D'you think I walked here?'

Norris shrugged.

'Whatever! Thought you lot could get away wi' it but Ah suppose times change...well, if you're no' havin' it, pour it in there—'

He pushed his glass across and Cook lifted his own, pouring the un-drunk contents into Norris's. The latter lifted it and took a large swallow.

'Ahh, that's good, cann'ae beat The Famous Grouse...'

Cook made to stand up, then stopped himself, looking down at the glass. Norris followed his gaze and gave a leering grin.

'Whit, Billy Boy?'

Suddenly, Cook leaned across the table and grabbed the glass, throwing it down on the floor where it smashed noisily into fragments. The barman looked over, as did a couple of hard-looking individuals seated in the corner; they rose from their seats but Norris smiled and signalled to them to stay where they were.

'S'all right, lads, Billy here just had a wee accident. Anyway, he's leaving now, before he has another one...'

He stared across at Cook, the evil grin still present; it didn't reach his eyes.

'D'you no' fuckin' trust me, Cook?'

Billy Cook glared back.

'Best not to leave anything that can prove I've been here, Norris. You know the score...'

Norris raised his hands, indicating the drinkers, whose eyes were turned towards them.

'There's a few witnesses...'

Cook stood up.

'I'll take my chances.'

He looked about, then leaned over to John Norris, lowering his voice. He was feeling decidedly nervous—he was a long way from his home territory.

'D'you think I'm stupid, John, leaving a glass covered in my prints? You know I'll do my best; always have done.'

Norris sneered as Cook stood back up.

'Aye, I know you will, Billy Boy; because you just can't resist those pretty young Thai lady...'

Cook leaned over the table for a second time, now lowering his voice to a rasping whisper; he was shaking with suppressed rage.

'...listen, just because I take your money doesn't mean I have to like you, Norris. In fact, you can go and fuck yourself!'

He turned and strode out, leaving Norris staring after him. Once the door closed, the barman came over and sat down.

'Awright, John?'

Norris grinned.

'What a fuckin' tosser, Cammy. Thinks he's so fuckin' clever...'

Very carefully, he lifted the plastic bag that had contained the Thai currency, holding it up by the corner.

'You see, all you need to do is take his eye aff the ball...'

CHAPTER 6

'Where's the boss, Sarge?'

It was a reasonable enough question; unfortunately, it was one that DS Briony Quinn couldn't answer.

'Em, I think he's got some personal business to attend to, Faz.'

'Oh, right.'

Briony knew that the whole team were curious about their boss's absence at this stage in a murder enquiry, especially one that didn't seem to be proceeding particularly well. She stood up and addressed them.

'Right, let's see if we can't have a pleasant surprise waitin' for him when he gets back. Come on; Faz, have you checked HOLMES this morning?'

'Em, not yet, Sarge, just logging on now...'

'Listen, I need to go...'

As Grant extricated himself from Delia Donald's somewhat passionate embrace and headed for the door, he felt as if he was being torn in two. There was no doubt that she was an extremely attractive and sexy woman, not to mention being a pretty good cook; his house was cleaner and tidier than it had been in ages! So, what was the problem, he asked himself as he climbed into the sanctuary of his Toyota pick-up? He banged his fists on the steering wheel in frustration.

Fuck!

Of course, he knew *exactly* what the problem was...

As he drove down the narrow country road towards the busy A737, he tried to analyse his situation in an unsuccessful attempt to keep his mind from the forthcoming meeting; unfortunately, the previous day's conversation with Louise Thackray insinuated itself into his thought process...

'Louise? Louise, what is it? What's wrong?'

She managed to stop crying.

'It's Finn.'

'Finn! What's happened to him?'

'He's in trouble at school, Grant. He's being bullied...'

Grant could feel his temper rise; if there was one thing he abhorred it was bullying.

'Louise, I'm so sorry—'

She cut him off, the words tumbling out in a semi-incoherent jumble.

'Those wee...wee bastards, they've been calling him names for ages, just because Brian was a policeman. He's managed to cope... but then they must have found out what happened. Yesterday one of the little shits passed Finn in the corridor and started sniffing...'

More sobbing.

'...then he shouted to his mates "can you smell roast pork about here, guys?" And they all thought this was hilarious. Poor Finn had had enough and he lashed out and punched the little...the little..'

Grant had gritted his teeth; if he was being honest, he would probably have done the same.

'Louise, calm down, please. Listen, I know that kids aren't meant to retaliate but he was provoked, for God's sake, surely...'

'But the problem is he didn't stop; he knocked the little bastard down then started to kick him; that was when the head teacher caught them. Now it's Finn's that's the "big baddie" and I've been "requested" to attend a meeting with the sanctimonious little woman this morning to discuss his so-called "violent tendencies". The stupid bitch is even suggesting anger management...'

'What? Jesus, after what they said to him...tell me, Louise, had you reported the bullying before?'

'Loads of times, with the usual fob-off, you know "we're dealing with it," all that crap. But obviously they weren't "dealing with it" and I'm beginning to think she's actually afraid of these boys herself. Finn says they're a pretty rough lot, come from a bad background. He thinks they might be dealing drugs as well.'

Grant sighed; drugs were becoming an issue in too many primary schools.

'Louise, I'm so sorry; listen—'

'Can you come with me, Grant? Please, I don't know what the hell I'm going to say and maybe...'

'Louise, I'm in the middle of a murder enquiry, I can't just drop everything...'

There had been a meaningful pause, then Louise replied, her tone cooler and her emotion suppressed.

'Well, I suppose if you're too busy...'

Fuck...

'What time are you going in?'

'She said first thing so I'll be there at nine.'

There was another pause, then he let out a long sigh.

'Okay, I'll be there. I'll meet you in the car park at five-to.'

Grant pulled his pick-up in a few spaces along from where Louise was parked then walked across to meet her. Her eyes were red and puffy but she had made an effort and she looked smart and pretty, if a little gaunt and considerably strained. They hugged.

'Right, let's get this over with. I'll let you deal with it unless, or until, I think it's necessary for me to intervene. Just introduce me as a family friend, or as Finn's godfather, whatever; don't mention that I'm a cop. What's this woman's name again?'

'Mrs Alexander. Her first name's Doreen but, apparently, no-one ever calls her anything other than Mrs Alexander.'

'Hm. Right, let's go.'

The office was small, neat and tidy, as was the woman sitting across the desk from them. Doreen Alexander favoured her guests with a prim smile as she introduced herself, although Grant almost felt as if he was the one in trouble! He placed her in her early fifties, with bobbed grey hair and pale blue eyes that had a cold expression. He had a great respect for teachers and didn't envy the task they were faced with. Still...

'...and you're a "friend" of Mrs Thackray, I believe?'

The slightly disapproving emphasis on "friend" annoyed Grant but he merely replied

'Actually, I'm Finn's godfather.'

'Oh, I see,' she responded, seemingly placated. Right, let's move on, shall we? Well, Mrs Thackray, I have to say that we're lucky that Darren Barrowman's parents have decided not to take the matter further...'

Grant furrowed his dark brows.

Barrowman...that rings a bell...

'...but that doesn't alter the fact that your son, Finn, committed a serious assault on school premises...'

'Mrs Alexander, do you know what they said to my son?'

'Mrs Thackray, I am well aware that there has been a bit of an issue with bullying but—'

'My husband, who was a serving police sergeant, was killed in a car crash; his vehicle exploded with him inside. These little... monsters walked past him making comments about "roast pork"...'

Grant could see the tears welling up in Louise's eyes.

Keep it together, girl...

'Mrs Thackray, whatever they said, Finn should *not* have acted the way he did. He should have come straight to me...'

'He'd done that repeatedly, Mrs Alexander, and, as usual, you failed to act...'

The head teacher raised her voice.

'How dare you! I take this matter very seriously, Mrs Thackray, and I've already warned these boys about their behaviour. Now, if Finn had...'

'Mrs Alexander, what is it going to take? How many times must my son have to listen to these vile comments before you actually do something?'

Grant could see the colour rise in Doreen Alexander's cheeks. As she pointed an accusing finger at Louise, he reached slowly inside his jacket.

'Now you listen to me, Mrs Thackray. I am not going to tolerate any more of this; your son is obviously a violent young man with a dangerous temper. I am not going to allow such behaviour in my school and I am most certainly not going to allow you to come in here and accuse me…'

Grant took out his Police Scotland identity card and placed it on the table; Doreen Alexander stopped mid-sentence and stared at it. Grant glowered across at her as he spoke, his voice calm but authoritative.

'Right, I've listened to enough of this. First of all, Mrs Alexander, Brian Thackray was my detective sergeant. He was an excellent police officer and it grieves me deeply to hear the insults that his son has had to bear.'

'Well…I quite understand, Mr Mc…'

'Detective Chief Inspector McVicar, actually. And, as I am sure you are aware, Police Scotland take a very dim view of bullying, more so in schools and especially when it concerns the children of one of their own.'

'Yes, but…'

'Mrs Alexander, I'll be frank with you; I've heard enough here to know that, despite repeated complaints from Mrs Thackray, neither you nor your school have taken the necessary action to prevent this incident from happening. Finn Thackray is clearly the victim here; he has been subjected to ongoing verbal abuse and bullying which, despite Mrs Thackray's repeated attempts, has gone unchecked. His reaction was quite predictable and, whilst I do not in any way condone it, had you acted appropriately the incident would never have happened in the first place.'

Doreen Alexander opened and closed her mouth like a fish on dry land.

'Now…now just a min…'

'No, Mrs Alexander, you will hear me out. I will speak to Finn personally and advise him to modify his behaviour, although the poor young lad was undoubtedly pushed to his limit. You will deal with this bullying issue and ensure that it is eradicated. Rest assured I will be reporting this to the local community officer and, should I hear of any further incidents, there will be an immediate intervention by the police. Not only that, the matter will be reported to the relevant Education Authorities. I am sure that you don't want the bad publicity, not to mention the investigations, that will necessarily ensue. Do I make myself clear?'

The head teacher stared at him, an expression of rage and shock on her face. He raised his voice a notch.

'Do I make myself clear, Mrs Alexander?'

With considerable reluctance, the woman nodded.

'Good. Then we're done here. Louise?'

They said nothing as they walked out of the school and across the car park, although there was the trace of a smile on Louise Thackray's lips. Grant noticed three late-comers approaching and Louise whispered.

'That's one of them, Grant, that's the Barrowman boy in the middle. He's the ring-leader.'

Grant glared at the malevolent-looking youth, his nose swollen and bruised from Finn's punch, earning a dirty look in return; there was a vague familiarity about his features. Without further thought, he turned away from Louise, pulled out his warrant card once more and flashed it in front of Darren Barrowman's face, bending down as he hissed.

'You're on *my* radar now, sunshine. Any more of your nonsense and you'll have me to deal with.'

He strode across to where Louise was standing without a backward glance, which was probably fortunate, given the gestures that were being made towards him.

Sandie Pollock looked at herself in the mirror; she seemed to have aged by about ten years since last week. Her eyes were puffy, her face careworn; she felt desolate.

Neil had been up early, leaving just as she came downstairs. No "Love you, Sweet Pea", no warm hug, just a simple "might be late again tonight—I'll call you..." Where the hell had it all gone wrong? And just how wrong *had* it gone...?

She had phoned the pharmacy, claiming a deterioration of yesterday's feigned illness, although the truth of the matter was that she most certainly wasn't fit for work. She straightened her shoulders and gave her hair a final brush; she knew what she had to do, no matter what the consequences may be.

It was nearly eleven before Grant arrived at Osprey House; he and Louise had sat in his pick-up, discussing Finn, Brian, life in general...finally she had left, but not before eliciting a promise from him to come for dinner on Sunday. Just how the hell he was going to explain that to Delia was anyone's guess...

As he walked into the meeting room, there was a definite atmosphere, akin to static electricity, immediately signifying that something was afoot.

'Mornin' Boss. Everythin' okay?

'Morning Bri, aye, I suppose. So, what's happening? Something's up, would anyone care to enlighten me?'

He sat down and waited for a few seconds before Grace Lappin smiled across at him.

'Had a very interesting phone call, Boss.'

'Oh?'

'A woman presented herself at Mill Street first thing this morning with information on the murders...'

Mill Street was Paisley's main, and better-known, Police HQ; he could feel the hairs on the back of his neck stand up.

'And...?'

'Well, she seems fairly certain that she knows who our mystery blonde is...'

Forty-five minutes later, Grant, Briony and Grace pulled off Paisley's rather-exclusive Craw Road and scrunched into the gravel driveway of a beautiful, blonde-sandstone detached villa. It reminded Grant of another house, one in Glasgow's East End, one with a very different set of occupants...

No, Grant, don't...

Even as he suppressed the thought, he remembered that he was still planning to attend a funeral the next day; yet another event that he'd rather have avoided. Before he could press the doorbell, the oak door, complete with its original stained-glass panels, opened. Grant showed his ID.

'Oh, hello, thanks for coming over.'

Briony scrutinised Sandie Pollock's face. Mid-fifties, she guessed, and attractive, although the woman looked extremely distressed and had obviously been crying. As she walked past and into the tastefully decorated hallway, she detected a faint whiff of alcohol and she caught Grant's eye; he raised an eyebrow, obviously having noticed it too. Sandie opened the door to the lounge.

'In here, please...'

They entered the bright, spacious room, where Sandie invited them to sit on the large settee as she took her own usual seat in the armchair. Briony sat nearest to her as Grant looked around enviously at the furnishings and the decor; it was the kind of home he would have loved, rather than his own "work-in-progress!"

*Maybe I **do** need a woman...!*

'Can I get you anything?'

'No, thanks, Mrs Pollock,' he replied, trying to emulate his sergeant's sympathetic tone.

'Sandie, please. Mrs Pollock sounds so formal.'

'Okay, Sandie. Anyway, I'm DCI Grant McVicar, this is DS Briony Quinn and DC Grace Lappin; it was Grace who took the call from Mill Street.'

'Oh, right; I just thought that was where you went! I didn't even know you had another office.'

'Yes, Osprey house is where we're based, the Major Incident Teams HQ. But you were right, we don't actually have any public access there.'

'Oh, I see' Sandie replied, in a disinterested tone. 'Actually, I thought that what I told you colleague would be sufficient...I didn't realise you'd want me to go through it all again.'

There was a slightly awkward pause then, by pre-arrangement, Briony leaned towards Sandie Pollock, speaking in her soft Fife-shire lilt.

'Sandie, what you told the other officer wasn't really a statement as such, it was passed on to us to follow it up. I know this must be difficult for you, but if you could please tell *us* the whole story; an' take your time, eh?'

They could see the emotion on the woman's face; hurt, fear, something else; Grant wasn't quite sure what it was—guilt, perhaps? But guilt for what? Sandie Pollock lowered her head and stared at the carpet.

'Oh God, where do I start...'

'At the beginnin', Sandie.'

She told them about her husband, Neil, about their seemingly wonderful marriage, the kids, the grandchildren. She told them about the house, about Neil's love of art. Then she paused, fighting her emotions.

'So, what is it, Sandie? What's happened?' asked Briony.

'Oh, it was that bitch McKillop, it was her who sowed the seeds...'

Her voice was wavering and Grant was worried that she would break down completely. Sandie related the unpleasant phone conversation with Dr Carole McKillop, telling them how those very seeds of doubt had been sown. Briony was now holding the woman's hand, stroking the back of it very gently; once again, Grant envied the ability of his detective sergeant to calm down a near-hysterical witnesses. Sandie continued, her voice less shaky.

'And then I... I caught him out. He said he was at a conference in Edinburgh and I phoned up the hotel; but he wasn't there,

there was no conference, it was all a lie. He was lying. Neil was lying. He was cheating...'

Finally, she started to sob and Briony immediately knelt down on the floor beside her.

'There now, love, there...just breathe, that's it, you're nearly done.'

As they waited for a few minutes, hoping Sandie would recover a modicum of composure, Grant wondered where this tale of a shattered domestic idyll was leading.

'I'm sorry, it's just so...well anyway, he phoned me to say he was staying an extra night...'

'Sandie, was that unusual?' asked Grant, his patience with the near-distraught woman starting to slip away. Briony gave him a rather dark look.

She looked up at him as if she had forgotten he was there.

'What? Oh, no, sometimes if they asked him to go into the Edinburgh office the next day, he stayed; it made sense, rather than travelling home then back through...'

'And can I ask what weekend this was?'

She gave him a slightly puzzled look, as if he was missing the point.

'The one just there; he went through last Friday night and came home on Monday afternoon. That's what made me wonder...that and...'

Briony interrupted.

'What, Sandie? What else?'

Sandie grabbed Briony's hand and held it tightly as she mumbled.

'The cupboard.'

'I'm sorry' asked Grant. 'The cupboard, did you say?'

The distraught woman looked up again, staring at him through her puffy, narrowed eyes.

'Yes, you see. Neil has this cupboard in his art room; one that he keeps locked... to stop the grandchildren taking out paints and stuff...'

She cast her eyes back down as if ashamed.

'What is it, Sandie? Tell us; what's in the cupboard?'

'Well, I figured out the combination for the padlock...'

Grant was slightly surprised.

'You mean you didn't know it?'

Sandie shook her head.

'No, but it turns out it was the name of a band... Anyway, I'd always respected his privacy...but, after the weekend, I wondered...'

'Can I ask what was in it?' asked Grant.

Sandie looked up as if dumbstruck, then managed to mumble 'You'd better come and see...'

~~~

They climbed the elegant stairway and entered the rear-facing room, bright despite the overcast sky; it was filled with the paraphernalia of the artist and in one corner there was a built-in cupboard, secured by a small hasp and a combination lock. Sandie seemed to shy away from it as if the contents were, somehow, evil. Grant and Grace pulled on their thin forensic gloves as Briony stood with her arm protectively around Sandie's shoulders.

'Right, Sandie, before we have a look, can you tell me exactly what happened?'

The woman stared at him, her eyes wide.

'Sandie' whispered Briony, 'you need to tell us, please.'

'Well...so, after I'd worked out the combination on Saturday, I opened it and found... things; things that really upset me. I hadn't a clue about this secret life he seemed to be leading...but it was when I opened it again on Monday night, there were other... they hadn't been there before...and that policewoman on the television had said—'

This time she broke down completely and Grant looked at Briony in near despair. He spoke softly.

'Bri, I need the combination.'

Despite her upset, Sandie heard him and managed to mumble 'Seven-three-nine-six.'

'Right, thanks Sandie, well done. Grace?'

DC Grace Lappin stood beside him as he turned the little wheels and pulled the lock apart, removing it from the hasp; he opened the door gently and they looked inside.

CHAPTER 7

Christine Duff sat in her neat lounge, her hands clasped around a Dunoon China mug containing un-drunk, cold tea as she stared disconsolately, and with unfocussed eyes, at the black screen of the television. Her husband, Colin, was back at work; of course, he bloody was! He and Amanda had drifted apart over the last few years, latterly seldom communicating with one another apart from the occasional screaming match.

She wondered if he actually had any feelings left for the poor, dead daughter who had once been the apple of his eye; in fact, she wondered if he had any feelings left for *her*. Then there was all that crap about "bad genes"...she placed the cup carefully on the glass-topped table and closed her eyes, wishing it would all go away. She hated death; it was fine for those who had died, their worries were over. No, it was the ones left behind who suffered; the grief, the trauma, the anger...she picked up her mobile phone, hesitating only very slightly before pressing the dial icon.

~~~

Sandie and the three police officers stared into the depths of Neil Pollock's cupboard. It appeared to have been fitted out as a small wardrobe and there were a number of items of women's clothing hanging in it, with more garments neatly folded on the upper shelves. Several pairs of high-heeled shoes sat neatly in the base. Sandie looked shocked.

'But...but...they were there; on Monday! I saw them with my own eyes...that's why I...'

Briony gently took the woman's shoulders, turning her to face her.

'What was there, Sandie; tell me?'

'The clothes.'

'What clothes?

'The clothes that policewoman said the suspect was wearing; and the blonde wig...'

Grace was carefully examining the contents of the wardrobe.

'Sandie, do any of these clothes belong to you?'

The woman shook her head miserably.

'No.'

'So, who *do* they belong to?'

'To Neil. To my bloody husband.'

Grant turned and looked at Briony, raising his eyebrow as he spoke.

'Your husband dresses up in woman's clothes, Sandie; is that what you're saying?'

Sandie Pollock collapsed against Briony's shoulder, nodding her head in assent as she started to howl yet again.

They were back in the lounge; Grace had made them tea and they were sipping the comforting drinks in a slightly uneasy silence. Sandie had finally stopped crying and, once she had placed her mug on the table, Briony took her hand once again.

'Sandie, can you tell us exactly what happened?'

'Okay, I'll try.'

She blew her nose.

'So, on Saturday I'd phoned the hotel in Edinburgh where Neil was supposed to be staying and it turned out there was no conference, no-one of that name booked in. I realised he was lying and, coming after that other phone call, I realised he must be having an affair. I'd never actually looked in his cupboard—I had no reason to—but when that bitch phoned, well, I started to wonder...but I didn't look, I still trusted Neil.'

Briony let Sandie pause for a moment.

'So, what did you find on Saturday night?'

'Clothes. It was full of women's clothes, all in what I would imagine is Neil's... size.'

She started to falter, then pulled herself together.

'There was underwear, sexy, slinky stuff...even a couple of bloody bras'

She actually smiled at this, although Grant thought it appeared slightly manic.

'...trousers, tops, a couple of skirts...'

'And you're absolutely sure they're his?' asked Grant. 'There's no chance that they belong to another woman?'

Sandie shook her head.

'I don't think so...anyway, it was the shoes; they're a size eleven. Do you know any women with size eleven feet?'

'Em—'

'And if they belonged to another woman, why would they be in his cupboard, locked away?'

She had a point, Grant realised. Briony put her finger to her lips, cautioning her boss to be quiet, then lowered her voice.

'So, you'd looked in the cupboard on Saturday, Sandie, but what about Monday? What was different—what did you find then?

'Oh God...well, it was after that woman had been speaking on television'

'Superintendent Minto? She's our superior officer' added Grant.

'Oh, I didn't know... Anyway, she said that you were looking for a woman in a blonde wig, who'd been wearing white trousers and a green top...I looked in the wardrobe and they were there.'

'What, Sandie? Tell us specifically?'

'There was a pair of white jeans hanging up, next to a green, silky top; and, on the shelf, there was a shoulder-length blonde wig, exactly like the woman—your boss—said; and exactly like Carole McKillop saw getting into Neil's car...'

She started to cry again.

'You're quite sure?' asked Briony gently. Sandie nodded.

'Yes. I... I didn't know what to do...I was going to confront him but then, what if he *was* the mur... No, I can't say it! But I was so scared.'

'Tell me, has he been acting strangely in any way?' asked Grant.

Again, she looked at him as if she had forgotten he was there.

'Em, yes, that's the other thing, he's been acting *really* strangely; Neil's normally sweet and loving but he's been withdrawn, he's been so moody, nothing like the Neil I know...or knew. Oh Christ, surely he wouldn't...'

Sandie's shoulders started to heave and Briony knelt in front of her, trying to console her. She turned to Grant as he spoke.

'We're going to have to find him, Bri. It looks like our mystery blonde woman might actually be a man...'

~~~

DC Cliff Ford stood poised in front of the two white boards, waiting for his boss to continue. Grant was staring down at Sandie Pollock's statement, rubbing his short beard thoughtfully. Finally, he spoke.

'Right, put this Neil Pollock down as our prime suspect, although at present we're going solely on his wife's suspicions.'

Cliff started to write.

'He's an IT consultant with the NHS, works in...'

Grant turned and looked at Briony.

'Meridian Court, the NHS offices in Cadogan Street, Glasgow. Near Central Station, I think.'

'Okay; he drives a yellow Porsche...'

'Must be doing all right' murmured Faz.

Grant raised an eyebrow at his DC.

'...aye, and don't you be getting any ideas, sunshine! Registration...?'

Again, he looked at Briony, who rhymed off Neil Pollock's private registration, then added.

'Apparently, he's managed to wangle a parkin' permit, seems the parkin's pretty limited. It's a basement car park below the office buildin.'

Cliff continued to scrawl on the board.

'Are you going to bring him in, Boss?'

'We'll head up to his office after this briefing and take it from there, Kiera. His wife is adamant that the same clothes worn by this blonde person, along with the wig, were in his cupboard on Monday night but they're certainly not there now. Apparently, there's a holdall missing as well and we've got a couple of SOCOs over having a look at the other stuff as we speak; hopefully they've been discreet, don't want word getting out just yet, you know what the press are like.'

He sat down, staring at the floor, as Cliff finished off adding the fresh information. When he spoke again, it was almost as if he was talking to himself, although Briony knew that he was really just thinking out loud; that was how he operated.

'So, what've we got? Neil Pollock, possibly having an affair and apparently a cross-dresser, absent on Friday through to Monday night, not where he told his wife he would be and unexpectedly staying an extra day, wherever he actually was. That could be anywhere, of course...'

'What about the place he stayed before, Boss?' asked Grace Lappin.

Grant looked up; his train of thought broken.

'Sorry...what place?'

'Well, remember Sandie said she'd had a phone call from an acquaintance—a GP, didn't she say— claiming she'd seen a blonde getting into Neil Pollock's Porsche. From the description, it could actually have been him dressed as a woman, getting into his own car. Would it be worth checking to see where that was? Maybe he used the same hotel again...just a thought.'

'Hm, you could be on to something...listen, could you phone Sandie Pollock and see if she remembers exactly where it was. If not, we'll have to check with the GP who phoned her.'

'Don't think that'll go down too well, Boss' interjected Briony.

'I know, but needs must, Bri. Hopefully Sandie'll remember where it was, though.'

Grace got Sandie Pollock's number and made the call as Grant continued.

'Right. Pollock comes home on Monday night, he's in a strange mood, Sandie gets suspicious and, once he's safely tucked up in bed, looks in this locked cupboard of his; there, she claims that she found the outfit worn by our suspect, along with a blonde wig, all of which fits with both the CCTV and the witness statements. Unfortunately, this evidence has now disappeared...'

Briony suddenly looked up at him, a look of alarm on her face; the penny dropped with Grant as she spoke.

'You don't think he's planning another killing, eh?'

'Shit! That's just crossed my mind too; right, troops, we need to—'

Briony's phone rang and she looked at the screen.

'It's her—Sandie.'

Grace looked across at them.

'I've been trying her number, it's been engaged.'

Briony answered the call and spoke for a few minutes; all eyes were on her.

'Listen, Sandie, calm down, calm down, it's okay...I know... right...you're sure you'll be okay? Good, good. You take care, ma dear—'

Grant frowned at her.

'What?'

Briony ended the call.

'Her husband's just phoned her; says he's been called back through to their Edinburgh offices at The Gyle to deal with some software fault. He's staying over and won't be back until tomorrow afternoon.'

'Shit! Did she say if he'd actually left work?'

'She didn't know; he'd just called to say he wouldn't be home. She said he sounded really withdrawn, as if he was worried or stressed.'

'Christ, no bloody wonder if he's planning another murder! Right, we need to get up there fast and see if we can get a hold of him before he leaves. Have you got the exact address of his office?'

'Aye, on my phone.'

'Right, come on; Bri, can you call Sandie on the way, see if you can get his work number; maybe they can delay him, although we need to be careful that we don't warn him off. Cliff, Kiera, you come too—might need to have a look at his office, if he has one. Grace, Sam, I think it would be best if you head back over and have a chat with Sandie, see if you can get the address of this hotel that he stayed at; and see if she'll let you have a look through his personal stuff, receipts, a credit card statement, anything that might give us any clues as to where he's been. If she refuses, I'll get the Mint to arrange a warrant. He must have left a footprint somewhere and, if we miss him at his work, we might just be able to pick him up, wherever he's headed.'

'On it, Boss,' said Sam as the two girls stood up.

'Faz, see if you can track down anything for Neil Pollock; any history, see if he comes up on HOLMES in relation to anything else. I'm not liking the sound of this guy...'

$\sim\!\!\sim\!\!\sim$

'I'm sorry Sir, but Mr Pollock has left the building.'

Following Briony's call to the office, Grant was already aware of this fact.

'Yes, but can you tell us how long ago?'

The slightly-officious young man at the reception desk consulted the visitors' book.

'Let me see...everyone must sign in and out...ah, here we are! Neil Pollock, left the building at two twenty-seven.'

Grants pursed his lips in frustration; Pollock would be well on his way to wherever he was headed.

'Fine. Right, can we have a look at his office?'

'That's out of the question, I'm afraid.'

DCI McVicar drew himself up to his not inconsiderable height.

'Listen, Mr...' he looked at the ubiquitous lanyard around the receptionist's neck. '...McMillan, we're conducting a murder enquiry and it's imperative that—'

Gavin McMillan folded his arms and returned the policeman's fierce stare.

'Chief Inspector, I understand that you're doing your job; but you need to understand that I'm also doing mine. As I'm sure you are aware, this is an NHS facility and our computers have access to highly sensitive patient data, not to mention the entire national NHS database. Now, I fully appreciate that you have a job to do but, unless you have a warrant, then I'm afraid that there is no way that I can allow you to access Mr Pollock's workspace or any of his data...'

'Fine, Gavin, I understand...but, in that case, can I speak to your manager, please?'

Lynne Kilpatrick regarded the tall, bald and not-unattractive man who was glowering across at her; although she sympathised with his predicament, she was adamant.

'I'm sorry, Chief Inspector, but my word is final. Gavin is completely correct, without a warrant I'm afraid that there is no way that I can either allow you to access any of our systems or to examine Mr Pollock's workspace.'

'But, surely—'

'That's my final word. Come back with a warrant and we'll certainly allow you access; but, until them, I'm sorry...'

Fuck...!

'She's right, Boss.'

'Aye, I know, but it's so bloody frustrating; I mean, for all we know, this bastard is about to commit another murder and we haven't a clue where the hell he's headed. And, as far as we know, there was no request from the Edinburgh office for him to go through; at least they've checked that much for us. It all looks pretty bloody suspicious, if you ask me...'

Grant paused and thought for a moment.

'Right Bri, let's not wait till we get back; can you phone the Mint and get a warrant to search his office? The sooner we have a look the better; and we need to get his registration out to all the Central forces—it's a yellow Porsche he drives, isn't it? Phone it in and get the details out, see if anyone can locate him and where he's headed.'

'On it, Boss...'

'And we'll need to get in touch with Gordon Harris, see if he's found anything of interest at Pollock's house?'

Briony nodded; her boss seemed to have suddenly switched into overdrive...

<center>~~~</center>

They had arrived back at Osprey House; Grace and Sam had returned from their interview with Sandie Pollock and had managed to obtain the information that Grant had sought.

'Sandie says that the GP saw the blonde getting into Neil's car at a hotel down in Leith. I've checked and I'm pretty sure it must be the Premier Inn.'

'Good job, Sam. Listen, I know it's a bit of a trek, but could you and Grace head through, he might just be there, although it's a bit of a long shot. Anyway, you can at least try and find out who stayed there on the night that this GP saw him.'

He thought for a moment.

'Mind you, there's a chance that he might not have booked in under his own name; in fact, he might even be dressed as a woman. Anyway, if you can just get a list of the guests, that'll be a start. You know what we're looking for.'

'Okay, Boss. We'll head off now and let you know.'

The two DCs stood up, ready for their journey east, then Grace stopped.

'Boss...what if he *is* there? I mean, maybe this is where he goes to...well, I don't know, but—'

'Hm, fair point. Right, if, by any chance, he is, then phone me immediately. I'll request uniform back-up and we'll head through. But don't tackle him yourself, okay?

Grace smiled.

'Don't worry, Boss, we won't! We'll wait for you...'

Grant turned his gaze to Cliff Ford.

'Anything from the SOCOs, Cliff?'

'Aye, I had a chat wi' Gordon Harris, Boss'

'Good; anything of note?'

'Aye, well, first of all, Sandie told him that her husband is left-handed...'

'Really?'

'...yup; and he also found a drawer containing rolls of brass picture-wire—you know, the stuff that...'

'I know what it is, Cliff. Does he think it could have been used to strangle the victims, though?'

Briony gave her boss a glare—she didn't like when he was abrupt with his team. Cliff seemed undaunted, however.

'Possibly; he's taken it away an' he's goin' to check with Nippy to see if it could have caused the neck injuries. It's somethin', Ah suppose.'

'Aye it is, Cliff, and it's all starting to stack up against Pollock; unfortunately, we haven't a bloody clue where he is!'

Grant's phone buzzed and he looked at the screen.

'It's the Mint, requesting my presence...'

Briony smiled.

'Good luck, eh, Boss!'

Superintendent Patricia Minto sat at her desk, her head resting on her hands. She was weary; the years of leadership, the often seemingly futile fight against crime, the management issues, they had all taken their toll. And now...well, her consultant had told her that the prognosis wasn't exactly positive...

She recognised the sharp, rhythmical rap on her office door and smiled. "Shave and a haircut..." only DCI Grant McVicar announced his presence in such a manner! For a moment, she was tempted to respond with two knocks of her own "Two bob" but, instead, she responded with her usual "Come".

'Afternoon Ma'am.'

'Grant. Have a seat.'

'Thanks. Em, Ma'am, are you okay?'

'Yes, thanks Grant, just a bit tired, I've not been sleeping well. Anyway, this murder investigation—'

"Is this the beginning, or is it the end..."

Sandie downed the last mouthful of vodka and cola then shook her head; "When Will I See You Again" by the Three Degrees was firmly lodged in her brain. She gave a grim smile at the irony; murder in the third degree...

She laid her head back against the comforting tweed of the chair and closed her eyes. It was all out of her hands now; Neil wasn't coming back, that night, the next night...the police would undoubtedly arrest him when he returned to work, he would be remanded...that nice sergeant, Briony, had explained the process. Patiently and calmly, but leaving Sandie in no doubt that her husband was now the prime suspect for the two supermarket murders.

All thanks to me...

She sat forward and reached for her phone; she desperately needed to talk to someone and she knew exactly whom she would call.

A beginning...yes, definitely a beginning...

Wherever Neil Pollock was, it wasn't at the hotel in Leith. Sam and Grace had discussed the new arrivals with the manager, who had been on duty all afternoon. No-one answering Pollock's description, either as himself or posing as a woman, had booked in that day. After no little persuasion he had reluctantly accessed the register for the weekend that Pollock's car had been spotted; needless to say, his name didn't appear anywhere.

The hotel had been full that weekend and the list of guests was extensive to say the least. They were returning with the information they had gleaned and would trawl through it, looking for anything of interest. The Mint had finally managed to obtain the necessary warrant and, as Meridian Court closed at seven p.m., they had resorted to using their blue lights to ensure they arrived in time, abandoning the pick-up on the pavement outside. Lynne Kilpatrick wasn't particularly enamoured at their arrival and subsequent request to search Neil Pollock's office.

'Chief Inspector it's nearly seven now and we've all got homes to go to; can't this wait until morning?'

'No, I'm afraid it can't Mrs Kilpatrick...'

'Ms, if you don't mind.'

'...sorry, *Ms* Kilpatrick; we'll be as quick as we can.'

'And can I ask what, exactly, you're looking for? Neil Pollock is a highly respected member of our team, I'm quite sure he wouldn't...'

There was an element of bloody-mindedness in Grant's reply; Lynne Kilpatrick's earlier refusal to allow them access, whilst undoubtedly for legitimate reasons, had cost them time. He hoped it wouldn't cost someone their life...

'I'm sorry, Ms Kilpatrick, but I can't divulge the nature of our enquiries at this stage. Now, if you could just show us to where Mr Pollock works...'

'Oh, very well, follow me, please...'

Nothing.

Grant and Briony were driving back to Osprey House in a slightly troubled silence, which Briony finally broke.

'There's no' much we can do, Boss.'

'Aye, I know, Bri, but it's not looking good, is it? He's away with that outfit and the blonde wig. We don't know where the hell he actually is. He's been behaving strangely...God, if he commits another murder then I'll only have myself to blame...'

Briony could see Grant descending into the familiar spiral of self-doubt and self-pity.

'Oh, come on, Boss, this is all conjecture. For all we know, he might not even be our murderer...'

'Cheers, Bri, that's a big help; so, if it's not him, then who the fuck is it...?'

She remained silent for the rest of the journey. DCI Grant McVicar could be a right awkward sod sometimes.

$$\sim\!\sim\!\sim$$

Lachlan Dallas took a long, slow sip of his gin and tonic, allowing himself time to think; he would need to consider his next move very carefully.

Sandie Pollock's head was lowered slightly; her large baby-blue eyes looked forlornly at him from under her ash-blonde fringe, their appeal currently heightened somewhat as they were brimming with tears. She had nice full lips, a pretty smile (alas, noticeably absent due to present circumstances) and, having once played opposite her "Sally Bowles" in a production of "Cabaret", Lachlan was only too well-aware of her rather voluptuous and extremely sexy figure. Tales of her, and her husband Neil's, physical exploits were somewhat legendary in their parochial and indiscreet little Theatre Group but he had learned long ago that it was often the ones that boasted most who "performed" the least. Still, as far as he was aware, Sandie had always remained faithful to her husband, a fairly uncommon trait in theatrical circles. He liked Sandie—in fact, he liked her very much— and he suspected the feeling was mutual. Over the years there had been a couple of wine-fuelled and rather intense conversations, filled with innuendo and some heavy flirting, although nothing more. He swallowed his gin, placed his glass on the table and rubbed his chin; the absence of his little goatee, shaved off the previous Christmas for his part as a pantomime dame, still took him slightly by surprise. Perhaps he would grow it again, he felt that it suited him! A reasonably accomplished amateur actor, Lachlan was acutely self-aware and carefully cultivated the image of a suave, debonair star of the stage. Tonight might just be the performance of his life, in more ways than one...he adopted his most sympathetic expression and looked across at his host, sagely shaking his head.

'I can't believe it, Sandie. I mean, I don't really know Neil that well, but surely... No, I just can't get my head round it.'

Sandie snuffled as she stared down at her hands; it was rather appealing, he thought, and she looked at her most vulnerable; but, just like acting, it was all about timing...

'I know, Lachie, I can't either. But after finding those clothes... well, it all pointed to him, didn't it?'

What, exactly, is she looking for here? Reassurance? Something else...?

'Well, I suppose...and, although there's nothing really *that* wrong with it, I would never have had your Neil down as a cross-dresser, far less a...'

'Oh, don't say it, Lachie, don't...'

She looked over at him, her eyes moist, her lips parted; then, like the leading man that he undoubtedly was, he rose from the couch and played his opening gambit...

∿∿∿

He was in a troubled sleep; fitful fragments of dreams played through his brain, with flames, drowning and women whose identity he couldn't quite resolve...someone was shaking him.

'Grant. Grant, wake up, your phone's ringing!'

The voice was sleepy-soft and husky; who did it belong to? He wasn't sure but the shaking became more urgent.

'Grant—och, it's stopped now. Oh, for God's sake, it's away again...'

Suddenly he was awake; Delia was still shaking him as he sat up and mumbled.

'Sorry, Dee, was in a deep sleep...'

He lifted the phone from the bedside cabinet, fearing that the murderer had struck again but, when he saw that the call was from Louise Thackray, his stomach lurched; this could be worse...

'Louise; what the hell's wrong?'

She was incoherent at first but, eventually, he managed to calm her down enough to understand what she was saying. Finally, he ended the call and climbed out of bed. Delia looked at him, wide-eyed, tousled and questioning.

'Sorry, Dee, I need to go out. That was Louise.'

'Louise?'

'Yes, Brian's wife—remember, my sergeant, he was, em...killed.'

'Oh, yes, I'm with you. But what's happened?'

He frowned as he pulled on his jeans.

'Some bastard set her garden shed alight. The fire service has put it out but she's in a hell of a state so I'm heading over for a while; try and calm her down.'

He leaned across the bed and kissed her.

'Listen, you try and get back to sleep, don't know when I'll be home.'

∿∿∿

Grant could feel the rage building inside him; the fire service had left, having doused the fire and checked the charred remains of the shed and its contents for any smouldering debris. The air was heavy with the smell of burnt wood and plastic although, fortunately, the shed was at the back of the garden and the damage was limited to the adjacent wooden fence. They had found the partially-melted remains of a plastic fuel can next to the ruin, clearly indicating arson; however, the main cause of his fury was what had been left on Louise's doorstep.

As he held the near-hysterical woman close to him, he glared menacingly at the small jar of cheap apple sauce that now sat on the table. He had not the slightest doubt who had left it, presumably after having doused the shed in petrol before setting it alight. He was equally certain that the jar would have been well-wiped, thus avoiding any incriminating fingerprints, although he would send it to forensics, just in case. Nothing he could say seemed to calm Louise and he desperately wished that Briony was with him. She'd know what to do...or say... Gently, he stroked her blonde, curly hair.

'I'm so sorry, Louise. Will Finn and Callum be okay?'

She managed to stop crying for a moment, mumbling into his shoulder.

'I think so; my mum's taken them so at least they're safe. Oh Grant, what if it hadn't been the shed, what of they'd poured petrol through the letterbox, we'd all be dead...'

She was off again.

'We'll get them, Louise, don't worry; this was probably just retaliation for what happened this morning. Anyway, they wouldn't dare try anything worse.'

The words sounded hollow as he spoke them; he knew only too well what families such as the Barrowmans were capable of. Louise was mumbling again.

'What, sorry, Louise?'

'Please, Grant.'

'Please what?

'Please stay with me tonight. Don't leave me alone...Please Grant. I just need to be with someone...'

Oh fuck...

CHAPTER 8

'*He's a bit of an* odd bugger, isn't he?'

DC Fazil Bajwa and DC Grace Lappin were sitting in Faz's car, sipping their takeaway coffee and eating their breakfast. Despite Neil Pollock's claim that he wouldn't be back until the afternoon, Grant had instructed them to keep a discreet watch from seven a.m., when the offices opened. The dashboard clock showed six-fifty but already several people had entered the large, nondescript building. Faz washed down a mouthful of sausage roll as he considered Grace's question; he answered somewhat defensively.

'I kinda know what you mean, Grace but, well—'

She turned and coquettishly arched an eyebrow; she was rapidly learning how to manipulate the handsome young Sikh. He responded with his customary wide grin.

'What?'

'I get the feeling there's a story here; aren't you going to tell me, Fazil?'

She poked him in his reassuringly muscular stomach and he laughed.

'Don't call me that—you sound like my bloody mother!'

He took another drink of coffee.

'To be honest, Grace, I don't actually know the full story; I do know that his previous sergeant was killed in a car crash, apparently he'd been drinking heavily and there was a rumour going about that the boss had been having a "thing" with the sergeant's wife. Seems he blames himself for what happened.'

Grace frowned.

'And do you believe the rumour?'

Faz stared out of the rapidly steaming-up windscreen; he switched the blower on to clear it.

'I'm not sure; thing is, the boss has always been pretty fair by me. Sure, he has his moments but I reckon he's a pretty decent guy with a bunch of demons that he seems to be fighting. Sometimes it spills over and he turns up in a mood, although the sarge seems to be able to handle him pretty well; he's been much better since she arrived.'

He gave a shrug.

'Overall, I think it's unlikely; as far as I know, he's unattached, although he never talks about his personal life. But he doesn't really seem the type, somehow...'

He turned and looked at Grace, smiling again.

'I think you're becoming the new favourite, though!'

'What? Don't be daft, Faz! I'm the rookie!'

'You think? No, the boss has definitely got his eye on you...'

He saw the slightly shocked look on her face.

'Not like that, you muppet; no, I mean professionally. Leave the other stuff to me'

'Get your hand off, Fazil, we're on duty!'

'I thought we were on surveillance? We need to blend in, remember, and not look like two cops staking out a building!'

Grace laughed.

'Staking out! Where do you think we are, Faz—New York? It's a cauld, dreich Thursday mornin' in doon-toon Glasgow, it's no' a frickin' stake-oot, ma man...'

~~~

Briony Quinn took one look at her boss and instantly knew something was seriously amiss. He was un-shaved, un-kempt and he looked as if he had hardly slept. She opened her mouth to ask but, remembering his mood on the previous evening, decided against it. He sat down wearily on the nearest chair, the other members of the team studiously avoiding his glare.

'Anything?'

'Nothin' Boss' Briony replied. As instructed, Faz and Grace are up at Pollock's offices, just in case. Anyway, you left instructions that we were to be phoned immediately Pollock arrived.'

'Aye, I know, but I don't think Lynne Kilpatrick was exactly happy about the situation. Pollock seems to be a bit of a favourite up there.'

Briony raised an eyebrow.

'What, you don't think...?'

'Oh, God knows, Bri, but she certainly was pretty defensive about him. Let's just hope she *does* call us when he turns up and doesn't bloody warn him off.'

'I don't think she'd dare, Boss. Goes by the book, that one, I doubt she'd try anything so stupid.'

'Hm, you'd be surprised. Anyway, I take it there's been nothing...?'

She knew what he meant.

'No, fortunately, there's been no report of any murder, we've already checked on HOLMES.'

'Thank Christ. Right, keep me posted, I'm getting a coffee...'

Wearily, he stood up and left the meeting room. Sam, Cliff and Kiera gave her a look but she shrugged her shoulders; she certainly wasn't going to get involved in a discussion with them about DCI McVicar's demeanour. She gave him five minutes then followed his example, making herself a coffee before walking along to his office. She entered without knocking, closing the door behind her, only to find her boss sitting at his desk, slumped forwards with his head resting on his arms; she wondered if he was asleep.

'Boss?' she said quietly.

'Mm?' he mumbled, without looking up. She sat down across from him, noticing that there was no coffee mug; he must have gone straight through to his office. She placed her drink beside his elbow and patted his arm.

'Looks like your need is greater than mine, eh?'

Finally, he sat up; she realised that he was a mess, both physically and emotionally. She remained silent but raised her eyebrow questioningly. He sighed and picked up the coffee.

'Cheers, Bri.'

She gave him another minute.

'Right, Grant. It's time.'

'For what, exactly?'

'You know damned fine, Grant McVicar. I don't know what the hell's going on but you need to talk about it and you need to do it now, before it starts to affect—'

'...my judgement? Like last time? Go on. Say it. I know that's what you're thinking— what everyone's thinking...'

She could feel her hackles rising.

'No, you bloody don't! That's not what I'm thinking at all!'

'Aye, right! So, what *are* you thinking, Sergeant?'

That was it; her temper snapped and she stood up.

'Oh, for fuck sake, don't start all that crap again, that "sergeant" nonsense. I thought we were past all that; I thought we were friends; but if you can't confide in me now, when you need it the most, then maybe I was wrong.'

She turned to leave, with one parting shot.

'You need to catch a bloody grip, DCI McVicar. You need to wise up and start trusting the people who care about you...'

She got as far as the door before he spoke.

'Briony!'

She stopped, standing with her back to him.

'Bri, I'm sorry. You're right...'

As bloody always...

'Please, come back...'

Ronnie Pettigrew was worried; of course, she was naturally sad at the death of her father, Michael but, in a way, it had been a blessing. Since the brutal killing of her older brother, Ricky, a number of years previously, her father had been a broken man and, in the last few years, the onset of Alzheimer's had rendered him little more than a shell of his former self. She had frequently implored her mother to put him into a home, where he would receive the care that he needed, but to no avail. Helena Pettigrew had been adamant; Michael was her husband and she would care for him as long as he lived. Admirable, perhaps, but it was an enormous burden, one that she unavoidably shared, living in the same household. Hence her feeling of relief, a feeling that her mother didn't seem to share; that was what was worrying her.

'Mum, are you okay?'

'Whit? Eh, oh, aye, hen, Ah'm... Aye, Ah'll be fine.'

'The car's booked for two-thirty; you'll need something to eat...'

Her mum shook her head sadly.

'Ah cann'ae, Ronnie, Ah've nae appetite. Anyway, there's bloody hours to go before the—'

She stopped, as if unable to mention her husband's funeral.

'I know Mum, but you can't go on like this. You need to take care of yourself...'

'Whit for? Michael wis ma life; whit's left fur me, now he's gone?'

'Me, mum. I'm still here, I'm still your daughter.'

Helena Pettigrew gave her a strange look; somehow, Ronnie got the feeling that her mother was keeping something from her.

'What is it, Mum?'

'Em...nothin', Ronnie. Nothin...'

'Fine. Right, I'm going to have some breakfast. Come on, Mum, have a bit of toast, something. Please?'

'Aye, maybe'

~~~

Ronnie Pettigrew contemplated her reflection in the bathroom mirror; the grey eyes that looked back at her were her father's, the thick mane of dark hair her mother's. Not an unattractive combination, she thought, although the lines of care were exclusively her own, of her own making...

Christ, Ronnie, don't bloody start...

As she began to apply her make-up, she was suddenly aware of her mother talking downstairs; she stood up, walked quietly across the room and opened the door. Helena's voice was low and Ronnie couldn't make out what was being said, although it seemed to carry a sense of urgency. Curious, she tiptoed across the landing just as her mother finished the call; Ronnie heard her say "Bye Teeny" before silence fell once again.

Teeny...? Who the fuck is Teeny...?

~~~

It took all of fifteen minutes; Briony Quinn sat in silence, stunned by her boss's emotional outpouring. In the time she had known him, as far as she was aware, he had never been on a date, far less in a relationship of any sort; she had assumed that his short, but disastrous, marriage to solicitor Jackie Valentine had put him off women for life! During their previous murder enquiry, there had been a chemistry of sorts between Grant and Delia Donald. However, once the attractive owner (of what had turned out to be an escort agency) had re-located to her mother's house in Dumfries, Briony had assumed that that was an end to things; obviously not... She expelled her breath slowly, choosing her words very carefully. Well, her word...

'Wow!'

'Aye, "wow!" It's a fucking mess, Bri, that's what it is.'

'Those little bastards, poor Louise...but nothin'...em, happened with her?'

He looked at her in surprise, then shook his head.

'Nope, absolutely not. I slept on the couch—well, when I say slept, I managed to doze for a while. Came straight in, haven't even shaved...'

He rubbed his head, where the dark stubble was already showing at the back.

'And Tina? Why the hell did you go out with her on Saturday night when Delia was in your house?'

She had just managed to stop herself from adding "and in your bloody bed...". He shook his head.

'God only knows; I didn't want to hurt her feelings; I didn't want to let her down at the last minute. Anyway, I'd been going to ask her out for weeks, just hadn't quite got round to it. Then, like I said, Delia turned up out of the blue, we ended up—'

He closed his eyes, dropping his head on to his hands and mumbling from between his fingers.

'...well, you know. When I woke, the bloody taxi was outside, what the hell could I do?'

He took a deep breath and let it out in a long sigh.

'I mean, how the fuck was I to know Tina would turn up on my bloody doorstep on the Sunday, with a bottle of red wine to thank me for the evening! Delia said she was so polite, so nice... Christ, poor woman, it must have been bloody humiliating...'

He screwed his face up; although Briony could see the pain in his features, knowing how much he must have hurt Tina Sturrock, she wasn't feeling particularly sympathetic at this point.

'And Delia? Is there a future there, do you think, eh?'

He shook his head forlornly.

'Oh, I don't bloody know, Bri. She's sweet, she's sexy, she's a good cook...But I don't know if...aw fuck, I don't bloody know anything, do I?'

'Oh, don't start, Grant; let's face it, you've been a total arse here. You need to sit down and ask yourself a few difficult questions. One—do you love Delia? Two—do you want to be with her? Three, what do you feel for Tina Sturrock? Four—what do you intend to do about it, eh? And that's just your starter for ten...'

'Huh - "nothing" to the last one at any rate; I very much doubt Tina would have anything to do with me after what happened and I don't blame her. Can't even go back to training—she made that perfectly clear in the text message she sent me on Sunday night.'

'Talk to her.'

'Why? What good will that do?'

'It'll clear the air. If it was me, I'd be beating myself up, wondering just how long you'd been leading this double life. Come clean, tell her that Delia turned up out of the blue, that you didn't want to let her down...'

She paused; her own relationship was on pretty shaky ground at the moment and she strongly suspected that her rugby-playing boyfriend was "playing the field" in more ways than one. She couldn't help but feel great sympathy for Tina Sturrock; and, to an extent, for Delia Donald. The poor girl had been through enough shit with deceitful men...still, Grant *was* her friend...

'At the very least it might give the poor woman a little bit of closure.'

'You think?' he replied miserably.

She couldn't help herself; she raised her voice, glaring across at him.

'Put yourself in her place, Grant, and stop feeling so bloody sorry for yourself. No-one's done the dirty on you, after all!'

He sat back in his chair as if she'd slapped him.

And maybe that's what he bloody well needs...

She backed off a bit, realising that she'd probably overstepped the mark.

'Sorry. Anyway, what have you got to lose?'

'Fuck all, I suppose. Might be worth a try...'

He sighed and stood up.

'Right, let's get on with the job in hand.'

'Aye, good idea, Boss.'

As he reached the door, he turned and looked directly into her eyes.

'I don't know if I've said this before, Bri...

She held his gaze expectantly.

'...but I don't know just what the fu...aw shit...'

His phone was ringing and the moment had passed.

∿∿∿

They were back in the meeting room and Grant was now fully alert, the conversation with Briony seemingly forgotten.

'Right, Kiera, what did he say exactly?'

Kiera Fox had just received a phone call from the manager of the hotel in Leith.

'Well, Boss, naturally, he was chatting to his staff this morning, seems our visit yesterday is the talk of the steamie...'

She paused but Grant gave her a stony look.

'And?'

'...well, em, he mentioned the sighting of the blonde woman, you know, by the GP...'

'Aye, I know, Kiera. Can you get to the point?'

Briony felt like kicking him; instead she simply hissed

'Boss—'

He turned and looked at her, then back at his DC, shrugging slightly by way of apology.

'Sorry, Kiera, didn't sleep well...anyway, go on, please.'

Briony gave Kiera a look and shook her head very slightly.

'Well, it seems that a couple of the staff remember the woman—or man, I suppose; their description's pretty much the same as what we have from the CCTV and the witness reports. Also, one of them remembers the yellow Porsche—this guy's a bit of a petrol-head apparently, could rhyme off the make and model.'

'Good; so, we've got as near to a definite identification as we could hope for?'

'Yes, but there's more...'

Grant silently raised a dark eyebrow.

'The woman...or man, was with another man and they had a double room booked for the weekend; that's why the staff remembered the booking. They were certain at the time that the blonde was a man dressed as a woman and they were...well, let's just say they were intrigued! I'm not sure if sexual emancipation has quite reached Leith yet...'

This time Grant didn't interrupt the slight pause; Kiera continued.

'Unfortunately, they have no way of knowing what name they were registered under, although it definitely wasn't Pollock. But I suppose we can wade through all the bookings, try and find contact details for the guests who stayed. We'll probably need a warrant to get the relevant personal information...'

'That shouldn't be a problem, Kiera; good job. I'll speak to The Mint and, once we've got the warrant, you two head back through and see what you can find. Have a chat with the staff who saw her...him...whatever. Get a statement then bring the details back through. Hopefully we're on to something here.'

<center>~~~</center>

He had spoken to Superintendent Minto, who was now in the process of obtaining the necessary warrant to search the hotel records. Faz and Grace still had nothing to report; as expected, Neil Pollock hadn't yet arrived at the office. Briony crossed to where Grant was sitting.

'Boss, there's no' goin' to be much happenin' until Pollock shows up; Kiera and Sam will be headin' back through to Edinburgh as soon as we get the warrant, Cliff and I can hold the fort...'

He looked up at her with bloodshot eyes.

'...why don't you get down the road, freshen yourself up and have a wee rest. Anyway, don't you have a funeral to go to this afternoon?'

He let out a groan.

'Aw shit, I'd completely forgotten...'

'Do you really need to go, Boss?'

'No, of course I don't, Bri, but it's always good to get a look at the West of Scotland's criminal elite; after all, it's not often they're all assembled in the one place. You never know who you'll bump into; some of these guys are pretty reclusive, only appear at funerals.'

'To gloat over dead rivals, eh?'

'Aye, something like that. Anyway, it'll only be for an hour or so, I'll just head to the graveside, don't think I'd be too welcome at the service, do you?'

Briony smiled.

'Aye, and you're no' exactly inconspicuous, Boss. Look, get yourself down the road and just come back after the funeral. If anythin' happens, I'll call you right away.'

He sighed wearily and stood up.

'Fair enough, but let me know if you hear anything.'

'Will do; you can trust me.'

As he turned to walk away, he looked back at her.

'I know, Bri, I know I can...'

She smiled and shook her head.

Christ, he's an awfy man...!

Grant sat in the warmth of his pick-up, the heater blasting the windscreen in an attempt to clear the condensation. He had taken off his sodden jacket, throwing it on the back seat, but the trousers of his suit were uncomfortably damp and his shoes were caked in mud. As the glass began to clear, he gazed out at the bleak, grey cemetery. He hated funerals; they brought back too many memories, resurrected too many ghosts...

And it had mostly been a waste of time; he had stood at a safe distance from the cortège, scanning the faces; most he recognised (despite the ravages of age coupled with an unhealthy, stressful lifestyle) although there were a few new, younger attendees, either newcomers at the foot of the ladder or the next generation of the existing families; he made a mental note as best he could. These were men and women who lived in the shadows of the underworld, brought together in a public showing of grief for one of their own; driven by respect, relief or even fear—absences would certainly be noticed and noted. Then, presiding overall, with a surprising calm dignity, was the slightly bent and considerably careworn widow, Helena Pettigrew; she had aged visibly since he had last seen her and he very much doubted that she would be requiring the services of any more young men...

Finally, and as he had expected, the matriarch was accompanied by the younger and considerably more attractive Veronica, her position as the head of the powerful Pettigrew crime dynasty now firmly established. He shook his head sadly,

Oh Vera...you've come a long way, baby...

The mourners were starting to dissipate, a sea of black-clad figures bowed against the rain, jackets pulled over heads in a vain attempt to keep them dry; they resembled rooks searching for worms, he thought. He looked in his rear mirror, noticing that one of the figures had detached itself and was walking towards his vehicle. He considered driving away but it was too late now, the opportunity for escape had passed; well, if it was escape he had wanted...

The passenger door opened and the figure slid into the passenger seat, turning to face him. Her hair was protected by a black hat and her grey eyes held his through a veil of black lace. As always, despite the circumstances, Ronnie Pettigrew managed to look as if she had stepped off the pages of a fashion magazine. Her cheeks were moist; tears or raindrops...Grant couldn't quite determine. They sat, silently regarding each other for a few moments then, to his great surprise, she reached over, took his hand and squeezed it.

'Thanks for coming, Grant. That was very considerate of you. Surprising, but considerate.'

He looked away and stared out at the seemingly relentless rain; he wasn't quite sure what to say.

'Aye, well, I felt I should...'

'Why? You never met my dad.'

He looked at her again—her expression was impossible to read.

'No, Ronnie, I didn't, although God knows I knew enough about him. No, it was, em...'

She contrived to look surprised.

'...for me?'

He sighed heavily.

'I suppose...'

They sat for a few minutes, staring at the rivulets of rain streaming down the windscreen; she continued to hold his hand and, somehow, he was reluctant to break the contact. Finally, he spoke.

'How's your mum?'

Ronnie Pettigrew sighed as she shook her head.

'Devastated. Latterly, he was her sole purpose in life, even though he hadn't a bloody clue what planet he was living on, far less who she was. But she never gave up on him, wouldn't hear of putting him in a home.'

'What happened in the end?'

She removed her hand; his own suddenly felt cold.

'A stroke. He just keeled over, hit his head on a table. By the time the paramedics got him to hospital, he'd gone. Probably best, though, it would have been worse for mum if he'd lingered...'

He turned and looked at her again. She was a striking-looking woman, the mane of dark hair, the grey eyes, the full lips; there had been a time when...

No... don't go there...

She seemed to be aware of his gaze and she, too, turned, smiling at him.

'What?'

He felt his cheeks redden, like a schoolboy caught staring at the class beauty.

'Em—'

'Tell me? What were you thinking, Grant the Vicar?'

The corruption of his name took him by surprise, took him back. She laughed at his ill-concealed discomfort.

'Oh aye, I remember all right, that night at the Albion Vaults, when you so dashingly rescued me from the baying mob! You were a good-looking bugger back then—actually, you're still not too bad...'

'Don't Ronnie. We can't turn back the clock...'

She laughed again, this time with a hint of bitterness.

'Huh, you're right there; but it *was* fun, while it lasted...'

She moved her face closer to his and looked into his eyes; he could smell her perfume and he felt the hairs on the back of his neck tingle. She parted her full lips and lowered her voice to a husky whisper.

'Wasn't it, Grant McVicar?'

Shit...!

He held her gaze as he answered.

'Aye, Ronnie, I suppose it was...'

She sat back and smiled wickedly.

'...listen, I have a favour to ask...'

~~~~

She considered him with her grey eyes, the smile still playing on her lips.

'Hm, this *is* a very interesting situation, Grant, especially as I seem to remember asking *you* for a favour not that long ago...'

'As I recall, it was more a case of attempted blackmail, Ronnie,' he replied, a troubled look appearing on his face; he was regretting his actions already.

'Aye, whatever; anyway, I'm not sure exactly what you're asking here; I mean, what has this got to do with me? I'm just a businesswoman, after all.'

He looked into her eyes again and shook his head very slightly.

'Aye, I knew it was a mistake; listen just forget it, Ronnie...'

She sighed.

'Oh, Grant McVicar, you're bloody hopeless sometimes, you know that? Especially when it comes to dealing with women...'

She was probably right, he considered, given his current situation.

'...look, I'll see what I can do, but I'm not making any promises. What was the name again?'

'Barrowman. The son's called Darren, the father's name's Jack— or Jake—a small-time, em...operator out in Johnstone. There's an older brother too, Derek, or Deek, they call him...'

'Not really my part of the world, to be honest; still, I'll see if someone can have a word. But you owe me, Grant, and I'll not forget that!'

Aye, I bet you bloody won't...

As he drove out of the cemetery, he dialled Briony's number, while a single thought kept repeating in his head.

'Grant McVicar, just what the fuck have you done...?'

Briony Quinn knew that her boss was keeping something from her; after he had enquired about Neil Pollock's arrival, to which her reply was negative, she had asked about the funeral.

'Bit of a waste of time, to be honest; the usual suspects, all looking a bit long in the tooth, a couple of new kids on the block, paying their respects...'

'An' did you bump into the delightful Miss Pettigrew?'

The directness of the question caught him slightly off-guard.

'Em...well, just saw her in the distance, at the graveside. I sat in the car. It was pissing with rain...'

'Didn't get to speak to her then, eh?'

'No... I mean, why would I, Bri?'

Why indeed...and why lie to me...?

Briony was aware of the history between Grant and Ronnie Pettigrew and she was worried that he was making a serious error of judgement. She decided to leave it be meantime; better to talk face to face.

And harder to tell lies...

'Listen, Bri, I'm just going to head over to Pollock's offices, surely to God he'll there any time now. Faz and Grace are there anyway so I've got back-up, but call me if there's any news.'

～～～

The traffic in Glasgow was starting to build in preparation for the usual end-of-day gridlock but, finally, Grant pulled up in Cadogan Street, about a hundred yards along from Faz's car. After reluctantly leaving the warmth of the pick-up, he rapped on the DC's window and it slid down, a strong smell of chips wafting outwards and causing Grant's mouth to water.

'Been having a snack?' he asked drily.

'Well, it's been a long day, Boss.' Faz replied, slightly defensively.

'No sign, then?'

'Nope, nothing. Plenty of folk going in and out, of course, but no sign of Neil Pollock.'

'Okay; listen, I'll head over in case they've heard anything from him. Could you phone head office and ask Sergeant Quinn to go over to Sandie Pollock's house, in the off-chance that he decides to go straight home; she can take Kiera with her. Oh, and can she also see if Sandie has a spare set of keys for Pollock's Porsche, just in case he plays awkward buggers? We'll need to get forensics to have a look.'

'Will do, Boss.'

Grant dodged the traffic that was winding its way along the rain-slicked street and entered the building; once again, Gavin

McMillan was behind the desk, busy signing for a parcel. He looked up at Grant with a slightly supercilious smile.

'Afternoon, Inspector. Can I help you?'

'Good afternoon, Gavin, I'm just checking to see if there's been any word of Mr Pollock.'

Gavin McMillan gave him an odd look.

'I'm sorry, I don't understand...'

Grant frowned; he didn't warm to the young man.

'You don't understand what, exactly?'

Gavin looked at his watch.

'Two of your men arrested Mr Pollock about...em...forty-five minutes ago...'

CHAPTER 9

'*Looks like she's got company,* Sarge.'

As Briony and Kiera turned into Sandie Pollock's gravel driveway, they were confronted with an unfamiliar black Jaguar SUV, its private registration bearing the initials LAD

'That plate must've cost a bob or two, eh!' remarked Briony. Wonder who it belongs to?'

'I daresay we'll find out, Sarge.'

'I daresay; right, let's go.'

They heard the sonorous chime of the doorbell, then they waited for a good minute before Sandie Pollock appeared behind the stained-glass and opened the door. She was wearing a dark-red satin dressing gown and she looked slightly flustered, Briony thought. She certainly didn't look like the grief-stricken wife of a possible double murderer.

'Hello again, Sandie, sorry to bother you. This is DC Fox. Can we come in please? I'm afraid we need to ask you a few more questions, if that's okay...'

'Oh no, no, it's quite inconvenient at the moment, I'm afraid...'

'Sandie, this is very important. Your husband still hasn't turned up and we need...'

'No, I'm sorry.'

A deep and pleasant voice resonated from within the house.

'Everything okay, Sandie?'

Sandie Pollock looked from Kiera to Briony as her face reddened.

'Em...em...oh...'

'I think we'd best go inside, Mrs Pollock,' said Kiera decisively as she side-stepped the stuttering and obviously highly embarrassed woman.

∿∿∿

The situation was bizarre, Briony thought. It was only a day since Sandie Pollock had brought her tale of betrayal and suspicion to their attention, playing the part of the wronged, anxious and law-abiding wife with aplomb. Yet, here she was, seemingly caught "in flagrante delicto" with the distinguished-looking, leonine-haired Lachlan Archibald Dallas, who was currently sitting relaxedly in a white towelling robe whilst sipping a large gin and tonic; somehow, he seemed to be in his element.

'Mr Dallas.'

He turned on what he obviously believed to be his irresistible charm.

'Och, Lachie, please.'

'Very well, Lachie, how do you come to know Sandie?'

He smiled at Briony and took another sip of gin.

'Through the theatre, my dear...'

She gritted her teeth...she wasn't his "dear".

'...you see, we're both in "Stage-Right", a select little theatre group. Sandie is a wonderful actress, you know...'

Oh really...?

'Is she now? And tell me, do you know her husband Neil as well?'

She had emphasised "husband" and looked across at Sandie; the woman seemed to be doing her utmost to vanish inside the armchair.

'No, not really, we met once or twice at after-show parties but I hardly knew him; no Thespian aspirations, alas.'

Hm, wouldn't necessarily say that...

'I see.'

She paused; she could see that, despite the gravity of their investigation, Kiera was struggling to keep a straight face. She daren't look...

'So, Lachie, are you stayin' here at the moment?'

For the first time he faltered.

'I... em, well, not exactly...You see, Sandie, well, she was...'

Finally, in a quavering voice, Sandie Pollock interrupted.

'I was upset, Briony, and I needed someone to comfort me. Lachie's an old and very close friend. Have you any idea what it's like to discover that your husband is cheating on you, that he's a transvestite and that he may well have killed two innocent women?'

She started to cry.

'You have no bloody idea how hard this has been for me...'

Briony felt a modicum of sympathy for the woman; she was correct, despite her own relatively minor troubles, she had no idea whatsoever.

'I'm sorry, Sandie, I understand...'

'No, you bloody don't.'

'Well, I understand your position, let's say, and how hard it must be for you. But you've not heard anythin' from your husband; from Neil?'

'No, not a bloody thing. I don't know where he is, I don't know who he's with...'

She broke down completely; Lachlan Dallas stood up and crossed over, kneeling on the floor in front of her; in the process he inadvertently managed to catch the hem of his dressing gown on the table, giving Briony and Kiera a brief glimpse of his not inconsiderable hidden talents...

'They WHAT?'

Gavin McMillan took a step backwards as DCI McVicar loomed over the desk and shouted at him.

'What the fuck do you mean, arrested him? *We're* in charge of this case and none of my team have arrested anyone, for the simple reason that you didn't bloody phone us...'

A door opened behind the now-trembling young man and Lynne Kilpatrick appeared, an expression of fury on her face.

'Excuse me, Chief Inspector, but I must ask you to keep your voice down and watch your language...'

'Excuse me, *Ms* Kilpatrick, but your "boy" here has just...'

She raised her voice to match his; Lynne Kilpatrick wasn't easily intimidated. She worked for the NHS, after all...

'Don't you *dare* refer to Gavin as "a boy". He is a professional young man and...'

'Okay, I'm sorry; nonetheless, Gavin has just advised me that Neil Pollock was apparently arrested about forty-five minutes ago, when I had left clear instructions that we were to be phoned as soon as he arrived here.'

Lynne turned and frowned at Gavin, who now appeared to be on the verge of tears.

'Is that correct, Gavin?'

'Em, well, they came in just after Mr Pollock arrived, they showed him their identification, I think, and then they took him away. They handcuffed him too...'

Grant raised his voice a further notch.

'They handcuffed him? For Christ sake, we don't just turn up and handcuff folk, not unless they turn violent...did *you* not think to ask who they were?'

'Well, they seemed to be police officers...'

'Oh, they bloody "seemed", did they? And just how did they "seem" to be police officers? Did they approach you? Did they show their identification to you?'

'Chief Inspector, I must ask you to stop this...RIGHT NOW!"

By this time a small crowd had gathered and was watching the proceedings; one was surreptitiously recording it on their mobile phone and Lynne Kilpatrick lowered her voice slightly.

'Perhaps we'd better continue this conversation in my office.'

Grant glared at her.

'Fine.'

As she turned away, he dialled Faz's number.

'Yes Boss?'

'You and Grace get your bloody arses over here, NOW. I want to know just exactly what the fuck you've been doing for the last hour...and it better be a bloody good explanation...'

~~~

It took about five minutes for Neil Pollock to recover from the shock of his sudden arrest and removal, in handcuffs, from Meridian Court. It took about another minute for him to realise that the two dark-suited men who had "arrested" him probably weren't actually police officers.

It took only a few seconds more for him to realise that he was in very deep trouble. He turned to the tough-looking man next to him, who stank of stale sweat and cigars.

'Just what the hell's going on...aaagh...'

The question was cut short with a hard punch to the side of Neil's face. The man didn't even turn to look at him as he spoke, his voice full of menace, his accent broad Liverpudlian.

'Just shut the fook up, will ya, there's plenny more where tha' came from.'

'But...'

Another punch, harder this time.

'Ah fookin' told ya, shut the fook up.'

Neil swallowed the blood that was filling his mouth, nearly choking in the process, but he remained silent. He desperately wanted to rub the side of his aching face and to check if any teeth were loose, but his hands were still securely cuffed behind his back. He tried to remain calm and consider his options, but they were limited. He couldn't escape, that was for sure; he could possibly try and attract the attention of another driver when they were stopped at traffic lights but the thug beside him would undoubtedly notice and he didn't want any more punches to his face, or anywhere else for that matter. He decided to wait; once they arrived at wherever they were headed, he might have a better chance. Then again, he might not...

$\sim\!\!\sim\!\!\sim$

The traffic was heavy and everyone appeared oblivious to his plight, busy concentrating on the traffic, listening to the radio and intent on getting home. Home to their loved ones, to a hot dinner, some television, maybe sex...everyday things that he had taken for granted for so long, for too long...he tried to focus on the route they were taking but it was dark and he hadn't the faintest idea where he was, other than it seemed to be in the North side of the city—they certainly hadn't crossed any of the Clyde bridges or gone through the tunnel. Then, without warning or indication, the car turned off the main road and into a quiet side street; a couple more turns and they pulled into the yard of a dilapidated industrial unit.

The driver stopped, got out and pulled up a roller shutter before getting back in and driving inside the abandoned building, which appeared to have been a factory of some sort. The car stopped once more and the driver switched off the engine before getting out. Neil heard the sound of the shutter being pulled back down then suddenly, the rear door of the car opened, he was roughly hauled out and thrown onto the concrete floor. Before he could get up, he was kicked viciously in the stomach; the pain was intense and he started to vomit. Another kick, he screamed; a punch to the mouth, this time knocking out at least one tooth. The blows and the kicks started to blur into one another until, mercifully, everything turned black...

He was back in the car; everything ached, every part of his body was screaming with pain. He could taste blood; he could smell urine; he must have wet himself. He managed to open one swollen eye; he was sitting in the driver's seat this time, the handcuffs still on his wrists but now securing him to the steering wheel. He tried to free himself but they were too tight. The door opened and one of his assailants threw liquid in his face; at first, he thought it was water and that the man was trying to revive him, but the stinging of his eyes and the smell quickly told him that it was petrol. His captor leered at him but said nothing; instead, he opened the back door and placed the green plastic container upside-down on the seat. Neil could hear the petrol gurgling out, he could feel the panic rise inside him. He started to scream and pull frantically at the handcuffs.

'No, please, I've got a wife. I've got kids, please...'

The man put his head inside the car and said something—it sounded like a name— but Neil paid little attention; he was still desperately trying to free his hands but to no avail. The driver's door was slammed shut and, as he looked in the mirror, he could see the two men walk slowly towards the shuttered entrance, dribbling petrol from another can as they went. Finally, they threw away the empty container then, slowly and inexorably, the shutter opened...

Neil Pollock stopped screaming as the panic subsided and a feeling of grim finality descended; there would be no escape. Maybe he'd pass out from the petrol fumes; he tried breathing deeply but his body was still too sore from the brutal beating. Maybe he could hold his breath until he became unconscious; no, that too was physically impossible. Then, as he realised that it was all futile, he started to cry, his tears mixing with the blood and the petrol before dripping onto his already heavily-stained white shirt. He had never really feared death but he had always imagined that being burned alive would be a terrible way to go; now he was about to find out. He stopped struggling and, to his great surprise, the only thought filling his mind was of his wife Sandie; and, as he waited for the terrible, final agony that would inevitably ensue, he muttered softly

'Oh, Sweet Pea, I'm so, so sorry...'

∿∿∿

Briony had never seen her boss so angry; he had stormed into the meeting room, causing Sam, Kiera and Cliff to jump in alarm. Faz and Grace were nowhere to be seen. He paced about for a minute or so until Briony spoke.

'Boss, please, calm down...'

'Don't fucking tell me to calm down! If anything's guaranteed to raise my blood pressure even further, it's you telling me to bloody calm down!'

She shook her head angrily, realising that there was absolutely nothing she could say or do. His phone rang and he glowered at the screen.

'It's fucking Minto.' he mumbled.

He stormed back out, leaving the four officers gaping at one another in a mixture of shock and disbelief.

∿∿∿

'DCI McVicar, I should bloody well suspend you right this minute.'

'With all respect, Ma'am...'

'RESPECT! You don't appear to know the meaning of the bloody word, Grant. I've just had Lynne Kilpatrick on the phone, reading the riot act and threatening to take the matter further. I've had to eat a huge helping of humble pie on your behalf...'

'But Ma'am...'

'Don't interrupt me! Not only have you verbally abused a member of NHS staff, you have cursed and sworn in front of them, you have used abusive language towards your officers and, to top it all, one of the other staff has apparently videoed the whole thing! It'll probably be on YouTube before the day's out and I'll have the Divisional Commander screaming at me, not to mention the press baying for your blood...God Almighty, Grant, what the hell were you thinking?'

'Can I speak, please, Ma'am?'

She sat down with a sigh and what looked to Grant like a grimace of pain.

'Very well, let's hear what you have to say for yourself.'

~~~

Superintendent Patricia Minto steepled her fingers; she was still furious and she could do without all this, especially now, but her DCI did have a point.

'Well, it still doesn't excuse your behaviour but this is obviously a very serious and troubling situation, Grant. For a start, why is Pollock on someone else's radar as well as ours; in fact, more to the point, *how* is he on their radar? And whose radar is he on, that's the sixty-four-million-dollar question, isn't it? The fact of the matter is that they managed to get to him before we did—and, yes, I appreciate that we should have been informed as you had instructed, but how the hell did they find out about him in the first place, whoever *they* are?'

Grant remained silent; he had been asking himself the same question since he had left Meridian Court and he didn't like the answer.

'So, what do you have in place, Grant?'

'Well, Ma'am, I've left DC Bajwa and DC Lappin up at the office, checking the CCTV...'

'Oh, and while we're on that subject, just how in the name of God did they manage to miss Neil Pollock, not to mention his captors, entering and leaving the building?'

He paused before replying.

'Em, they needed a... comfort break.'

She gave him a dark look.

'A comfort break? Together? And for how long? The whole bloody point of having two officers on surveillance is to prevent this very thing from happening. Listen, I know you're protective of your team, Grant, and rightly so; but they've fallen down badly here. You need to have a word; well, some very strong words—and not specifically four-letter ones, I may add...'

'Don't worry, Ma-am, we'll be having the conversation as soon as; but the fact is that they did miss him, although hopefully they'll find some images for us to work with. And we've got the receptionist's description, he says that they had quite broad English accents, possibly Birmingham or Liverpool, he wasn't sure...'

His phone was buzzing and he looked at the screen.

'That's Faz now, Ma'am; can I take this, in case he's got something?'

Superintendent Minto sighed wearily.

'Oh, go ahead.'

～～～

He had finally calmed down.

'Listen, I'm sorry, guys. I totally lost it but, in my defence, there was a fair bit of justification.'

There was an audible sigh of relief from the team. Briony smiled

'Och, you're alright, Boss, we're kinda used to you by now...'

He managed a rueful grin in response.

'Cheers. Okay, there's things to be done. Faz has got an image of the car that we believe Pollock was abducted in and he's managed to redeem himself a bit by getting the registration. We need to trace the owner, although it may well have been stolen, and we need to get this city-wide right away, in case anyone's seen it. We have a pretty good description of the two guys, as well as some decent CCTV images, we know that they spoke in either Birmingham or Liverpool accents, although the witness isn't entirely sure. Other than that, they could be anywhere so let's get the information out there. Bri, did you get the keys of the Porsche?'

She delved into the pocket of her jeans and pulled out a fob.

'Yup, all here, Boss.'

'Great. Right, let's head up and see if there's anything of interest in it; we can call the SOCOs en-route. Guys, run a trace on the registration, get this information out to all areas and figure out how far they could have got in a couple of hours. Check with the motorway police too, if the abductors *are* from down south, then they might well be headed back down the M6. Oh, and I suppose we'd better let Sandie Pollock know that someone's abducted her husband, because it appears that's what's happened. Cliff, you get on with things here, Kiera, Sam, can you head over...and tread lightly, it'll be a shock...'

Briony gave him a look.

'You think, Boss?'

He gave her a questioning glance.

'Don't you, Bri? Anyway, let's go, chop-chop...'

Grant and Briony were heading back up the M8 towards Glasgow; rush hour was over; the evening traffic was light and they were making good time.

'So, what's the story, Bri?'

'Well, you were in such a state earlier that you never heard what happened at the Pollock residence.'

He gave her a sideways glance.

'So, it seems that the poor, long-suffering Sandie has another man in tow already...'

'What? You're joking?'

'Nope. Kiera and I turned up this afternoon, she was in her dressin' gown and wasn't goin' to let us in. No bloody wonder; a Mister Lachlan Archibald Dallas was makin' himself very much at home, similarly clad in a rather revealin' robe and calmly sippin' his G and T whilst claimin' to be comfortin' his friend. Oh, and a friend whom he states is a very good actress...'

Grant considered this new information.

'So, what are you suggesting, Bri?'

'Nothin' exactly, but it shows her in a different light, doesn't it, eh? Makes me wonder if there's been a very slight degree o' pre-meditation; you know, husband gets arrested for murder—well, we hadn't even got that far—Mr Dallas immediately appears on the scene. I mean, who put these bogus cops up to it? Who else had access to all that information?'

He looked at her and raised an eyebrow.

'Aye, who indeed, Briony? Who else knew? Who else was at Sandie's interview, apart from you and I—think about it...?'

Her eyes widened as she realised the implication of his words.

'What? No way, Boss—Grace?'

'Well, she was there, wasn't she? She heard everything that we did; not only that, she and Faz mysteriously disappear just before Pollock arrives back and gets abducted. Faz says that it was his suggestion but he's bloody infatuated, if you ask me, and I'm wondering if it was actually Grace's suggestion and that he's covering for her. I mean, we don't really know that much about her background, do we?'

Briony was stunned; she really liked Grace.

Surely not...

'And have you seen the motor she drives? A brand-new Mini Cooper? On a detective constable's salary? Listen, I'm just saying, Bri, but she's ticking a good number of the boxes for a snout.'

Briony was speechless; she hated the idea but, unfortunately, he had a point; in fact, a few points...

∿∿∿

Having managed to gain access to the underground car park, they approached Neil Pollock's car, one of the few now remaining.

'Nice' muttered Bri, her mind still dwelling on their earlier conversation.

'Aye, well, let's take a look.'

Briony pressed the remote and the lights flashed. They pulled on their forensic gloves and opened both doors; the interior smelled pleasantly of aftershave and leather. They looked about but there was nothing of note, it was almost fastidiously clean and tidy.

'Nothing here, Bri. Maybe the SOCOs will have more luck.'

As she backed out, something caught her eye.

'Boss, look.'

On the rear of the driver's seat, a single, long blonde hair was caught under the headrest. She lifted it carefully and put it in an evidence bag.

'Looks like it could be from the wig, eh?'

'It does indeed; right, let's see what's in the boot—which is at the front, I think.'

They unfastened the catch and raised the large sheet of shiny, yellow metal. The space was small but roomy enough to contain a red Nike holdall.

'That's the bag that Sandie said was missin', Boss'

He took it out and Briony held it by the handles, avoiding any contamination from the garage floor. He unzipped it carefully and slowly, then pulled the top open...

~~~

Sandie Pollock was hysterical; Sam had been suitably primed by Kiera that the woman was an accomplished actress, but they could both see that this was most definitely no act. Even the ministrations of the now rather-drunk Lachie Dallas had little effect.

'Oh, come on, Shandie, they'll get him, don'choo worry...'

He looked at the two constables with slightly bloodshot eyes but Kiera just gave him a cold stare in return; she didn't like this man. He spoke, breathing gin-laden fumes in her direction.

'But how the fu...hell did you allow thish to happen, girlsh?

Kiera's hackles rose further, but she bit her tongue.

'Weren't you shupposhed to be watching the place, or shomething? Bloody incompetent, if you ashk me...'

Her stare turned to a severe glare. She wasn't exactly sure how drunk he really was, or if he was attempting to emulate Sean Connery's famous lisp. He *was* an amateur actor, after all.

'Mr Dallas, we suspect that someone has been providing information to these bogus policemen, information that allowed them to carry out the abduction...'

Sandie burst into a further paroxysm of grief at Kiera's use of the word.

'...and we intend to find out who, exactly, it was. It must be someone who is anxious to see Mr Pollock out of the way, even if by dishonest means, someone that might have a vested interest in seeing Mrs Pollock alone and vulnerable. Now, Mr Dallas, I'd like to take a statement from you...'

For the second time that day she struggled to contain herself at the sudden, stricken look that appeared on Lachie Dallas's face as it suddenly dawned on him that the petite red-head that he was attempting to intimidate was now treating him as a suspect.

'Wha...but...but...Sandie, tell her, I mean, surely...'

The lisp was now notably absent.

'If you'd just come through to the kitchen with me, Mr Dallas, and we'll leave DC Tannahill to take care of poor Mrs Pollock...'

That'll fix you, you slimy old bugger...

~~~

'Well, well, well!'

The holdall contained a number of items; the blonde wig sat on top of a green satin blouse, under which was a pair of white jeans, both neatly folded. A pair of black, patent high-heeled shoes in a size eleven sat in the base, each shoe containing a black hold-up stocking. There was also a black padded bra and a pair of slinky, lace-trimmed red briefs, along with a make-up bag containing a fairly extensive, not to mention expensive, selection of cosmetic products. Briony's eyes widened.

'Christ, this is makin' me jealous, Boss—he's got more stuff than me!'

The holdall also contained some more mundane items, such as a pair of gents' underpants, socks and another, smaller toilet bag with a razor and some deodorant. There were also a few rather interesting sex toys; Grant had seen, and used, some of these before, long ago...

No, Grant, not now, for fuck sake...

Briony raised an eyebrow and gave a wry smile.

'Looks like a fun time was had by all, eh?'

Her boss was rather more serious.

'Aye, well, we need to find out what the hell he was up to, and with whom...wait, There's another pocket...'

He unzipped the little compartment on the end of the bag and put his hand in; there was something stuffed down at the bottom...

He pulled it out and held it up between his latex-gloved fingers; they both stared at the item.

It was a black, skimpy, ladies' thong.

He handed it to Briony, who took it with some distaste; she wasn't smiling anymore. She examined the small, triangular front and gingerly sniffed it, screwing up her face as she did so.

'Well, I'd say they've been worn, Boss, but they sure as hell aren't Neil Pollock's size, are they?

He shook his head.

'No. But are they Natalie Wheeler's size, maybe?'

She held them up again and nodded.

'Yup, I'd say so...'

CHAPTER 10

Grace Lappin and Fazil Bajwa were driving back along the M8 in an awkward and rather gloomy silence. They had managed to get sufficient information from the CCTV images and they had finally left Meridian House, avoiding any further contact with their superior officer; they had had quite enough for one day. Grace stared down at her knees as she spoke.

'He thinks it was me.'

'What? Thinks *what* was you?'

'He thinks it was me that tipped off...well, whoever abducted Neil Pollock.'

'What—the boss? Don't be daft, Grace, of course he doesn't...'

She turned to face him but he kept his eyes fixed firmly on the road. Had he looked; he would have seen the tears of frustration running down her cheeks.

'Yes, he bloody does, Faz. You saw the way he looked at me in there, the things he said about how we just happened to be away when Pollock was taken. He thinks I've been tipping somebody off.'

'You're being a bit paranoid, Grace. There's no way the boss suspects you...'

'Well, who the hell was it then?'

DC Fazil Bajwa didn't have an answer for her...

~~~

The SOCOs had arrived; Grant and Briony were heading out of the car park when both their phones pinged, indicating a number of missed calls and messages. Grant looked at his screen.

'Shit, there must have been no reception down there. Cliff's been looking for us; urgently, apparently.' He dialled the number.

'Cliff? Sorry, we were in the car park and there was no service.'

He listened for a moment, his expression darkening.

'Okay; send us the address, we'll head straight there.'

He ended the call and looked at Briony.

'They've found Neil Pollock...'

~~~

They pulled into the dingy side street leading to a small industrial estate, created on a part of the old railway works at Springburn; Grant showed his ID at the inevitable cordon and was waved through.

'Left, then first right, Sir; it's a dead-end and you can't miss all the lights.'

'Aye, cheers.'

There were several fire appliances, as well as numerous police cars and an ambulance. They pulled up behind one, where a couple of firefighters were busy packing up.

'Right, let's see what the hell's happening, Bri.'

They stepped over the hoses that snaked along the ground as they headed towards the dilapidated industrial unit, its shutter up and exposing the now-floodlit interior. A uniformed inspector came towards them.

'DCI McVicar?

'Yes, and DS Quinn.'

The inspector extended a hand.

'Inspector Carol Wylie...'

Grant was looking over her shoulder towards two paramedics, who were pushing a stretcher trolley towards the ambulance.

'...aye, that's your man, Sir; and the luckiest bugger on the planet too, if you ask me...'

∿∿∿

On the way back to Osprey House, Grant had stopped to collect a takeaway curry for the team, safe in the knowledge that he would regret it later. Once the two bags of food were safely deposited at Briony's feet, she had asked

'Won't Delia have somethin' ready for you, Boss?'

There was a pause.

'Em, she's gone...'

There was a further pause as Briony stared at him.

'Gone? God, what happened, eh?'

He rummaged in the pocket of his jacket, handed Briony a slightly crumpled piece of paper then started the engine and drove off. She pulled out her phone, switched on the torch and started to read

My dear, dear, Grant.

I'm so sorry that I don't have the courage to speak to you face to face, but I've never been good at this.

Over the years I've had a lot of shit in my life, as you know. I probably should never have turned up on your doorstep unannounced but the truth is that, after all the terrible things that happened last year, there hasn't been a day gone by when I didn't think of you.

I understand what happened with Tina and, to be fair, I was in the wrong; like I said, I should never have just arrived out of the blue, with no warning. God knows what the poor woman must have thought when she found me in your house. But when your friend Louise called last night, you disappeared, you never came back, and I had no idea where you were! Well, that was the last straw, I'm afraid.

I can't do this, Grant. I can accept all that comes with being a policeman's...

The next word was heavily scored out; Briony suspected it might had said "wife".

...partner, I can accept your moods, your ups and downs and I know why you are sad sometimes. But I can't and I won't share you, not after all my other disastrous relationships. I'm sorry.

Although I've not officially started my new job, I've managed to get the keys to the flat early, although I don't think it's fully decorated yet. But I think it's best, although it's breaking my heart.

You're a good man, Grant McVicar; kind, considerate and way too self-critical. You need to face your demons and be honest with yourself...and those around you. I'm not the only one who loves you, you know... Take care, my sweet, sweet big guy. And never forget, you're my hero.

You've got my number. But think long and hard before you phone me.

With all my love,

Delia.

xx

She turned off her torch but remained silent, not trusting herself to speak. As they headed down Inchinnan road and turned into the Osprey House car park, Grant glanced at her.

'You okay?

'Hm. Are you?

'Fuck knows, Bri. Ask me next year. Right, let's get inside and have a confab; I'm starving and I need a coffee. Actually, I need something a hell of a lot stronger...'

~~~

As the team tucked into the assortment of Indian takeaway treats that Grant had brought them, he related the latest instalment in the Neil Pollock saga. Only Grace Lappin appeared to have little appetite, studiously avoiding her boss's glance.

'So, following Cliff's phone call we headed straight over to Springburn and arrived at the scene; as Inspector Wylie put it, Neil Pollock is probably the luckiest guy on earth at this point in time...'

As the abductors' car had pulled into the abandoned industrial unit, on an adjacent piece of waste ground, Paddy Cloherty, a spry octogenarian with a thick Irish brogue, had been closing up his ramshackle pigeon loft, home to about sixty of his beloved avian friends. He hadn't paid a lot of attention; it wasn't anything that concerned him and he was old enough and wise enough to keep out of other people's business. But when he saw two men come back out, pouring petrol along the ground, he knew something was seriously amiss. He had called the police on his ancient Nokia phone and raised the alarm, but they would still have been too late had it not been for one simple fact.

When Springburn Chemical Enterprises had suddenly ceased trading several months previously, the premises were vacated without disconnecting the highly-efficient fire sprinkler system. The trail of petrol had, indeed, been lit, the two men entering a second vehicle before driving rapidly back along the street. But as soon as the flames reached the shutter and crept underneath, the sprinkler system was immediately activated, dissipating the fuel across the concrete floor and leaving Neil Pollock battered, bruised, severely traumatised but very much alive. There was a fire station nearby and, having been alerted by the police, they had arrived within minutes, ensuring Pollock's safety.

Grant's narrative was greeted by a slightly astonished silence, broken only by the scraping of metal curry containers. Cliff drank some cola then asked.

'So where is he now, Boss?'

'In Glasgow Royal Infirmary, Cliff. He's been pretty badly assaulted, by all accounts, and he's in a state of shock. No bloody wonder; even if he is our killer, that must have been an absolute nightmare...'

His voice tailed off; only Briony knew that it was, indeed, one of Grant's own nightmares.

'Anyway, now that we've stuffed our faces, let's see where we're at.'

The assembly mumbled their thanks for the food and cleared the containers away.

'Right, at least we now have our suspect effectively in custody; There's a couple of uniforms stationed outside his door...'

He cast a frown in Faz and Grace's general direction but they studiously avoided his gaze.

'...although I very much doubt he's capable of going anywhere at present. There's no point in trying to interview him tonight, there isn't a hope in hell that we'll be allowed to talk to him. Sam, Kiera, I know it's getting late but could you go back over to Sandie Pollock's house and let her know that we've got her husband. Mind you I'm not entirely sure she'll be that pleased...'

'Boss!'

'Sorry, Bri, but you know what I mean. Right Cliff, any joy with the abductors' car?'

'Aye, Boss an' needless to say, it wis stolen. Taken from the services at Strathclyde Park on Wednesday mornin', owned by a civil engineer, Peter Shapiro—he'd gone in for breakfast, came out an' his motor had vanished. He reported it straight away, but that's it, Ah'm afraid.'

'Okay, fair enough. Right, my assumption is that our two abductors came up the M6 in another vehicle, stole this one then one of them drove off in it. They must have stayed overnight somewhere but that could be anywhere, unfortunately. And, of course, they must have known about Pollock, his place of work, they must have known that he was away from his office but due back sometime yesterday...'

This time he looked directly across at Grace, her face colouring noticeably.

'...and I'd very much like to know how they got that information. Now, after a bit of cajoling, Paddy, our reluctant witness, has divulged that he managed to get a partial on the numberplate. He saw our two suspects get into a car that was parked further up the street so there must have been a good bit of pre-meditation and organisation here. He says he thinks the car was silver, or white, although it was parked under a broken streetlight, and he thinks it might have been a Merc, but again he's not sure; to be honest, I'm not sure how much he *can* see. But if we could get anything else from CCTV at the services where they stole the second vehicle, we might get the whole registration. Thing is, if these two guys are heading back South, then they've had about...'

He looked at his watch.

'... shit, nearly five hours; that could take them down to the Midlands. Chances are this car is stolen too so it's unlikely that we'll find them now.'

He sat down wearily.

'Faz, I know it's getting on but can you head over to the services at Strathclyde Park; there's bound to be CCTV, see if you can catch sight of them stealing the car...'

He looked at Grace, then turned his gaze to Cliff.

'...and can you go with him, Cliff?'

DC Ford gave Grant a slightly surprised look.

'Em, aye, no problem, Boss.'

Grace Lappin stood up suddenly and stormed out of the room. There were a few questioning glances but Grant said nothing as the members of his team started to head off on their allotted tasks. Once they had gone, Briony turned to him.

'Wasn't exactly, subtle, eh Boss?'

'What? I never said anything, Bri.'

'Hm. You didn't need to...'

He stood up and glared at her.

'Listen Briony, someone's been feeding information to persons unknown that nearly resulted in our prime suspect being roasted alive. I want to find out who the hell it is and, at the moment, Grace Lappin seems to fit the bill.'

'Aye, guilty until proved in...'

'Don't give me that crap, Bri. Who else could it be?'

The problem was, she didn't know.

Grace Lappin sat in her car, the tears streaming down her face. It was so unfair; she loved this job, she thought—no, she knew—she was good at it. Look at how she had handled her first body; she had been proud of her insight and she knew that the boss had been impressed. But now? There seemed to be no doubt in his mind that she was the "leak", the one who had fed all their information to some third party. Even Faz was acting strangely; did he suspect her too?

She blew her nose; this wouldn't do. *Come on, girl, you don't give up that easily. You can do this...*

She turned the key in the ignition; she'd make an early start on Friday and make a few enquiries of her own. Anyway, there was always someone who said that they'd help her if she really needed it...

Grant lay on his back, contemplating the ceiling and regretting the curry. The bed seemed cold and extremely lonely, as had the house when he had finally called it a night and returned home. He sat up, swinging out his long legs and desperately hoping that there were some indigestion tablets in the bathroom cabinet. He picked up his phone and scrolled to Delia's number, his thumb hovering above the call button. Should he...?

~~~~~

The team had assembled early the next morning; Cliff was busy updating the whiteboard with fresh information and Grant was sitting, coffee in hand, his dark brows furrowed in thought. Briony sat down beside him.

'Penny for them. Boss?'

'Eh? Och, nothing really, Bri. Didn't sleep well again...'

She raised an eyebrow.

'Lonely?'

'Huh., could say that; plus, the indigestion...'

'You really should get that seen to, Boss. Could be an ulcer or something...'

He grimaced.

'And it could just be the curry at nine o'clock last night! Right, let's get on.'

He stood up.

'How'd you get on at the services, Faz?'

The young DC looked up wearily from his laptop, the customary grin noticeably absent; as was Grace Lappin, Grant realised.

'Well, we had to trawl a bit but we finally managed to catch some images of our two abductors, although we don't have a clear shot of either of them. But we eventually managed to get the number of the second car, Boss. I ran a trace and, as you guessed, the vehicle was reported stolen; from Liverpool, apparently, on Tuesday night.'

'Hm, not much help there then, other than we now know where our two bogus cops probably came from. Did you get it out to the relevant divisions?'

'I did, but there's been nothing back yet.'

'Have you put in on HOLMES?'

'When I came in, about an hour ago. Listen, Boss, I'm really sorry...'

'Faz, save it until the operation's over, we'll discuss it then. By the way, where's Grace?'

There was a pause.

'Em, she had stuff that she said needed to be done, first thing.'

Grant raised his voice in annoyance, ignoring Briony's stony look. He had had his own "stuff" to attend to, after all...

'Stuff? It's a bloody double murder and an abduction with attempted that we're investigating. What the hell is "stuff", exactly?'

'Sorry, Boss, that was all she said...and that she'll be in as soon as she can.'

'Hm; well, if I'm here, send her straight in to me. This just isn't good enough, especially after yesterday. Right, Kiera, how did you get on with Mrs Pollock?'

Kiera wasn't looking particularly happy either.

'Well, she seemed mightily relieved, Boss. There was no sign of the redoubtable Mr Dallas, although his car was still there. I suspect he was sleeping it off. Sandie had obviously had a few too, although I think she can hold her drink pretty well. She's a funny one, that...can't quite make my mind up about her.'

'No, neither can I. Well, we'll leave her be for the moment. Right, first thing on the agenda, we need to speak to Neil Pollock, attempted murder victim or not. Bri, we'll head up and see if they'll let us talk to him. Faz, you and Cliff chase up the stolen car, try and get hold of the cop in Liverpool who's dealing with it. I doubt they'll be able to help us much but we need to follow everything up. Give them descriptions of the two abductors, see if it rings any bells with them. Right, I've got to see the Mint, keep her updated. I'll be back down shortly and we can head over to the Royal.'

~~~

The interview with Superintendent Minto had been mercifully brief, although it left Grant with some grave concerns over his superior officer's health. He was sure that the woman wasn't well and the last thing he needed at this point was having some new Super foisted upon him, intent upon making their mark and "tightening things up", an all-encompassing phrase that usually spelled trouble. He headed back downstairs and into his office; he had just sat down when there was a knock at his door.

'Aye, come in.'

The door opened; it was Grace Lappin. Her eyes were red and puffy and she looked exhausted; he experienced a slight pang of sympathy, for he knew exactly how she felt.

'Grace.'

'Boss. Can I have a word, please?'

'Have a seat.'

She crossed over and sat across from him. He tried to read her expression, wondering if she was here to hand in her resignation.

Only one way to find out...

'I noticed you were absent earlier this morning, Grace. Would you mind explaining why?'

She looked across at him, but said nothing; instead, she handed him a sheet of A4 paper, printed on one side.

Here we go...

He took it and looked at it for a moment then glanced back across, a puzzled expression on his face. It certainly wasn't what he was expecting.

'What's this, Grace?'

'That's your man, Boss.'

'My "man?" What do you mean, exactly?'

'Your man. I know that you thought it was me, but it wasn't. *That's* the man who's been feeding information to those responsible for Neil Pollock's kidnap, not me. Unfortunately, I can't tell you who "they" are; but Sergeant William Cook might be able to.'

She sat back in the chair and folded her arms defiantly; suddenly, he felt great admiration for this pretty, petite officer, despite his earlier suspicions. He started to read what she had written as she sat, arms still folded and glaring across at him.

He finished, put the paper back down on the desk and looked over at her, rubbing his beard thoughtfully as he regarded her.

'And you're sure?'

'As sure as I can be, Boss; that's where I was this morning. Like I said, I made a few enquiries at Mill Street, found out who had initially spoken to Sandie Pollock when she came in to report her suspicions about Neil. Then I gave her a call and that's when I started to suspect him. She told me Cook had taken a really detailed statement from her, which he had no need to do as it was being referred to us anyway. That was why she seemed slightly surprised when we interviewed her; he'd already asked her absolutely everything.'

'I see. You appreciate that this a pretty serious allegation?'

'It was a pretty serious allegation against me, Boss.'

He hardened his voice slightly.

'There was never any allegation, Grace.'

She pulled a face; there was a trace of bitterness as she spoke.

'Oh, come on, give me some credit, I'm a bloody detective, you thought it was me—didn't you?'

He paused for a moment. Of course he had...

'Grace, I'm sorry, but everything seemed to be pointing to you...'

'I know, and that was why I had to clear my name. But it was my old boss, Sam Williams, who clinched it for me; he made a few discreet enquiries, found out that this guy has been under suspicion before. Cook also has a penchant for Thailand, apparently; God knows what he's up to out there but it probably won't come cheap!'

'No, I wouldn't imagine so. Grace, I'm going to have to take this further, you know that? You'll certainly be interviewed, possibly even called as a witness.'

'That's fine...'

She paused for a moment.

'...can I speak freely, Boss?'

'Of course.'

'Okay. First of all, I love being a cop...'

He raised an eyebrow but remained silent.

'...no, seriously. My dad was a cop, a good friend of Sam Williams, in fact. I've always believed in... well, "right and wrong" I suppose. I could have done other things with my degree but I really wanted to join the force; and I really wanted to be a detective. I don't know, it's always appealed to me...'

'Well, from what I've seen so far, Grace, you're bloody good at it.'

Her cheeks coloured slightly.

'Em...thanks, Boss. So, when I saw my chance being taken away, when I saw your obvious suspicions, I had to do something. And I'm sorry that I took the time off this morning but, let's face it, if I was under suspicion, then I wasn't going to be much use to you anyway, was I? I'd have been sitting here twiddling my thumbs because you didn't trust me.'

'Fair point. Right, Grace...'

'I haven't finished, Boss...'

He looked across at her; there was more?

'I'm really, really sorry about what happened yesterday.'

He raised an eyebrow.

'I know Faz said it was his idea but it wasn't. We'd been stuck in the car all day, we were stiff, sore and hungry. It was me who suggested we nip out and stretch our legs, get a fish supper. Faz said one of us should stay but I said it'd be fine because they were going to phone when Pollock arrived anyway. I had no idea that... well, you know...'

He regarded her for a moment; it took a lot of courage to admit a mistake to a superior officer, far less take the full blame and apologise. He was impressed.

'Ok, Grace, apology accepted. You've learned your lesson and we're just lucky it turned out the way it did. Had Pollock been killed, the implications would have been much worse, as I'm sure you realise. We'll leave it at that, but don't bloody let it happen again!'

She gave him a rueful smile.

'I won't Boss, I promise.'

'Good, let's move on then; you've done a really good job here, you've shown great initiative, which I appreciate, and I'm sorry if I doubted your integrity. But, as I said, this matter will need to be referred and I'll have to speak to the Mint. Unfortunately, once I've done that, it'll be out of our hands and we won't be able to speak to Cook, although it's highly doubtful that he'd tell us anything anyway. Right, we've got a busy day ahead...'

They both stood up but, as they reached the door, he stopped.

'Grace.'

'Yes, Boss?'

'Em, there's an expression that I've been known to use although, to be honest, I don't really like it...but it's "never assume—it makes an "ass" out of "you" and "me"...'

She cocked her head to one side.

'Hm, haven't heard that one before, Boss.'

'Well, you won't hear it again; not from me, anyway. But let's just say that, on this occasion, I'm the ass; right, the sergeant and I need to go and speak to our prime suspect...'

~~~

Grant seriously disliked hospitals; the smell, the sounds, like funerals, they brought back too many unpleasant memories. Needs must, however, and after waiting nearly ten minutes whilst one of the duty nurses had sought permission for their visit from the ward Doctor, they were approaching the room currently occupied by Neil Pollock. There was a uniformed constable standing outside, who nodded and asked for their ID.

'On your own, Constable?'

'Em, yes Sir, my mate's away to get us a coffee.'

'Fair enough. I take it no-one else has been allowed access?'

'Just his partner, Sir. He's still in with him, actually,' was the reply.

Grant stared at the man in disbelief.

'His *what*? What the hell are you talking about?'

The young constable looked slightly taken aback.

'Em, he turned up very early, Sir, and the doctor said that, under the circumstances, he was effectively next-of-kin so he was entitled to visit...'

Grant appeared to be speechless, although Briony suspected he was bighting his tongue following the previous day's outburst. She spoke before he said something else that he might regret.

'Constable, Mr Pollock is a married man; just who, exactly, is this "partner" you're referring to?'

Grant interrupted.

'There's one way to bloody well find out...'

He shoved past the slightly shocked young constable and barged into the room, closely followed by Briony. Neil Pollock was propped up on his pillows, hooked up to the ubiquitous medical apparatus; he was a mess. Both eyes were swollen and red, what they could see of his face underneath the various dressings was badly bruised and there were bandages around his chest and upper arms. But, beside the bed, holding Neil Pollock's hand, was a rather striking-looking, grey-haired man. As he looked up at the sudden intrusion, Grant thought that his face looked familiar. Nonetheless, he growled at the stranger

'And just who the hell are you?'

The man released Neil's hand and stood up, extending his own towards Grant.

'Nicholas Hogarth; and you are...?'

Grant took the man's hand but continued to stare at the face as he realised he was talking to a prominent member of the Scottish Government. Finally, his power of speech returned.

'Em...DCI Grant McVicar, Sir. This is my sergeant, Briony Quinn.'

Nicholas Hogarth turned the full benison of his not inconsiderable persona towards Briony.

'I'm very pleased to meet you, Sergeant and I'm glad you're both here. Now, I'm quite sure you have a number of questions so why don't we all have a seat.'

He practically ushered Briony to where he had been sitting then fetched another couple of side-chairs, setting them down on the opposite side of the bed. He sat down on the one nearest Neil Pollock, taking his hand once more.

'That's better; now, officers, where would you like to start?'

Grant and Briony exchanged a look, then Grant spoke.

'Well, first of all, is Mr Pollock able to answer any questions himself at present?'

Neil Pollock turned his head towards Grant; it was obviously an effort but he managed to speak, albeit rather indistinctly.

'Yes, Chief Inspector, I'm just about capable of speech, thank you.'

'Good. Right, Mr Pollock, first of all I must caution you that anything you say...'

Hogarth frowned as he interrupted.

'Excuse me, Chief Inspector, I'm at a loss as to why you are about to caution Neil, but let me make you aware of the fact that, until recently, I was Minister for Justice for the Scottish Government and, as such, I am a senior QC. You can consider me to be Neil's legal representative. If it's necessary, that is, and I can't see any reason why it should be.'

'Fair enough, Mr Hogarth. I take, then, that you're unaware of why we're here?'

Nicholas Hogarth gave Grant a dark look; Neil Pollock, even within his limited range of expression, looked perplexed to say the least. It was Hogarth who replied, anger in his tone.

'What, apart from the fact that Neil has been abducted, beaten and, but for the Grace of God, he'd have been burned alive? My assumption was that you were here to interview him in order to further your enquiries about the perpetrators of this brutal and vicious attack which, I may add, is quite obviously an attempted murder.'

Grant and Briony exchanged another look; was this a bluff or did Hogarth really have no idea?

'And what about the two constables outside, Mr Hogarth? Did you not wonder why they were posted?'

Again, that intimidating stare; Grant certainly wouldn't care to be cross-examined by this man!

'I assumed that they were there for Neil's protection; obviously the attempt on his life failed, presumably you suspected another attempt may be made?'

Shit...!

'Well, not exactly, Sir. I take it that you're aware of the two recent murders in Asda and Tesco's Linwood branches.

'Of course—a terrible affair...'

Suddenly, Hogarth's bushy eyebrows shot up.

'Wait, you're surely not suggesting...good God Almighty, you are!'

It was Hogarth's turn to look astonished, but he rapidly regained his composure.

'But wait, these murders took place last Sunday, didn't they?

'Yes Sir, they did.'

The man relaxed visibly.

'I see; well, in that case...'

Neil Pollock interrupted.

'No, Nicky, please, don't...'

'I'm sorry Neil, but this is complete and utter nonsense. Officers, I can provide Neil's alibi; he spent the weekend with me, in a small and rather discreet hotel through in North Berwick. Neil and I are lovers, you see...'

'I have to go Lachie.'

'No, you don't, Sandie. They think he's a bloody murderer, not to mention some kind of sick pervert...'

Sandie gave him a look that silenced him.

'He's still my husband, Lachie.'

'I know, but...'

'No, I'm going. No matter what he may or may not have done, no-one deserves to be kidnapped, no-one deserves to be burned alive...it's just too horrible to contemplate. Anyway, now that they've got him, it's time...'

'For what, may I ask?'

'For the truth, Lachie, for the truth. Now, will you stop pawing me, get yourself dressed and give me some space to get ready.'

CHAPTER 11

'Right bloody mess!'

'Aye, Sarge. Waste o' a good Merc too; bloody joy riders.'

'Did you run a check on the plate?'

'Aye, nicked from outside a bloke's work in Liverpool a couple of days ago. Suppose we'd better let the poor bugger know we've found it.'

'I suppose; right, let's get back to the car, bloody freezin' up here.'

Constable Pete Jones and Sergeant Lucy Barcroft headed back towards the comfort of their Police BMW. The burnt-out wreck lay beside the narrow B-road that ran from the peaceful little Cumbrian village of Orton across to Greenholme, smashed through a fence and sitting on a patch of moorland, the surrounding grass charred and littered with debris. The recovery vehicle was already at the scene, about to lift the remains of the Mercedes onto the back of the truck. As they closed the door of their car, Pete rubbed his hands together and turned to his sergeant.

'D'you think it's worth passin' it any further up the line, Sarge?'

She thought for a moment; she had recently applied to become a detective and she was already starting to think differently about things.

'Aye, maybe, Pete, you never know, it could well have been used for a robbery or summat. I'll get the recovery guys to keep a hold of it for a day or two, we can shove the reggy on HOLMES and see if anyone takes the bait. After all, they couldn't walk anywhere from ere, must've had another vehicle somewhere. Pity about the rain, it'll have washed away any tyre-tracks. Come on, I'll treat you to a coffee at Tebay Services before we catch bloomin' hyp'thermia.'

Under the watchful eye of Nicholas Hogarth, Grant and Briony had started to take Neil Pollock's statement. The long and short of it was that the two men had been having a clandestine affair for almost a year, meeting secretly at a variety of locations spread across the Central belt. Hogarth claimed that all of these would be easily verified by the hotels, having been booked for business purposes in the name of a public relations company that he had set up some years previously. With some reticence, Pollock admitted that he was, indeed, a cross-dresser, often arriving "dressed" for Hogarth's benefit. Unfortunately, from Grant's point of view it raised more questions than it answered. In one final attempt to connect Pollock with the murders, he asked.

'Mr Pollock, we found a red Nike holdall in the boot of your Porsche; can you confirm that it's yours?'

Neil Pollock sighed; the words were obviously an effort and Grant knew they wouldn't be allowed much longer to question him.

'Yes, Chief Inspector, it is.'

'And the clothes?'

Another pause.

'Yes, they're mine, too.'

'And you claim that you were nowhere near the scene of the...'

Hogarth interrupted angrily.

'Chief Inspector, we've already established that Neil and I were in North Berwick last weekend. Of course, he wasn't in Linwood, he was with me—as he was the night before last—and that can easily be verified. Or are you doubting my word?'

Grant wasn't going to be intimidated; he ignored Hogarth and stared keenly at Neil Pollock.

'We found an item of clothing in the end pocket of the bag. Mr Pollock. An item of ladies underwear, to be specific, in a considerably smaller size than I imagine you would wear...'

Nicky Hogarth raised his voice.

'Just what are you insinuating, Chief Inspector? We've already established the facts. I don't know what you've found but it certainly didn't belong to Neil; or to me, as you can probably gather.'

'No, I don't believe it belonged to either of you, Mr Hogarth. The item is currently being tested for DNA, as it has clearly been worn, although I can't be more specific until we get the results. However, I believe that the item may have been taken from one of the victims.'

A tense silence ensued, relieved only by the soundtrack of hospital life. Hogarth glared at Grant.

'This is absolute nonsense, Chief Inspector. I haven't the faintest idea how this item came to be in Neil's bag, but I can assure you that he had nothing, I repeat *nothing* to do with these murders. I resent the...'

There was a sudden commotion outside and all four occupants turned towards the door as the lone constable raised his voice.

'Ma'am, I'm sorry...'

The door burst open and Sandie Pollock stormed into the room, the young constable immediately behind her. He looked at Grant apologetically.

'I'm really sorry Sir...'

Sandie froze, staring at her bruised and bandaged husband, his right hand still being held tenderly by Nicky Hogarth. Briony stood up, ready to intervene but, without saying a word, Sandie turned and stormed back out, slamming the door behind her. Briony ran after her, leaving the constable gaping in astonishment; he felt that it was proving to be an extremely bizarre day...

~~~

Briony hadn't yet returned, leaving Grant to assume that she was trying to placate Sandie Pollock; no easy task, he imagined. He sat with the two men in an increasingly embarrassing silence until, finally, the door opened and Briony re-entered, a charge nurse immediately behind her.

'Right, gentlemen—and lady of course—I'm going to have to ask you all to leave.'

Grant hadn't finished with Neil Pollock

'Excuse me, but...'

The nurse gave him a look.

'No "buts", I'm afraid. Doctor is on his way so you all need to leave. You'll be able to visit later...'

Grant wasn't giving up.

'This isn't actually a visit, this is a...'

The nurse raised her voice.

'With all respect, I don't care what it is. Mr Pollock is badly injured, as I'm sure you are aware, and the doctor needs to examine him. So, I'll ask you again...'

Grant grunted something, stood up and joined Briony, leaving Nicky Hogarth bidding farewell to his friend. Just as they reached the door, Neil Pollock spoke.

'Em, Chief Inspector.'

Grant turned.

'Yes?'

'I know we haven't yet discussed my, em, abduction...'

'Yes, Mr Pollock, I'm well aware of that; we'll come back later, but is there something you wanted to say?

Nicky Hogarth turned to his friend.

'Neil, careful!'

'It's okay, Nicky, it was just that one of the men said something, just before...'

Grant could see the man struggle as he relived his ordeal, but he managed to retain his composure.

'Well, it was odd, really, I think he said that someone had sent their regards.'

Grant felt the hairs on the back of his neck tingle; this could be important.

'Really—who exactly?'

'That's the thing, I just can't remember, I'm afraid. If it comes back to me, I'll let you know.'

Sandie Pollock had, somehow, managed to drive back to Paisley without incident; she had cried, she had sobbed, screamed, hit the steering wheel... the cross-dressing she could tolerate, understand even; in fact, in a peculiar way she thought it might be fun! An affair? Well, that was hurtful, deceitful, horrible, but it happened and people managed to work their way through it. With another woman she could always try harder, up her game; but with another man? How the hell could she compete...?

She screamed again.

'Neil Pollock, you bloody, fucking...oh, you bastard...'

She sat in the car, trying to control her feelings. Lachie's Jaguar was still sitting in the drive; no doubt he was reclining on the couch, gin and tonic in one hand, the TV remote control in the other...

She opened the door and strode purposefully toward the front door. She had had *quite* enough of men...

∿∿∿

'But...but, Sandie, I've had a wee drink...'

'I don't give a monkey's, Lachie. I want you out...now.'

'But what about the car...'

'Get a bloody taxi; I don't care. Go on, get out, Lachie.'

'Och, come here, my dear...'

She screamed again then raised her hand, slapping him so hard that he staggered and nearly fell over.

'What the...Jesus, Sandie, that was sore! What...'

Another slap.

'All right, all right, I get the fucking message, you crazy bitch...'

Lachie Dallas had spoken the wrong line...

∿∿∿

The team of detectives were assembled in their small meeting room. There was an air of expectancy as they sat, waiting for Grant to speak; in the last hour there had been a considerable amount of information to assimilate. Although yet to be corroborated, Neil Pollock appeared to have an alibi, in the form of Nicholas Hogarth QC, for the period in which the murders were committed. Not only that, upon their arrival back at Osprey House, Faz had reported that there had been a tag on their HOLMES report that the stolen Mercedes had been found, burned out, in the Lake District. Grace Lappin had brought the team up to date with her own enquiries and told them the identity of the alleged informer. Grant was staring at the floor, deep in thought; finally, he stood up.

'Right, lots to do...ready, Cliff?'

He paused as the DC stood up, marker pen at the ready.

'So, we have a statement from Pollock and his friend, Nicholas Hogarth, and they appear to have a pretty solid alibi. Pollock wanted to keep this Hogarth chap out of the limelight, frightened it would affect his position...'

'Surely that's pretty unlikely in this day and age, Boss?'

'You'd have thought so, Bri, but Pollock was really reluctant to drag Hogarth into it all. Anyway, we'll need to check with this hotel they claim to have stayed at, of course; then there's no explanation as to where the item of ladies' underwear came from but they claim that neither of them knew it was there. I suppose it's possible that it belonged to Pollock's wife—Bri, could you check with her; we should have a photo of the item.'

Briony nodded as Cliff's pen squeaked across the white board. Faz's phone started to ring and Grant glared across at him.

'Do you want to answer that, Faz?'

'Yes, sorry...'

Faz took the call, then looked up at Grant, his broad grin returned.

'That was forensics down in Carlisle. They've got a couple of prints from a pair of sunglasses—they were inside a case in the side pocket and survived the fire relatively intact.'

'Excellent. Have they run a check on them?'

'Yup, they belong to one Marcus Malone, from Liverpool.'

The name meant nothing and Grant shook his head.

'Hm; do we know anything about him?'

'Well, they've made a few enquiries, seems that he's a real nasty piece of work. He's done time for GBH and robbery, as well as having a load of charges that he's managed to wriggle out of. They have a last known address for him and they've given me a contact in Liverpool that we can call for more information.'

'Good, you away and phone, see what you can find out about him.'

He sat down and rubbed his beard.

'Right, Sam, Kiera, you take a run through to this hotel in North Berwick that Hogarth claims they stayed in. We need to check Pollock's alibi and we need to be absolutely sure that it's watertight. We need to find out more about Hogarth as well; is he married, does his wife know what's going on? Do a bit of research on the man, see what you can come up with. But if the alibi holds, then it's back to the bloody drawing board as far as the murders are concerned.'

'Boss?'

'Yes, Grace?'

'Well, it's starting to look as if someone's trying to frame Neil Pollock for these murders, doesn't it?'

He nodded.

'Yes, it does. But who, that's the bloody question? And, of course, why? It brings us back to whether the victims were chosen randomly or not and it also brings us back to why someone else wanted to impose their own form of justice on Pollock; not to mention who...'

He leaned forward, his elbows on his knees, and dropped his chin onto his balled fists; his head was reeling. After a minute or so he looked back up at his team, then stood up once more, his manner now more decisive; he paced back and forth as he spoke, rubbing his hand over his shaved head.

'Right, let's look at it all again, from the start. Two female victims, either chosen at random or possibly targeted. A killer dressed as a blonde, making little attempt to hide their identity, thereby implicating Neil Pollock. Our killer must know Pollock, must know that he's a cross-dresser and they must have seen him dressed in the wig, the white jeans and the shirt.'

'If Pollock's alibi does hold, then they must have been aware of his movements too, Boss,' said Kiera. 'If he was off with this Hogarth guy and wanting to keep it secret, they must have known, surely? If he'd been at home with Sandie then it would have been pointless—she'd have given him his alibi.'

Grant considered this; his dark brows knotted together.

'True, Kiera. So, Sandie Pollock knew that he was away, that he wasn't where he said he would be and she also knew that he was cheating on her...'

'And she also knew what he wore when he dressed as a woman' added Sam.

There was an ominous silence, then Sam continued

'And then, as soon as she's given us the evidence, knowing we'll most likely detain him, she invites this Lachlan Dallas over for a bit of...well, extra-marital fun, I suppose.'

Grant pursed his lips and exhaled. He and Briony exchanged glances.

'What do you think, Bri?'

She frowned.

'I'm not sure, Boss. Dallas said she was a great actress, certainly. But would she kill two innocent women just to get revenge on her husband for cheatin'?'

She shook her head slowly.

'Then there's that bit o' underwear. She would have been the only other person with access to Pollock's bag; mind you, we don't know for certain whose it is yet...'

'But then who tried tae kill Pollock?' asked Cliff. An' why? Surely it must've been something to do wi' the victims, or one of them at least; Grace says that this Cook character passed on Pollock's details, but who did he pass them on tae?'

He paused, thinking.

'Can we no' have a word with Cook, Boss?'

Grant shook his head.

'It's got to be reported to the Anti-Corruption Unit, Cliff, we can't get involved.'

'Aye, but have you reported it yet?' the DC asked, a slightly mischievous look on his face.

'No, I'm going to see the Mint after we're finished here.'

'Could you no' delay it?'

'Cliff, don't be daft' interjected Briony. You could get into a lot of trouble...'

'Sarge, I could just have a wee word wi' him; after all, he effectively took a statement from Sandie Pollock so all I'd be doin' was askin' him tae corroborate it; anyway, at this point in time, we're only goin' on what Grace has told us so, technically, it's only her suspicions that point tae Cook bein' the informer—wi' all respect, Grace.'

Cliff winked at his colleague and Grace grinned back; she was obviously thinking along the same lines. Grant wasn't convinced.

'Em, well, I suppose, but...'

'Listen Boss, just give me an hour before you pass it on; anyway, the Mint won't know when Grace actually gave you the information.'

Grant considered Cliff's request.

It might work...!

'Okay, but tread very carefully, Cliff...'

Grace Lappin's grinning countenance caught his eye.

'Aw, bugger it, you may as well go too, Grace, probably be better with the two of you. Keep me posted.'

～～～

Grant and Briony were sitting in the now-deserted office, both deep in thought; the door opened and Faz walked in. Grant looked up.

'Well?'

'Spoke to a DCI Owen down in Liverpool, Boss, and she knows all about this Malone character...'

'Great. We'll need to get them to detain him...'

'Well, when I say "all about", unfortunately that doesn't extend to actually knowing where he is.'

'Shit! Why the hell not?'

'Seems he keeps himself well below the radar. They're after him for another attempted murder and a couple of serious assaults, but he's one of these guys who's able to disappear at will.'

'Bugger. Anything from the description of the other one?'

'She thinks it could be a Gary Hopkins; apparently they've been known to work together but she doesn't know where he is either. She's going to make some enquiries for us but she's not hopeful, I'm afraid.'

Grant was annoyed but there was little he could do.

'Anything else, Faz?'

Briony's phone rang and she turned away as she answered it.

'Only that they're both known to be "for hire" as she put it; paid thugs, assassins, enforcers, whatever. Malone is certainly suspected of at least two gangland murders, unproven, of course...'

'Of course. What, Bri?'

'Forensics, Boss; about the underwear we found in Pollock's bag.'

He raised an eyebrow.

'Already? That was bloody quick.'

'Natalie Wheeler's; there's pretty much no doubt. They've not done the DNA yet but they've matched some pubic hair...'

'Fuck.'

♒︎

'Mum, will you tell me the hell's going on? Where's Dad? Mum...'

Sandie Pollock seemed incapable of speech; Dawn, her eldest daughter, sat across from her at the slightly-battered pine kitchen table, the silence broken only by the excited shrieks of Sandie's grandchildren as they played in the garden with Rufus, their new spaniel puppy.

'Mum...?'

Sandie looked up at her daughter, a distant, blank expression on her face. Dawn got up and walked round the table, taking Sandie's hand before bending down and looking into her mother's eyes.

'Mum, you're scaring me; what the hell's going on?'

Sandie remained silent as Dawn moved closer.

'Mum, have you been drinking? I thought you said that you'd stopped?'

Sandie bit her bottom lip as she looked away. Dawn's tone became sterner.

'For God's sake, Mum, will you talk to me...Christ, who the hell's that at the door?'

Sandie made no attempt to move and Dawn stood up, letting go of her hand.

'I'll get it then, shall I?'

She barged out of the kitchen and strode angrily along the hallway as the bell chimed for a second time. She could see two figures on the other side of the stained-glass as she turned the handle and pulled the heavy oak door open. A tall, dark-bearded man with a shaved head and an attractive dark-skinned woman with very short, curly black hair looked at her, their expressions serious and, immediately, Dawn Brodie realised that something was amiss. The man was holding up a small identity card as he spoke.

'DCI McVicar—this is my sergeant, DS Quinn. We'd like to speak to Mrs Pollock, please.'

Dawn gaped at them; she could feel a sense of panic rising.

'Wha...em...oh God, is it Dad...has something happened...?'

Briony gave her a faint smile as she edged towards the open door.

'Can we come in, please, and we'll explain. Can I ask what your relationship is to Sandie? Are you her daughter?'

'Em, oh yes, I'm Dawn, the oldest. What is it, what's happened, please...?

They were interrupted by a slightly slurred voice from the other end of the hall.

'S'okay, Dawn, we're already acquainted. Come into the lounge please—you too, dear, you may as well know...'

It took all of fifteen minutes to explain what had transpired; Dawn sat staring at the two officers as if they had just announced an alien invasion. Finally, she shook her head in apparent disbelief.

'No, that can't be right, not Dad, he'd never...

Sandie interrupted.

'Dawn, M'afraid Briony's right. Your dad's having an affair with...another man, apparently he dresses up as a woman...'

Her voice started to falter.

'Oh, I'm so sorry that you had to hear all this; but can you imagine how I feel, being abandoned for...for a bloody man.'

Dawn seemed to be made of sterner stuff that her mother.

'Oh Mum, don't worry, it'll be some stupid phase that Dad's going through, a mid-life crisis or something. Men are all the bloody same; I'll talk to him, knock some sense into that stupid, arty-farty brain of his. That's what it'll be, he's probably got some ridiculous notion that artists need to be bloody quee...well, you know...'

Sandie was shaking her head. Grant and Briony exchanged a glance at the younger woman's slightly homophobic point of view.

'No, it's more than that, Dawn...'

Her daughter interrupted; her voice harsh.

'It won't be, Mum. Where is he—I'll speak to him...'

'Mrs Brodie, I'm afraid your father is in hospital,' interrupted Grant. 'He was the victim of a serious assault and an attempted murder...'

Dawn's jaw dropped in surprise.

'What? Why...I mean, what happened?'

Grant explained the sequence of events that had led to Neil Pollock's hospitalisation; her expression of disbelief returned.

'Wait, you're saying that you thought my dad killed these two women? For God's sake, that's completely ridiculous, Dad wouldn't hurt a fly, would he Mum? Mum?'

Sandie was staring vacantly out of the window.

'What, dear? Oh, sorry, was miles away...'

'And why on earth would someone try to murder him?'

Briony answered.

'We think that some unidentified party believed your dad to have been the killer and we presume that it was a revenge attack, although at this point it's mostly conjecture, I'm afraid. Your dad's in the Glasgow Royal Infirmary.'

Dawn stared at Briony for a moment then lowered her voice, as if afraid to ask.

'Is he okay?

'Well, he's been badly assaulted, as DCI McVicar said, but he'll recover. He's lucky to be alive, though.'

They sat in silence for a few moments as Dawn tried to come to terms with what she'd just heard. Finally, Grant turned towards Sandie, who was still gazing unseeingly out of the window.

'Mrs Pollock?'

'What? Oh, sorry! Yes, em...Chief Inspector?'

'Mrs Pollock, can you account for your movements last Sunday?'

She stared at him as if she didn't understand the question.

'Sunday? My movements? What do you mean, exactly?'

Dawn turned and gave Grant a decidedly hostile look.

'Yes, Chief Inspector, what *do* you mean, exactly?'

Briony intervened.

'Sandie, we just need to know what you did last Sunday, if you were with anyone; did you go out, did you stay in...?'

Sandie gaped at her.

'But...em, well I was in the house all day, I don't think I went out...'

She frowned, shaking her head.

'No, no, I just stayed here...'

She turned toward her daughter.

'You phoned, dear, didn't you, to tell me about the puppy...?

'Yes, Mum, but that was about seven at night, we'd just got back from collecting Rufus...'

She turned back towards Grant.

'Why are you asking my Mum to account for her movements?'

Grant ignored the question.

'Mrs Pollock, is there anyone that can corroborate your claim that you stayed here?'

Sandie shook her head.

'No, of course there isn't; my husband was...well, you know perfectly well where he was, he was with that...that...'

Briony and Grant exchanged another look; was the woman acting?

'Mrs Pollock, did you at any point leave the house? Specifically, did you go to either Asda or Tesco at Linwood?'

Sandie's eyes widened but, before she answered, Dawn interrupted, her expression now furious.

'Just what the hell are you suggesting, Chief Inspector? That was where those murders happened, wasn't it? Christ, don't tell me your now accusing Mum of those...'

Grant raised his voice.

'Ma'am, we're not making any accusation at this point in time but we need to establish whether or not your mother can be ruled out of our enquiries. There is considerable evidence to suggest that she had the opportunity, the motive and the knowledge to have carried out these attacks...'

'Motive? God all bloody mighty, what motive could Mum possibly have for killing two innocent women! As far as I can gather, my dad seems to be favouring men at the moment so why the hell would my Mum kill two women... anyway, she could never do a thing like that—could you Mum? Mum...?'

Sandie Pollock seemed to be lost once again.

'What, dear?'

'I said, you'd never...oh Christ, never mind...'

'Mrs Pollock, I think it would be best if you accompany us to our offices where we can conduct a formal interview and take a statement. However, I must caution you that you needn't say anything but if...'

Dawn Brodie jumped to her feet and screamed.

'WHAT!' You're bloody arresting my Mum? Don't be fucking ridiculous...'

Grant stood up, towering over the seething woman.

'I must ask you to try and remain calm, madam. We're not arresting your mother; we simply wish to interview her in the course of our enquiries and we have to caution her as a matter of course. As I said, I think it would be best if she accompanies us to our office; she is entitled to have her solicitor present if she has one, if not we can appoint someone to act on her behalf...'

Sandie continued to stare out of the window as Dawn lowered her voice to an angry hiss...

'Solicitor! Oh, you can count on that, Inspector...'

The hiss lasted for only a few seconds then she started to shout again.

'...and he'll have your bloody guts for garters by the time he's finished with you; wrongful arrest, intimidation...'

She was now punctuating her words by jabbing her finger angrily towards Grant's face. Briony placed her hand gently but firmly on the woman's shoulder.

'Dawn, calm down, please.'

'Don't you bloody tell me to calm down, you fucking black bi...'

It was too late; Dawn Brodie raised her hand to her mouth but the words were out; they stared at each other in a tense silence for a moment, then she spoke again, her voice almost a whisper.

'I'm sorry...I'm so, so sorry, I didn't mean...oh God...'

She started to cry. Grant looked at Briony and mouthed 'You okay, Bri?'

She nodded but he could see the anger on her face.

'That was uncalled for, Mrs Brodie, but we'll say no more, put it down to the heat o' the moment, eh.'

Grant spoke with an authoritative tone.

'Mrs Brodie, your mother is coming with us, whether you like it or not. If you want to arrange a solicitor, then by all means go ahead.'

Grant crossed over to where Sandie was sitting.

'Mrs Pollock?'

Sandie looked up, her eyes glazed and unfocussed. Her head was starting to loll from side to side.

'Yes, dear?'

Briony looked across at Dawn Brodie, who was sitting with her face buried in her hands, sobbing quietly. She turned her gaze towards Sandie and frowned.

'Boss?' she whispered.

Grant turned away from Sandie, who was still staring inanely up at him. Her eyes were starting to close and she looked as if she was about to pass out.

'What Bri?'

She beckoned for him to approach; reluctantly he obeyed, glowering down at her.

'What?'

'Listen, Sandie's either very drunk or else she's having a breakdown of some sort; either way, I think we're wasting our time...'

'She's a bloody good actress, Bri, remember that.'

'I know but, seriously, I think we should leave it for a wee while, see how things go...'

His phone was ringing; the display indicated it was from Mill Street police office. He slid his thumb across the screen and lifted it to his ear.

'McVicar.'

He listened to the caller on the other end, shaking his head as he pursed his lips. The call ended and he looked at Briony.

'What, Boss?'

'Lachie Dallas had just turned up at Mill Street, accusing Sandie Pollock of assaulting him and demanding that we press charges...'

He looked at Sandie, the inane smile still on her face, her eyes now closed. Suddenly, she slumped back in her chair, mouth wide open, dead to the world but snoring like a pig. Grant shook his head as he muttered

'Fuck me.'

CHAPTER 12

Sergeant William Cook rubbed his hand nervously over his thinning, slightly greasy hair as he regarded the two young detective constables seated opposite him. Did they know? And, if so, how much did they know?

'I'm no' exactly sure what you mean, Constables' he stated, emphasising the last word in an effort to pull rank; after all, he *was* a sergeant...

'We just need to corroborate the statement that you took from Mrs Sandie Pollock, Sir,' said Grace, a sweet, innocent smile on her face. Cliff cast a sideways glance at his colleague, realising that that same sweet, innocent expression was likely to stand her in very good stead in the future.

'Em, aye, okay, just let me get my notes...'

Fifteen minutes later, Cook had read out the statement he had taken; it corresponded exactly with what Sandie had told them. Grace made a show of consulting the notes she had taken, chewing the end of her pen as she did so.

'Right, Sir, that all ties in. Just one more thing.'

'Yes, Constable?'

'Mrs Pollock was making this statement implicating her husband as a double murderer, yes?'

There was a pause; Cook realised it was a question.

'Em, yes, just as I told you.'

'And she made you aware of her suspicions at the outset?'

'Yes, constable. Look, I'm a busy man...'

'And you were aware that we were already conducting an investigation into those murders?'

He glared at Grace; he decided that he didn't like this girl and his reply was terse.

'Of course; why would I refer it to you otherwise?'

'Exactly Sir...'

She closed her notebook and glanced at Cliff.

'And, that being the case, why did you take such a full statement when you were only too well aware that we would be questioning the witness ourselves?'

~~~

'You were bloody brilliant, Grace!'

'Cheers, Cliff. Don't know how much further it'll get us but there's not a shadow of doubt that he's guilty of passing stuff on.'

'Aye; so, what now?'

'We wait; he might not do anything but my guess is he'll go and see his contact, with us tagging along behind. He's not going to chance a traceable phone call after our visit, is he?'

'Nope; excitin' stuff, this!'

'Yes, it is rather...hang on, there he is; right, Cliff. Just take it easy. Don't get too close...'

'Och, away, Grace, Ah'm a dab hand at this sort o' thing...'

~~~

'Didn'ae expect to see you so soon, Billy Boy; everythin' okay?'

John Norris stared up at Cook; the policeman's hands were shaking and, despite the coolness of the day, there were beads of sweat on his forehead.

'No, Norris, it fucking well isn't okay. I think they're on to me.'

'Who's on tae you, Billy? The polis?'

He gave a humourless laugh. The pub was fairly quiet but a few worthies were ensconced at the bar, watching the proceedings with disinterest; there was football on the television, after all.

'The bloody CID, or whatever they call themselves now. Came round asking all sorts of questions, why I took the statement, that sort of thing.'

'So, what the fuck are you dae'in here, Cook? Leadin' them straight tae ma door, that's what, ya fucking wanker.'

Norris stood up; he was a burly, muscular man, a good few inches taller than Cook, who now looked nervously up at him.

'Get tae fuck oot ma sight.'

'But...but, I gave you the information you wanted; what about the rest of my...aagh...'

John Norris had grabbed Cook's arm and twisted it up his back. As he walked the policeman to the door, one of the worthies crossed the room to hold it open for him. Norris let go of Cook's arm and pushed him out.

'You bastard, Norris!' Cook shouted, as he stumbled forward. He would have fallen had he not been caught and steadied by the two figures standing in front of him. He looked at them, an expression of shock on his face. Norris glowered at Cliff and Grace.

'Who the fuck are you—wait, don't tell me, mates o' this piece o' shit, eh? Well, youse can bugger off too, you're no' welcome around here...'

Cliff held out his identity card as Billy Cook squirmed free before running off in the direction of his vehicle; the constable frowned up at the man despite his menacing demeanour.

'You're John Norris, aren't you?'

'Who the fuck wants tae know?'

Several of the worthies had gathered behind Norris, their interest now thoroughly aroused. Cliff grinned wickedly.

'Here, Ah mind ma old man told me about you; wasn't there something about a lassie at school—whit was her name? Oh aye, Mary Ross; it wis her dolly you took, wasn't it...'

Norris's eyes widened.

'How the fuck...'

Cliff held his card higher; John Norris peered at it then took a step towards the constable.

'Ford...ya wee bastard...'

One of the worthies grinned, revealing rotten teeth stumps.

'Whit wis the story son? Sounds like a good yin...'

Norris turned and glared at the man, who immediately shut his mouth and took a step backwards. Grace was smiling, less sweetly this time.

'Right, we're done here. John Norris, then. Good, I think we've got all we need...'

Billy Cook had already entered his car and driven away with a screech of tyres; Grace and Cliff walked briskly back to their own vehicle and, once inside, Grace burst out laughing.

'What, in the name of God, was that all about?'

Cliff was grinning too.

'Well, ma old man worked the East End but he grew up an' went tae school here as well, pretty much knew everybody. He used tae tell the story about this guy Norris, one o' these stories that wis kinda local folk-lore, if you know whit Ah mean. So, Norris took this lassie's doll one day, but what he didn't know was that Mary Ross wis a right wee hard ticket; her dad wis one o' the local tough nuts an' he'd taught his daughter a thing or two. Anyway, she an' her pals chased Norris an' when they caught him, they stripped him bare naked an' tied him tae a lamp-post wi' their skipping ropes.'

'Oh my God,' exclaimed Grace. 'They'd end up in court for that nowadays...'

'Aye, but that's no' all. It wis hot, the middle o' summer, an' one o' them got her jeely piece...'

Grace frowned.

'Her what?

'Jeely piece? Her jam sandwich!'

'Oh, right.'

'Anyway, she rubbed jam all over his...em, private parts, an' they went away an' left him. By the time his pals got tae him, he'd been stung a couple o' times on his...well, you know...an' he wis crawlin' wi' flies.'

Grace looked at Cliff in astonishment.

'Seriously? So, what happened then?'

'Sweet eff all! Like Ah said, Mary Ross's Da wis too tough to touch. Norris wouldn't come out o' his house for weeks, apparently, he couldn't handle the humiliation, especially with it bein' lassies.'

'Wow! No wonder he was upset when you mentioned that wee gem, what a brilliant story; anyway, let's get back to base and let the Boss know. If we can track down who Norris is working for, then we'll have a pretty good idea who carried out the assault on Neil Pollock.'

Cliff winked at her.

'It's the East End, Grace, there's really only one family he's likely to be employed by...'

After some careful consideration, Grant and Briony had come to the conclusion that Sandie Pollock had been drinking heavily and wasn't suffering from a breakdown of any sort; she was currently sitting in the chair, still comatose and still snoring like a pig. A chat with the daughter, now effusive with her apologies for her racist outburst, had elicited the information that her mum had struggled with a drink problem over the past few years. Dawn Brodie had assured them that she'd put her mum to bed, make sure she stayed at home and keep her away from the bottle. As the two officers had taken their leave, she had said.

'You know, there is no way on earth that my mum is capable of doing anyone any harm; she's a sweet, kind person, really...'

Briony had touched her on the arm, the jibe apparently forgotten.

'We're not accusin' her, Dawn, we just want to eliminate her from our enquiries. Just you keep an eye on her an' we'll come back later, eh?'

As they had driven back to Osprey House, Grant's mobile had rung.

'See who it is, Bri.'

She lifted his phone.

'It's Louise. Will I answer it?'

He felt his stomach lurch.

What the hell's happened now...?

'Em, no, I'll call her back when we get to the office.'

Briony gave him a surreptitious glance; there was a tone in his voice that worried her.

Grant finished the call to Louise and stared out of his office window. He slumped forwards on the desk, leaning on his elbows and rubbing his hands over his face; just what the hell had he done...? His troubled reverie was interrupted by a knock at the door; he sighed and sat up, trying his best to appear normal.

'Aye, come in.'

Grace Lappin and Cliff Ford opened the door and entered the room.

'Have a seat; you two look like the proverbial cats who got the cream. Okay then, let's hear it...'

<center>~~~</center>

Grant regarded the two enthusiastic young officers seated across from him; there had been a time when it would have been him sitting in front of his then boss, DI Jacky Winters, desperate to impress...all a distant memory, distant and dark...

No, Grant, don't...

He spoke, his voice stern.

'You realise that you put yourselves at considerable risk?'

'Och no, really, Boss. Ah mean, they weren't goin' to do anythin' in broad daylight...'

Grant decided that a little bit of authority was warranted.

'You don't know that, Cliff; you don't know what these people are capable of. You were way off your home turf, you were way out of line...'

But then, despite himself, the image of John Norris, a "weel kent" hard-man, tied naked to a lamp-post with jam smeared over his privates, insinuated itself in his mind and he smiled.

'Oh, for God's sake...still, you got away with it. Right, I'll need to report all this—well, an edited version— to the Mint. Presumably Cook hasn't gone back to Mill Street so we'll need to get his address...'

Grace interrupted.

'Em, Boss?'

'What, Grace?'

'Should we maybe put out an alert at the airports, in case he decides to bugger off somewhere? I heard he's already got a trip to Thailand booked; he might try to leave early.'

Once again, Grant was impressed.

'Good point, Grace, you can get on to that. I'll speak to the Mint and we'll get it passed on to the ACU.'

He shook his head.

'You're a right pair...but that was bloody good work, very well done. Right, off you go...'

As Grace and Cliff reached the door, the young constable turned back.

'Just one more thing, Boss.'

'Aye, Cliff?'

'Well, oot in that part o' the world, you know who Norris was most likely to be workin' for?'

Grant just stared at his DC; his thought process hadn't got that far.

The two constables left Grant's office with ear-to-ear grins; DCI McVicar wasn't usually so liberal with his praise. Had they looked back, however; they would have seen a dark, troubled expression appear on their boss's face.

'Mum, come on, sit up and drink your coffee.'

Sandie Pollock looked a mess; her normally well-coiffured hair was dishevelled; her make-up was smeared and her breath smelt foul; Dawn tried not to wrinkle her nose in disgust. Her mother had been her rock throughout her life but now...

Sandie managed to prop herself up on the pillows, taking the coffee and draining half the mug in one long, thirsty gulp. She looked at her daughter.

'Oh Dawn, I'm so sorry, what a bloody mess.'

'You're right there, Mum. How long has all this, you know, with dad and... Well, how long's it been going on?

Sandie averted her eyes.

'I don't know, Dawn. Months, years, who knows? Your dad just seemed the same, sweet kind man he'd always been. It was only in the last few days, since…oh…'

'Since those murders?'

'Oh God, I suppose so. When I found that stuff in his cupboard, then when the policewoman on the TV gave the description, especially the bit about the blonde wig, well…'

She swallowed the rest of the coffee.

'Then when Neil…Dad started acting really strangely, I just put two and two together, I suppose. It all seemed to fit.'

Dawn looked at her mother; she seemed to have aged considerably in the last few weeks. She lowered her voice, trying to sound sympathetic

'And when did you start drinking again?'

Sandie shook her head.

'After that bitch McKillop phoned to tell me she'd seen a tarty blonde getting into your father's car; the joke is, it was probably your dad dressed up…'

Her eyes filled up but she managed to hold back the tears. Dawn squeezed her mum's hand.

'It's okay, Mum…'

'No, it's not okay. How can it ever be okay, Dawn? Another woman, well, maybe, but a man? How can I compete with that unless I get a bloody sex-change?'

Mother and daughter looked at each other…and burst out laughing!

The tears had passed; tears of laughter, of sorrow, of love, they had done their job. Dawn's husband had arrived to collect the children and the puppy; mother and daughter were sitting at the kitchen table, Sandie now showered, sober and looking almost back to her normal self. They were chatting easily as they sipped their second coffee, then Dawn put down her mug in a decisive manner.

'Right, we'd better call this detective guy and get it over with. Listen, I'll ask if he can conduct the interview here; after all, you really *have* got nothing to hide. I'll stay with you, make sure they don't bully you, then I'll go up and see Dad.'

Sandie's smile disappeared.

'Oh! Em, are you sure, dear?'

'Mum, for God's sake, no matter what, he's still my father.'

She paused.

'Listen, why don't you come too?'

Sandie shook her head.

'No, no I can't, not yet. Anyway, what if...if he's there?'

'If he is, then he'll get a piece of my mind, Mum, don't worry. But fair enough, I'll go by myself, then I'll come back here.'

'Och, There's no need...'

'Yes, Mum, there *is* a need, especially tonight. Anyway, it'll be nice to be back in my old room, and it'll give you peace of mind...

And me, for that matter...!

'Right, let's get this over with...'

Grant pulled up outside the Pollock residence, closely followed by Briony; they had driven separately as he had decided to pay a visit to Louise on the way home. The afternoon hadn't turned up anything conclusive. Sam and Kiera had returned from North Berwick, where the hotel had confirmed the reservation, in the name of Nicky Hogarth's company, but no-one seemed to be able to recall much about their guests, other than they had requested breakfast in their room and hadn't used the hotel dining room at all. No-one seemed able (or willing) to pass any further comment on the two reclusive occupants of room 5. Not for the first time, Grant felt that the case was grinding to a halt; he had reported to Superintendent Minto, who had set the wheels of the Anti-Corruption Unit in motion. Cook's house was being watched and an alert had been put out to Glasgow, Edinburgh and Prestwick airports, in case he decided to make his escape. However, even without Cook in custody, Grant knew that Cliff was correct; it was highly likely that John Norris was in the employ of the Pettigrew family, in which case why had they wanted information on Neil Pollock, the man the police had assumed to be the murderer? Why had they taken out a contract on him? Finally, where the hell did that leave him...?

Grant and Briony had left the team looking for some connection between the victims and the Pettigrew family but, so far, their search had been fruitless. He climbed wearily out of the pick-up; he had already decided that, after he had taken his leave of Louise, he would walk down the Howwood's Railway Inn, where his two friends, the Reverend Fraser Ballingall and Father Eddie McKee would undoubtedly be found. If ever he needed the company of the Holy Trinity, tonight was the night...

∿∿∿

'Well?'

The interview was concluded and Briony was sitting in Grant's vehicle. She shook her head.

'Honestly, Boss? I don't think Sandie had anything at all to do with the murders.'

He gazed out of the window, along the wide, tree-lined thoroughfare. Not too long ago it would have been well-lit in a soft, orange glow but the recent fitting of harsh, white LED lamps had created pools of darkness between the lamp-standards.

Aye, saving money at the cost of safety...as always...

'To be honest, neither do I. Either that or she's a *really* good actress. But it's this bloody item of underwear that we know belonged to Natalie Wheeler—I mean, where the hell did that come from? The only people with access to his holdall were Sandie, Neil Pollock and Nicky Hogarth.'

Briony frowned.

'And the staff at the hotel in North Berwick.'

He looked at her.

'Hm, fair point. Mind you, they said that Hogarth and Pollock didn't come out of their room.'

'No Boss, they said that they didn't use the hotel dining room. But they must have eaten somewhere, apart from breakfast. If they were out during the day, then the hotel staff would have access to their room; it wouldn't have been hard to place it in the bag and it's unlikely that Pollock would have noticed it.'

'Aye, I suppose... but where's the motive, Bri? What the hell is the connection with this hotel through in North Berwick and two random murder victims in Linwood; not to mention why would they try to implicate Pollock? We might need to conduct interviews with the staff, even if it's just to rule them out... listen, are you going back to the office?'

'Aye, I thought I'd look in and see what's happening.'

'Might be worth having another chat with Nicky Hogarth, on his own, find out exactly what they actually did over the weekend...'

Briony gave him a look and raised an eyebrow; he grinned back at her.

'Well, apart from that, of course...the thing is, their alibi holds water only because they say it does. If the hotel staff don't specifically remember them and if they can't prove what they were doing, especially on Sunday...'

'You think they might be in it together?'

'Don't know, but it's a possibility, isn't it? I mean, they could easily have driven through, done the deed, driven back. Hogarth could have been waiting in the car, ready to get Pollock out of the way...and it would explain the presence of the "trophy".'

The statement hung in the air as they both considered the implications. Grant breathed out noisily.

'What are you doing after you see Louise, Boss?'

He shrugged.

'Em, I was thinking of heading down to the Railway Inn...'

'I thought you didn't usually drink on a Friday now, since you started rowing...'

She stopped suddenly as she remembered.

'...oh, sorry...'

'No, it's okay, Bri, you're right, but there's no way I can show my face down at the rowing club. No, I'll go and see Fraser and Eddie, have a few, try and get my head straight.'

She looked at him in the harsh glow of the LED streetlight. He looked worn, troubled...and sad. She placed her hand on his arm.

'Don't overdo it, Grant. And don't forget what we're *really* investigating here...'

He turned and glared at her.

'What's that supposed to mean?'

She glared back; she was learning how to handle Grant McVicar.

'You know damned fine what I mean; we're investigating a double murder, not the bloody Pettigrew family...'

CHAPTER 13

'And you've opened it?'

Louise Thackray nodded.

Grant reached into his pocket, took out a pair of forensic gloves and pulled them on before picking up the grubby white envelope that lay on the kitchen table.

'Taking no chances, I see?'

He looked up.

'Just in case, Louise. Don't want my prints all over it.'

In the background he could hear Finn and his younger brother, Callum, playing some inane computer game; he reckoned it was safe to proceed so he looked inside the envelope then removed the contents; a bundle of well-used twenty-pound notes, wrapped in a scrap of lined paper.

'I reckon about five hundred quid, Grant. Didn't count it though, didn't want to get my hands dirty...'

He could see the look of distaste on her face; he read the single word scrawled in ballpoint on the torn sheet of paper.

"Shed"

He took a deep breath and exhaled slowly. He hadn't expected this.

'And the Barrowman kid just handed it to Finn?

'Yup, came up to him at lunchtime—he thought he was in for "a doing" as he put it—but Barrowman mumbled what Finn thinks was an apology then handed him the envelope, saying it was for me, apparently. Finn gave me it as soon as he got home. Oh, and the bullying seems to have stopped, thank God.'

She gave him a scrutinising look.

'Grant, what the hell prompted this? I mean, I hoped that your intervention might have stopped the bullying, but then there was the fire...and now this money... why?'

Aye, why indeed, as if I didn't know!

They sat in silence for a few moments, listening to the noise of the two boys happily zapping aliens.

'What do I do with it, Grant?

'Not sure, really. I suppose it's an admission of guilt but it'd be pretty hard to prove anything so it's probably not worth taking it any further. You could hang on to it...'

She shook her head violently.

'No, I don't want it; it's dirty money, Grant, you know that. They're crooks, those Barrowmans...men...Christ, I don't know what you call a crowd of them...'

Grant smiled—he hadn't actually thought of what to call the Barrowman family "en masse".

'...but it'll be drug money and I want no part of it. Anyway, the shed and the stuff in it are covered under the house policy. You take it.'

'Me! Not a chance! Listen, Louise, if you *really* don't want it— and, to be honest, I don't blame you—give it to a charity. At least that way it'll do some good work, even if it's "bad" money.'

She thought about it for a moment.

'Okay, fair enough, that's what I'll do. It'll need to be anonymous, though, can't just suddenly present anyone I know with five hundred quid, can I?'

'No, I suppose not; but that's probably the best course of action. Listen, leave that one with me, I've had a thought...'

Louise smiled at him and took his hand, giving it a squeeze.

'You still okay for dinner on Sunday? The boys are really looking forward to it.'

He had completely forgotten and, in an attempt to cover his embarrassment, he stood up, rather suddenly. It didn't work—her expression turned to one of sadness.

'You'd forgotten, hadn't you Grant?'

'Em, no, of course I hadn't; listen, Louise, I really need...'

Louise Thackray sighed.

'Yes, you need to go, don't you; you always need to go, Grant. Are you afraid of me, or something?'

Am I...?

'Don't be daft, Louise, it's just been one hell of a week. Actually, I'm going out for a drink with my mates...'

'Huh!' she exclaimed with a slight smile. The Holy Trinity? Well, there's no way I can compete with those two!'

~~~~

'Oh-oh, Eddie, here comes a man carrying the weight of the world on his shoulders...'

Father Eddie McKee turned towards the door of Howwood's Railway Inn, then turned back to his friend.

'Hm, we're in for a bit of a confession-session, if you ask me...'

He was correct. Half an hour, two pints of Belhaven and a double Macallan later, DCI Grant McVicar was beginning to feel ever so slightly relaxed; which was more than could be said for his two ecclesiastical friends. They looked at each other, a shocked look on both their faces, then Fraser shook his head.

'You couldn't bloody write it...'

Eddie managed a smile.

'Well, I probably could, with some of the confessions I've heard in my time, but I know what you mean, Fraser.'

Fraser Ballingall looked at Grant, currently draining his pint.

'I take it, then, that rowing's off the cards for the time being, Grant?'

Grant placed his glass on the table and wiped foam from his moustache.

'Yup. You ready for another...?'

And another...and another...it was nearly closing time and Eddie gave Fraser a look; unfortunately, their friend noticed.

'What? I'm bloody fine, if that's what you're thinking.'

'If you say so, Chief,' replied Fraser, with a smile. Grant had drunk a double whisky for each of their singles and he was showing the effects.

'How're you getting up the road?' asked Eddie, a note of concern in his voice.

'I'll walk; do me good.'

Again, his friends exchanged a look.

'Listen, Grant, come and stay at the manse, there's a spare bed always at the ready. I've got a wedding in the afternoon so you can lie on for a bit.'

'Cheers Fraser, but...'

'He's right, Grant. Honestly, I'd feel a lot happier if...'

Grant glared at Eddie.

'Why, do you think I'm going to do something stupid? For fuck sake...'

'Grant, that's not what I meant at all, it's just...'

Grant stood up, rather unsteadily.

'Like I said, I'll be fine. See you...'

He walked unsteadily towards the door, nearly knocking over a table on his way and leaving the other two members of the Trinity staring at his back in dismay.

Thankfully the rain had stopped and the moon was out, shining with a pale, watery light as Grant took a short-cut through Mid Gavin farm. His phone rang and he pulled it out of his pocket, gazing at the name displayed on the screen; it was Briony. Rather clumsily, he swiped it to answer but it slipped out of his hand, landing with a clatter on the tarmac of the farm yard.

'Shit!'

As he bent down to lift it, he could hear his sergeant's voice.

'Boss! Boss, are you okay?'

He picked it up and glowered at the shattered glass.

'Fuck! You fucking bastard!'

There was silence for a few moments.

'I beg your pardon?'

'Fuck! Aw, sorry, Bri, I dropped my fucking phone and I've broke the screen, sorry, wasn't you that's bastard, it's the phone...'

'Boss, what the hell's the matter; wait, are you drunk?'

He laughed manically.

'Aye, and why the fuck not, Bri? I mean, a man's entitled to get pissed...'

'Boss, for God's sake, pull yourself together. Jesus, I thought you were just havin' a sociable wee drink wi' the Trinity, I didn't think you were settin' out to get hammered...'

'Aw, don't you bloody start...I'm fine. Anyway, what the hell are you phoning me for...at this time of day for? You might have woken...em...me up...'

There was another frosty silence.

'Actually, I'm no' sure I should tell you, the state you're in.'

'Don't you bloody start...did I just say that? What is it, Bri?'

Another pause.

'I had a call from Neil Pollock earlier. I tried to call you but you didn't answer.'

'Aye, reception's crap in the Inn; so, what's he saying to it now?'

'He remembered the name.'

'Whose name?'

There was frustration in her voice as she answered.

'God! The guy who abducted him, Boss. Remember, he told Pollock that someone had sent their regards but he couldn't remember the name...'

Grant felt as if an icy wind was blowing over him; he started to sober up.

'Em, aye, got you now; so, who was it?'

The pause was longer this time.

'Bri?'

'Braid. He said that "Teeny Braid sends her regards".'

Grant stared at the moonlit farmyard as his brain went into overdrive; Helena Pettigrew's maiden name was immediately familiar to him from the previous case.

'You're sure? Teeny Braid?'

'Yup, that's what he said. He remembered "Braid" but wasn't sure what the first name was. It suddenly came to him this evening; he thought it was an odd name.'

'Definitely Teeny? I mean, he couldn't have misheard... maybe it was Ellie?'

'Definitely Teeny. Pollock said he went through the alphabet tryin' all the different name permutations; he got as far as Tina... oh...'

Grant didn't respond.

'...anyway, it suddenly it came to him. Teeny; he says it was definitely Teeny Braid...'

Shit...

'So we need to speak to Helena Pettigrew right now...'

'Don't be bloody stupid Boss, there's no way on this earth that you're goin' over there now, not at this hour and certainly not in the state you're in. I'll pick you up in the morning and we'll head over...'

'No, I'll come up to Osprey Ho...'

Her reply was stern.

'You bloody well will not, Boss! The way you sound it'll likely be lunchtime before you're fit to drive, eh. No, I'll pick you up at, say, ten o'clock, give you time to sleep it off. By the way, where are you, exactly? Is that a dog barkin?'

He realised that the lights in the farmhouse had come on.

Shit...!

'Em, aye, listen, Bri, I need to go—I'm walking home and I've just wakened the bloody farmer!'

∿∿∿

Dawn Brodie looked at her mum across the kitchen table then put her mug back down.

'Well, Mum?'

Sandie looked at her daughter with an expression of feigned innocence.

'Well what, dear?'

Dawn sighed; why was the woman being so obtuse?

'Are you going to see Dad today?'

Sandie lifted her mug slowly and deliberately.

'Mum?'

'Dawn, it's not so simple; you don't know what it feels like to be betrayed like this...'

'Oh, for God's sake, Mum, of course I don't but you've been married for over thirty years, the least you can do is talk about it; after all, he was nearly killed...'

They looked at each other, remembering the horror of what might have been. Sandie gave a weary sigh.

'I'll see, dear. I'll see how I feel later on...'

'He wants to come home.'

A look of shock appeared on Sandie's face.

'What? Home? What do you mean?'

'What do you think I mean, Mum. Home—the place he lives; here, in case you hadn't noticed. I mean, where else did you think he'd go when he got out of hospital. Which they think will probably be Tuesday, by the way.'

Sandie gaped at her daughter.

'Em...I hadn't given it any thought...I thought he'd go and stay with...'

'With that Hogarth man?' Dawn shook her head. 'No, he wants to come home, Mum. Hogarth has a wife, although Dad says he's planning on leaving her...'

'Huh! What, to move in with...'

It was as if she couldn't mention her husband's name.

'Mum, I don't know, but he's got nowhere to go. You need to go and talk to him; he's my dad—and he's your bloody husband!'

Sandie shook her head; Dawn looked down at the floor, twisting her hands together.

'Well, I suppose if that's your final answer, we *could* move the kids in together and he could come and stay with us...'

'No!'

Dawn looked up; her ploy had worked...

∿∿∿

Grant's head was pounding as Briony's car crawled along the eastbound M8, the traffic nearly gridlocked due to an earlier accident. She braked suddenly and he winced.

'You okay, Boss?'

His brain felt like it had become detached from the inside of his skull; he couldn't even risk shaking his head.

'No, not really. Did you say you had water?'

'There's a bag on the back seat, a couple o' bottles and a pack of croissants; I thought you'd be hungry eventually...'

He managed a slight smile in response to her grin as, very gingerly, he turned round and retrieved the bag.

'Aye, cheers...'

'No problem. Oh, and there's paracetamol as well...'

Serves you bloody right...

He had finished the water and the two croissants by the time they arrived at the Pettigrew residence in Glasgow's Mount Vernon area. The security gate was closed, Ronnie Pettigrew's Audi sports coupe parked safely behind it. As they stepped out of Briony's car, she looked at him.

'Tidy yourself up a bit, Boss, you don't want to make a bad impression wi' Ronnie...fasten your shirt properly; an' there's crumbs all down the front too...'

He glared across at her but managed to make the necessary adjustments to his appearance. The heavy metal gate slid open at their approach and, as they walked across to the front door, it, too, swung open. Ronnie Pettigrew was standing waiting for them, arms folded, as they mounted the stone steps.

'Well, well, what brings you to this part of the world on a Saturday morning? Suppose you'd better come in.'

As he passed her, she gave him a knowing look.

'Looks like someone had a rough night!'

Aye, you could say that...

He put his head down (rather ashamedly, Briony thought) as they entered the house, Ronnie holding the door open for them; as always, she was immaculately dressed. Smart, well-pressed grey trousers showed off her long legs and were topped with a tailored black blouse, the upper few buttons unfastened just enough to show some lacy underwear and the swell of her cleavage. Grant briefly wondered if she always dressed this carefully; he had never seen her in casual attire—well, not since...

No, Grant...!

Ronnie closed the door behind them then walked past and into the hallway; Grant caught the faint and alluring aroma of expensive perfume and, as he looked at her, she gave him a wicked grin and winked. He hoped Briony hadn't noticed.

'So, who are you here to harass today, officers, me or my poor mother?'

'We're here to speak to Mrs Pettigrew, Ronnie.'

The grin disappeared.

'Hm. Okay, you'd best go in, then, and I'll see how she is. But don't you dare upset her, she's very fragile, as you'd expect.'

Aye, right...!

They entered the now-familiar television room, sat down and waited. They could hear slightly raised voices then, after a few more minutes, Veronica came in, her mother behind her. Helena

Pettigrew had aged considerably since Grant had last seen her and, as she sat on the couch, he could see her hands shaking. He decided that he should probably stick to convention.

'Mrs Pettigrew, I'm here on...well, business, but before we start, I'm very sorry for your loss.'

She favoured him with a look of pure hatred.

'Don't give me that shite, McVicar. You never even met Michael an' if you'd known him in his prime, he'd have been more than a match fur you...sorry ma arse...'

'Mum!' Ronnie interrupted, raising her voice. 'Don't be rude, the Chief Inspector's just being...'

'He's just being his usual self, Ronnie. He doesn't give a fuck about Michael, just one less o' us tae worry aboot...'

She lapsed into silence as if all her malicious energy had been spent. Grant ignored the jibes; it was only to be expected, after all.

'Right, Mrs Pettigrew, down to business then...'

Two pairs of Pettigrew eyes swivelled to glare rather malevolently at him.

'I'm aware from our previous investigations that your maiden name was Braid and that you went under the alias of "Ellie".'

'It wisn'ae a fuckin' alias, it wis whit Michael called me...'

'Whatever. Can I ask you, Mrs Pettigrew, have you ever been known by the nickname "Teeny"?'

Ronnie frowned.

'Teeny? Mum's never been called that—have you, Mum?'

Helena Pettigrew narrowed her eyes as she averted them.

'Em, Ah don't know whit ye're goin' on aboot.'

'No? Think again, Mrs Pettigrew; "Teeny", as in "Teeny Braid sends her regards?"'

'Grant, what the hell are you talking about?' asked Ronnie, her tone angry. 'We've told you: my mum's never been called "Teeny"'

'Anyway, there's plenty o' Braids in the phone book, Mr Clever-Dick, why would it be me they were talkin' aboot?'

There was a sudden silence; Briony looked at Grant, then spoke.

"They", Mrs Pettigrew? We never mentioned a "they". We only asked if you had ever been called "Teeny". To whom were you referring?'

They saw Helena Pettigrew's eyes dart between them and her daughter; Ronnie was now frowning at her mother and Grant had the vague feeling that, whatever Helena's involvement, the daughter knew little or nothing of it. Before he could add anything, Ronnie turned back towards him and smiled, this time with a hint of menace.

'Officers, my Mum's really tired and she's due to take medication for her nerves. I think we'll call it a day at that, if you don't mind...'

'Actually, Miss Pettigrew, I do mind. As well as a double murder, we're investigating the abduction and attempted murder of one of our suspects. Unfortunately, we are also investigating the passing of sensitive information by one of our officers.'

Briony interjected.

'Are either of you familiar with a John Norris?'

This time, both women cast a fleeting, slightly anxious glance at one another. Ronnie recovered her composure first.

'I think that Mr Norris might work in one of our pubs...' she looked at her mother '...McTurk's, isn't it, Mum?'

'Whit? Oh, aye. Maybe, Ah don't have much tae dae wi' it these days...'

'I see' interrupted Grant. 'And will Mr Norris be there at the moment?'

Ronnie Pettigrew gave him a supercilious look.

'I believe Mr Norris is on holiday at present.'

Grant could feel his temper rising.

'Interesting; you're pretty vague about whether or not he works for you and yet you seem to know that he's just gone on holiday. Convenient.'

'As a responsible employer I like to keep in the loop, Grant.'

Aye, of course you bloody do...

He turned back to the mother.

'Mrs Pettigrew, do you know who Neil Pollock is?'

She looked genuinely surprised this time as she shook her head.

'Naw, never heard o' him.'

'I see. And did you at any time issue any instructions for harm to be done...'

Ronnie jumped to her feet, her long dark hair flicking angrily.

'That's quite enough, Chief Inspector, I'm not having you coming here and harassing my mother a week after she's lost her husband. She'll say nothing further without a lawyer present, so I suggest you leave us in peace and come back when you have something more concrete other than a handful of uncorroborated accusations...'

Grant stood up and held her gaze; for a moment, it was as if a spark of static electricity passed between them.

'Fine; we'll leave you be meantime but I can assure you that this isn't over.'

He strode towards the door, followed by Briony, who glanced down at Helena Pettigrew as she walked across the room. The woman had been biting her fingernails during the interview and, as Briony reached the door, she noticed a drop of blood run down Helena Pettigrew's finger and drip onto her trousers.

Christ, the woman's on a bloody knife edge...

As they reached the front door, Ronnie Pettigrew suddenly grabbed Grant's arm and pulled him towards her, bringing her full, red lips close to the side of his head. He could smell her perfume; he could feel her warmth... She hissed in his ear.

'You might have forgotten, Grant McVicar, but I most certainly haven't...'

He pulled away and strode down the steps without a backward glance, leaving Briony wondering what the hell had just happened.

∿∿∿

Ronnie Pettigrew closed the door, leaned against it and stood for a few moments, gathering her thoughts. Finally, she returned to the small room, where her mother was staring at the blank television screen, still biting what remained of her once-long fingernails. She glanced at her daughter as she walked across and sat down on the chair recently vacated by her adversary. Ronnie looked back at her and shook her head resignedly.

'Oh, for God's sake, mum, have a bloody cigarette if you must... even if it's just to stop you biting your nails...what a mess, look...'

But Helena Pettigrew wasn't interested; she rummaged in her bag, pulled out the crumpled pack of cigarettes and the lighter. A few seconds later, she took a long, deep draw before doubling up in a paroxysm of coughing. Another couple of draws and her breathing normalised as her lungs re-adjusted to the warm, nicotine and tar-laden smoke. Ronnie narrowed her eyes and wrinkled her nose as her mother exhaled.

'Thanks, hen, Ah needed that.'

'Mum?'

Helena inhaled again then gave a smoke-laden reply.

'Aye, Ronnie?

'Just who the fuck is Teeny?'

Grant had asked Briony pretty much the same question shortly before he fell asleep; she was now driving along Inchinnan Road to the accompaniment of his loud snoring, having decided that he would probably be the better for some rest. A few minutes later, she keyed in her code, the barrier lifted and, as she pulled into a parking space, he finally wakened.

'We here?' he mumbled in a thick voice.

'Yup. Feeling any better, Boss?'

He took a deep breath.

'Marginally; right, let's get inside and see what the hell's happening.'

He sipped his coffee as he surveyed his team; they were a good, loyal and dedicated bunch—maybe he should tell them sometime...

'Right, first of all, as you know by now Neil Pollock claims that one of his abductors said, "Teeny Braid sends her regards" just before they left him to his fate. And, as we also know from our last murder investigation, Braid was Helena Pettigrew's maiden name, although she was known as "Ellie" and not "Teeny".

He looked at DC Ford.

'Cliff, could you ask your old man if he remembers anyone ever calling her by "Teeny"?'

'Em, aye but he's away up north fishin' at the moment.'

'He's what? Can't you call him?'

'No, Boss, he always switches his phone off when he's away; he only takes it for emergencies. He swears the signal disturbs the fish...he's back tomorrow though, so Ah'll give ma Maw a buzz an' get her tae ask him tae call me when he gets home.'

Grant frowned; he really wanted an answer now but there was little he could do about it.

'Fair enough; anyone any closer to finding a link between either of the victims and the Pettigrews? I haven't the slightest doubt that they're behind Pollock's assault, the mother let slip something that pretty much implicated her...'

Briony had a doubtful look that Grant ignored.

'No, Boss,' said Kiera. 'We've checked all our information on both the victims and the Fielding woman, in case she *was* the intended victim, but there's no link that we can find. Amanda Duff had been in a few scrapes and was an occasional drug user, as we already know, but she's got no convictions so I doubt if she had any direct association with the Pettigrew family. There's nothing, I'm afraid.'

He grunted.

'Boss?'

'Yes, Sam.

'We were going to head back through to North Berwick for another word with the hotel staff. We thought the weekend shift might remember something.'

'Good idea; maybe best to wait until tomorrow in case they work to a regular rota. Call ahead first and see who'll be there, but that might just throw up something new. Faz, anything from Liverpool?'

DC Bajwa shook his head.'

'Nothing, Boss. I spoke to DCI Owen again this morning, they've looked in all the usual haunts but Malone and Hopkins have gone to ground somewhere. She says she'll keep looking but she's not hopeful, I'm afraid.'

'Bugger. Right, Bri, I think we need to have a chat with Nicky Hogarth; I'm beginning to feel far from convinced about this alibi of theirs.'

There was a look of relief on Briony's face; not for the first time she was concerned that her boss seemed to be expending more energy in finding a link with the Pettigrews than with the actual murder investigation. He addressed the team.

'Thing is, although they can prove the hotel booking, most of their time there is unaccounted for and they only really have each other as an alibi.'

He frowned.

'Kiera, how long did it take you to drive through to North Berwick?'

She thought for a moment.

'Just under two hours; a lot depends on the traffic, especially the Edinburgh City Bypass, but between about an hour forty-five and two hours fifteen, I'd reckon. Are you suggesting they're both involved?'

'I'm not sure yet, Kiera, but it's a distinct possibility. We've still got that item of Natalie Wheeler's underwear to explain, for a start. Then there's the fact that they seem to have spent hardly any time in the hotel and none at all in the dining room. That would leave them plenty of time to drive through, do the deed then drive back. We know that Pollock is left-handed, we know that the evidence suggests that the murderer was left-handed...'

'Oh, by the way, Boss, forensics called—they're pretty certain that the fragment of wire that Dr Napier recovered *is* picture-wire, although they can't say for definite if it came from the stuff we found in Neil Pollock's studio.'

'Okay, cheers, Kiera, it's something, I suppose...'

'But if it *was* Pollock and Hogarth, what's their motive, Boss?' asked Grace.

'Don't know yet,' he replied might just be some dark, perverse fetish, maybe they've developed a hatred for women for some reason; let's have a closer look at their marriages. By all accounts, Pollock's wasn't as rosy as first appearances might suggest and, as yet, we know absolutely nothing about Hogarth's...'

He stood up,

'...which brings us back to plan A. Right Bri, let's go and question him further, see if we can get a feel of how things are in the Hogarth household. Listen, the rest of you, if you can spend a couple of hours going through everything again, see if Merseyside Police come up with anything then call it a day. If we can be in for about ten tomorrow then we'll see where we're at.'

∿∿∿

'He's not here.'

Nadia Hogarth was a well-dressed and attractive sixty-something woman, strong featured and with an athletic build that suggested an expensive gym membership. She stood on the doorstep of the ground floor flat in Quarriers Village, the converted former children's home near Bridge of Weir. Grant waited for an invitation to enter but it wasn't forthcoming.

'I see. Could we come in please, Mrs Hogarth?

'What for?'

'Mrs Hogarth, we'd like a wee chat with you about your husband,' said Briony, her tone gentler that her boss'.

'What about my husband?'

'Mrs Hogarth, we can stand here if you like but it would be better off we come in rather than conduct an interview on your doorstep,' said Grant, a hint of authority in his tone.

'So, I'm being interviewed now, am I?' replied Nadia Hogarth, in an equally hostile tone. Briony tried again.

'Please, Mrs Hogarth...listen, can I call you Nadia?'

'No, you can't, actually. If this is a formal interview then let's keep it formal.'

She took a step backwards, her features contorted in an expression of annoyance.

'Hmph. I suppose you'd better come in, then.'

She turned sharply away from them and they followed her into the flat. Although spacious and tastefully furnished, it was, somehow, impersonal and very slightly unwelcoming, as if reflecting Nadia Hogarth's personality. She ushered them into the high-ceilinged sitting room, gesturing offhandedly towards a large but rather austere-looking leather settee. She sat on the chair opposite, crossing her legs and clasping her hands over one knee; rather primly, Grant thought. She glared at them, her hostility almost tangible.

Christ, another woman that seems to hate me...

'Well?'

Grant looked at Briony and nodded, although he wasn't entirely convinced that her charm would work on Nadia Hogarth.

'Mrs Hogarth, I take it you know about Neil Pollock?'

The woman narrowed her eyes.

'Are you referring to my knowledge of his affair with my husband or to his attempted murder?'

'Both, actually.'

'Then yes, I am aware of both facts.'

'Mrs Hogarth, are you aware of where your husband spent last weekend?'

'Yes.'

Briony sighed; she was losing her patience.

'Let me put our cards on the table, Mrs Hogarth. Neil Pollock is...was, our prime suspect for the two murders in Linwood. We believe that the murderer entered the changing rooms dressed as a woman and we believe that both the attire and the wig that the murderer wore were the same as those worn by Neil Pollock when...em...when he was with your husband.'

She looked at Nadia but there was no response; the woman's brows were knitted in a frown and her lips were pursed, but she remained silent.

'Your husband has provided Mr Pollock with an alibi, claiming that they were both in a hotel in North Berwick at the time. Can you corroborate this or do you have any doubts about its validity?'

Nadia's frown intensified.

'You are aware who my husband is?'

'Yes, we are.'

'And that he is a barrister—one of Scotland's foremost barristers, I may add.'

'Yes, we're aware of that also.'

Grant was equally aware that Briony was modifying her Glenrothes accent somewhat. She seemed nervous; he had never before seen his sergeant even slightly intimidated, but he decided to allow the interview to proceed...for the moment.

'I don't suppose you are aware that I am also a barrister?'

'Em, no, I wasn't.'

'No, I thought not. So, despite my husband's infidelity and depravity, I am not going to tell you anything that may incriminate either him or myself. I realise that I am not under caution and, presumably I am not a suspect...'

Given the woman's somewhat aggressive attitude, Grant wasn't entirely certain about this.

'So, there is nothing further that I am prepared to say.'

Grant decided it was time to take over.

'That's fine, Mrs Hogarth, you are within your rights. Can I ask, though, do you know where your husband is at present?'

Nadia Hogarth paused, considering the question.

'Yes. We have a flat in Highburgh Road, in Glasgow's West End. Our son lived there when he was at University and we retained it...'

She paused, her expression changing very slightly.

'I will tell you this much. Nicholas had recently stated that he was leaving me, that he was intending to live with this... Pollock person...'

She spat out the name as if it was poisonous.

'...following discussion, it was decided that I would retain the flat here and that he would take the flat in the West End to live with this "new-found love" of his...'

She italicised the phrase with her fingers as she spoke, a sneer on her lips. Then, to Grant and Briony's surprise, her veneer started to slip. She bowed her head as she half-mumbled

'Thirty-five years. Thirty-five bloody years and now he's decided he's gay...'

The mask returned; she looked up again.

'So that's it. I'll provide you with the exact address and I'll ask you not to trouble me any further...'

CHAPTER 14

En route to interview Nicholas Hogarth, they had taken a detour to Peckham's, one of Grant's, and Glasgow's West End's, favourite delicatessens.

'Aw, for fuck sake...'

Briony looked at the empty shop, the sign above the window still proclaiming its provenance.

'Looks like it's closed, Boss...'

He shook his head. It had been such an institution.

'What now?' his sergeant asked.

He didn't answer. He remembered the smell, the coffee, the staff...all gone.

Bugger...

'Don't know...drive on, let's see what else there is...'

Eventually they found a convenience store and, a few minutes later, they had picked up some sandwiches and were sitting in Briony's car, eating what seemed to Grant to be two pieces of cardboard filled with a meagre layer of limp bacon and dry, unappetising egg. At least he had a packet of tomato sauce crisps to look forward to.

'Just not the bloody same, this...' he mumbled.

Briony's egg salad wasn't much better but at least she didn't have to suffer the smell of Gorgonzola...

Thank God...!

Grant finished his crisps, washed them down with some Irn-Bru, wiped his hands carelessly on his trousers and said, 'Right, let's go and see what our friend Hogarth has to say...'

'Can I no' finish my lunch first, eh? No wonder you get bloody indigestion, Boss.'

'Isn't that what Rennies are for...?'

A few minutes later they set off for Highburgh Road. As expected, the streets were packed with cars, the only spaces available reserved for residential permit holders. Grant pointed to one of these.

'Pull in there, Bri, we can leave the mileage log on the dashboard, just in case...'

She frowned; the old dodge for illegally parking an unmarked police vehicle wasn't always known to work, especially with an embittered traffic warden. Still, there didn't seem to be any option.

'Aye, fine. Right, the entrance to Hogarth's tenement is just along there. Nice flats, always kinda fancied the West End, bit more up-market than Ibrox!'

'Bit pricier too, mind. Right, let's go.'

They headed along then turned into the entrance; the small front garden was neat and tidy, with slate chips, some in-season pots and a small bench, discreetly chained to the roan-pipe. They climbed the well-worn stone steps and looked at the list of names beside the controlled-entry door.

'There he is—top floor. Ready Boss?'

'Yup.'

They pressed the buzzer and waited for a few moments.

'Doesn't look like anybody...oh, here we go.'

Hogarth's deep voice resonated from the intercom.

'Who is it, please?'

'DCI McVicar and DS Quinn, Mr Hogarth. Can we have a word, please?'

There was a pause before he responded.

'Oh, very well, it's the top floor, left hand door.'

The lock buzzed and they entered a typical, Glasgow West End "close"; the walls were covered to dado height in what looked like the original green and brown highly-glazed ceramic wall tiles, embossed with an attractive Art Deco pattern. Above these was pale-cream painted plaster. It was spotless and smelled strongly of disinfectant.

'Not your usual student den of iniquity then' Grant mumbled, as they plodded up the scrubbed stone stairs. They arrived at the top landing, which was adorned with a variety of healthy pot-plants. However, despite Hogarth's invitation, the door was firmly closed.

'Hm, he doesn't seem particularly keen to see us, does he, Bri?'

'Nope.'

Grant gave his customary knock on the door and, for a moment, Briony, just like Superintendent Minto, was tempted to respond with two answering knocks. She smiled; somehow it reminded her of her childhood. As they heard footsteps approaching from within, Grant turned towards her, raising a dark eyebrow.

'What?'

'Och, nothin' Boss. I'll tell you later...'

The door opened; Hogarth was casually dressed in grey jogging bottoms and a Scotland rugby top. He noticed Grant looking at it and favoured him with a slight smile.

'Are you a player, Chief Inspector?'

'Used to be, at school and Uni; second-row forward.'

'Hm, tough position, I was a front-liner myself...anyway, you'd better come in.'

Although bright and spacious, the flat lacked the neat formality of his recently-estranged wife's more ordered accommodation; instead, it appeared cosy and somewhat cluttered with an eclectic assortment of books, antiques and rugby memorabilia. The walls were lined with an apparently haphazard array of paintings, prints and photographs. They were ushered to a slightly battered—but extremely comfortable—couch, over which was draped a large, tartan throw. Hogarth sat down and leaned forward in his chair, lowering his head and looking at them from under his bushy brows as he regarded them; Grant felt as if he was about to be cross-examined.

'So, officers, what can I do to help you this time?'

Hogarth emphasised the last two words. Grant wasn't quite sure where to start.

'Well, we've been to see your wife, Mr Hogarth...'

'I assumed as much, given that I didn't disclose this address. Go on...'

'Can you confirm that you and your wife have separated?'

Hogarth sat back with an indignant grunt

'God, she doesn't waste any time...yes, Nadia and I have gone our separate ways.'

'I see. Can I ask, is Neil Pollock planning on staying here?'

'You'd have to ask him. He is welcome, of course, but the final decision is his alone.'

'Fine, we'll be speaking to him later. Can we turn to the alibi that you have provided for Mr Pollock?'

Hogarth's expression became more severe.

Christ, I bet he's good in court...

'And why, may I ask? Presumably you've checked it with the hotel and I have no doubt that they have corroborated it.'

'They've corroborated that you stayed there, Mr Hogarth, but that's about it. Apparently, you breakfasted in your room, you didn't dine in the hotel restaurant at any point and no-one seems to have seen either of you during the day.'

Hogarth leaned forward again and Grant could see the colour rise in the man's cheeks.

'Just what are your suggestion *now*, Chief Inspector?'

'I'm not suggesting anything, Mr Hogarth. I'm merely stating that your alibi only covers the fact that you and Mr Pollock stayed in the hotel. Can I ask what you did for the rest of the time; on the Sunday in particular?'

Hogarth scowled.

'We went for a walk, if you must know; we drove to Dunbar and parked our car down at the harbour. We had lunch in a local cafe then walked along the shore and onto the edge of the golf course. It's a lovely, quiet walk, a good couple of hours if you go all the way along.'

Grant paused, then looked at Briony, who took up the questioning.

'An' that's it, Mr Hogarth? The two of you went for a walk; alone, presumably?'

'Of course, who else would be with us?'

'Exactly, Sir. Did you see, or speak to, anyone?'

'Not as far as I can remember; there may have been a few golfers out but it was a bit blowy, as I recall. Other than an occasional nod to a fellow walker, we spoke to no-one.'

'Hm, that is unfortunate, Sir, as it does leave your alibi pretty wide open, doesn't it?'

Hogarth dropped his head again and stared menacingly at Briony. Grant reckoned it was probably second nature to the man after years of intimidating the poor sods in the witness box...his sergeant, however, seemed impervious. Maybe Mrs Hogarth had been a good practise run for her...

'What do you mean by that, Sergeant?'

'Well, Sir, you breakfasted in your room, you left the hotel and drove to Dunbar, you went for a walk, unaccompanied by other persons...basically no-one other than you and Mr Pollock can corroborate your story...'

'We don't need anyone else, Sergeant...'

'You might, Mr Hogarth' interjected Grant. 'You see, if you think about it, there was plenty of time for you and Mr Pollock to return to Linwood, to...'

Nicky Hogarth jumped to his feet.

'How dare you? Neil and I had nothing to do with those vile murders and I strongly resent the insinuation. Now, if you have any evidence to back up your veiled accusations, then by all means take me into custody. If not, then I must ask you to leave...'

Grant remained seated.

'Mr Hogarth, I am not making any accusations, I am investigating the murder of two innocent women; and before we leave, can I ask you if you can give any further explanation as to how an item of underwear belonging to one of the victims came to be in Mr Pollock's holdall?'

Hogarth stared at Grant and sat back down, his anger subsiding. He remained silent for a few moments.

'No, Chief Inspector, I can't and, as a barrister, I have to admit that it is a pretty damning piece of evidence. But you have my absolute assurance that neither of us placed it there. As I have said, neither of us had any involvement in these dreadful murders...'

He paused again, a troubled look on his face.

'...actually, I've been giving it considerable thought. As far as I can see, the only people who had access to the holdall were either Neil's wife or the hotel staff. I think we can rule out the latter; after all, we had minimal contact with them and there is absolutely no reason why any of them should place the item in Neil's bag It was the first time we'd stayed there, they knew nothing about us; and, of course, by implication, they would need to have committed the murders, wouldn't they?'

Grant nodded his agreement.

'Yes, they would.'

'Which, assuming that to be highly unlikely, leaves Sandie Pollock...'

Aye, Sandie bloody Pollock...

Hogarth stood up again, less forcefully this time. Grant and Briony followed suit, realising that the interview was now over. As they were shown silently to the door, Grant turned.

'Of course, I must ask you not to go anywhere without informing us, Mr Hogarth. We may need to talk further about this...'

'I am fully aware of the situation, Chief Inspector. However, I have absolutely nothing to hide and I haven't the slightest intention of going anywhere, other than my place of work. Actually, I'm taking a few days off as I need to be available for Neil when he gets out of hospital, so I'll be here or hereabouts. Goodbye.'

The door closed with a solid thump. Grant and Briony exchanged a look.

'Well, that's us told...'

Grant had gone back into Osprey House to make an attempt at tidying his desk and was wading through the sundry paperwork that seemed to have accumulated during the current investigation. The building was quiet, his team having headed home for some well-earned rest. He sat back, his hands clasped behind his head; once it was all over, he should really arrange something better than a curry. Maybe they could go somewhere nicer for a change, something a bit fancier. He smiled; no, if they solved the case, a curry was the traditional thing...

The smile disappeared and he sat forward as it suddenly hit him.

"If" Grant? There's no bloody "if" about it. "When... I can't let the bloody side down...

After another half an hour he gave up and drove back to Bluebell Cottage. As he approached the dark, deserted cottage, his heart sank; despite the brevity of their liaison, he missed Delia. In fact, he missed her badly. He opened the door, feeling a chill as he entered the house. Had he forgotten to set the heating? A cursory examination of the boiler in the kitchen showed a number of red lights that looked entirely unfamiliar and, try as he might, it failed to operate.

Fuck...!

He went into his lounge, set a fire in the wood-burner and waited for the room to heat up. An hour later and it was reasonably cosy but he knew the rest of the house would be uncomfortably cold; it wasn't much of a prospect for a Saturday night. He sat on the couch and took out his phone, staring in dismay at the shattered screen. He scrolled to Delia's number and, once again, his thumb hovered over the call button...

She had cried; they had laughed a bit, they had talked, but forty minutes later he ended the call, his heart heavy. Delia had told him that she loved him, that she missed him, but that she felt that it had all happened too quickly and that they should take time to think about what each of them wanted. He knew that he had hurt her (just as he knew he had hurt Tina Sturrock) and there was little he could say. Sorry really wasn't sufficient...

He sat in the darkness, the flickering of the burning logs casting a warm glow in the room. He stared out of the patio doors, the lights of the various scattered houses and farm-steadings twinkling mysteriously in the valley below. He loved this view but tonight the magic failed to materialise. He realised that he was hungry but the thought of preparing a meal in the cold of his kitchen didn't appeal to him. He stood up; he would drive down to Lochwinnoch and treat himself to a black-pudding supper; to hell with heartburn...

'It's the good life...'

The Dean Martin song came into his head as he stood in the queue in La Dolce Vita, his local fish and chip shop. The smell was making his mouth water as he leaned his back against the wall, waiting for the fresh batch of hot, golden chips to be netted from the bubbling oil and tossed into the cabinet. He had nodded at one or two vaguely familiar faces, half-hoping and half-dreading meeting someone he knew...

He had toyed with calling Tina; maybe he could explain, maybe he could make amends but, in the end, he had decided against it. He had wounded this amazing woman, the woman that he had been so looking forward to taking for dinner, the woman he had hoped to...

'Puddin' supper?'

'Eh? Oh, aye, that's me.'

'Salt and vinegar, pet?'

'Aye, and a couple o' onions please.'

The condiments were liberally sprinkled, causing his mouth to water even more. He rummaged in his pocket for some change, adding two sachets of tomato ketchup to his order. Finally, he lifted the takeaway bag and headed back to his pick-up; should he take it back to his cold, lonely house?

Bugger that...!

Five minutes later, he was sitting in the dark, near-empty car park at Castle Semple Loch, staring out at its oily surface that reflected the few distant lights from the houses on the opposite hillside. He had driven to the far end, near the rowing club, its gate firmly closed and padlocked just like his memories of the previous year's tragic events; the water was calm and still—perfect rowing conditions. Suddenly, the clouds parted and the near-full moon revealed herself, shining silver on the loch's surface; it was a little piece of magic. He knew that a few of the more accomplished rowers occasionally went rowing in the moonlight, small cycle lights attached to both bow and stern of their boat. It was something he aspired to; one day, if he was proficient enough, experienced enough, he had hoped he might be invited. Now? Well...

He munched his way through his dinner, slugging yet another can of Irn-Bru and only too well aware that he would regret it later. Maybe Briony was right, maybe his digestion was faulty, but what the hell...

His repast was finished, the only reminder the smell of chips that would undoubtedly linger for a couple of days; there were a few cars further along the car park, presumably couples looking for a bit of privacy for amorous pursuits. He envied them; oh, to be young, carefree...and in love! Their headlights shone out on to the water, at one point illuminating a couple of swans gliding sedately across the loch, a lot more graceful than his rowing, he mused! The moon had hidden herself once more and he sat back, staring into the velvety darkness, lost in his thoughts...

He had never felt so lonely in his entire life...

He picked up his phone and looked at the cracked screen; three twenty-two and, as expected, his stomach was in turmoil. He sat up, immediately aware of how cold the house was without the heating. He pulled on his thick dressing gown and made his way to the bathroom, where relief was to be found; alas, the packet of Rennies was empty, as was the bottle of Gaviscon.

Fuck...

The last resort—some hot milk. He went into the kitchen, filled a jug and put it in the microwave, standing shivering as it heated. Once it had pinged, he poured the steaming white balm into a large mug and made his way back to the bedroom; it was uncomfortably cold. He realised that sleep would be some way off and he decided that the lounge may be marginally warmer. However, before he went through, he opened the drawer in the cabinet beside his bed and removed the little Chinese-silk bound diary; the book that contained his innermost thoughts. The last entry had been months previously; maybe it was time for an update...

So here we are again. O sleep why dost thou leave me...?

Well, tonight it's indigestion, of course. What else could it possibly be—apart from heartache, loneliness, guilt, misery...

What a fucking mess. Delia, Tina, Louise...Ronnie, even. Oh, and Jackie, my ex-wife; how in God's name did I forget that disastrous interlude? But Ronnie Pettigrew summed it up perfectly. "Grant, you're hopeless with women..."

She's right—I bloody am. And am I any better with my investigations, I ask myself? Where are we this time? I haven't a clue who killed these two women; theories, yes, but actual proof... no! And is my judgement being clouded yet again in my quest to implicate the Pettigrews? God only knows; maybe I should chuck it altogether, let the younger ones take over. Maybe I'm getting too old for this shit...maybe I'm just getting too old period...

O sleep why dost thou leave me, why thy visionary joys remove...
O fuck off...

~~~

Briony looked at her boss and immediately knew that he'd had a bad night. She was aware of many possible reasons and she knew that he'd come out of his mood eventually; as did the rest of the team, fortunately. They were a loyal group, she knew, and they were learning to cope with DCI McVicar's various moods. Basically, shut up and get on with it...

He was sitting, coffee in hand, staring morosely out of the window at the gloom of the spring morning. She shook her head; it was time for action, if not by her boss then by her...she stood up.

'Right, what's the plan today, Boss, eh?'

'What? Oh, em, right then...'

He rubbed his hand over his head.

'Okay, let's look over it all again...'

They had done this a good number of times, Briony thought. *Still, best keep him happy...!*

'Right, Hogarth and Pollock. An alibi, for sure, but a pretty weak one. Apart from the fact that they stayed in the hotel, there are no witnesses to confirm that they stayed in the area.

No motive as yet but plenty of circumstantial evidence; Pollock was left-handed, as was the murderer and he had access to brass picture-wire, at present the apparent choice of murder weapon. He has admitted that he owns the same clothes that the murderer wore and, "de-wigged," he pretty much matches the description from the CCTV. Then there's that item of underwear...'

He looked across to Sam and Kiera.

'Okay, once we're done, give the hotel a call and head back over too North Berwick, see if the weekend staff have anything more to say.'

'Sure, Boss' replied Kiera.

'Faz, any word from Liverpool on Hopkins and Malone?'

'Nope, Boss, nothing.'

'Bugger. I'd hoped we could get hold of at least one of them, although it's debatable if they'd give us any information on who actually took out the contract on Pollock. I take it she'll let us know if they find them?'

'Yes, DCI Owen said she'd keep trying...'

Grant knew it was a rather hollow assurance; his Liverpool counterpart's resources were likely to be as overstretched as his own and hunting for two suspects from an enquiry a few hundred miles away wouldn't necessarily make its way to the top of the priority list.

'Okay, maybe try again later. Cliff, any word from your Dad—is he home yet?'

His DC made an apologetic face.

'Sorry Boss, he messaged ma Maw, says he'll be coming down later now; apparently they had a skinfull last night and none o' them'll be fit tae drive until the afternoon.'

Grant scowled and seemed about to have a rant when he caught Briony's warning look.

'Em, right, can you let me know as soon as you get hold of him?'

'Aye, will do, Boss.'

He stared out of the window; a thought was beginning to take shape.

'Faz, we didn't get anything on CCTV showing the suspect getting into a car, did we?'

'No, Boss. We checked and double-checked, but there was no sign of Pollock entering a vehicle.'

'So, what if...what if Hogarth *did* drive Pollock to Linwood, dropped him at Asda then drove to Tesco to wait for him? It's a bit of a walk but it would explain the lack of a vehicle.'

'Or maybe he parked in one of the other car parks, Boss,' said Sam. 'Pollock could have walked from the Showcase Cinema or one of the other retail areas. Then there's the fast food outlets, they probably have cameras too. It's not far really, Hogarth could have waited there then driven Pollock across to Tesco.'

'Good point. Right, Faz, this is going to involve a hell of a lot of painstaking work but we need to try and get access to the CCTV in the locus between the two stores. Find out what car Hogarth drives; either phone him or his wife, although I doubt you'll get much joy with the latter. We know that Pollock drives a yellow Porsche so it should be easy enough to spot, although we'd probably have noticed it already. As you said, Sam, there's the cinema, there's a few food outlets and then there's all the garages...'

He paused, realising the enormity of the task he was setting.

'...actually, we need a plan...'

Ten minutes later, the plan was in place. As previously agreed, Kiera and Sam were to drive back though to North Berwick, having ascertained that some different members of staff would be on duty. Faz was going to do the rounds of the various locations where either Hogarth or Pollock may have parked; once each CCTV system was accessed, one of them would remain at each location to trawl through the images from the previous Sunday. Eventually, they should manage to cover them all. Eventually...

'Sorry guys, it's going to be a pretty miserable task, but hopefully it'll turn something up.'

The team were preparing to leave and Faz was packing up his laptop when his phone rang. He looked at Grant with an expression of anticipation.

'DCI Owen, Boss.'

He answered the call, spoke for a few moments, then said

'Right, I'll let you speak to my Boss, DCI McVicar. Cheers... and thanks very much, Ma'am, I really appreciate it...'

Grant took the phone, returning Faz's wide grin.

'Hello, Grant McVicar...'

Following what sounded like a car chase from a Hollywood blockbuster, Liverpool's finest had apprehended Gary Hopkins and were holding him in custody for a variety of offences, including those committed north of the border. DCI Lara Owen, by all accounts a competent and rather fearsome officer, had already interviewed the detainee but, at present, he was giving nothing away.

'He's a righ' tight lipped little booger,' she said, in her broad Scouse tones. Grant could have listened to her speak all day, the melodic, comforting accent reminding him of childhood days spent listening to Ringo Starr narrating "Thomas the Tank Engine..."

'Won't say a bloody word about who 'ired him. Listen Grant, I don't know if you want to coom down yersel', or send one of your officers; he's pretty immune to us but someone from up your way migh' just put the fear o' God into the little shit...'

Grant had ended the call with profuse thanks. He knew that someone such as Hopkins would be a tough nut to crack; hired professional thugs rarely gave away their employers, usually for reasons of self-preservation! But it might be worth the effort, the only problem being that his staff was now seriously depleted. He considered the situation for a moment as the four remaining officers awaited their instructions.

'Right, I'm going to stay up here. Faz, you still need to get on with the CCTV stuff. Cliff, you go with him as planned and I'll come along and do my bit...'

He looked at his sergeant.

'Briony, sorry, I know it's a trek and it'll mean a late night, but could you head down to Liverpool and interview Hopkins; as Lara Owen suggested, try and put the fear of God into him...'

Should I...?

He looked at Grace, who was standing with a slightly expectant look on her pretty face.

'...and you can go with her, Grace, it'll be good experience for you. The sergeant will keep you right on what to say and what not to say. If you're okay with it, that is?'

She smiled; Grant had his answer.

CHAPTER 15

'*Have you ever been to* Liverpool, Sarge?'

'Nope; always fancied it, mind you, seems to be a pretty cool place. What about you, Grace?'

'Went for the weekend once when I was at Uni. From what I recall, it involved quite a lot of alcohol!

She smiled at the memory—or lack of it, Briony supposed.

'Okay Sarge, left here. Corporation Road should be a couple of hundred yards...yup, there it is.'

It had been a long and tedious journey but the two officers had chatted easily, stopping briefly at Tebay Services for a coffee and some fast-food. However, they were glad to finally reach their destination, Merseyside Police's Wirral Custody Suite. They drew up outside the secure gates, set between high brick walls, and Grace turned to Briony with a wry smile.

'Sounds more like a hotel, Sarge; I mean, a bloomin' suite!'

'Maybe they look after them better down here, Grace, might not be a bad thing to paint a picture of life in Barlinnie...'

She announced their arrival in the intercom and the gate slid open; as they drove in and the gate shut behind them, the feeling of being locked up was tangible...and terrible.

～～～

Briony and Grace were seated in the hot, stuffy interview room number 2; it was little different from those in their local custody unit at Helen Street. Inside, the centre itself was clean and well-lit, the corridors bright and reasonably airy, the biggest difference being the accent of the various occupants!

Across the table, a truculent, gum-chewing man reclined in the chair, heavily-tattooed arms folded across a broad chest. His well-developed triceps were evident beneath the tight black Under Armour t-shirt and he wore a single gold earring in his left ear. Briony stared at him dispassionately; he was a fit, muscular and reasonably handsome man, probably in his early forties, but with an extremely hard, menacing edge. Clean-shaven, very short dark hair, piercing green eyes and thinnish lips, currently set in a supercilious smile as he eyed up Briony and Grace as if they were goods on offer. Apart from the fact that he was undoubtedly a "hard man" on the wrong side of the law, Briony took an immediate dislike to him, as did Grace, judging by her expression of distaste.

Seated beside him was his even harder-faced solicitor, an unnatural blonde, probably in her late fifties but vainly attempting to look ten years younger. Her pursed, thin lips and grey skin identified her as a heavy smoker, confirmed by her deep, throaty voice; she had introduced herself as the rather exotically named Carmen McGarrigle. Once the recording had started and the customary introductions made, she looked across at Briony.

'I'm afraid you've had a wasted journey, Officers. Me client has nothin' to say.'

Briony's gaze swivelled from Hopkins to his solicitor, whose accent reminded her of Lily Savage.

'And why is that, Ms McGarrigle?'

'Mr Hopkins 'as been residing in Liverpool for the last few months; he 'asn't been north of the border for years. We may as well terminate the interview...'

Briony turned away from the woman and addressed Hopkins directly.

'Mr Hopkins...'

He grinned at her, revealing expensive-looking teeth.

'Yeah, sweedheart?'

Briony paused but didn't respond to his deliberate attempt to rile her.

'Have you ever had any dealings with either a Helena, or Ellie, or a Veronica, or Ronnie, Pettigrew?'

He raised an eyebrow but remained silent as he continued to chew on the piece of worn-out gum.

'Hm. Can I ask, then, have you heard of a Neil Pollock?'

Hopkins grinned as he kept on chewing; he shook his head.

'Nope, love, never 'eard of 'im either.'

'I see.'

She paused and made a show of consulting her notes, then looked back up at Hopkins.

'I take it, then, that it wasn't you and a Mr...'

Again, she looked, unnecessarily, at her notes.

'...Marcus Malone who abducted Mr Pollock on...'

Carmen McGarrigle interrupted.

'I've already made it quite clear that me client 'asn't been in Scotland for years, Sergeant, so I suggest you don't...'

This time it was Grace who interrupted.

'You realise, Mr Hopkins, that as well as abduction and assault, you're facing a charge of *attempted* murder...'

Hopkins' smarmy smile faltered and his eyes narrowed very slightly. It was Briony's turn to smile.

'You see, Mr Hopkins, apart from having been rather severely assaulted, Mr Pollock is alive and well...and quite ready to identify the persons who beat him, threw petrol over him and told him that "Teeny Braid sends her regards..."

This time Hopkins turned and looked nervously at his solicitor but, before she could speak, Grace continued.

'You know, I'd have thought that any hired thugs worth their salt would have checked that the sprinkler system was switched off before they tried to burn their victim alive...'

Gary Hopkins just stared at Grace, his eyes widening as Briony continued.

'Yes, Mr Hopkins, that was pretty shoddy work, wasn't it, eh? Tell me, when you were contracted to kill Mr Pollock, did you offer a money-back guarantee to your employers...?'

~~~

They were sitting having a welcome coffee with DCI Owen, currently extolling the virtues of her beloved home city, when a uniformed constable sought them.

'Excuse me, but the prisoner is ready to see you again.'

'Thanks, luv, nice of him to fit us in...'

The constable grinned back at her as they rose.

'Righ', girls, away an' see what this piece o' work as to say for 'imself now. I'll be out 'ere somewhere...'

~~~

Grant rubbed his face, then his eyes, which were dry and itchy; someone had once told him that your blink-rate slows down when you stare at a computer screen and, after what seemed like hours, he could well believe it. He sat back and sighed. He had trawled through footage from nearly every camera angle outside the cinema, situated only a few hundred yards from the Asda store where the first murder had taken place, but there was no sign of Pollock (in either guise), of Hogarth or of Hogarth's silver Lexus saloon.

His stomach growled; he realised that, somehow, he had missed lunch and he stood up, massaging his aching shoulders. The cinema now offered a reasonable range of fast-food and drink, including alcohol; he'd stretch his legs and grab something to eat, then phone Cliff... again!

He was glad to get moving after being seated for so long. It was years since he'd had to spend time staring at CCTV footage and he remembered just how much he disliked it. He made his way out of the office and across the foyer towards the central counter; for some reason, he fancied a hot dog. As he approached, a woman picked up a bag of popcorn and a large drink container then turned towards him.

It was Tina Sturrock.

For a few seconds he froze, as did she. Then she looked away and made to walk past him, but he put out his hand, grabbing her arm lightly.

'Tina...'

She turned and gave him a look of pure loathing.

'Get your hand off me, Grant McVicar.'

He released his grip and took a step back.

'Tina, I'm so, so sorry...'

He was aware of a wiry, silver haired man watching the proceedings and recognised him as another member of the rowing club, presumably waiting for Tina. He felt his stomach clench very slightly as Tina hissed

'Frankly, I don't give a fuck.'

She turned away again, taking a few steps towards the man, who was now glancing at his watch.

'Tina, please, can I at least try and explain...'

She handed the popcorn to the man then turned back to face Grant. As she did so, she took the lid from the drink then, without warning, threw the entire contents straight into his face before striding angrily away, leaving Grant standing dripping ice-cold cola over his clothes, his shoes and the carpet. He stood, open-mouthed, as Tina and her date walked towards the auditorium, arm-in-arm. A few people were now watching with considerable amusement and, finally, he turned and made hastily for the sanctuary of the office, feeling angry, humiliated...and extremely jealous!

Once inside the small room, he realised that he would have to go home and change; he was both saturated and sticky. He had a brief word with the manager, making the excuse that he had spilled his drink, but he could see the disbelief on the man's face as he looked at Grant's cola-streaked face and soaking clothes. Anyway, like any such organisation, there was bound to be a healthy grapevine and, finally, he exited the warmth of the cinema, feeling his clothes sticking uncomfortably to his damp skin as the evening chill irrevocably set in.

~~~~

As soon as he entered Bluebell Cottage, he remembered that the heating wasn't operational; the house was chilled and unwelcoming. He entered the bathroom and turned on the shower, stripping off his wet clothes as he waited for the water to heat up. Finally, he stepped into the cubicle, letting out a cry as the icy cold jet sprayed onto his already goose-pimpled flesh; of course—the water wasn't heating either! He turned off the shower and stepped back out of the cubicle, then sat down on the toilet seat, cold, wet, sticky and miserable. He could have wept...

His phone was ringing and he stood up, rummaging amongst his cola-stained clothes. He pulled it out of his trouser pocket and looked in dismay at the cracked screen. He had completely forgotten; he was supposed to be having dinner at Louise's that night.

Fuck...fuck...fuck...

~~~~

Fifty minutes later, clad in an old tracksuit and with a change of clothes hastily stuffed into a bag, he arrived on Louise's doorstep, a bottle of wine in one hand and a sheepish grin on his face.

'Louise, I'm so sorry...'

She smiled and touched his cheek as he entered.

'Grant, I was married to a cop, I'm used to it...what the hell happened?'

The explanation of the spilled drink sounded thin and they both knew it but, thankfully, she accepted it at face value.

'Right, I've delayed dinner but the boys are starving. You away up and get a quick shower and you can eat when you're...'

She looked him up and down then grinned.

'...a bit more presentable!'

He ran up the stairs, half expecting Finn and Callum to be lying in wait for him, then entered the neat, tidy bathroom. He closed the door, relieved to finally be warm and looking forward to being clean. A large, fluffy white towel was draped over the radiator and he switched on the tap before stripping off once more, quickly checking the water before he entered, just to be on the safe side...

He took longer than usual, savouring the stream of hot, soothing water as it coursed over his tall, muscular frame. Finally, he turned it off, aware that the Thackray family were undoubtedly downstairs, impatiently awaiting their dinner. He turned and slid the shower door open, reaching for the towel. On the way up, he was sure he'd smelled roast beef...

~~~

'Well, I suppose that were to be expected, Briony.'

Briony Quinn tried not to show her annoyance.

'I know, Ma'am, but it's a pain; what's the chances of you picking up Malone, eh?'

DCI Lara Owen shook her head.

'Not good, to be honest. Catchin' Hopkins were a piece o' luck, really; the traffic boys saw 'im speeding, ran a check on the car – stolen, of course – then they chased 'im. But Malone could be anywhere—I know he's got family in Ireland; he might even have crossed the sea for all we know. It'll be even harder now if he knows we've got Hopkins in custody.'

Briony sighed; she had to agree with DCI Owen. Having found out that their intended victim had survived the murder attempt, it was always going to be likely that Hopkins would lay the blame at Marcus Malone's door, especially when the latter had vanished without trace. He now claimed that he had been employed only as the driver and had no prior knowledge of the identity of his employers, the victim or the reason for their remit to murder him. He would be held in remand as an accessory, not to mention for his other, local crimes, but without his testimony it was unlikely that any link to the Pettigrew family could be established. Briony knew that Grant would be bitterly disappointed.

'Okay, thanks, Ma'am. Listen, I'd best go and call my boss, give him the bad news...'

∼∼∼

Half an hour later, having bid their farewells to DCI Owen, they were back in Briony's car, pulling out on to Corporation road.

'Try him again, Grace. I'd have thought he'd answer; he'll be anxious to know what we've found out.'

Although I very much doubt he'll be best pleased...

Grace tried Grant's number but, after four rings, it switched to his terse voice-mail message

"DCI Grant McVicar. Leave your name, number and message. I'll call you back."

'Em, it's Grace Boss. We've interviewed Hopkins, if you'd like to give us a call. Bye.'

Briony frowned; where the hell was he?

∼∼∼

At that moment in time, Grant, having decided to switch off his phone, was actually beginning to feel human again. As always, the meal had been delicious—roast beef, Yorkshire puddings, an apple crumble to follow, the works! The boys had been in great form and Louise, who had finished a half bottle of red wine, had seemed almost back to her usual self. He knew that she had made an effort; her hair was shiny and nicely cut, she was wearing a navy shirt and nicely fitting jeans. She was a lovely woman and

any man would be proud to have her as his wife, his partner...
whatever...

Aye, any man except me...!

She looked at him and furrowed her brows slightly.

'Penny for them, Grant?'

'Och, nothing, Louise. Listen, that was a fantastic meal, I really
enjoyed it. I'm stuffed now!'

Finn suddenly grabbed at Grant's arm.

'Uncle Grant, Mum says that I can get a guitar—they're giving
lessons at school and it'd be really cool!'

Louise made a face; music didn't seem to run in their family.

'Nice one, Finn, that *would* be cool...girls really go for guys that
play an instrument, especially if you're in a band!'

Louise laughed at Finn's sudden expression of alarm; girls
weren't quite on her eldest son's radar yet...

~~~

It was time to leave; the boys were upstairs and Grant's eyes were
beginning to close. He stood at the door, feeling the chill of the
night air, reluctant to return to the greater chill of the currently
unheated Bluebell Cottage.

'Thanks Louise, that was just what I needed.'

'It's not that late, Grant. You're sure you won't stay, have a wee
nightcap? The spare room's always ready.'

He was torn; although very slightly false, the evening of family
life had stirred a vague longing somewhere deep inside him and
he was reluctant to end it. He shook his head.

'Best not, I'm pretty busy with this case...'

'Oh well...'

He reached forward to give her the customary "goodnight"
embrace and she did the same but, somehow, they misjudged it.
Unexpectedly, their lips met and, for a brief moment, they kissed.
He pulled away and mumbled "sorry" but she looked into his
eyes, shaking her head ever so slightly as she whispered

'Don't be, Grant...'

∿∿∿

Fifteen minutes later he was sitting just round the corner from her house, staring down the deserted Paisley street, his mind in turmoil. Had the kiss really been an accident? Had Louise planned it? And had the shadow at the top of the stairs been Finn, watching...hoping...

Shit...

He had never told Louise about Brian's final message where, having seen Grant's car outside the house, his friend had assumed that Grant and Louise were having an affair. He probably never would, but he was still ridden with guilt, wondering if Brian had driven his car into the wall deliberately; he would never know... and he could never be with her for that very reason.

He pulled out his phone and switched it on. Once it had booted up, he saw that there had been at least four phone calls and several text messages, all of which he had missed.

Bugger...!

The first two missed calls were from Briony and Grace, the second two from Sam. He dialled the first number and Grace answered, the background noise indicating that they were still on their way back from Liverpool. He listened to what his DC had to say and grunted his acknowledgement before hanging up. To be honest, he wasn't at all surprised, just extremely disappointed. He tried the second number and Sam's answer message came on, but he hung up without speaking; he'd try again later.

Par for the bloody course tonight...

As he pulled out and headed for home, his phone rang once more; it was Cliff this time. He pulled back in to the kerb and answered.

'Cliff. Hope you've got some good news; it's been a crap night so far as the case is concerned.'

Cliff laughed.

'Aye, well this might just cheer you up, Boss. Ma old man's home and Ah've had a word...'

∿∿∿

Despite the hour, Grant and Cliff were back at Osprey House, awaiting the arrival of Faz; a few minutes later the door opened and he walked in, the ubiquitous grin present.

'Developments, then, Boss?'

'You could say that; tell him, Cliff.'

'Well, Faz, Ah spoke to ma old man, asked him if Ellie Braid, or Helena Pettigrew, as we know her, had ever been known as "Teeny".'

He paused.

'And?' asked Faz.

'So, ma Da says, "Naw, her father always called her Ellie—that wis his pet name for her; it was her *sister* that wis called Teeny..."'

Faz looked at him in astonishment.

'Her sister?'

'Yup, her sister.' Grant interjected. Teeny, short for Christine. As in...'

'What...seriously? Christine Duff? No way...'

'Aye. We checked the registers, Christine Braid married a Colin Duff, had two kids, Amanda and Bruce. Helena Pettigrew is Christine Duff's big sister. No two ways about it.'

There was a pause as Faz considered this new information.

'Wait, so that means Amanda Duff is effectively Ronnie Pettigrew's cousin...?'

'No "effectively" mate, they're full cousins; Christine Duff is Ronnie Pettigrew's aunt and the deceased, Amanda, is—well, was—Ronnie Pettigrew's full, first cousin.'

'Bloody hell; surely that's got to be a motive for killing Pollock, hasn't it?'

A frown creased his brow.

'But...so you think it was Christine Duff that took out the contract on him? Surely not? I mean, how the hell would she... how could she...?'

Grant grunted.

'Hm! That's what we need to ascertain, Faz. To be honest, I had just supposed it would be Helena, or Ronnie even, but Pollock was definite about the name being "Teeny Braid", which pretty much puts Christine Duff in the frame. Mind you, I don't think there's any doubt that Helena Pettigrew must have been involved; like you say, how in God's name would Christine Duff have any idea how to take a contract out on someone. And how did she know who to take the contract out on in the first place? Anyway, there's only one way to find out. Come on...'

They arrived at the Duff family home and parked on the street outside. In the absence of all his team's female members, Grant had called for a female uniformed officer and the marked car drew up in front of them. He got out, made their introductions then issued instructions.

'Right, I doubt if there'll be any trouble, but if you could come in with Cliff and me, just to keep things right. Stay in the background, we'll handle things.'

'No problem, Sir' replied Constable Robertson. To Grant's relief she seemed a capable young woman; he knew this wasn't going to be the easiest of interviews. He turned to Faz.

'Faz, you wait outside with the other uniform, just in case; we shouldn't be too long. Let's just hope they're not in bloody bed.'

The curtains were drawn tight but he could see a chink of light as he rang the bell. The hall light came on and the door was opened; Colin Duff stood in the doorway, staring at them. He looked drawn and weary.

'Yes? What do you want now; more bad news for us?'

The sarcasm was understandable, Grant thought; unfortunately, Colin Duff was accurate in his statement.

'Can we come in, please, Mr Duff. We need to speak to your wife.'

Grant and Cliff were sitting in the comfortable lounge, now looking very slightly neglected, as was Christine Duff. Her hair was uncombed and there were a couple of stains down the front of the grey fleecy dressing gown that was wrapped tightly around her body despite the warmth of the room. There were dark circles under her eyes and she had aged visibly since their last visit. Constable Robertson stood discreetly beside the door, only Colin Duff seeming to be aware of her presence. As before, he had seated himself at the opposite end of the couch from his wife. He glared across at Grant.

'Well?'

Grant ignored him, looking instead at the troubled woman sitting across from him.

'Mrs Duff?'

Her eyes had a distant expression.

'Yes?'

'Can I ask, was your maiden name Braid?'

Colin Duff snorted.

'Oh, here we go; it was only a matter of time before that came back to haunt us.'

His wife turned and glared at him.

'Oh, shut up, Colin, you sanctimonious bastard. You've always held that against me...'

Grant tried to steer the conversation back to the matter in hand.

'I take it, then, that you were formerly Christine Braid?'

She looked at him.

'Yes, I was. So?'

'And Helena Braid, or Pettigrew, is your sister?'

There was a pause this time, before Christine Duff mumbled her reply.

'Yes, she is.'

Colin Duff gave another sarcastic snort but didn't speak.

'Mrs Duff, do you know who Neil Pollock is?'

She looked away and shook her head.

'No.'

'We believe you do, Mrs Duff. Mr Pollock was, at one point, our prime suspect for the murder of your daughter and we believe that this information was passed either to Helena Pettigrew, or to her daughter Veronica—your niece, I believe. We also have reason to believe that this information may have been passed to you, a result of which was that a contract was taken out to kill Neil Pollock...'

Colin Duff stood up and shouted.

'What? What the hell are you saying, Chief Inspector, that my wife hired a hit man to kill someone? Don't be bloody ridiculous!'

'Sit down please, Sir,' said Cliff, rising slightly from his seat as Grant turned back to Mrs Duff.

'Mrs Duff, did either you or your sister Helena take out a so-called "contract" to murder Mr Neil Pollock?'

There was silence, broken by the ticking of a clock on the sideboard.

'Mrs Duff?'

Colin Duff balled his fists in anger; he opened his mouth to speak again but, before he could, his wife mumbled.

'Yes.'

'Yes, Mrs Duff? You or your sister?'

'That's enough' shouted her husband. 'You're putting words into her mouth. This is bloody ridiculous—I mean, why the hell would my wife be involved...'

Christine Duff turned on him, her voice vicious.

'Oh, shut up, you prick. You never liked Amanda, you were so bloody disappointed that your first-born was a girl, not the boy you always wanted. When Bruce came along you practically ignored the poor wee lassie from then on—no wonder she had problems. This is all your fault...'

He screamed back at her.

'How dare you! My fault? Hah! I always said that her genes were bad...'

Before either Cliff or Grant could stop her, Christine Duff jumped up and flew at her husband, fists hammering at his face and head as she shouted

'You fucking...horrible...little...'

The door burst open and a good-looking young man entered; Christine Duff ceased her pummelling as they all turned to stare at Bruce Duff, who was standing in the doorway with an expression of profound shock on his face.

'Mum? Dad? What the fu...'

Constable Robertson immediately ushered him out of the room and Grant could hear her speaking gently to the young man as she attempted to explain what was happening. Colin Duff was dabbing at his bloody nose with a handkerchief as his wife took her place once more at the opposite end of the couch. Grant waited for a moment to make sure that it wasn't a temporary respite.

'Mrs Duff, I must caution you that...'

Before he could finish, she dropped her head, staring down at her lap.

'It was me.'

'You, Mrs Duff?'

'Yes, me. I loved that girl; and, yes, she had her issues, but she was just unlucky...'

She looked back up at Grant, tears now streaming down her cheeks.

'She didn't deserve to die like that, my poor wee Amanda, she didn't... Left there like a broken rag-doll, all alone, without even the money to pay for an outfit to go to a party...'

She turned to her husband, now sitting staring at her, open-mouthed.

'...it was you, Colin. You're responsible, just as if you'd put your hands round her throat yourself...you stingy, selfish...'

She broke down completely.

CHAPTER 16

Sandie Pollock wakened early. She opened one eye, then the other, waiting... Strangely, the headache didn't materialise; then she remembered—she had stopped drinking! Of course, it had been mainly at Dawn's behest...

'Mum, you need to stop.'

'Dawn, it's not a problem, really...'

'It quite clearly *is* a problem and you know it! Please, you'd promised me that you'd stopped last year. What happened?'

'Life, my darling girl, life. Maybe one day you'll understand...'

She sat up, tired but with a clear head; and if ever she needed a clear head, it was going to be over the next few days, tomorrow especially. She wondered how the hell she was going to cope without even a small measure of vodka...

Briony Quinn also woke early and, although she hadn't consumed any alcohol the previous evening her head was anything but clear. She was worried; about the case, about her own crumbling relationship but, primarily, about her boss, DCI Grant McVicar.

She lay in her bed, staring at the ceiling and listening to the drone of traffic that seemed to permeate her home life. Maybe she should move to somewhere more rural, like her boss had done. She took a deep breath, then let it out slowly, trying to slow down her chaotic and confused thoughts.

Grant McVicar; she had only herself to blame, after all. She had requested the transfer to Paisley, acting on the advice of retired Divisional Commander Alastair Young, her mother's partner. He had known Grant when he had worked as a young detective under the supervision of Jackie Winters, a hard-bitten detective Inspector whose alcohol-infused body had been dragged from the river Clyde. Young believed in Grant, he believed that he was a good cop who was struggling with a series of tragic incidents. He also believed that Briony, with a background in victim support, could help Grant get back on track; Briony had believed it herself, but now she was beginning to wonder if the task was just too much for her.

She was weary; weary of his moods, his lapses into a morass of self-pity and blame but mostly of his obsession with the Pettigrew family, Veronica in particular. She knew that there was a history, she was aware that he had had a relationship with Ronnie before he discovered her true identity. He also held them personally responsible for Jacky Winters' death; Grant firmly believed that his former boss was teetotal and had been plied with drink prior to being thrown into the Clyde, although she had heard rumours that the man was, in fact, a secret alcoholic. But his fixation was unhealthy and often overshadowed the real issue, the real investigation. And that was exactly what was happening this time, yet again.

He had phoned her last night after Christine Duff had been taken into custody; he believed that he finally had the link to the Pettigrew family that he had been seeking, although Duff claimed that she had acted entirely by herself, unlikely as it seemed. What concerned Briony most was that there had been no mention whatsoever of the ongoing and, as yet, unsolved murder case. She hoped the day would see fresh enthusiasm, renewed connection even, from her boss. She stretched and swung herself out of bed, wondering what the morning would bring...

'So where are you with the murder investigation, Grant?'

DCI McVicar turned towards Sheena McPartland, the Procurator Fiscal, as she asked the same question that he had been asking himself on the way in to work that morning.

'Em...'

'I mean, this is all very well. Naturally we all want to see the Pettigrews finally brought to justice but, at the moment, from what you tell me, Christine Duff is claiming that she acted without the knowledge of either Helena or Ronnie...'

'With all respect, Sheena, that's total crap; how the hell would she have the first idea how to hire a couple of contract killers; from Liverpool, I may add...'

'Yes, I know, but unless either Duff or this Hopkins character admit to the link then we have no evidence at all to implicate the Pettigrews, other than the fact that the two women are long-estranged sisters. But that's not what I'm talking about.'

'I agree with Sheena, Grant' interrupted Superintendent Minto. 'You're losing your focus on the real investigation, the murder enquiry.'

'But Ma'am...'

'Look, we've been down this road before; I know how desperate you are to bring the Pettigrews to justice—as am I— but you can't allow yourself to be side-tracked. At the moment, Christine Duff has confessed to contracting Hopkins and Malone to kill Neil Pollock...'

'Yes, Ma'am, but how in God's name did she find out about Pollock in the first place? We know that Billy Cook was passing information for money to John Norris, who is employed by the Pettigrews, and I very much doubt that Christine Duff was dealing with him directly. The information must have come through either Helena or Ronnie...'

Patricia Minto raised her voice, cutting him off.

'I appreciate that, Grant but, again, it's all circumstantial. We can't get hold of Norris as he's buggered off somewhere. Oh, and we managed to pick up Cook at the airport—that was a sensible suggestion from your new constable, by the way—but, understandably, the despicable little man is saying nothing. Bad enough being jailed as a corrupt cop, worse still if you're doing time having crossed the likes of the Pettigrew family. I very much doubt that he'll give us anything we can use.'

'We wouldn't have a case, Grant, I'm sorry' interjected the Fiscal 'especially when they've got that weasel Turnbull fighting their corner...'

Sheena McPartland's hatred of the renowned criminal defence QC, Bryce Turnbull, was legendary.

'...the thing is, I don't doubt a word of what you've said but, as there's nothing we can actually prove, then I agree with Patricia, you need to focus on this murder investigation. Are you any nearer an arrest?'

He stared at the desk.

Am I...?

'Grant?'

'Em, sorry Sheena...yes, I'm coming back to the theory that it was Pollock after all, but probably assisted by Nicky Hogarth.'

Sheena McPartland pursed her lips and exhaled.

'Well, if that's the case, the shit is really going to hit the fan... you're aware of who he is, of course?'

'Yes, and I'm treading as carefully as I can.'

'So, what makes you believe it's them?' asked the superintendent. 'As Sheena implies, we're going to have to be absolutely certain. I've come up against Hogarth a couple of times in the past, makes Turnbull look like Mother Theresa!'

'Yes Ma'am. I'm aware of that'

He paused. Was he certain...and why?

'The thing is, it comes down to this item of underwear. We know it was worn by Natalie Wheeler, the second victim. The evidence suggests that the killer tried to remove a similar piece of underwear from the first victim, presumably as some sort of perverse trophy. I believe that Amanda Duff wasn't actually the intended victim, that it was Susan Fielding; she'd have been wearing the red dress, it would have been easy enough to remove her underwear. The fact that we found it in Neil Pollock's bag is what implicates them; unless Sandie Pollock placed it there, how else did it get in the side pocket of his holdall?'

'What about the hotel staff? asked Sheena. 'Surely one of them could have put it in his bag?'

'There's absolutely no motive, though. It was the first time Pollock and Hogarth had stayed there, they didn't eat in the hotel, the staff had virtually no contact with them. No, I'm pretty certain that we can rule them out. Then there are the other factors; Pollock was left-handed and Dr Napier has said that the killer was left-handed. The evidence suggests picture-wire was used to strangle the victims and we found a roll of the stuff in Pollock's studio; forensics have said that the fragment we found probably comes from the same roll. Plus, all the footage shows the suspect wearing the same clothes as Pollock wore when he was...'

'Yes, and I accept all that,' said the Fiscal. 'But, as I said before, it's all circumstantial and Turnbull...'

She sneered as she spat out her adversary's name.

'...would tear our case to ribbons. No, we need something more tangible, a witness who actually saw them, fingerprints...what about the murder weapon? Any sign of that?'

'With respect, Sheena, even if we did have the murder weapon, it's highly unlikely that we'd get any usable prints from the picture-wire.'

'What about the changing cubicles; did the SOCOs check for prints there?' asked the superintendent.

'Yes, of course, but Pollock's weren't there. We don't have Hogarth's on file but I don't think he's the actual killer. There are plenty of other prints but far too many to isolate—they'd just be from customers, presumably.'

There was a pause; Grant stood up.

'Right, I'd best get on, if that's okay?'

Patricia Minto looked at him with a thin-lipped smile.

'Yes, but I must ask you to focus on these murders; leave Christine Duff be for the meantime, she's in custody and she's admitted to being behind the assault and the attempted murder...'

She paused for a moment,

'...God knows I don't condone it but if someone killed a child of mine then...well...anyway, off you go. Keep me informed.'

'So, what did she say, Boss?'

'Who, the Mint or Christine Duff?'

Briony smiled.

'Both, I suppose. But Christine Duff? That was a bit of a shock.'

Aye, you could say that...!

'Yup; all down to Cliff's dad, too. He remembered that there was a sister; actually, Cliff, I wouldn't mind a wee chat with your dad at some point, just to thank him.'

'Aye, sure, Boss, he'll be happy tae talk to you. Think he still misses the job, for some strange reason!'

Briony looked at Grant, wondering if there was an ulterior motive. Cliff's dad had worked in Glasgow's East End—Pettigrew territory—and she suspected he was still on a quest to find out what really happened with his former boss, Jacky Winters. The DCI had been found in the River Clyde, drowned and sodden with alcohol, and Grant had always believed that Ronnie Pettigrew was behind his death. She said nothing as Grant continued.

'Anyway, Christine Duff—or Teeny Braid, as she seems to have called herself—claims that she alone took out the contract on Pollock for killing Amanda.'

'But how the hell would she know about any of that, Boss?' asked Kiera. 'None of it was public knowledge.'

'My point exactly; it must have come from her sister, via our friends Cook and Norris, although Christine claims that she's had no contact at all with her sister since she started going out with Michael Pettigrew.'

'Do you believe her, Boss?' asked Sam.

'No, but she's adamant. She lifted most of the family savings—apparently the going rate for a "hit" is about a hundred grand, cash. I thought Colin Duff was going to have apoplexy when he heard that. Christine blames his tight-fistedness for all poor Amanda's troubles; I don't think it's exactly a happy household, do you, Cliff?'

'No, Boss. Mind you, none of the ones in this case seem tae be, do they?'

'No.'

He paused and let out a weary sigh; Cliff's statement could equally apply to his own domestic situation.

'Anyway, you'll probably be relieved to hear that I've been instructed by the Mint to forget about the abduction and Pollock's attempted murder in the meantime, now that Christine Duff's in custody.'

Briony rolled her eyes slightly.

About bloody time, Boss...!

'Right...' Grant clapped his hands together as he stood up.

'So, my money is back on Pollock, but possibly assisted by Hogarth. Motive? Well, I'm not sure but I'd certainly be prepared to say that neither man was in the happiest of relationships...'

'I'd agree, but it's not exactly a motive for killing two women, Boss' interrupted Briony.

'No, but it could just be a reason, Briony. Maybe a long-standing resentment grew into a hatred, a need for revenge against women in general...anyway, there's plenty of other circumstantial evidence to implicate them, we just need to get a bit of solid proof. And speaking of which...Sam, Kiera, how did it go in North Berwick yesterday?'

Sam shook her blonde curls.

'I'm afraid there's nothing to report, Boss. As before, it appears that Pollock and Hogarth had very little contact with the staff. One of them did wonder if the blonde was actually a man but they weren't sure.'

'Bugger; not much help, is it?'

'There's one more receptionist still to interview though,' said Kiera. 'She was on holiday last week, flew back in to Newcastle about one a.m. this morning. She's on duty today from twelve— will we head through again and interview her?'

Was it a waste of time? He rubbed his beard.

'Do you know if she was on duty on that Sunday, Kiera?'

'Yes, the same shift as today, apparently. Twelve till eight. But if Pollock and Hogarth *were* out all day and had their dinner elsewhere, then she probably wouldn't have seen them at all.'

'No, probably not; still, I suppose we shouldn't just assume; you know what *that* makes...'

There were a few smiles.

'Okay, can you go back through and have a chat, just to make sure there are no loose ends.'

He looked at his watch.

'May as well leave now, the traffic will probably be worse today, being Monday. Give me a call if anything turns up.'

'Will do Boss,' said Kiera as she and Sam stood up.

'Right, I'm afraid we're going to have to keep looking at those security videos...'

There was a groan from both Faz and Cliff.

'...I know, it's a pain in the arse, but if we can get an image of either of them, or their vehicles, then it ties them to the crime scene. Take Grace with you, a fresh pair of eyes and all that. By the way, I hadn't finished in the cinema, one of you'll need to head back there and round it off.'

He knew there was a chance that the story of his drenching would become public knowledge, but it was a risk he had to take. Once the three remaining DCs had left, he sat down again, the memory of the humiliation and the hurt showing on his face.

'What is it, Boss? asked Briony, recognising the symptoms.

'Och, nothing, Bri...'

'Bollocks...to coin a phrase! Come on, out with it!'

He managed a wry smile.

'Well, it'll probably come out once they've been at the cinema... what the hell...'

Briony felt heart sorry for Grant; sure, his behaviour had been far from exemplary but he didn't deserve to have cola thrown over him, certainly not in the middle of a public place. She briefly considered suggesting that he charge Tina Sturrock with assaulting a police officer, but thought better of it; if she was honest with herself, she might well have done exactly the same thing!

'You need to try and speak to her, Grant. There's always going to be a chance you bump into her, in the village, in the pub. You can't go around scared to show your face.'

'And just how the hell do I convince her of that, Bri? After what happened, it's quite clear that I'm "persona non grata" as far as Tina Sturrock's concerned.'

He stood up.

'Anyway, I've been thinking, let's head over and have another chat with Mr Nicholas Hogarth. Last time we spoke, he was simply Neil Pollock's partner, but he's recently been promoted to prime suspect number two. Come on...'

Briony knew the conversation was over; whether headway had been made or not remained to be seen.

~~~

Veronica Pettigrew wasn't a woman who was easily surprised; she had seen and done many things in her life, some good, more bad. She managed to think of herself as a businesswoman for most of the time but, in those dark, sleepless moments that come to such people in the wee, small hours, she was only too well aware of what she *really* was and what could happen as a result. Hence the security cameras, the alarms, the gates...

But today? She sat in the conservatory, staring silently at her mother in disbelief; finally, she regained her power of speech.

'Let me get this straight, Mum; you're telling me that I have... well, had now, I suppose, a full cousin? And that she was murdered a week ago?'

'Aye, Ronnie, that's whit Ah'm tellin' you.'

Ronnie stared at her mother again; why was the woman so infuriatingly calm?

'And that you have a sister, an aunt that I didn't even know existed?'

She was trying not to raise her voice; God knew her mother had been through enough recently, but she was angry. Angry and worried...

'Aye.'

'And she was arrested last night, apparently having taken a fucking contract out on this Neil Pollock person? A person that Grant Mc-Bloody-Vicar was here asking about only a few days ago?'

Helena Pettigrew nodded as she bit at her one remaining fingernail.

Ronnie's temper finally snapped.

'For fuck sake, Mum, just how the hell did this bloody aunt of mine find out about Neil Pollock and how in the name of God did she manage to get hold of a couple of hired thugs to take him out? Is there some fucking instruction book available on-line or something—how to take out a fucking contract...'

'Ronnie, Ah'm sorry, hen...'

'Sorry? Mum, McVicar's going to be over here as fast as his clapped-out pick-up will carry him, asking just how the hell this sister of yours got all her information. God almighty, woman, we could all end up in the fucking jail...what were you thinking?'

She fell silent for a moment.

'And, anyway, why did you never tell me?'

Helena had the good grace to look very slightly apologetic.

'What difference would it have made, Ronnie?'

Her daughter shrugged.

'I don't know, Mum, I don't know... Maybe it would have been nice to have had a cousin, someone to talk to after...'

The phrase "after Ricky was killed" had played on her lips but she realised that raking up the memory of her brother's brutal death would have served no purpose.

'Anyway, we're going to have to think about what the hell we say to McVicar when he comes calling, which I'm sure he will. How much has your sister told him, do you know?

'Bryce Turnbull's goin' over tae see her this mornin'...'

Ronnie's voice notched up a tone.

'What, him? Christ, that's going to point the finger straight at our involvement...wait a minute...'

She stared at her mum, her frown deepening.

'So, if Turnbull's going over today, who the hell was there last night when she was charged.

Helena looked away.

'Wan o' his assistants, I think. Bryce wisn'ae available...'

Ronnie shook her head violently.

'God, this just gets worse...why the fuck did you phone Turnbull in the first place?'

This time it was Helena who raised her voice.

'For fuck sake, Ronnie, whit wis Ah gonn'ae do—she's my bloody sister, for Christ's sake...'

Ronnie was furious.

'Your sister? Aye—so tell me, when was the last time you spoke to her; before all this carry-on, I mean...?'

~~~

Ronnie sat in a slightly stunned silence as her mother told her the story. Ronnie knew about her grandparents, of course, although they had both died when she was still a child. She knew that they had come from a reasonably respectable lower working-class background and she knew that her grandfather had strongly disapproved of Helena's relationship with Michael Pettigrew. Helena's eyes had a distant look as she spoke of her deceased husband.

'He wis a right looker, wis Michael; he wis a boxer, he used tae go tae the gym before it became the "in thing" an' he always dressed really well. Thick black hair that we wore in a quiff, a smile that made me go weak at the knees...'

Ronnie saw tears rolling down her mum's gaunt, grey cheeks.

'He wis bad, Ronnie, an' Ah knew he wis bad, but it wis...och, Ah don't know. The thing is, ma mum an' dad wis poor, an' Ah *mean* poor! Ma mum used to shop at Paddy's market—you know, in the railway arches behind St Enoch's—an' Ah had tae make do wi' cast-offs that she washed and altered tae fit me. But when Ah started goin' out wi' Michael? Well, it wis different then, he had plenty o' ready cash an' he wis happy tae spend it on me; an' Ah wis happy tae accept, of course.'

She paused and gave her daughter a pleading look; Ronnie shook her head.

'Oh, go on, if you must.'

Helena lit a cigarette and inhaled deeply, her cheeks hollowing as she greedily sucked in the smoke. Ronnie tried not to show her distaste as her mother continued, each word emitting a small puff of tobacco smoke.

'Ma dad didn'ae like it, he tried tae stop me from seein' Michael but...well, tae be honest, it really *wis* love...Ah suppose.'

She shook her head sadly as she took another drag on her cigarette.

'Ma mum said it wis ma relationship that killed ma dad; Ah don't think it wis, mind you, he wis a heavy smoker...'

Ronnie raised an eyebrow.

'...aw, don't start. Anyway, he passed away an' Teeny— Christine—blamed me. We'd already started driftin' apart an' when Michael and I got engaged, that was it; over. She wanted nothin' more tae dae wi' me an' after she met that wee prick Colin Duff, Ah never saw her again. Never wanted tae either, stuck-up little bitch.'

Ronnie shook her head in amazement.

'So how come she get back in touch, Mum?'

Helena inhaled again.

'She'd heard that Michael had died; she knew where Ah stayed, mind you, we've been in this hoose since we were married. Ah got a wee note wi' her phone number an' Ah decided tae give her a call. Wi' Michael gone and Ric...well, apart from you, pet, there's no-one...'

There was a pause as Helena dabbed at her eyes.

'And then?'

'Aye, well, Ah wisn'ae tae know that poor wee Amanda wis goin' tae get herself murdered, wis Ah? That wis when things started tae get complicated...'

Grant and Briony had left the meeting room and were heading along the corridor, en route to interview Nicky Hogarth; his phone buzzed as he received a text and he took out the handset. Briony could see his brows furrowing as he read the content. He looked up.

'Sorry, need to make a call...'

Without further explanation, he strode back to his office and slammed the door shut.

A couple of minutes later, he re-appeared, a thunderous look on his face.

'You okay, Boss...?'

He walked past, muttering as he went.

'Got to go out...you wait here...be back as soon as...'

∿∿∿

Grant couldn't actually remember the old Erskine Ferry, the Clyde's chain-operated vehicular crossing that had existed before the Erskine Bridge was built. However, he remembered driving down with his parents and gazing in childish terror at the disused slipway, the rusting ferry chains still in place, as it disappeared into the murky depths of the Clyde. His father used to let off the handbrake, the car rolling forward alarmingly and, although he had thought it was funny, it had given Grant nightmares. The thought of the brakes failing and his father's old Hillman Minx careering irrevocably down the ramp, into the dark, flowing water, had always scared him and, today, as he sat outside the old East lodge of Erskine House, he could still feel that strange, irrational fear well up inside him. He looked in the mirror as the black Audi coupe drew in behind him.

Maybe I should just let off the handbrake, roll down the ramp and into the river...

She got out; glamorous, elegant...evil. Her hair was tied in a ponytail and, unusually, she was wearing dark jeans, a hoodie and trainers. Somehow, it suited her, normalised her...

Don't...

She opened the door of the pick-up and slid in, turning to smile at him. She saw the slight wrinkle of his nose as he detected a smell underlying that of her expensive perfume.

'My mum! I hate it but, well, under the circumstances...'

He nodded, almost afraid to speak. He was in an extremely difficult situation and he was all too aware of it. They sat for a few moments, staring at the water as it flowed to the sea, then she reached down and took a small box from her bag; he stared at it—he knew what it was...she handed it to him and he looked at her.

'A gesture of faith, Grant.'

He gave her a cynical look.

'Huh. How many copies do you have?'

She shook her head.

'Always so bloody suspicious, McVicar. Just the one.'

'Aye, right.'

She turned angrily.

'Aw, believe what the fuck you like. I don't care. But there was only ever one copy and the only person who's ever seen it is me...'

Her expression changed and she smiled; he couldn't decide if it was evil or...sexy?

'Actually, it's pretty raunchy...'

He could feel his face redden as he held the little digital video cassette in his hand. He slid it into his pocket and mumbled.

'Thanks'

'What was that?'

He looked into her eyes.

'I said "thanks", Ronnie. I appreciate that.'

She shook her head and sighed.

'Finally!'

They stared at the water again. A ship was travelling upstream, a rare event nowadays. They watched it pass, the waves lapping greedily up the ramp, then he turned towards her again.

'So, what do you want now?'

She looked back at him.

'I think you know. Actually, I'm surprised you haven't been hammering at our door already!'

He shrugged.

'Warned off—well, when I say that, my boss said I've to concentrate on the murder enquiry at the moment...'

'Oh, yes, those two girls...that was just awful...'

He noticed her expression; to his surprise she looked sad.

'Did you know?'

'About what?'

'That you had a cousin...an aunt.'

She shook her head, her ponytail flicking from side to side.

'No. First I heard of it was this morning, when my mum told me. I couldn't believe it; I mean, to find out that I had a cousin and then to hear that she'd just been murdered...'

Somehow, he knew her expression wasn't feigned. She seemed genuinely upset.

'I'm sorry, Ronnie, really. That must have been horrendous, especially coming after...well, you know. The thing is, I don't think she was actually the intended victim.'

Ronnie's eyebrows shot up in surprise.

'What?'

'Listen, I can't say too much, but I think Amanda was just in the wrong place at the wrong time. She had gone into another changing cubicle to...'

'To what, Grant?'

'Nothing, never mind. She was just unlucky.'

'Huh—unlucky! You could say that.'

'Sorry. But you know what I mean.'

'I suppose...but it was a shock, even to a hard bitch like me...'

She smiled at him and raised an expectant eyebrow but he remained silent.

'Oh well...'

Another silence. Finally, Ronnie spoke again as she stared out of the window.

'So, Grant, you'll remember that you owe me a favour?'

Here we go...

'Ronnie listen...'

'Hear me out, Grant.'

'No, Ronnie. I shouldn't have asked you; and God knows what you did, but Louise Thackray certainly wasn't looking for money...'

She looked at him in surprise.

'Money? There was no mention of money.'

'Well, the Barrowman boy handed her son an envelope with about five hundred quid in it...labelled "shed".'

She smiled.

'Well, I'm sure she can put it to good use...listen, Grant, please, I'm not asking for much. This aunt of mine—Christine Duff—appears to have confessed to instructing a couple of professional thugs to murder your suspect. And, yes, how the hell would she know, etcetera etcetera. But you have a confession, you have her in custody, what more do you need? Leave it at that.'

He pursed his lips; Ronnie Pettigrew was starting to sound like Superintendent Minto!

'I don't know, Ronnie, once these murders are solved...'

She turned and glared at him.

'Oh, for Christ's sake, Grant, what would you have done? Her daughter is brutally murdered by some psychopath dressed as a woman; you know what the bloody justice system can be like. Chances are he'd have got off because...oh, I don't know, because his mum dressed him in a frock for a school play or some such rubbish. But she's left with a dead daughter and he'll be out in ten to fifteen years, probably having had a great old time in prison...'

'No-one has a great time in prison, Ronnie, believe me...'

'Oh, for God's sake, you know what I mean! Grant, you owe me; I delivered, all I'm asking is for you to drop any further investigation, give my mum a break. She's been through enough already! Anyway, by all accounts my "Aunty Christine" isn't going to implicate anyone, why do you need to waste time and resources? Is it just revenge? Do you hate me that much?'

Do I...?

He gazed at the river, a dark and mysterious ribbon. The tide was on the ebb, a few pieces of flotsam heading slowly westwards, towards the estuary. The water looked inviting, somehow...all he had to do was let off the handbrake...

'I wasn't responsible, you know.'

'What?'

'For Jacky Winter's death. I know you think I was but, honestly, the man was an alcoholic; I've told you already. He had a few too many and fell off the bridge, as far as I know. But I wasn't behind it. Believe me or not, Grant, I've done a few things...but this wasn't one of them. And I'm sorry I sent you that card. I was younger, impetuous...it wasn't nice...I was just hitting back at you...'

He looked at her.

'For what? What did I ever do to you? Or was it just because I was a cop?'

She gave a sad smile and shook her head.

'Oh, never mind...'

Could he believe her? He didn't know.

'Why did you do it?'

'Oh, for fuck sake, I've just told you...'

'No, not that. Why did you sort out the Barrowmans?'

She didn't respond at first.

'I don't know; old times' sake, maybe.'

'Was it just so that you'd have something else over me?'

'You see, there you go again. No, it bloody wasn't, Grant.'

Suddenly, just as she had done at her father's funeral, she took his hand; as before, he didn't resist.

'The truth is...'

She sighed heavily.

'The truth is, since we were, well, you know...there's never been anyone...aw, fuck, Grant the Vicar, you're a bloody hard act to follow...'

He couldn't believe what he was hearing. She let go of his hand.

'Anyway, I've asked you to repay the favour. What you do is up to you, I suppose. But I won't forget it, either way.'

Then, to his utter astonishment, she leaned over, pulled his head towards her and kissed him hard on the lips; before he had a chance to respond, she opened the door and, without a backward glance, she was gone.

He waited a few minutes until her Audi had disappeared up the narrow Ferry Road, then he turned his pick-up and drove slowly after her. His senses were reeling.

∿∿∿

Briony Quinn was sitting in her car, parked in the lay-by under the access road for the Erskine Bridge. She recognised the black Audi as it sped by, heading for the M8. A few minutes later, Grant's pick-up followed, driving in the opposite direction back to Paisley. She sat for a few moments longer, staring at his lights as they disappeared round the corner.

Grant, Grant, just what the fuck is going on, my friend...?

∿∿∿

"Red rain is falling down, red rain; red rain is falling down, falling down all over me...!'

Oh Peter Gabriel, it is, it is...but why does it have to end like this? Why couldn't it just be simple, just her and me, forever? I thought she loved me, even though she never told me. I suppose I should never have assumed...

"...I tasted life. It was a vast morsel. A Circus passed the house— still I feel the red in my mind..."

CHAPTER 17

It really was a lovely dress...and red *was* his favourite colour, after all!

Nicky Hogarth hung the pretty scarlet garment back up on the rail above the mirrored wardrobe and smiled. Of course, he knew Neil's size and he knew that it would fit; a bit tight round the middle, perhaps, but he didn't mind that too much. He lifted the bag containing the set of rather exotic and very expensive underwear; maybe he should wrap it—after all, it was a "moving in" gift!

Nicholas Hogarth, QC, had never really questioned his sexuality, having always accepted that he was, quite simply, "sexual". Sure, he liked men, always had; but he liked woman too (after all, he had married—hadn't he...?) and this was where Neil Pollock had been a highly entertaining and extremely accommodating partner, happy to satisfy Nicky's every demand. A relentlessly ambitious political animal, Hogarth had always kept his preferences strictly confidential; but times and attitudes had changed and the pendulum had very much swung the other way...he smiled at the allegory. Maybe it was time to come out, now that Neil was about to move in.

He licked his lips lasciviously at the thought. A phone call to the Royal Infirmary, a bit of judicious name-dropping, and he had found out that Neil would probably be released that afternoon, not the following day as originally planned. As always, there was an NHS "bed-crisis" and his friend was deemed to be well enough to face the outside world once more. He hoped that Neil's clinging and rather fatuous wife, Sandie, wouldn't get wind of it; he had left instructions with the ward that he would be collecting his friend that afternoon but he knew that such messages often got overlooked or ignored.

He decided that he really should wrap the underwear and he walked through to the recently cleaned and tidied kitchen; afterwards, he would head out to his favourite delicatessen to purchase an appetising selection of delicacies and fine wines. Then he would drive to the local supermarket to stock up on the more mundane items; Neil liked his food and hadn't been overly-impressed with what the NHS had to offer!

Yes, a clean house, a nice meal and a sexy wee surprise...need to make a good first impression, after all...

As he lifted the exquisite combination of black silk and satin, he wondered if (and perhaps for the first time in his life) he was actually in love...

∿∿∿

Briony arrived back at Osprey House, noting that Grant's pick-up was already parked rather carelessly in the middle of two spaces. She was deeply troubled, having spent the journey back from Erskine exploring all the possibilities as to why Grant had suddenly headed off to meet Veronica Pettigrew. Unfortunately, none of them yielded a positive outcome. There was only one thing for it.

His office door remained firmly shut as she approached with two coffees and a packet of biscuits. She tapped on it with her toe, trying to sound cheerful as she called.

'Can you get the door, Boss? My hands are full.'

She heard footsteps and the door opened; he looked awful. Without waiting for an invitation, she walked past him, placed the coffees on his desk and sat down. He closed the door and sat opposite her, lifting his mug gratefully.

'Cheers Bri.'

She waited a few minutes, then spoke, as gently and unemotionally as she could manage.

'Just what the hell's goin' on Boss, eh?'

He glowered at her.

'What do you mean?'

She shook her head.

'Listen, I know where you were...'

He slammed his coffee down on the desk, oblivious to the liquid that splashed onto some adjacent papers.

'What? You bloody followed me? I thought I told you to stay here!'

She raised her voice to match his.

'Aye, an' it's obvious why you did! What the hell are you doin' meetin' that woman...'

'None of your damned business, that's what.'

'Oh, don't give me that crap, Grant. If it's anythin' at all to do with the investigation, then of course it's my business; if it's not, then it's none of your business either and you shouldn't be puttin' yourself in what could be a very difficult position.'

She waited for the tirade, but it wasn't forthcoming. Finally, he spoke, staring out of the window as if his mind was elsewhere.

'Aye, well, I'm already in that position, aren't I...'

~~~

Briony could hardly believe what she was hearing. When he had finished, she sat in silence, at a loss as to what to say. Finally, she took a deep breath.

'Christ, Grant, that's not good.'

'Tell me something I don't know.'

'Why in God's name did you ask her to intervene? Could you not have...'

'Briony, we're overstretched as it is; There's barely enough uniforms to go round without someone having to sit outside Louise's house, waiting for those bastards, the Barrowmans, to show up. I mean, it was the shed last time—next time it could be petrol through the letterbox, or the car set on fire. They may be small-time but they're a nasty shower of bastards. Louise was in a hell of a state...'

He stopped; Briony thought he was going to break down but he seemed to recover.

'...after what happened to Brian, I couldn't let anything like that happen to them...I hadn't thought about it really, but when Ronnie came over after her dad's funeral, well, it just kind of slipped out. I thought she'd just get someone to have a quiet word, scare them off. As soon as I said it, I knew it was a bad idea...'

'And the money? What's happened to that?'

He shrugged.

'Louise doesn't want anything to do with it; she's going to give it to charity—anonymously.'

'Well, at least that's something.'

He looked across at her; she had seen him in many moods but never like this.

'Briony, what the hell am I going to do?'

She shook her head; she honestly didn't know...

~~~

They were driving through the Clyde tunnel, sitting in a somewhat strained silence. In the end, they had decided that doing nothing was the most sensible option...for the time being, anyway. As Grant had been left in no doubt by both Sheena McPartland and Patricia Minto that he needed to press ahead with the murder enquiry and reach a timely conclusion, Briony had thought it best to proceed on that basis. They were now on their way to interview Nicholas Hogarth as originally planned. Finally, they arrived at Highburgh Road and, to Grant's surprise, he found a space just a few yards from the entrance to Hogarth's flat.

'Suppose it's a working day, everyone'll be away' he commented, his voice flat.

'Hm. Okay, Boss, let's see what he has to say.'

They walked across to the entrance, pressed the buzzer and waited; nothing. They pressed it again—still no reply.

'Will *he* no' be at work, Boss?

'No, did he not say that he was taking some time off to get settled in; and to visit his, em, friend.'

She nodded as she recalled Hogarth's statement.

'Worth headin' over to the Royal then, kill two birds with one stone? If that's where he is, of course.'

He considered it, then shook his head.

'Maybe, although, to be honest, I'd rather get them both on their own first; Hogarth's a clever bugger and Pollock is more likely to let something slip when he's alone. No, let's go and grab something to eat...'

He pulled a face as he remembered that his deli of choice had closed.

'I suppose it'll have to be another cardboard sandwich... Hang on. There's a place down near Dumbarton road, Matonti's, I think it's called...'

Given the events of the morning, she was surprised that he had any appetite, but she agreed; her own stomach was rumbling.

They were sitting outside the little cafe cum delicatessen. It had had been about to close but, with a smile, the handsome, bearded young Italian had managed to rustle them up a couple of ciabattas and two cans of San Pellegrino to go. Grant was half-heartedly chewing his as he stared out of the pick-up's rather dirty windscreen at the grey, leaden sky.

'Try and let it go, Boss. We'll deal with it all later.'

He turned and dropped the remains of his rather late lunch into the plastic bag.

'I don't know... I mean, am I fit to continue—'

'Oh, for God's sake, don't start; of course you are. This isn't influencin' the murder enquiry and, to be honest, unless Christine Duff comes clean about her sources or changes her plea, then it's highly unlikely that we'll be able to link her to her sister or her niece anyway. As the Fiscal says, it's all circumstantial.'

'Aye, maybe. Fuck, I was such an idiot...'

'No fool like an old fool, eh?'

He managed a smile.

'Less of the old...mind you, I bloody feel it today! Right are you done? Let's go and see if Hogarth's back.'

He wasn't; they returned to the pick-up and sat for a few more minutes.

'So, what now, Boss?'

'I suppose we might as well go and interview Pollock again. Let's just hope bloody Hogarth isn't there as well.'

He pulled out and started the journey across the city towards the large edifice that was Glasgow's Royal Infirmary. If he'd known how bad the traffic was going to be on Great Western Road, he might have taken a different route and spared his blood pressure!

'He's what?'

'He's gone, I'm afraid.'

'Gone? Gone where—I thought he wasn't getting out until tomorrow?'

The pleasant young nurse smiled sweetly up at him; she had dark curly hair and her resemblance to Delia Donald caused his stomach to churn very slightly.

'Aye, but it's the same old story, Chief Inspector, There's a shortage of beds. Mr Pollock was fit enough to leave so he was discharged...'

She was interrupted by a considerably sterner and care-worn charge nurse, alerted by Grant's raised voice.

'Is everything all right, Madeleine?' she asked, with a hint of an accent.

'Aye, I'm just telling the Chief Inspector here that Mr Pollock was discharged earlier.'

The senior nurse looked at Grant and nodded

'Mm, yes, you're a bit late; but I was close to calling you out earlier on, what a dreadful carry on that was...

They were in the staff room, sipping a coffee. Marta Janiec put her mug down.

'Oh Lord, I still miss a ciggy with that...anyway, your friend Neil Pollock...'

She smiled. Her face lit up; the stern expression gone.

'...although I'm assuming he's no friend, right?'

Briony smiled back.

'No, Marta, he's not; so, tell us what happened...

~~~

It appeared that, despite Nicky Hogarth's exhortations, the ward *had* phoned Sandie Pollock to tell her that her husband was being released that day. She had duly arrived, noticeably harassed, and it was immediately apparent to the staff that the relationship between husband and wife was considerably strained; they were just leaving the ward when, unheralded, Nicky Hogarth arrived.

'Well, you could see right away that the man was not happy. He started shouting, firstly at Mr Pollock then at his wife. Mind you, she gave as good as she got—the term homophobia certainly springs to mind.'

She paused, knitting her brows.

'This man looked sort of familiar; I wondered if he'd been on the telly...anyway, poor Mr Pollock finally got a word in, said he was going home with his wife. Well, this other guy went off at the deep end, started ranting about what he'd done for Neil, hurling abuse at the wife. That was when I called for a couple of porters; I tried to intervene myself but that other guy seemed to be a bit of a bully and, to be honest, I was starting to worry that he'd turn violent. Eventually the porters calmed him down—well, me threatening to call your good selves helped, I suppose.'

'And was that an end to it? asked Grant.

'Pretty much. The big guy stomped off but he gave a parting shot, something along the lines of "you'll regret this, Neil." Oh, and something about making sure of it. Empty threats; it sounded nasty but emotions were obviously running high.'

She grinned at Briony.

'I take it there's a bit of a "love triangle" going on there—only with poor Mr P in the middle, with his wife and the big guy fighting over his affections, right?'

Briony smiled back.

'Somethin' like that, Marta. Listen, you've been a big help. By any chance, do you know if they were headed home?'

Marta shook her head.

'I assumed so; he was pretty exhausted looking by the end of it but they didn't say specifically. It's a shame, Neil seemed such a nice guy...'

A nurse put his head round the door, a serious expression on his face.

'Sorry, Marta, there's a patient gone into arrest'

'Oh shit! Coming, Jordan.'

She jumped up, resuming her more stern expression.

'Duty calls, guys, but feel free to come back if you need any more info, right? Bye.'

$\sim\!\sim\!\sim$

They were sitting in Grant's pick-up in the Royal Infirmary car park, discussing their next move.

'Well, that explains where Hogarth was, Boss. Will we head back over and see if he's home yet?

'May as well...'

He had just started the engine when his phone rang; he pulled it out and peered at the screen. The cracks were definitely getting worse, he'd need to do something...

'It's Kiera.'

He put the phone on speaker.

'Kiera, anything new?'

There was a slight pause; when she spoke, he could hear the excitement in her voice.

'Yup. Spoke to the receptionist, Sonia Thewlis.'

'And?'

'Well, as expected, she didn't see anything of either of them for the first few hours of her shift, although they'd certainly been a topic of conversation amongst the other staff. Pretty much what we already found out, they reckoned that the blonde woman was actually a man.'

'Aye, Neil Pollock, presumably. Go on.'

'Well, it was later in the afternoon, she thinks somewhere around half-past three. The blonde rushed back in, on her own. She said she needed to go back to their room, that she'd forgotten something and that she'd left the keys in the car.'

Grant didn't speak, but Briony could see his shoulders tense up.

'So, the receptionist fetched the spare key—they keep a spare for every room—and gave it to her. The woman, or whatever, was only up for a few minutes, then came down and handed back the key.'

'Anything else?'

'Yes, Sonia says that she seemed really agitated, upset almost, wouldn't make eye contact and, when she left, just mumbled a "thanks". She thought her behaviour was really odd; you see, she's not really supposed to give out the spare, in case it's someone trying to get into a different room but, from what everyone else had been saying, she knew immediately who the woman was, so she thought it'd be okay.'

'We need to get that key, check it for...'

'Done, Boss. Safely stowed in a nice wee bag.'

He smiled; he should have known Kiera would have it covered.

'Good stuff; right, get back over as soon as you can, get it to forensics. We need to find out if the prints are Pollock's and what the hell he was doing back in the room, although I've got a good idea...great job, Kiera, well done.'

He finished the call and looked at Briony.

'Well?'

'The timing certainly fits, Boss; if he'd driven through from Linwood, he wouldn't have got back until mid to late afternoon. But why didn't he have the key? What did he need to go back to the room for and why was he so agitated?'

Grant furrowed his dark brows.

'Aye, exactly, was he putting Natalie Wheeler's underwear into his holdall, perhaps? So, the question is, was he acting alone after all? Hogarth has given him an alibi, but did he know that Pollock had gone back across to Linwood, or is he covering for them both? Was Pollock hiding his actions from Hogarth? We still need to speak to Hogarth, see if he knew anything about Pollock's wee trip up to the room with that borrowed key. Right, if Sandie got him from the hospital, presumably she's taking him home. Change of plan; I think we need to speak to Pollock first so we need to get back over to Paisley...'

He rubbed his hand over his head.

'...the net's closing, Bri; thing is, I don't know if we've got one fish or two...'

They were sitting in Craw Road, a few hundred yards along from the Pollock household; it was in darkness and Sandie's car was nowhere to be seen.

'Where the hell have they got to?'

Briony didn't bother answering and Grant took out his phone, speed-dialling Cliff's number. He had recalled the three DCs from CCTV duty, instructing Cliff and Faz to drive to Hogarth's flat, with Grace heading to Mrs Hogarth's house in the off-chance that her husband decided to return there. They had instructions to phone him as soon as they reached their destinations and he thought that they should have arrived by now.

'Cliff? Are you not there yet?'

'Just comin' up now, Boss, road was hellish busy for some reason and we had to drop Grace at the office to get her car. Faz is just lookin' for a space...oh, here we go.'

'Right, I want you to go up and question him...'

He explained about Pollock's return to the hotel room and the incident at the hospital.

'We need to find out if Hogarth knew about Pollock's return to that room; my guess is that he didn't, if Pollock didn't have the key. I suspect the threats he made at the hospital were in the heat of the moment but watch how you go.'

'Right, Boss, we'll head up now, I'll keep you posted.'

'Good man.'

He ended the call and turned to Briony.

'I'm going to phone the Mint, we may need warrants now to search their houses; it was fine when it was just Sandie but now that Pollock's back home, he might resist; and if Hogarth thinks we're on to him, I'm pretty sure he'll not let anyone in...'

He gazed out into the dark street and muttered.

'The wife picked Pollock up from the hospital ages ago; where the hell are they?'

If I bloody knew that, Boss...

~~~

Sandie and Neil Pollock were sitting in Sandie's car, parked in the near-deserted car park atop Greenock's Lyle Hill. The tall, dark shape of the Cross of Lorraine, the memorial to the Free French troops killed in the Second World War, loomed to their right but, in front of them, the lights of the suburban sprawl that was Gourock twinkled cheerfully below, as did the more distant little pinpoints that were Dunoon and Craigendorran, far away across the mighty Clyde.

They had come here when they were courting, sitting happily in Neil's pride and joy, his green Ford Escort, complete with two chrome Cibie spotlights. They had held hands, snogged and, occasionally, gone "a bit further". Happy times, happy memories...

The blower was on, clearing the condensation from the two takeaway coffees. They sat in a silence that was neither comfortable nor awkward, just natural. Finally, Neil put his cup on the floor.

'Sandie...'

'What, Neil?'

'I... I don't know where to start, how to say I'm sorry...'

'You've already started, Neil.'

He looked at her in the darkness.

'What do you mean?'

He could just make out the faint smile on her lips.

'You're here, aren't you; not with...anyway, that's a start, isn't it?'

He smiled back, although it was still painful.

'Yes, I suppose it is.'

They spoke for over an hour; of love, of life, of hopes attained, of dreams shattered. They talked about the children, about Neil's painting. They talked about sexuality, about acceptance...

Finally, she took his hand and gave it a squeeze.

'So, what now?' he asked, his voice slightly more buoyant than when they had arrived. She sighed.

'Neil, you're my husband. I love you, I've always loved you, although it doesn't mean I like some of the things you've done. But, let's face it, none of us are perfect and life's too bloody short...'

There was another silence as they gazed at the magnificent view; Neil spoke again, his voice husky, a whisper, almost.

'You know, Sandie, when I was...well, you know, handcuffed in that car...'

She shuddered at the thought.

'Oh, don't Neil, it terrifies me...'

'I know, but when it seemed certain that it was all over, that I was going to die, there was only one thought in my mind.'

She squeezed his hand tight but remained silent.

'All I could think about was you; about how much I loved you and how sorry I was for what I'd done to you. It was you, Sandie, just you...'

He started to cry.

'Oh, you big lump, Neil Pollock. What am I going to do with you?'

He squeezed her hand back.

'Take me home, Sweet Pea, just take me home.'

'Where the hell are they?'

Finally, Briony snapped.

'If I bloody knew that, I'd tell you, Boss, save you askin' me every five minutes...'

He looked at her as if she'd slapped him.

'Sorry, was I repeating myself?'

She laughed.

'Aye, just a bit—it's like the kids in the back seat askin' "are we there yet!"'

He laughed too; it had been a very long day.

'Nothing from Cliff either. God, where the hell's Hogarth... shit, sorry.'

There had been a reasonably regular procession of vehicles passing along the dark, leafy street but none had turned into the Pollocks' drive. A fresh set of lights approached and indicated.

'Oh-oh! Here we go...'

The car turned into the short driveway and the lights were extinguished.

'Right, let's wait until they're inside; be easier, just in case Pollock tries something stupid. Oh, for God's sake, what the hell's keeping them now?'

They watched Sandie Pollock's car for another five minutes; finally, the passenger door opened and the figure of Neil Pollock climbed out, his movements indicating that he was still stiff and sore from his beating. He closed the door as his wife got out, then started to walk towards the house; as he did so, a dark shape seemed to detach itself from the adjacent hedge; Grant saw an arm raise, he saw the glint of metal as it reflected the streetlight; the arm scythed down hard, it was raised again, it fell...Sandie Pollock screamed...

'What the fu...Jesus Christ, Bri...'

They were out of the car in an instant and running across the road; Neil Pollock was on the ground and the shadowy figure was running back along the street. The figure appeared to be wearing a dress, now unceremoniously hoisted above the waist, revealing strong legs and trainer-clad feet. As the assailant ran, Grant called out to his Sergeant.

'See to Pollock; I'll get after this bugger...'

'On it!'

The figure was about thirty yards ahead of him but stopped suddenly, wrenching open a car door; Grant realised that the engine was running and, before he could catch up, it sped off with a screech of tyres.

'Fuck!'

He ran back to the pick-up, which was parked facing in the opposite direction. He started it, pulled the wheel hard over and did a u-turn, narrowly avoiding a taxi that gave him a long blast on its horn. He switched on his concealed blue lights, then wound down the window and shouted.

'Bri, call it in; dark grey Volvo saloon, last three letters Uniform Hotel Papa—couldn't get the rest. Get as many cars as you can, I'll keep you posted on where we're headed. And let the others know...'

Before she could reply, he hit the accelerator and gunned the pick-up along the quiet, sedate street, his tyres squealing, the concealed lights flashing and the siren blaring.

"...with your hands and your feet and your raiment all red..."

CHAPTER 18

The Toyota pick-up wasn't the fastest pursuit vehicle Grant had ever driven but he had managed to keep the dark coloured saloon in sight. His phone was on the seat beside him, Briony having called him back once she had reported the incident.

He could see a couple of sets of distant flashing blue lights in his rear-view mirror; at least he had back-up. Down through the streets of Paisley they sped, the vehicle in front weaving alarmingly in and out of the traffic, attracting angry horn blasts as cars braked and veered out of its way. Grant was surprised by the driver's skills—at least he had the benefit of his blue lights and siren! Eventually, there was only one direction in which the car could be heading. He shouted above the roar of the engine.

'Bri, we're heading towards the St. James roundabout...'

Her reply crackled inaudibly then he heard the continuous drone of the "disconnected" tone.

'Shit!'

The car in front approached the lights, currently showing red; the driver disregarded the signal, speeding through the steady flow of traffic to an accompaniment of yet more horn blasts. Grant managed to follow suit, narrowly avoiding a collision with a car transporter; he was beginning to wonder if the driver had a death wish.

'Fuck!'

The Volvo took the slip-road for the M8, accelerating down the ramp towards Greenock and, once more, Grant followed. As they came onto the motorway itself, a large articulated timber lorry was overtaking a slower-moving tanker. The car tried to pull out but the tanker was boxed in by the artic, the lorry driver blasting furiously on his horn as the car veered towards him before finally pulling away to the left. It careered across the hard shoulder, narrowly missing the start of the crash barrier before disappearing down a slope beside the railway embankment, which ran parallel to this section of the M8. As the lorries sped off, Grant pulled his pick-up onto the shoulder and jumped out, aware of the sirens getting nearer.

He looked down; the car had nose-dived into a mud-filled ditch but he saw the door open and the driver scrambled out, stumbling through the scrubby undergrowth before hoisting up the red dress once more and climbing over the wire fence at the foot of the railway embankment.

As Grant set off down the slope, he was aware of a whining noise overhead, rapidly increasing in volume. He looked up; he was immediately beneath the approach to Glasgow airport and a large jet was coming in to land, its landing lights blazing as it approached the runway. Ignoring it, he reached the foot of the slope, sinking up to his ankles in the cold, muddy water. He waded through it then started to scramble up the overgrown railway embankment; the plane was now directly above him and the noise was almost deafening. He looked up; the figure in the red dress had stopped and was staring down at him, face hidden by long blonde hair that flicked in the wind. He was about to set off again when another noise sounded from his right. The figure turned away from him to face the source of this new sound, arms spread wide like some bizarre scarecrow. As Grant lunged up the steep embankment, he suddenly realised what this new noise was; the frantic blasting of a horn, together with the metallic squealing as the driver applied the brakes—a Glasgow-bound train was rapidly bearing down on them. With a final grunt, Grant dropped his head and charged up the last few feet of the embankment then, with a brief glance to his right, he dived across the tracks, knocking the figure over and falling in a heap between the two sets of lines. A few seconds later, the train thundered past, sparks flying from the brakes and the horn still sounding; he caught a brief glimpse of the driver's horrified face, then turned to look at the person he had just saved. As he did so, a foot caught him squarely in the mouth, sending him flying backwards on to the ballast as the rapidly-slowing train thundered past.

'Bastard!'

He scrambled to his knees, spitting out a mouthful of blood and hoping there were no teeth in it. Quickly, he ran his tongue around the inside of his mouth—fortunately, he couldn't detect any spaces. He looked across the other railway track; the figure had disappeared, presumably down the other side of the embankment. He stood up and followed, quickly checking for any trains approaching from the opposite direction; one close shave was quite enough...as he looked down, he saw a blonde wig lying on the tracks and he picked it up, shoving it as best he could in the pocket of his trousers.

The embankment fell away towards a large, uncultivated field, across which the driver of the car was now running. In the darkness, he could just make out that the red dress was still hoisted somewhat ridiculously up to waist height. Grant set off down the bank and over the fence but, as he reached level ground, he stopped to catch his breath for a moment. He set off again and, to his surprise, his own running seemed to come more easily that he'd expected. He was gaining on the shadowy figure, his breathing was regular, his legs weren't tiring...suddenly, he realised that the months of rowing training had finally paid off. Then, in a brief but astonishing moment of clarity, he thought how proud Tina Sturrock would have been of him...and just how much he wanted her to be proud...

Ignoring the clenching of his insides, he put his head down and made his final drive. His mind briefly flashed back through the years to his school rugby-playing days and he altered his pace very slightly, timing it as best he could. Twenty yards, ten yards, finally he dived, catching the figure round the ankles, just as he had done all those years ago as a second-row forward. They plunged down on to the soft muddy surface, the smell of the earth, the feel of the grass and the mud both familiar and strangely comforting. He pulled himself quickly to his knees, grabbing the nearest wrist of the prone figure and twisting it upwards in a firm arm-lock; this time there was no resistance. Grant could hear shouting and he turned to see a number of uniformed cops running across the field. He looked back down at his captive, moved his head closer and, with a sneer of satisfaction, growled

'You're bloody nicked...'

Then he laughed out loud—he *never* said that!

As his captive was handcuffed and led away by two uniformed cops, Grant stood up and stretched, groaning as he did so; his body was sore and he realised that, as well as the kick in the mouth, he was most likely bruised from his fall on to the sharp stones of the railway ballast. Not only that, that he was covered in scratches from his climb up and down the embankments. Once again, he ran his tongue around the tender interior of his mouth, just in case...

Nope, still nothing missing, nothing broken...

He shuddered as he realised just how close to death he had come under the wheels of the train; no doubt one more memory that would haunt him in the wee, small hours!

The evening's earlier events flickered into his mind, until now driven away by the adrenaline of the chase. He decided he'd better check in with Briony and he put his hand in his pocket to remove his phone—it wasn't there. He pulled out the blonde wig, checked again...no phone.

Shit...!

Realising that it had probably fallen out during his earlier scuffle at the top of the embankment, he set off back towards the railway. A uniformed cop was approaching and Grant accosted him, pulling out his Police ID... Just in case.

'Haven't found a phone up there, by any chance?'

The cop gave a rueful grin and delved into his own pocket.

'Wouldn't be this one, by any chance, Sir?'

Grant looked at the phone in dismay; the smashed screen was gone altogether, revealing a display of electronics.

'Shit—aye that's the one. Listen, could I borrow yours a minute?'

The constable pulled out his own phone.

'No problem, Sir.'

He activated the dial screen and handed it to Grant, who looked at it, his brows furrowing; the constable smiled again.

'Aye, I know the feeling, Sir. Lost my own a few months ago, all my bloody numbers were on it, wasn't backed up...'

Grant shook his head as he realised that he didn't even know Briony's mobile number.

'Em, Sir?'

He looked up.

'Mm?'

'Who are you trying to contact? I could probably reach them on the radio...' he grinned, 'you know, the old-fashioned way?'

A few minutes later, the constable had managed to have his radio patched through to one of the uniforms that was attending the incident at Neil Pollock's house. Finally, they tracked down Briony and Grant took the handset.

'Briony?'

A crackly voice responded.

'Boss? You okay?'

'Aye, just about; long story, I'll tell you later. Listen, how's Pollock?'

There was a pause before she responded.

'He didn't make it, Boss; Neil Pollock's dead.'

<center>~~~</center>

Grant's head was aching; in fact, his whole body seemed to be throbbing, despite having been on the receiving end of the ministrations of Karen Walker, his some-time adversary. Although they had their differences on occasion, the paramedic had been extremely gentle with him.

'God, you're in some bloody mess, Grant McVicar. Looks like somebody pulled you through a hedge backwards. Best get to a dentist an' all, just in case there's somethin' loose inside that big gob o' yours...'

The slight jibe had been delivered with a kindly smile and a gentle squeeze of his arm and, finally, he had been deemed fit to leave. The M8 had been closed due to the incident and he had to drive a few miles further towards Greenock before he could turn eastbound and along the old A8, trailing tediously back through the village of Bishopton along with all the other diverted traffic. Eventually he re-joined the eastbound M8 and headed for Glasgow, the prisoner already having been despatched to the Helen Street offices. He could barely concentrate, although not specifically due to his physical discomfort...

<center>~~~</center>

Interview room one; stuffy, windowless, bleak...as it probably should be, he considered. The obligatory duty solicitor had been summoned, a tired, cynical-looking man in his early sixties.

A pair of heavy, black spectacles sat at the end of his nose as he consulted some notes he had made, shaking his head very slightly. Grant sat down at the bleak metal table and looked at his own notes for a few moments, then turned and spoke quietly to Grace Lappin, who had been recalled from Mrs Hogarth's house and was now seated beside him.

'Ready?'

She gave him a brief smile of assent; of course, she was!

The recording started; the identities of the occupants were stated. Grant paused again and looked at the short-haired woman opposite him, noting the almost lifeless eyes; *was* she suffering from post-traumatic stress disorder? Had those eyes seen too much tragedy, too much pain...? He'd probably never know. He cleared his throat.

'You are Kimberley Margaret Montgomery Smart...'

CHAPTER 19

'And who the hell is this Kimberley Smart?'

Sheena McPartland, the Procurator Fiscal, scowled at Grant as she asked the question; somehow, she always managed to give the impression that he wasn't coming up to her required standards. He had been called in to see Superintendent Minto first thing that morning but the Fiscal had been delayed and was clearly in an extremely bad mood. He didn't ask why...

'She's the manager of the clothing department in Tesco Linwood, Sheena. She was the one who found...well, claimed to have found Natalie Wheeler's body.'

'So, from that I take it you'd already interviewed her?'

'Yes, but...'

'And yet you failed to take any subsequent action, resulting in Neil Pollock's death...'

'Now, Sheena, that's being a bit unfair' interjected Patricia Minto. 'I've already discussed this with Grant and there was no reason to consider her a suspect at that time. Her story stood up—she had simply gone into the changing room to ensure that it was tidy and discovered Wheeler's body.'

'But surely...'

Grant wasn't going to be intimidated.

'With all respect, Sheena, at that point the suspect we had from the murder in Asda was a long-haired blonde who was subsequently seen in Tesco. We had no reason at all to suspect Smart.'

Sheena McPartland sighed.

'Hm, well I suppose that is fair comment, Grant. So, what's her story?'

In the end, the story was relatively straightforward; Kimberley Smart had been Neil Pollock's lover, until Nicky Hogarth arrived on the scene. They had met years ago apparently, when Pollock used to surreptitiously browse in the ladies' clothing department, occasionally making a purchase. Eventually, Smart had tumbled to the fact that the clothes he bought were probably for his own use. She had finally approached him and, after his initial denial, he had admitted that he liked to cross-dress, something that Smart found herself attracted to. Grant paused his narrative.

'Actually, she gives me the impression of being unsure about her own sexuality.'

'What do you mean, exactly?' asked the Fiscal, with a frown.

'Well, I think she liked men—she certainly liked Pollock—but I suspect that she hankers after women too and the idea of combining both—well...'

As he said it, he realised that that was exactly what had attracted Hogarth to Neil Pollock. He continued the sorry tale.

The relationship had lasted for several years. Smart would buy clothes for Pollock and they would meet at her house in nearby Kilbarchan. Grant had wondered if these visits had coincided with previous "trips to Edinburgh", although it was unlikely that he would be able to tie down any dates now that Pollock was dead. Then, suddenly and without warning, their relationship was over; Pollock had simply told her he wasn't seeing her again, with no explanation. Kimberley Smart was devastated; she had become very fond of Pollock, although Grant doubted that she was capable of "proper" love...

Whatever the hell that means...

Pollock was true to his word, never returning either to Tesco or to Smart's house. She had tried repeatedly to phone him but he never answered and never returned the calls. Finally, she had started to stalk her ex-lover and it didn't take her long to discover his relationship with Nicky Hogarth; she had been dumped for another man! Her hurt had turned to jealousy, then to a deep, burning hatred for both Pollock and Hogarth. And so, the plan was hatched...

'The strange thing is, when it came down to it, she couldn't bring herself to actually harm Pollock; at first, anyway. I think she really did love him...well, within her own terms of reference, I suppose...'

Sheena McPartland gave him a questioning look.

'I think she may be suffering from post-traumatic stress disorder; she certainly displays the characteristics, the withdrawal from reality etcetera, but I do think she was genuinely fond of him...'

He paused, torn again between justice and sympathy.

'Her original plan was to kill the girl in Asda, remove her underwear then plant it in Neil Pollock's luggage.'

Patricia Minto gave him a sceptical look.

'How the hell was she going to manage that—I mean, how would she know where he was going to be that weekend?'

'She'd followed them when they went through on the Friday night. As I said, she was stalking him by this time and she'd become pretty proficient, by all accounts.'

'Really? God, she certainly took her revenge seriously.'

'She did; it was all very carefully planned and she was just waiting for the right opportunity.'

'But all this palaver with the dresses—surely that was never going to be easy,' interjected Sheena.

'Aye, but remember she was the manager of the clothing department in Tesco, she knew her stuff and she was used to handling stock, putting it out on display. No-one would take any notice and it would have been relatively simple for her...'

'But why two killings, Grant' asked the fiscal. Why not just the first one?'

He shrugged.

'The first one went wrong.'

'Wrong?'

'Yes. It was supposed to be the Fielding woman, she had been trying on the red dress. Naturally, Smart was under considerable stress, knowing what she was about to do. When the cubicle became occupied again, she assumed it was Susan Fielding back with the other dress. But it wasn't—she hadn't reckoned on a thief going through her intended victim's handbag. Of course, once she realised her mistake, she had to carry it through; couldn't very well leave poor Amanda Duff as a witness.'

'So, the girl really was just in the wrong place at the wrong time?' asked the superintendent.

'I'm afraid so. Smart did try to remove Duff's underwear but Amanda was wearing tight jeans and trainers which made it impossible. Smart was working to a very tight schedule as Susan was due back at any minute, she gave up and walked out; but she was smart...sorry...'

Neither woman reacted to his unintentional pun and he continued.

'There was always a chance it might go wrong so she had the same arrangement in place in Tesco. Of course, she'd have to be more careful, it being home territory, so to speak. But she entered as the blonde then, once the deed was done, she quickly changed in the public toilets, dumped the stuff in her locker, went on duty then "discovered" the body.'

'Hell of a risk' mumbled Sheena McPartland, half to herself.

'Murder always is, I suppose, Sheena. But generally, it's in desperate circumstances, even if these are only in the mind of the murderer. And, of course, she had no idea who Amanda Duff was related to, or of what trouble she'd be bringing upon her ex... well, apart from being arrested on suspicion of murder, I suppose. That was her plan and she certainly didn't figure on him being abducted and burned to death...'

He paused again as they considered the implications.

'So, you're certain she's guilty, then?' asked Sheena.

'Absolutely. She left work that Sunday, not long after we'd interviewed her; actually, the store manager sent her home, which was completely understandable given what had happened. She drove through to North Berwick, changed in the car then entered the hotel, pretending to be Neil Pollock—dressed up, of course. Once she'd got the keys to the room, she planted Natalie's underwear in his bag then made a hasty exit. We looked in her locker at work, she'd put the clothes back in it the following day; the green blouse and the white trousers, they were both there— and she was wearing the blonde wig when I chased her...'

He hadn't mentioned the incident with the train; now wasn't the time.

'...it fell off as she crossed the railway. But it's all there, just as we have on the CCTV. Oh, and we found the murder weapon in her house.'

Sheena McPartland's eyebrows raised as Superintendent Minto gave a knowing smile.

'Really? Thank God—what was it?'

'Just like the doctor surmised, it was brass picture-wire. It was looped at each end over a couple of pieces of what looks like a broom handle, as if they'd been cut off. Some of my team are still at her house as we speak, no doubt we'll get more evidence later; and it turns out she's left-handed, again as the doctor suggested. It all fits.'

The two women mulled over the information, then Sheena looked back at him.

'But why red? The dresses, including the one she was wearing when she was arrested, were all red. Any particular reason?'

'She said that it was Neil Pollock's favourite colour. She hated it, said it reminded her of blood, of death...you see, she left the fire service after a particularly traumatic, fatal house fire and I think that red brings back some horrific memories for her. I suppose it became symbolic in a way—well, to her, at least. I think it was easier for her to kill someone in red...'

Patricia Minto gave him a shrewd look.

'You feel slightly sorry for her, don't you, Grant?'

The question took him by surprise; he thought he had managed to mask his emotions. He took a deep breath and let out a long sigh.

'I don't know, Ma'am. Maybe, in a way, she was a victim herself. At the end of the day, murder is murder but I suppose it *was* a crime of passion; and she's seen some pretty awful things in her career...'

'So, have you, Grant,' interjected Sheena, 'and you don't go about murdering people. At least I hope not!'

The sudden spark of dark humour took him by surprise; despite himself, he grinned.

'Not yet, anyway; but that's pretty much it. We're going over all the case notes, we'll see what else we find at her house, but she's admitted to the two store murders and we witnessed her stabbing Pollock anyway so, unless she changes her plea, it's pretty much a closed case.'

They sat in silence again for a few moments, before Patricia Minto spoke again.

'And then we've got this situation with Christine Duff to consider. Anything further?'

He shook his head. He had discussed it with Briony and they had decided it was best to say nothing about his involvement with Ronnie Pettigrew. Briony had reasoned that, as Christine Duff seemed to be taking sole responsibility, it would serve no purpose other than to create a great deal of trouble for him. He felt extremely guilty as, by implication, Briony had become involved but, once again, his sergeant had demonstrated great loyalty to him—something he wasn't entirely sure he deserved.

'Grant?'

'Oh, sorry...no, nothing, Ma'am. She's adamant that she acted alone and we can't prove a link to her estranged sister or to her niece. Cliff and Faz are interviewing her again, I'll keep you posted.'

Sheena McPartland gave an impatient grunt.

'Hmph. The whole thing's highly improbable, if you ask me. There's no bloody way the woman could have acted alone.'

'Of course not, Sheena, but if that's what she claims and we can't prove otherwise, then what can we do? Gary Hopkins certainly isn't going to give us anything and, even if the guys down in Liverpool managed to arrest Malone, I doubt if he will either. These guys may be career criminals but they're not stupid.'

The fiscal shook her head angrily.

'I suppose you're right...'

She certainly didn't make him *feel* right...

'...still, it's a bloody shame.'

He sat back in his chair, emotionally drained; he should have felt a sense of elation but, instead, he felt slightly nauseous. If he'd acted sooner, then perhaps Neil Pollock would still be alive. Before he could descend into further self-blame, Sheena McPartland stood up.

'Well, it seems pretty cut and dried as far as Kimberley Smart is concerned...and Duff, unfortunately. Let's get them charged, get the hearings over with tomorrow. Are you sure they'll both plead guilty?'

He nodded.

'Yes, I don't think there's any doubt. As far as Smart's concerned, her life's over—as is what she considered her "work". At the end of the day, it was a case of "if I can't have him, then nobody can...". Unfortunately, that now includes Sandie Pollock.'

∿∿∿

Grant had made to follow the Fiscal out of Superintendent Minto's office but she motioned for him to stay. He sat back down, looking questioningly at the deeply-lined face of his superior officer. Finally, she took a deep breath.

'Grant, I don't know if you've noticed, but I've not been in the best of health recently.'

He nodded slightly.

'I had wondered, Ma'am.'

'Yes, well, it was hard to hide at times.'

She paused, a sad expression on her face.

'The thing is...'

She shook her head then looked directly at him. He could feel the hairs on the back of his neck stand up; somehow, he knew it wasn't going to be good news.

'I'm afraid it's cancer; they reckon I've got about six months at the most.'

He stared at her, not knowing how to respond; he mumbled something meaningless and she smiled.

'Yes, I know, what the hell do you say to someone with a death-sentence? Anyway, I'm leaving, with immediate effect; well, I'll see these charges out, of course, tie up a few loose ends, but I'll be gone by the end of the week. I want to spend as much time as possible with Alan, see more of the grand-kids, all that sort of thing...'

Her voice tailed off; he thought she might be fighting back tears.

'I'm so sorry, Patricia.'

She looked up at him and managed a smile as he continued

'I know we've had our moments but you've always had faith in me, even when I probably didn't deserve it...'

She let out a small chuckle.

'You could say that, Grant!'

'...but you've always been fair, supportive. I'll miss you...'

'And I'll miss you too, DCI McVicar. In spite of yourself, you're a bloody good cop—don't ever forget that!'

He smiled.

'I'll try not to.'

'Oh, and could you keep this to yourself for the moment, please? I can't abide sympathy; anyway, bugger all use it'll be, in the long run...'

He saw the pain and sadness in her careworn face.

'Of course; em, I don't really like to ask, but...do you know who's replacing you, Ma'am?'

She stood up, indicating that the interview was over.

'Yes. He starts on Friday, just an interim appointment but he may stay on.'

Grant raised a questioning eyebrow as he, too, stood up.

'I think you know him, Grant; Keith Kilgour...'

Grant closed his eyes.

Aw fuck, no...

He sat despondently in his office, staring out of the window; why did it have to be Keith Kilgour? The man was an arrogant, pompous prick, playing what Grant considered a political game in an attempt to reach Divisional Commander level at the very least. Then there was the fact that he had been involved in the investigation into Jacky Winters' death... murder...

Whatever...fuck...

A knock on the door brought him back to his senses.

'Aye, come in'

Faz and Cliff entered and Grant regarded them; the two young DCs obviously got on well together, a fact that would help them through the difficult times, just as he and Brian had done. He was mildly surprised that he was now able to think of his relationship with his late partner without shying away from it.

Progress, maybe...?

'Well, how'd it go?'

The two had been to interview Christine Duff one final time; Grant gestured and they sat down, Faz giving his customary grin.

'Well, you've got to hand it to her, Boss. Sticking to her story like glue.'

'Aye, like she would know where tae get hold o' a couple o' would-be assassins!' interjected Cliff.

'So, we're no further ahead then?'

'Nope, Boss. Says she acted entirely on her own and completely refuses to discuss how she found and contacted Malone and Hopkins.'

Grant gave a grunt; had the woman decided to implicate her family, it could have made things decidedly awkward...

'And no doubt she was suitably coached by Bryce Turnbull?'

The two constables looked at each other; this time they both grinned.

'Okay, what?' asked Grant, intrigued.

'She absolutely refuses to let Turnbull represent her,' answered Faz. 'She's using the lawyer who dealt with her first...em...'

He looked at Cliff, who smiled across at Grant.

'Shelley Crook!'

'You're bloody joking?'

'Nope, Boss,' continued Faz. 'Some name, eh? But apparently when Turnbull arrived, she spent all of five minutes with him then sent him packing, said she wasn't dealing with that...how did she put it, Cliff?'

It was like watching a double act, Grant thought, with an inward smile. Somehow, the company of these two enthusiastic and loyal young men improved his spirits.

'Em...oh, aye "an odious little upstart who makes his livin' by keepin' the guilty out o' jail". The duty constable said that Turnbull wisn'ae best pleased!'

'I bet! Anyway, basically she's still not giving us anything we can use and she's admitting full guilt?'

'Seems that way, Boss. Sorry.'

He was torn between disappointment and a strong feeling of relief, although he tried to exhibit the former. It would certainly make his life considerably easier, at least as far as Ronnie Pettigrew was concerned. Anyway, he very much doubted if Keith Kilgour would sanction any further unproductive investigation into the matter. It would be a waste of the taxpayer's money, after all...

'Don't worry, Faz, it's not your fault. Right, I suppose we'd better prepare charges and get her out of the way. Are Briony and Sam back yet?'

'No, they're still at Sandie Pollock's house' replied Faz.

Briony had insisted on going to see Neil Pollock's widow and he hadn't had the heart to refuse; by all accounts, the woman was devastated, having decided to give her husband a second chance. Grace and Kiera were still at Kimberley Smart's house, along with the SOCOs, and he was awaiting their return before finally proceeding with the charges against the distant, uncommunicative woman who appeared to have been obsessed with Neil Pollock. Somewhere deep within his soul, he *did* feel a vague pang of sympathy for her...he wondered if Keith Kilgour would be as observant as Patricia Minto had been.

Aye, like fuck he will...

'Right, let's get it all rounded up. Once the others are back, we'll proceed with the charges against Christine Duff and Kimberley Smart. Good job, lads.'

~~~~

Grant was back at Helen Street, accompanied once more by Grace Lappin. He had discussed this with Briony and they had both agreed that, as the young detective constable had shown considerable insight and fortitude during the investigation, it would be good for her to attend the actual charge. Briony and Cliff were in a separate room, charging Christine Duff.

Grant nodded at the two uniformed constables then opened the door and entered the stuffy, slightly odorous interview room one, followed by Grace. He saw his DC wrinkling her nose and smiled to himself.

The aroma of incarceration...she'll get used to it...

Kimberley Smart was sitting, composed and aloof, beside her weary-looking solicitor, his expression one of apparent disinterest; his involvement would now be minimal. Grant and Grace sat across from them and he started the recording, making the usual introductions. He paused and looked down at the sheet he had placed on the table, then turned his gaze back to the woman seated opposite him. She appeared calm and resigned to her fate; her eyes seemed like dark pools, deep and without sight of the bottom, dead, almost. He found it quite unnerving but, somehow, he knew that there would be no histrionics here.

His team had made a number of further discoveries that morning. They had found a particularly accomplished and highly erotic charcoal sketch of her, signed by Neil Pollock; it had been professionally framed and hung with brass picture-wire, the two ends still attached where the remainder had been cut off. Inside a cupboard they had found a broom with evidence of the handle having been cut (including traces of sawdust in the corner of the kitchen floor). The spare room contained a fairly extensive wardrobe of clothing and lingerie, in a size that would have fitted either her or her former lover. Neil Pollock's prints were found both on the hangers and on the wardrobe itself, inside which was also one pair of ladies' size eleven shoes. Smart's fingerprints had also been found in the Asda changing room, placing her irrevocably at the scene of the first murder.

The woman had, indeed, been a respected member of Scottish Fire and Rescue but had left front-line duty following a particularly harrowing house fire, in which two young children and their father had died. She had attended counselling sessions for a few months but had finally been invalided out, leaving the service altogether soon afterwards. Again, he felt a wave of sympathy; he had seen some pretty awful things in the line of duty, God only knew what this woman had witnessed. Still, murder was murder, leave the sympathy to the judge and the jury...

He cleared his throat then, with a brief sideways glance at Grace, he spoke, his voice clear and level.

'On the morning of Sunday...

...you, Kimberley Margaret Montgomery Smart, did place a ligature around the necks of...

...and you did murder them.'

CHAPTER 20

Saturday...

A perfect morning...

Somewhere an alarm was sounding, dragging him once again from the morass of sleep. He opened his eyes, blinked a few times then he sat up. The sun was streaming through the crack in the curtains and he could make out a clear blue sky beyond—it was, indeed, a perfect rowing morning...

Then, as ever, reality crashed head-on into his senses as he realised...

It was all over.

The week had finally played itself out; Kimberley Smart had been charged with, and pled guilty to, three counts of murder. Christine Duff had been charged with, and likewise pled guilty to, conspiracy to abduct and to commit murder. Both women had been remanded without bail. Fiscal Sheena McPartland had seemed reasonably pleased with the proceedings, which was always a bonus. The team had been in high spirits, rightly congratulating one other on a job well done.

Despite his best intentions to go elsewhere, they had all gone out for the seemingly obligatory curry on the Friday night, although Grant hadn't really been in the mood. It wasn't so much the case; Friday had been Patricia Minto's last day and although he had seen other superior officers come and go, this was the first time he had said farewell with the near-certainty that the next time he encountered The Mint would probably be at her funeral. It wasn't a cheering thought.

As expected, Superintendent Keith Kilgour had been his usual smarmy, supercilious self. All handshakes, arm patting, insincere smiles... 'Good to be working with you again, Grant; I'm very much looking forward to leading the team...'

Aye, that'll be fucking right...

Grant yawned and lay back down, squeezing his eyes shut as he tried to block out his bleak thoughts; he hadn't slept well, the curry causing the usual early-hours indigestion. Maybe Briony was right, maybe he should have his guts checked...

And, of course, rowing was yet another closed chapter. Tina Sturrock had made it quite clear that he was no longer welcome at Castle Semple Rowing Club. He swore under his breath, swung his legs out of bed then padded through the cold house to the kitchen, where he filled the kettle and switched it on. The heating engineer was coming to fix the boiler that morning; that was something, at least ...

∿∿∿

The day had dragged tediously by. He always felt this way when a murder case was finally closed; a feeling of anti-climax, of emptiness, almost. Although they had achieved the desired result, the ripples continued to fan out, affecting the families of the victims, of the villains, of his team. And although justice had been done, so had damage. No matter how he viewed it, three people were dead, lost forever to their devastated families; another two people were locked away in the purgatory that was prison—where was the satisfaction in that?

Still, the boiler was finally mended, the house was warm and there was hot water on tap once again. The weekly shop had been bought and stowed away and he had managed to summon enough energy to make a start on clearing the accumulated junk from one of his spare bedrooms. This had lasted all of an hour before he became weary; he had headed back to the lounge, settling down on his comfortable couch and gazing rather wistfully out at the sunlit view as his eyes started to close...

He woke with a start, remembering the one remaining highlight of his otherwise mundane weekend; the planned assembly of the Holy Trinity in Howwood's Railway Inn, this evening with the added presence of honorary member, Briony Quinn. Finally, he smiled.

After a light, bland meal (in deference to his still-tender stomach), he changed into a set of clean and slightly smarter clothes then set off for the two-mile walk to his hostelry of choice. It was a fine evening and, in the hope that it remained so, he was wearing a light hoodie over his short-sleeved shirt. He duly arrived outside the recently-painted frontage and pushed open the door; the sound of laughter, of cheerful, drink-fuelled conversations and the enticing clinking of glasses reached his ears; he felt like he was coming home...

$$\sim\!\!\sim\!\!\sim$$

The bar was unusually busy but Father Eddie McKee and the Rev. Fraser Ballingall had managed to procure a table at the far end of the small room and they waved across cheerfully as he entered. He was a familiar enough figure now that the assembly no longer turned and stared at him and he walked across, grinning at his two friends as he held out his hand.

'Great to see you, guys.'

Eddie stood up and gripped his friend's hand in a fierce, bone-crushing handshake.

'You too, my friend. Where's Briony?'

'She's making her own way down, getting a taxi.'

'Good, good...'

'Pint, Grant?'

'Aye, Belhaven please, Fraser, cheers.'

They had taken their first sip of their drinks when Grant heard the door opening behind him; Eddie looked past him and smiled, once again raising his hand in greeting.

'Briony! Lovely to see you!'

For some reason, the hint of Irish brogue in Eddie's voice always seemed stronger when he was addressing Briony Quinn. Grant stood up, as did his friends; the two clergymen each hugged Briony warmly, Eddie's embrace seeming very slightly longer than Grant might have thought appropriate. Finally, his sergeant turned and smiled at him.

'Evenin', Boss!'

Fraser laughed.

'Oh, for goodness sake, you two, you're off duty...'

Grant and Briony finally gave each other a fierce hug; as they did so, he whispered softly in her ear.

'Thanks, my friend; good job.'

She nodded silently into his shoulder. He was about to pull away when he noticed a table of three smartly-dressed women in the corner. One of them lifted her drink and looked up, inadvertently catching his eye. His heart plummeted; it was Tina Sturrock. Briony immediately sensed that something was amiss.

'What is it, Grant?'

He sat down and she followed suit, as Eddie fetched her a drink.

'Tina bloody Sturrock, sitting over in the corner with a couple of friends...don't look...'

Briony managed to stop herself and smiled.

'I doubt she'll try anythin' tonight; you've got back-up!'

Eddie returned with Briony's lager and they toasted each other, the case, friendship...

They made small-talk for about fifteen minutes but Grant was sure he could feel Tina's eyes boring into the back of his skull.

'Oh, for God's sake, Grant...oh, sorry guys...try and ignore her... look, she's leavin', you're in the clear...'

Before Grant had time to breathe a sigh of relief, Briony frowned.

'What?'

'Em, I think she wants to talk to you...'

Grant turned; Tina was standing, stony-faced but beckoning him over; her friends had already left. Reluctantly, he stood up and walked across.

'Em, Tina...'

She turned and walked towards the door and he followed, bracing himself for a fresh onslaught. The door closed behind him and he noticed Tina's friends getting into a taxi as she turned to face him. She took a deep breath.

'Listen, what I did in the cinema...that was...'

'No, Tina, I probably deserved it...'

She glared at him, raising her voice.

'*Probably*! Christ, you...'

She stopped mid-sentence, shaking her head.

'No, you didn't deserve that. It was just immature and I let myself down, so I'm sorry.'

'Please, there's no need...listen, Tina, I'm sorry too...'

She held up her hand. One of her friends called out that they needed to be on their way.

'No, not here. But I've decided I'll give you a chance to explain yourself. Just one, mind—any hint of bullshit and we're done. For good. Understood?'

'Understood.'

She turned and walked towards the waiting taxi; when she reached the door, she looked over her shoulder at him.

'And I expect to see you back at training on Tuesday.'

Without a further word, she clambered into the taxi and she was gone.

'Well?' asked Fraser.

'At least he's dry,' chuckled Eddie.

Grant couldn't suppress his own wide grin.

'She's agreed to let me explain what happened; and she's said I've to go back to training on Tuesday.'

Fraser threw back his head and stretched out his upturned hands.

'Oh, thank the Lord!'

Eddie let out a guffaw.

'Yes, we've had quite enough of your moping, Grant McVicar.'

'Moping? I don't bloody mope, Eddie.'

'You think?' laughed Briony. 'Grant, you could mope for bloomin' Scotland...'

Another half hour of banter, gentle teasing and laughter ensued but once the four friends moved on to smaller measures of more potent alcohol, the conversation inevitable turned to the recent investigations.

'Been a pretty bizarre case this, Grant?' stated Fraser, placing his whisky glass back on the table.

Grant nodded as he rolled the twelve-year-old Glenlivet around his palate.

'Aah! Aye, you could say that, Fraser. One of the weirdest I've investigated, I think.'

'I see Nicholas Hogarth has stepped down, as of this afternoon.' he added.

'Really? I've not heard the news. Did he give any reason in particular?'

'The BBC said it was for "personal reasons," covers a multitude of sins, that!'

'Indeed,' said Grant. 'He's one strange bugger, that man, totally egocentric and extremely manipulative. Mind you, you could say that about half of our politicians, I suppose.'

'I take it he's what's classed as "pan-sexual?" asked Eddie.

'I'm no' so sure about the "pan" Eddie,' Briony replied. I think the man's just interested in the sex itself, as opposed to the person he's having it with. By his own admission, he's a highly "sexual" person, Neil Pollock was just another conquest, it seems. Like Grant says, all he thinks about is his own gratification.'

'But wasn't Pollock supposed to be moving in with him?' Eddie continued.

'We'll never really know' answered Grant. 'Hogarth's a fantasist in more ways than one. He certainly seemed to be of the opinion that Pollock was going to stay in his flat, but I suspect it had never really been determined one way or the other until Sandie turned up at the hospital.'

'How is she, by the way?' asked Fraser, a note of concern in his voice.

'Devastated' replied Briony. 'The poor woman's a hopeless romantic, I think, always lookin' for the happy endin' despite her brief interlude with that idiot, Lachlan Dallas. She told me that they'd decided to start again, move on from all the upset. Mind you, there's little doubt that Neil was a bit o' a philanderer himself but maybe he was about to turn over a new leaf. We'll never know that now either...'

Briony's voice tailed off sadly and she took a sip of her whisky.

'But surely it was a good result for you, Grant? You've charged the woman who committed the murders— Smart, wasn't it?'

Grant sighed. If only he'd caught her sooner, Neil Pollock might not...

No, don't, Grant...

'Aye, Kimberley Smart. Another troubled character, an ex-firefighter...I think she might be suffering from PTSD...'

He looked at Briony, who nodded her agreement.

'So, goodness knows what she's been through. Still murder's murder, at the end of the day. She seemed to take it all in her stride, the charges the hearing...no emotion. Sad, really...'

'Why?' asked Fraser.

'Why "sad?"'

'No, why did she do it?'

Grant didn't reply immediately; it was the same question he always asked himself and the answer was usually pretty unsatisfactory.

'She'd had an affair with Pollock for years then he dumped her for Hogarth. It was just revenge, plain and simple. She tried to implicate him in the murder, she went out of her way to make it look like it was him, even down to making sure she was seen on CCTV in the clothes that he sometimes wore; that was why she didn't wear a jacket. She'd only intended to kill once but it went wrong and she ended up killing the wrong person. That meant she couldn't get the necessary evidence...'

'The underwear, you mean?' asked Fraser.

'Exactly. So, she had a back-up scheme ready, in her own store.'

'Bit risky that' interjected Fraser.

'Yes, but remember, she was the manager of the clothing department. The changing room had been left open because they were short-staffed so all she needed to do was lock it behind her when she'd committed the murder and removed the necessary item of underwear. It was just a standard Yale lock, after all. Then she got changed, dumped the clothes in her locker and reported for work, as normal. The first thing she did was to unlock the changing room again and "find" the body...'

He took a sip of whisky.

'So, once she'd killed poor Natalie Wheeler and got what she needed, all she had to do was wait.'

'For what?' Eddie asked.

'To be sent home; she'd given us a good statement, her boss seemed to be more shocked than she was, naturally he wouldn't expect her to stay at work—she'd have been counting on that, probably. She drove through to North Berwick, changing back into her alternative outfit somewhere along the way. She went into the hotel, pretending to be Pollock, she got a set of keys and planted said underwear in his holdall. No wonder the receptionist thought she seemed nervous, mind you!'

'It was all very well planned then?'

'Aye, Eddie,' responded Briony. 'She's smar...em, clever, she had it all planned out, includin' the back-up in Tesco; that was more o' a risk, as it was her own shop, but she was very careful. Her experience in retail meant it was easy for her to change all the dress sizes. Apparently, it wasn't the first time she'd had it all prepared.'

'Really?'

'Yup. She's admitted that she was stalkin' Pollock, she knew mostly when he was away with Hogarth. She'd set the whole thing up about six weeks before, changed sizes on a different set o' clothes—red again, of course—but the opportunity didn't present itself on that occasion. Bein' manager of the department, she just changed the sizes back an' no-one was any the wiser. But second time round, she decided that it was too risky in her own store, so she decided to use somewhere else, with her own as a back-up, just in case.'

The two clergymen shook their heads, astonished once more at the lengths a woman, hell-bent on revenge, would go to. Grant continued.

'Anyway, it seemed that her plan hadn't worked, Pollock was released from hospital, free to return home. She'd assumed he'd have been arrested by then, although she didn't know that we were waiting for him outside his house. When she realised that Neil was actually leaving Hogarth and going back to his wife, that was the tipping-point. She reckoned that she was about to lose him forever, so she decided that if she couldn't have him, then no-one was going to. Terrible thing, jealousy...'

He took a sip of whisky; it had been a particularly trying case, for many reasons...he continued.

'To be honest, I get the feeling it's probably the first serious relationship she'd ever been in; as for Pollock, I think it just suited him. I don't think he had any particular feelings for the poor woman, it was just a means of living out his own particular fantasies. But there she was, involved with a man, albeit a married one, enjoying an active, if slightly bizarre, sex-life, then out of the blue he goes and dumps her for another man...'

Briony shook her head and scowled.

'You know, I've asked myself how I'd react in that situation. Actually, Sandie and I spoke about it, poor woman.'

She drained her whisky and gave a heavy sigh.

'If your partner has a fling with a woman, well, it must be horrible, hurtful, the feelings of betrayal...'

From the way she spoke, Grant sensed that there was something else underlying her words. Now wasn't the time, however.

'...but if you *do* decide to forgive, then I suppose you can always try harder to make it work. But if it's a man you're competing with, what the hell can you do?'

She banged her empty glass down on the table, causing a young couple nearby to look across.

Bloody men...!'

The last phrase was made with such anger that the three members of the Trinity looked at each other in an embarrassed silence. Finally, Eddie spoke.

'And I heard you'd charged this other woman—Duff, wasn't it— with the murder attempt on Pollock?'

'Aye,' Grant mumbled into his whisky glass. 'But it's a pity we never...'

'Oh, don't bloody start, Grant, eh!' interjected Briony, the anger still in her voice. 'There's nothin' more we can do. Anyway, it's probably for the best...'

She raised an eyebrow at him.

'Hm,' said Eddie, 'I think there's more to this story than you're letting on; care to enlighten us?'

Grant and Briony gave each other a look and shook their heads. Eddie sighed resignedly.

'Oh, by the way, I almost forgot...'

Grant delved into his pocket and removed two envelopes, handing one each to Fraser and Eddie.

'That's a wee charitable donation from a friend...'

Briony gave him another knowing look. For some reason, he felt she was angry with him.

'...just to whatever you like; Church roof fund...'

Finally, they all laughed, the awkwardness evaporating; apparently the "roof fund" was a thing of the past! Fraser seemed about to ask where the money had come from but Grant held up his hand.

'Nope—ask no questions...'

'Oh well, tell your donor thanks very much, Grant. It'll be put to good use. Right, another one...'

~~~

It was nearly closing time and Grant was pleasantly inebriated; "glowing" his friend Brian used to call it...the evening had gone a long way to restoring his faith in humanity. Briony stood up.

'Right, I'd best call a taxi; I'll away outside...'

Eddie McKee jumped to his feet, almost knocking his chair over.

'I'll come out for a breath of air...'

As the door closed behind them, Grant gave his remaining friend a questioning look as he drained the dregs of his Glenlivet.

'*Is* there something going on there, Fraser?'

The minister shrugged.

'Damned if I know, Grant. I've known Eddie for a good number of years and never once had reason to question either his faith or his celibacy. But he often mentions her; I mean, how many times has he asked you if she's coming to join us?'

Grant considered this.

'You're right, I never really thought about it, but I suppose he has...'

~~~~

Despite Fraser's offer of a bed for the night, Grant set off on his walk home to Bluebell Cottage. The truth was he enjoyed it; the peace, the quiet of the countryside, the soft, velvety darkness, they acted like a salve for his troubled psyche; and he enjoyed the exercise. He made his way carefully through the farmyard, hoping not to waken the dogs, and he was soon tramping along the last quarter mile, aware that the stars had disappeared and there was the first hint of rain in the air. Suddenly, without warning, the faint precipitation turned to a heavy downpour and he pulled up his hood, regretting not having taken a rain jacket.

Still, at least the heating's working...

He approached his house, it's dark bulk just visible through the gloom, solid and comforting. But before he entered the driveway and triggered the security light, he stopped and turned, facing back down the valley. Even through the rain he could just make out the twinkling lights of the various farms and houses, the distant glow of the great Glasgow conurbation. He loved this view, come rain or shine; it made him feel at home. He turned and looked down to his left, where Castle Semple Loch lay unseen; still, dark, waiting...

He smiled to himself as the rain coursed down his face. Maybe life wasn't so bad after all...

FIN

If you have enjoyed reading this book, please consider leaving a review. Some sites rate books by the number of reviews they get and, without your help, a really great book can be left to languish unseen.

Acknowledgements

Once again, I experience a sense of wonder at seeing my name in print! I am eternally grateful to my publisher, Lesley Affrossman at Sparsile Books, for having faith in me, and to Jim Campbell, for his assistance and his incisive editing (considerably less this time, I may add!). Thanks also to Davy for keeping me right on Police procedural detail. For scene setting at Meridian House, grateful thanks to my awesome rowing friend, Lisa Hopcroft.

To everyone else who has supported me, at the launch of "Drown for your Sins" and throughout my writing journey to date, I am extremely grateful. I hope I have lived up to your expectations.

Finally, to Joanie, Kirsty and Lindsay, thank you for putting up with me and for allowing me to take over the dining room with my computer, books, notepads etc. Much love!

Further Reading

The Promise
When promises can cost lives

Simon's Wife
Time is running out, and history is being rewritten by a traitor's hand.

The Unforgiven King
A forgotten woman and the most vilified king in history

American Goddess
Ancient powers and new forces

L. M. Affrossman

Kindred Spirit
A dead man with unfinished business

Stephen Cashmore

Science for Heretics
Why so much of science is wrong

The Tethered God
Punished for a crime he can't remember

Barrie Condon

Two Pups
What makes us different. What makes us the same.

Seona Calder

Pignut and Nuncle
When we are born, we cry that we have come to this stage of fools
King Lear

Des Dillon

Comics and Columbine
An outcast look at comics, bigotry and school shootings

Tom Campbell

Drown for your Sins
DCI Grant McVicar: Book 1

Dress for Death
DCI Grant McVicar: Book 2

Diarmid MacArthur

www.sparsilebooks.com